T0162678

# Given A Second Chance

*Burning Memories*

Pat Gillespie

iUniverse®

**GIVEN A SECOND CHANCE**
**BURNING MEMORIES**



*iUniverse books may be ordered through booksellers or by contacting:*

*iUniverse*
*1663 Liberty Drive*
*Bloomington, IN 47403*
*www.iuniverse.com*
*1-800-Authors (1-800-288-4677)*



*ISBN: 978-1-4917-7333-8 (sc)*
*ISBN: 978-1-4917-7335-2 (hc)*
*ISBN: 978-1-4917-7465-6 (e)*

*Library of Congress Control Number: 2015911918*

*Print information available on the last page.*

*iUniverse rev. date: 9/30/2015*

To my daughters, Laura and Jennifer, for your part in my stories. Thank you. And Jennifer, a big Thank You for all the long hours of proofing, while working full time, and taking care of your family. Rest up, sweet girl, there's nine more to proof, and you have the last series to help write, all because you wouldn't let me retire.

# Chapter One

"Lori," Kyle groaned, frustratedly, "why can't you see that I love you?"

"Now who's blind?" she cried, shaking her head.

"No." Taking her hand, he put it to his heart. "Here. In your heart," he explained to the girl he had loved, since high school, only to have nearly lost her, when her parents' car went out of control, while driving through the Smoky Mountains on their family vacation, a few years back, just before she was to go off to college.

Due to the awful accident that had nearly taken all but one life, Lori Roberts, now twenty-two, with sandy blonde hair, and blue eyes, once known for having been the prettiest, had lost her sight when the car went up in flames. Luckily, a passer-by saw the horrible accident and called it in just before risking his life to pull them out of the burning car to safety. Her younger brother, unfortunately, didn't make it, when the car exploded, just as the man was about to go back to get him.

"Lori, what had happened to you and your brother, Sam, was awful. But that doesn't change, and never will change, the way I feel about you."

"How can you say that? My eyes! I can't see! And from what the doctor told my parents, I never will again!"

"Maybe not, but that doesn't mean you have to stop feeling, does it?"

Unable to respond to that, she turned away to hide the pain, just as a friend of theirs called out from across the busy main street of Camden, a fairly small, but prosperous city just east of Springfield, Illinois, where they have lived most of their lives.

"Hey, Tate," Kyle called back, seeing his friend with a larger than life smile, as he crossed the main thoroughfare of town. Not going too far from her side, Kyle greeted his old high school pal, a young man, now in his early twenties, like the rest of them. Only, unlike Kyle, his friend stood a bit shorter than Kyle's six-foot frame. "How's it going?"

he asked, while extending out a warm hand to the curly brown haired youth, wearing wire-rimmed glasses.

"It couldn't be better. Susan has gotten herself a job, working for the Chronicle, as their head reporter."

"Still digging up hot stories like back in school, huh?" he teased, knowing how their other friend liked being in the midst of things.

"Don't you know it," he returned, looking over Kyle's shoulder at Lori, who stood back wiping away the remaining tears that had fallen, before he had gotten there. "Lori..." Tate spoke up, going around his friend to greet her with a hug. "Hey there. How has it been with you?" he asked, pulling back to look at her, only to see her look away, while trying to seem happy to hear a familiar voice.

"It's been..." she shrugged, "well, okay."

"You know," Kyle jumped in, while coming around to place a caring arm around her shoulder, while seeing how hard she was struggling to hold it together in front of their friend, "work and all."

"Oh? And how are things at home? Your parents, how are they?"

"They're fine!" Lori returned, gathering her strength. "Dad has more clients than he knows what to do with. And mom," she tried to laugh, "well, you know, teaching is what she lives for."

"Isn't that the truth? Then I guess your dad's law firm has grown quite a bit since, well, you know?"

"Sam's death?" she asked, knowing their friends rarely felt right by bringing it up.

"Yes, sorry."

"No, it's okay, though that's how dad deals with Sam's death."

"And I guess your loss of sight, too?" Tate offered, sympathetically.

"No," she shivered upon feeling the cool fall breeze, as it picked up some, "he and mom have been a great help by giving me space to learn my way around things."

"Good!" He turned to Kyle, feeling like a total jerk for having opened his mouth in the first place.

"Hey," Kyle chuckled to lighten the subject, but seeing she was chilled he dropped it all together, "what do you say, we go and get some coffee? I think a certain lady here could use something to warm her up."

"Sure, just let me give Susan a quick call to let her know where I'll be," Tate smiled.

Doing so, Kyle turned to Lori to offer both arms to help warm her. "Does that help any?" he asked, wishing her pain away.

"A little!" she replied, taking in the soft scent of his cologne, when laying her head against his warm chest.

Having finished with his call, Tate put his cell phone back into his inside jacket pocket. "Well, are we ready for that coffee?" he grinned.

"Sure thing," Kyle smiled, while giving his lady a tight squeeze, before turning to head for their favorite coffee shop, which was two doors down from her father's office.

Once there, having taken the same table they had always taken, Lori excused herself to go to the ladies room.

"Wow, I'll never get over how she does that," Tate laughed quietly, as the two watched her make her way successfully.

"She's been coming here for years. And since the accident, the owner refuses to change a thing so she wouldn't have any trouble finding her way around!"

"I can see why. Sam worked here, and they really liked him."

"You could say that, and more. Having lost their own son, Todd, due to Desert Storm, Sam was like a replacement."

"Man… that had to have been a real blow to have heard about the accident, then."

"Sure was," he groaned inwardly, when the owner's wife, Emily, appeared with their usual, one piping hot black coffee for Kyle, and a peppermint tea for Lori.

"What can I get for you?" she asked Tate, while taking out an order pad, and pencil, after setting the cups down.

"Coffee. Black," he smiled.

"Kyle," the buxom woman turned back, does Lori want her usual Danish today?"

"I'll have to ask her, when she gets back. She hasn't been sleeping well lately," he explained, with concern etched across his brow.

"The dreams…?" Tate asked, when Emily walked away, having heard all about them from his wife, having been Lori's best friend.

"Yes, and they don't seem to be letting up any."

"Is she still blaming herself for what had happened?"

"Yes, all because I didn't want her to go!"

"I remember that. Just about the time the two of you were about to become engaged."

"Yeah, and what timing, just when her parents sprung the news about the Florida trip."

"Yes, and then the blinding storm that had to hit when they were half way through the Mountains."

"Yes," Kyle's voice became ridged.

Then it hit, seeing the look of anger come over his friends' face, Tate knew. "Oh, Lord, you're blaming yourself too for that accident, aren't you? If it weren't for you wanting her to stay, she wouldn't have had that argument with her parents about going, and they would have left on time."

Not saying a word, Kyle looked up to see Lori talking to Emily, at the counter.

Later that day, after taking Lori back home to her parents house, Kyle went back to the office to get started on a file that Jason needed right away.

Sitting there, staring at the papers in front of him, his mind went back to that awful day after their graduation. *'Lori,'* he recalled their conversation painfully, *'why do you have to go? Can't they just let you stay with Susan?'*

*'You know better than that! It's my Aunt's wedding. I wish I could stay, but mom wants me there to take pictures!'*

Shaking his head, sadly, while running a hand over his dark brown hair, he broke himself free of what was to play next. That being the scene of the argument with her parents, when reminding her of her scholarship, to study more photography, having been rated the highest for the photos she had taken of several riots, which took place, since the war of Desert Storm. Not to mention, the return of their soldiers during that time.

Meanwhile, as his blue eyes clouded with emotions, unaware he was no longer alone in his meek little office, while sitting behind his desk, Jason Roberts walked in with some more papers to add to the file Kyle was working on.

Seeing the look on the young man's face, Jason became concerned. "Kyle?" the graying haired attorney, in his early fifties, called out from the doorway. "Kyle?" Breaking into his deep thoughts, Jason asked, walking up, "Where were you just now?"

"W...what?" he asked, looking up, startledly.

"You looked as though you were miles away. Did you find out anything on our Philips vs. O'Connely's case?"

"No. Not as of yet," he explained, looking back down at the file.

"You want to talk about it then? What has you looking so upset?"

Not wanting to drudge up sad memories, he shook his head sadly, while getting up to go over and look out the window. "It looks like rain, doesn't it?"

"Kyle, did you and my daughter get into another one of your deep discussions? If so, what frame of mind did you leave her in when you took her back home?"

"She..." he began, when Jason walked up beside him. Instead, he shook his head defeatedly.

"Give her time. She'll remember what the two of you had, before all of this other stuff took place."

Shocked by his candor over his son's death, Kyle turned to study his expression. What he saw in his blue eyes was a sense of peace. *'Had he put it all behind him?'* he wondered. *'If so, how... when he and his son were so close...!'*

"Kyle, what is it?"

Shaking his head again, "I don't get you. How is it that you put the death of your son behind you, and yet so soon, as well as the loss of Lori's sight?"

"Kyle..." Jason was about to say.

"No, it isn't just stuff." He turned angrily and walked back over to the desk. "The two of you were so close," he cried, looking back at him.

"Yes, we were, and God has taken him. Now life must to go on."

"Just like that...? Aren't you angry, or something?"

"Angry? At first I was very angry. I asked myself, why would God do this to an innocent boy like Sam? But then it hit me."

"What?"

"God has His reasons."

"His reasons...? Well if it weren't for me, wanting Lori to stay home, she wouldn't have gotten into that fight with you and your wife. Then the four of you would have left on time, and maybe missed that storm altogether."

"And maybe not," he corrected, while leaning back against the window frame, with his hands resting on the windowsill. "Kyle, no one knows why things happen the way they do, only God. And as for that dreadful day..." He stopped to collect the building of emotions.

"What? What were you going to say?"

Pushing away from the window, Jason went over to take a seat in one of the chairs in front of the desk.

Seeing the look on his face, Kyle took a seat, as well. "What is it?" he asked.

"A few years back, before the accident, Sam was playing ball."

"Sure, I remember. He fell, while running in home!"

"Well, it was later, while at the hospital, the doctor came out with news of his injuries. It wasn't good." He looked sad, just then.

"What did he have to say?"

"He," Jason began, when running a hand over the back of his neck. "He couldn't find any broken bones, just some mild abrasions. But then when he asked Sam to stand, he tried, but started to fall."

"Fall...? But why...?"

"The doctor didn't know at the time. He said he would have to do some blood work to see if there was some other reason for why he wasn't able to stand too well."

Growing concerned, Kyle asked, "And was there? Some other reason, that is?" When he didn't answer, Kyle looked hard at the man's face. "Oh, Lord, there was, wasn't there? What did he find out?"

"Sam had a bone disorder. Nothing could have been done about it. With that, my wife and I took it as a sign, when we had the accident."

"A sign...?"

"He didn't want him to suffer."

"He, as in God?"

"Yes."

"And Lori..., what about what she went through, in the name of God?"

"We don't know. Perhaps it was His plans not to have her see her brother die that way, or any other way, as far as that goes. As for Jamie and I, we have come to except God's plan and are moving on."

"But to have her eyesight taken away for good...?" He wanted to scream. "And now... of all times, just when she was about to further her interest in photography...? Not to mention, we had planned to get married and have some kids after she got out of college."

"Well, you still can get married and have kids, that is."

"Yeah. Right. Just not the way she's feeling."

With a chuckle, Jason got up to head for the door. But then Kyle remembered something he had seen that had been slipped under his door when he had gotten there, after dropping Lori off. "Mr. Roberts. Wait."

"What have I told you about calling me Mr. Roberts?" he turned back.

"Jason. Sorry. This must have been slipped under my door by mistake," he explained, getting to his feet, after picking up the white envelope from his desk, to give to him. "It's addressed to you."

Taking it, he hesitated.

"What is it?" Kyle asked, seeing the look of fear come over his face.

"It's nothing. I got one of these before, and a phone call before that."

"What about?"

Going to the door, Jason opened it to look out.

Thinking he was about to leave, Kyle went to stop him, when sensing something was gravely wrong.

Instead, he turned back, closing the door behind him. "Take a seat," he ordered sternly, while doing the same. "What I am about to tell you does not leave this room. You understand? Not even Lori or my wife is to know about this, or any other letters, and or phone calls. Your word, Kyle, I have to have your word."

"Sure. You got it!"

"This case we're working on."

"Yes, the Philips vs. O'Connely's case. What about it?"

"Philips. It started when he came in to see me a few weeks ago, wanting me to drop it. But I wouldn't hear of it. Then the threatening phone calls came, saying if I didn't, he would have me blown out of the water. I still refused, and now the letters."

"What are you going to do about it?"

"I placed a call, to a friend of mine, back in Indiana. He once worked for the County Sheriff's Department, and now he is a Federal Marshal."

"Who is he?"

"He's better known as, Detective Alex Storm. You may have heard me mention him."

"The guy with a list of enemies to choke a horse?" he laughed.

"Yes," he shook his head, laughing, as well. "He's coming in to go over our plan of strategy." At that time, looking at his watch, he got up to leave the room.

"What?" Kyle asked, while getting up to follow.

"He should be here at anytime now. So I had better be going to see if he has arrived yet."

"Yeah, sure, okay!"

# Chapter Two

Stepping out into the hall of his plush office building, Jason was met by a tall, masculine-looking man, dressed in black, with graying hair, and a pair of sunglasses that made him seem more powerful-looking, when walking up to greet him. "Jason…!" he spoke up, sounding even more powerful, while reaching out to shake his old friends' hand.

"Alex…!" he grinned proudly, happy to see him. "Hey, what do you say we go into my office and get caught up on old times first, before diving into why you're really here?"

"I'd like nothing more, but for safety sake let's leave out the name, in case you're being watched," he suggested strongly, while looking around the corridor.

"You're right, it wouldn't look good if seen talking to a Federal Marshal right about now," he grinned. "But it's safe to say my partner is in court right now. So how about we take this to my office anyway to get comfortable?" he gestured down the hall from where they stood.

"Sure."

Just as they were about to head that way, Kyle spoke up curious to know about some of the stories he had heard about this man. "Excuse me, sir," he looked around them quietly, before going on, "I just have to know, is it true what they said about the Belaro and Delgado case? Was Belaro really buried beneath the rubble of your nephew's old farmhouse? And Delgado, is he still a threat to you and your other nephew?"

"Who is this?" Alex turned to Jason.

"My intern, as well as my runner, and…" he laughed, "my daughter's boyfriend, Kyle Moorsted. Kyle, this is the man I had mentioned to you earlier. As for the tales…" he grinned, looking at Alex.

"They're true," Alex laughed, proudly.

"And your nephew's spirit?" he lowered his voice even more. "You really saw it?"

Looking back to his friend, he laughed even more, "Jason, just exactly what all have you told him?"

"Not everything!" he chuckled. "I was afraid he might have flipped out hearing *all* about it!"

"What, there's more…?" Kyle laughed quietly.

"Later," Jason smiled, patting him on the back, just as the two turned to go to his office.

"Are you really going to tell him?" Alex asked, as they walked into a well-furnished room, with its own wet bar off in one corner.

Closing the door behind him to secure their privacy, Jason went over to pour them each a cup of coffee. "Good, Lord, no," he roared, "I think I'll leave that to you. Not to mention, the look on his face, when he hears the spirit of your nephew, Craig, is alive and well, and living out the rest of his life in the body of the man Tony was supposed to have killed in the first place. What's it been, three years ago, now?" he asked, handing Alex his cup. "Oh, but I was right about the coffee, wasn't I? Or should I have poured you something stronger?"

"Coffee's fine. And when the time is right, beer is what I drink."

"Still into that beer, huh?"

"Yep! And yes, it has been three years, now."

"Lord, when you called and told me about Craig. Man…!"

"Yeah, finding him dead on his farmhouse floor, when it was David, we thought that Tony's boss had ordered a hit on. And David having been eaten up with guilt those two years that Craig had been gone."

"Yes, and to hear an angel took David's spirit home after he and Craig went and switched places, before the house collapsed in on Tony. Wow."

"Yes," he returned, quietly, while taking a drink of his coffee.

"How is he doing?" he asked, in reference of the tall, brown hair, blue eyed nephew of his, who looked a lot like his other nephew, Jarred, both tall and in their forties, with wives that were a set of cousins, as well.

"Married and helping out around the Inn, when not out working a construction job," he grinned, thinking about Craig, and his wife, Jessi, an Irish tempered, brunette. But then, with a silent chuckle, he turned, thinking of his own wife, Beth, a thirty-two year old, strawberry blonde, with baby blue eyes, who gave up being a cop to marry him. The two were now expecting their second child, a son they planned to name after David, who gave up his own life so Craig could have his back. But not before doing one last heroic deed. Saving Jessi's life, just as Craig's old house began to shake, as beam from one of the upstairs bedroom ceiling began to fall, and beneath it she stood. Seeing this, David threw himself into its path to push her out of its way. *'Pushing her out of its way,'* Alex groaned, silently, thinking back on that day, July 4th, three years ago, when a man in his forties with a strong likeness to Craig's, except for his nephew's crooked smile, took the hard blow to the head, before falling to the floor in what would soon have been a pool of blood. Though, with a bullet in his own shoulder, given by Tony's gun, before Tony ran from the room, Alex got up to help Jessi move the heavy beam, before rolling David over onto his back.

"Thinking about that day, three years ago?" Jason asked, seeing Alex's faraway look.

"Yeah, how did you guess?"

"Oh, you just had that look on your face, is all. Hey, didn't you say you and Beth were having a baby boy now?"

"Sure did! Little David Alexander," he spoke proudly of their son.

"Named after your nephew's friend, and yourself, huh?"

"Craig, too. Alexander is his middle name, as well! But when we're out around others, we call him David, because of how he got here."

"Yes, I can see why."

"Yeah, well the truth would only turn this whole thing into a media circus if it were to get out."

"Yes, well you guys don't need that, and Ted, what of my replacement after I had left?"

Laughing, Alex shook his head, "Oh, he's still around. In fact he will be joining me shortly at this cheesy motel, outside of town."

"Oh…?"

"Yeah." Looking at his watch, Alex sighed, while getting himself another cup of coffee, before the two went over to the couch to take a seat. "So, where are these letters you were telling me about?"

"Here," he announced, pulling them out of his suit pocket, where he had kept them for safe keeping

After reading over them, Alex concluded, "You're not kidding, the man is really upset that you didn't take his bribe, nor heed his warnings!"

"What am I going to do? I'm concerned he may go after my wife or daughter now."

"Well..." Once again Alex laughed, when a thought came to him.

"What?" Jason laughed. "You have an idea, don't you?"

"I just might, but first I have to put it passed some people. The first time I tried doing something like this, I nearly got my head bit off by the owner of the Inn!"

"The one you stayed at, while working those other two cases?"

"The very same!" he roared. "And now my nephew is there, running it with her, while my wife is helping out in the kitchen."

"Sounds like fun!"

Going on with their plan, Alex couldn't help but picture Jessi's angered expression, when all he was trying to do was protect her and her family from Tony and his side-kick, Harry, when they stayed at the Inn, waiting to make right a hit that went bad years ago on David McMasters.

Later that afternoon, after arriving at his motel room, Alex went in to make his calls. One to his old Commander, the other to the Serenity Inn Bed & Breakfast, to ask Jessi if he could send a few people her way to stay for a while, just until the case was handled. However, instead of telling her the truth, he conjured up another story to avoid having his proverbial head chewed off again.

While waiting on the call to go through, there came a knock at the door. "Damn," he grumbled, getting off the bed to peer out the window. Seeing his old partner, a tall, distinguish-looking, black male standing outside his door, he called out, opening it. "Ted... get on in here!"

"Alex," he greeted, quietly, walking in.

"Take a seat, I'll be right with you," he ordered, pointing out a chair, near a corner table, while closing the door behind him.

Seeing that Alex was on the phone, Ted did just that. Taking a seat, he kept watch out the window, while Alex went on with his call.

"Commander," he spoke softly into the phone, "it's Alex. I have a favor to ask of you."

"For you, Alex, anything," Commander Jamison returned, while looking over some files on his desk.

"I need to borrow Jarred."

"Why? What's going on?" he asked, shutting a folder he had just opened, to listen more intently.

"I'm working on a case in Camden, Illinois, and I'm going to be sending three people over to stay at the Inn. While they're there, I'm going to need Jarred to stay and keep an eye on them."

"Well," he laughed, "this certainly sounds a bit all too familiar! Are you sure that's a good idea? And have you talked it over with the Innkeeper? You do recall the first time you were there, right?"

He roared, laughing. "Oh.... yeah, I painfully remember that visit. And no, I was just about to call her next, but I wanted to put it past you first, before talking it over with her."

"I don't have a problem with it. Do you want Marcose on it too?"

Remembering his other good right hand man that was a part of taking Belaro and Delgado down, he looked to Ted and laughed. "Sure, why not."

"What about Ted? Is he there with you now?"

"Yes, just got in," he announced, thinking about the others, aside from Ted, being one of his first of elite team players to bring down Tony Belaro, an Italian drug runner, and Vince Delgado, another runner, working for Chicago's Mob Lord, Martin Santose, Marcose, Beth, Baker, and Jarred, were all a part of his team back when he had to deal with Tony, and Vince, who is presently serving time for his crimes, and didn't look to get out for another ten years. Now bringing everyone back together again, he had another case for them to work on.

"Good," Jamison laughed. "Well, if there is ever anything else I can do for you, you know to just call."

"Sure thing," Alex smiled, hanging up.

"Well, I know it isn't Delgado we're going after. So what's going on?" Ted asked, when turning back to face him.

"I'll fill you in shortly. Just let me make this next call, before I lose my nerve."

"Jessi, I take it?" he laughed, remembering those times, as well.

"Yes," he grumbled, humorously, while punching in the number on the key pad.

"This ought to be good," Ted held back a laugh, while leaning back in his chair, wondering what Alex was going to tell her to get her to agree to his plan this time.

Meanwhile, back in Indiana, at the Inn, Jessi, Beth, and Jessi's two best friends, Ashley and Renee, who she used to work with some years ago at their local Wal-Mart store, were now sitting in the turn of the century's old Inn's boutique and coffee shop having coffee and cappuccino, while talking about none other than Alex, himself.

"What do you think he's doing now?" Ashley, an average height, brunette in her forties asked, while getting up to get them each a refill.

"Talking to Ted and getting settled in, I hope!" Beth exclaimed, while rubbing a hand softly over her eight and a half month round tummy.

"Don't worry," Jessi, the thirty-eight year old, Irish tempered, brunette, offered smiling, "he'll be calling you soon, you'll see."

And call, he did, when Lora, Jessi's eldest of two girls, took the call, while working the front desk. "Hello, Serenity Inn! How may I help you?"

"Lora?" Alex's voice came over the other end.

"Hey there, Alex, your ears must have been burning!" the light haired brunette, laughed.

"They're talking about me, aren't they?" he too laughed, along with Ted, who could only guess what was going on back home.

"Oh... yeah. Anyway, are you calling to talk to your wife, or my mom?"

"Both, but first my wife, to let her know that Ted and I are just now getting settled in."

"Okay." Taking the phone into the boutique that was located across from the Inn's office, Lora laughed at the group sitting at the far table, nearest to the coffee bar.

"What is it, Lora?" Jessi asked, seeing her expression.

"It's Alex. He wants to talk to Beth first, and then you."

Getting to her feet with some help from Ashley, Beth went to the kitchen to take the call so not to tie up the line. "Alex," she smiled, "how are things there?"

"Quiet for now. I had just gotten in a little bit ago from seeing Jason Roberts, and Ted is sitting here now. How are you and Bethany doing?"

"Bethany is out with Cassi. And me..., well... pregnant," she laughed. "And when little David isn't doing his back flips or running a marathon, hungry. You would think I was doing all the work myself."

"Yes, but you are taking it easy with this one, aren't you?"

"Yes."

"Hey, I hate to cut this short, but I need a favor from Jessi. Is she nearby?"

"No, but I'll get her for you. Just a minute."

While waiting on her, Alex filled Ted in on what was really going on.

"Charges of embezzlement...?" Ted asked.

"Yes, against his partner. And to make matters worse, he tried bribing Jason first to drop it, before threatening to blow him out of the water."

"Jason? Roberts...?" he asked. "As in your first long running partner, before me?"

"Yes."

"Wow, how things seem to always get back to old times around you," he laughed, just as Alex heard Jessi's voice come over the other end.

"Alex, what's up?"she asked, suspecting already what the call was about.

"Do you have a couple of rooms available? I need to send, or I should say Jason Roberts, an old partner of mine, wants to send his wife, daughter, and if possible, the daughter's boyfriend over to stay awhile. I should tell you, though, the daughter was in an accident, which resulted in losing her eyesight. Worse yet, her brother was killed in that accident when the car they were in blew up, before they could get him out."

"Oh, Alex, how awful for them," she offered, pushing aside her suspicions for what she had just learned. "Well..., sure," she replied, glancing over the reservation book to see what she had available. "It looks like the main floor guest room is available, and if we don't have any other rooms inside, we have a couple of cabins available, as well. Would that work?"

"It should. Oh, and Jessi, Jarred and Marcose will be staying to help out, as well."

"What?" she asked, when all sense of suspicion came flying back upon hearing Marcose's name. "Alex...?"

"I can't explain now. Just take good care of them, as you always do. And thanks, Jess," he said, quickly getting off the phone.

"Jessi?" her friends all asked, while gathering around in the foyer, when seeing that all too familiar look come over her face, as she went to hang the phone up.

"That rat!" she groaned. "He's doing it to me again!"

"Doing what?" Renee, Jessi's Hispanic friend asked, with her usual quirky grin, while being the jokester of the group, since they all first met.

"He's threatening to take over the Inn again, saying he needs to send a few people out to stay for awhile. Oh, and let's not forget that Jarred and Marcose are going to be staying here, as well, or at least until things cool off."

"Did he say all that?" Beth asked.

"No. But after all this time that I have gotten to know the way he works, and that this all has something to do with why he's in Illinois, working that case, I'll just bet on it."

"Bet on what?" came a man's voice from behind her.

Turning to see, not only her husband, a tall, handsome, blue eyed, forty-eight year old, standing in his work clothes, but his cousin, too, who looked a lot like Craig. Beside him was Marcose, an average height, Hispanic, in his late forties. "Well, well, well, if it isn't Jarred," she laughed bittersweet. "It's so nice to see you. And you too, Marcose," she turned, smiling, knowingly.

"Uh, oh," Marcose grinned. "If you'll excuse me, I think I'll just wait this one out on the front porch," he laughed, leaving the men to face her temper alone.

"Jessi…" Jarred began, grinningly.

"Oh, no you don't," she shook her head slightly. "You have heard from Alex today, haven't you?"

"Yes. That's why Marcose and I are here."

"And Jodi, will she and the girls be coming too?" she asked, referring to Madison and Kyleigh, who weren't far from her own girls' age.

"Just as soon as she gets through at her antique store."

"Good. Now back to why you're here. You know what's really going on, don't you?"

"Yes. You have company coming, and Alex wants us here to chaperone them."

"Is that what he is calling it? And guns…? There will be no guns 'a blazing, or lives at stake here, right…?"

"Nope! Just making sure they're taken good care of, is all," he fibbed, knowing how bent out of shape she would be if there were any trouble at her Inn.

# Chapter Three

Back at Jason's office, Jason went back in to see Kyle.

Closing the door behind him, Kyle looked up to see concern written on his face. "What is it?"

"It's nothing. But I do have a serious request to ask of you."

"Sure, anything."

"I wanted to say something earlier, but…"

"Jason, spit it out!"

"All right, how soon can you be packed and ready to go?"

"What?"

"You heard me."

"Yes, but where am I going?"

"I can't say out loud, but you won't be alone, Jamie and Lori will be going with you. So again, how soon can you be packed and ready to go? Your ride will be here to get you within the hour. Will that give you enough time?"

"Yeah, sure! But what's going on? Did you get another threatening call?"

"No. Alex feels I should send my family away, until this whole thing blows over."

Seeing how this was really bothering him, Kyle rounded the desk to offer him a caring shoulder.

"Damn him anyway…! First my son, and now my family…?"

"Jason, they'll be safer if they weren't here."

"They darn well better be," he grumbled angrily, while the two stood there, knowing of each other's pain.

In the meantime, back at the motel, Alex was just rapping up on telling Ted what their part in all this was going to be.

"A disguise again, huh?" Ted laughed. "Let me guess, your old alias, 'Jake Green' again?"

"No. He's in retirement for now. I think, maybe this time I'll be Jordan Scott, Attorney at Law. And you," he thought a moment, "Taylor Green, my investigator. How does that suit you?"

He laughed. "Well, I just knew 'Green' was going to be in there somewhere."

"Well, it's worked for me a time or two. Now, it's getting close to that time for you to go and pick up his family. Get Kyle first so Lori won't be frightened, knowing she is about to go to a strange place."

"Sure thing. And you? What will you be doing, while I'm out?"

"Tailing you to make sure you aren't followed. And when we get back, it's work around the clock again, as usual."

Heading out, the two stayed several car lengths away from each other, with Alex in his specially equipped, bullet proof, black Chevy Blazer, and its tented windows, and Ted in his black, Chevy, 4X4.

Arriving outside the Law office of Roberts & Epstein, the two went in to meet with Jason, who was on the phone with his wife, telling her to be ready. "A man named Ted Jones," He looked up seeing Alex, "will be there to get the two of you."

"What will he be driving?" his wife, a sandy blonde, with blue eyes like their daughter's was, asked.

"Just a moment, I'll ask. They're here now."

"Ask what?" Alex inquired, when hearing the tail end of their conversation.

"What they will be riding in."

"Is the line secure?" he asked, cautiously.

"Yes. It's my private cell phone."

"I'll be driving my black Chevy 4x4," Ted announced from the closed door.

"Is that going to be roomy enough for the four of them?" Jason asked.

"Sure, it's a four door," Ted smiled. "Though it does come with a cage in behind the driver's seat for when I have to haul a possible criminal in it. Will that be a problem?"

"No. Kyle can ride in the back seat with Lori, while Jamie sits up front, if you're all right with that."

"Sure. It's not often I get to have a lady in the front seat with me," Ted teased to lighten the mood.

"Thanks," he smiled, laughing. "And you, Alex? What are you in now days?"

"You mean, what am I still in?" he teased.

"What? You still have that Blazer after all these years?" he laughed, knowing how much Alex loved his vehicle.

"It's not the same old one. It's newer. And are you ready for this? It's equipped with bullet proof, tinted windows to help keep me alive, longer."

At that, they all laughed, while Jason went back to telling his wife what to watch for. Then with her still on the line, he went over to get a current photo of Philips and O'Connelly to give to Alex. Pointing them out, he told them which was which.

Looking the two men over, Alex and Ted saw the difference, Philips, the one embezzling money off his partner, was the average height, muscle bound one, with thinning blond hair. The eyes told them both he was cunning, as well as dangerous if crossed. As for O'Connelly, he was more of a family man, tall, husky with brown hair and eyes. Both men, though, looked to be in their late fifties.

"Okay," he was saying, when hanging up his phone. "Well, they'll be waiting. I told her not to open the door for anyone, but you or Ted."

"Does she know that Kyle is going too?" Alex asked.

"Yes. I mentioned it, as well."

"Good," Alex returned.

Turning, when hearing someone approach the door, the three stood tense at what they weren't sure of. But then there came a knock, followed by the familiar sound of Kyle's voice, as he went to slowly open it.

At that, the three exhaled heavily.

"Kyle," Jason scolded.

"What?" he asked, having sensed some tension in the air, when walking in.

"I was expecting Cindy to announce you, when you got here."

"She wasn't at her desk!" he exclaimed, when setting his bags down to meet Alex's old partner. "You must be Ted, Jason's replacement after he left the force."

"Yes," he returned, taking the young man's hand firmly in his own. "And am I to understand you will be riding along with the Roberts' family and I?"

"Yes, and staying on, while they're there to help make it easier on Lori."

"Well then, are we ready to go?" he asked, turning to Alex.

"Let's hit it!" he ordered, turning back to Jason. "Stay here, a man in his late thirties will be posted outside your office, incase Philips or one of his cronies shows up."

"And afterwards?" he asked, puzzledly.

"Your bodyguard will take you home, and stay with you, until we get back. After that, Ted will be your personal guard, while I watch from a safe, but close distance."

"What? Not like the old days?" he teased.

"Sorry, but if I were the one guarding you, I'm afraid I wouldn't be as effective."

"You're right. If something was to go down, and we were to miss it, because we were too busy talking about what was, and not what is, someone could get hurt or worse," he agreed regretfully. "So you guys had better be going, while it's still early yet."

"Yes, and Jason," Alex turned to assure him, "we'll talk when I get back," he announced on their way out to the lobby, where Cindy was still nowhere to be seen. However, once there, one of Alex's new men was standing guard, along with his bomb sniffing K-9, as he was assigned to do.

"Is that him?" Jason asked, seeing the German Sheppard sitting by his man's side.

Seeing the familiar face of Jacob Manning, a tall, well built officer, wearing street clothes and a hint of a bulletproof vest under them, he nodded his head. "He's one of our best, and a former Marine. Manning," Alex called the man and his dog over. "This is Jason Roberts. Stay with him until we get back. And, too, you are to escort him home, and have the dog do his job, sniffing out the house and grounds, before letting him in. For now, go with Jason back to his office until he is ready to go home. This way your presence wouldn't be noticed, unless you have already been seen."

"No, sir, not by anyone looking like an Attorney, that is," he returned respectively.

"Good. Jason, we'll be in touch," Alex turned, patting him on the arm assuredly.

"Alright," he nodded, and turned to go back into his office with his bodyguard and K-9.

Once the door was closed, Alex, Ted and Kyle were about to leave, as Alex stopped, when looking back at Cindy's empty chair.

"Alex?" Ted spoke up, suspecting trouble in the way he was staring at the desk.

"Don't you find it a little puzzling that she would still be away from her desk at this time of day?"

"Yes, and to make matters worse, it's too quiet for being in the middle of the day."

At that moment, the two reached into their jackets where they kept their weapons, when going to the front door to look out.

Seeing nothing out of the ordinary, Alex turned back to study the empty chair once more. "Kyle," he spoke carefully, "what does Cindy look like? Isn't she somewhat tall, with long dark hair and glasses?"

"Yes. Why?"

Turning to Ted, he ordered him to stand ready.

"Already there. Are we expecting trouble?" he asked, unsnapping his weapon from its shoulder holster, before pulling it out, when seeing the muscle along Alex's jaw line tighten.

"Expecting it? I feel it," he explained, while quietly pulling out his own weapon. Just then, out of the corned of his eye, he saw a figure move in behind some filing cabinets, next to the desk. "Damn…" he growled, shoving Kyle in behind some chairs, while he and Ted took cover along with him.

"Where," Ted asked quietly.

"The filing cabinet," he pointed.

Getting up, the two moved in slowly to overpower the person hiding.

"P…please, d…don't hurt me…!" the lady cried out in horror, as Alex pulled her out from behind one of the cabinets.

"What were you doing behind there?" he demanded, as Manning and Jason came rushing out of the office, just then. "Answer me."

"Cindy..." Jason looked surprised, "what is going on out here?"

"M...Mr. Roberts..., I...I saw them come in, and thought they were here to hurt you. And then shortly after, I saw him coming up with his dog, so I hid!" she explained, while still feeling Alex's grip tight on her upper arm. "I'm sorry...!"

"Cindy, this is a friend of mine. And the man with him is a friend of his. They're not here to hurt me, just to help me with another case I'm working on," he explained, while quickly covering his tracks so as not to let on to what was really going on.

"Then why is Kyle going with them? And why are his bags packed? And that man...," she indicated toward Manning, "why is he here?"

"First of all, Kyle is being taken off the Philips case, and working on a new one. So he'll be away for awhile to gather some information for me. And these two are here to take him. As for Jacob, well..." he had to think quickly.

"I'm filling in, until one of them gets back," he offered, looking down at his dog. "And this, here, is Aramis, my service dog. He won't hurt you."

Satisfied, she looked to Alex. "Can I have my arm back, please...?"

"Sure. Just don't hide like that again, unless your life is really in danger."

"Sure. Okay! But what's with the guns?" she pointed out, while rubbing her arm.

"Security," he said, pointedly, while they put them away.

Shaking her head, she returned to her desk to finish up on some work, in which Jason had been waiting on.

"Sorry," Jason offered, while walking them to the door, with Manning at his side.

"Just stay out of the open. You got that?" Alex ordered quietly, while looking back at Cindy.

"Sure will."

Saying their goodbyes, Alex walked out first. After giving him some time to get to his Blazer, it was Ted and Kyle's turn. However, just as they were about to leave the building a black sedan came around the corner, and the man in it looked an awful lot like Philips. Seeing it, Ted pulled Kyle back inside to where they could take cover in behind some artificial foliage, just inside the doorway. While there, taking out his radio, Ted called Alex.

Hearing this, Manning too, came up to see what was going on.

"I see him," they both replied.

In a matter of minutes, the car, with its driver, was gone, but not before Alex could get off a good description, along with its plate number.

"Alex, were you able to see the man more clearly?" Ted asked, while instructing Kyle to wait inside.

"Yes, and that's our man all right."

"Which one was it?"

"Philips."

"Great. Now what?"

"Have Manning stay alert. I'll get some extra men to help watch Jason, until we get back. Speaking of which, we had best be hurrying over to Jamie's in case our friend was to head over there."

"I hear you." Turning back to Manning, Ted asked," Are we square on what's going on?"

"Yes, sir," the guy nodded.

"Good. Kyle?"

"Yes. Let's go."

In the meantime, at the Roberts' house, Jamie and their daughter waited with bated breath, as they saw the same black sedan go by. Fortunately, Jamie was smart enough to keep the curtains pulled, when to her relief, Alex and Ted didn't waste any time getting there.

Seeing the same sedan parked up the road, Alex called out to Ted to warn him of their so called friend. "Don't move a muscle. Let's wait and see what he does first."

"Yeah, you're right, I can see him clearly from here. And it looks like he's watching their place," he commented, having parked one house shy of the Roberts' four bedroom ranch home in its quiet suburban neighborhood, while Alex hung back a bit further.

"I'll call Jamie and tell her to wait until I give the all clear. Once I do, we'll have no time but to rush them out of there."

Hearing this, Kyle asked to be the one to call, since they knew his voice. "If the phone is tapped, I'll be cool about what I say and how."

"Alex, he has a point. Let's have him make the call."

"Go for it, but be careful, Philips just might be listening."

Meanwhile, inside, Jamie was peering out her living room window.

"Mom, what's going on? Is our ride here yet?" Lori asked, from the living room doorway.

"No, honey, not yet," she fibbed, seeing Kyle and Ted sitting quietly in the 4x4, as if watching something down the street.

Just then the phone rang, scaring her away from the window.

"Mom...?" Lori cried frightenedly.

"I'll get it, dear. Just make sure you have everything you want to take with you," she explained, while waiting on her daughter to leave the room, before picking up the phone.

By the fourth ring, she had finally answered it, only to hear Kyle's voice. "Mrs. Roberts," he asked, "is Lori home?"

"She's in straightening up in her room," she returned, while going back over to the window to see for herself that Kyle was on his cell phone. Seeing this, she knew something was wrong, since he knew Lori was home.

"Oh, I was hoping to talk to her. Can she come to the phone?"

"I'm sorry, no," she replied, not wanting the call to end. Stopping to think of something quick to say, a thought came to her. "Kyle, listen," she instructed carefully. "Do you remember the crack you put in our front living room window the other day?" Seeing him turn to look at the house, she smiled and nodded her head.

"Yeah, sure!" he returned, seeing how they were in sync on what was going on. "There's this guy I know up the road from your place, waiting on me now. I'll just go and get him to help me fix it."

Worried that he would be made, while parked, listening to their conversation, Philips pulled away before Kyle was to supposedly show up.

Seeing this, Alex and Ted were impressed with their quick thinking, without wasting any time, they pulled up to the house, they got out quickly and ran up to the door to get everyone out to the vehicles, before Philips was to return.

"Jamie," Alex grinned, when she opened the door to see her husband's old partner, "how have you been?" he asked, stepping inside to gather up their things to carry out to the Blazer.

"Wow, Alex, it seems like old times, seeing you again," she smiled happily.

"Yes, and you haven't lost your touch either," he continued to grin, having been told her end of the conversation, while on their way up to the house. "Are we ready?" he asked, having gathered up the last of their luggage.

"Yes," she replied, when turning to see her daughter in the arms of her true love. "Oh, yes," she nodded, "we're ready."

"Ok. Ted," Alex turned, "do a quick sweep of the house and garage and make sure everything is secured for when Jason and Manning get here."

"All right," he returned, heading for the back door, while they went on out to Ted's truck.

Once done, they were on their way.

# Chapter Four

The ride to Langley, Indiana was a successful one. Though, having pulled into the driveway of the turn of the Century old Inn, for Alex it was tough to say if it were as successful for him. “Craig, Jarred,” he called out, shutting off the Blazer, before getting out, when seeing his two nephews walk out the front door to greet him. *Or was it to warn him of Jessi's wrath,* he wondered, when seeing Jarred smile. “Is Marcose here?” he asked, meeting them halfway.

“Yes,” Jarred laughed.

“Oh? What's so funny?”

“You'll know soon enough. Until then, you *are* wearing your bullet proof vest, aren't you?”

“Come on, it can't be all that bad, is it?” he asked, not seeing the beautiful Innkeeper yet.

Craig laughed. “Oh, you're safe for now. She's tied up on the phone, in her office. But I'm sure when she gets through… Well, let's just say, you will think you have had it.”

Seeing Alex out front, talking to his nephews, Jessi was certain they were warning him of her wrath. *'So, my darling husband, you're warning him, huh?'* she teased him in their special way of communicating, while the two continued their ability of picking up on each other's thoughts, along with perceiving troubled spirits, from the time they met, when his own was in question.

*'Well someone has to protect him!'* he laughed, quietly, while Jarred held Alex's attention.

*'Oh, sure…!'* she laughed as well, keeping the next thought to herself, while not wanting anyone, including her husband, to know what she was up to next. *Just you wait, Alex Storm. When you least expect it, I will*

*lay into you then,* she went on grinning, till the time was right to go out and greet them.

Until then, they went on talking about how the additions to the Inn were looking pretty good.

"Finished up the main floor guest room just after you left," Craig went on saying.

"Looks good. And the last cabin, how is that going?" he asked, knowing how the last few years his nephew's construction business had taken him a while to get caught up on other work.

"Had to put it off, but now that Jarred is going to be around to give me…" He hesitated to say what was really on his mind, due to their new guests. "Well, you know."

Looking from one nephew to the other, Alex was quick to pick up on Jarred's part in being there, as an undercover officer, playing the part of a handyman. *And play it well, he will,* he grinned, while they headed on up to the porch, where Jessi was then coming out to greet them with her usual bright smile.

"Good day! I hope your trip was a pleasant one. As for your rooms," she went on smiling, "I have our newest guest room, here on the main floor, ready for the two of you ladies, while you," she turned to Kyle, "may want a cabin, or a room on the second floor. It's up to you."

"Alex?" Kyle asked unsuridly.

"You heard her! It's up to you."

"Lori?" he turned back.

"I…" she began.

"Kyle," Jamie spoke up for her daughter, "how about staying close by for now. You know, until she feels a little more secure with her new surroundings."

"That's a wonderful idea," Jessi agreed, sensing the girls' discomfort about being in a strange place. "And if there is anything we can do to make your stay a more pleasant one, just ask," she offered, turning to go back in to get their keys. "Oh, and you will love our cook, Annie, and her helper."

"Oh?" Jamie asked, looking to Alex.

"The helper is my wife, Beth, and she's pregnant with our second child."

"Oh, and then there's our stable hand, Hank, who is a lot like a grandpa," Jessi added, smiling, when returning to hand them their keys.

"Thank you," Jamie offered. "We had just lost my father not too long ago. He and Lori were pretty close."

"I'm sorry to hear that! Alex," Jessi turned, "why don't you guys go and get their things brought in, so they can get settled in."

As they were about to do that, Alex stopped, when seeing his wife come up the hallway.

"Alex...!" she called out, seeing him standing on the front porch.

"Hey, sweetheart, did you miss me?" he teased, while going up to hold her.

"Yes!" she cooed, before letting go to be introduced to the others.

"This is an old friend of mine's wife, Jamie, and their daughter, Lori. And this," he pointed to the young man, standing by Lori's side, "this is Kyle. He's here to help make her stay..." He paused for a better way of putting it, "more fun!"

At that, they all laughed at seeing Jamie's expression.

"Okay, well maybe mothers can't always be a barrel of laughs, but we can sure try," she went on laughing with them.

"Yes, well if you will excuse us," Alex smiled, "we have to get your things brought in so you can get settled in."

Once that was done, Alex couldn't stand suspense any longer of hearing Jessi's wrath. So instead of waiting until she was going to lay it on him, he pulled her into her office to get it over with.

"Alex... what are you doing? We have guest to attend to," she teased, while the others went off to take care of other things.

"Oh, no you don't," he grumbled, closing the door behind them. "Woman, I've been driving myself crazy on the drive here, wondering what waits for me when I got back. So let's have it."

"Have what?" she asked, calmly, while folding her arms in front of her.

"You know what. The hell that I'm about to put you through once again. And how you don't want your family or the guests' lives here put into any kind of danger."

Shrugging her shoulders, she said with a smirk, "What is there to say? Looks like you got it all covered!"

"What…?" he nearly lost it, while out in the foyer, some of the guys, hearing the commotion, laughed, while gathering around to hear what was going on in the office.

"Man, she is letting him have it," Jarred teased.

"No," Craig laughed, "Alex is letting himself have it this time. And I'll lay you odds, she's eating it up in there, knowing he was just waiting for the bomb to drop. Instead, he was fooled."

Just then, the door opened, and Jessi walked out, smiling.

"Now just wait one minute there," Alex groaned with disbelief, while following her out. "You're not going to argue this out like you usually do? What's up with that?"

"Alex, what's the point? You said it all just fine. And now if you will excuse me, I have work to do." Turning to the others, she grinned mischievously. "Well now, what's going on out here?"

Laughing, they all went their separate way, while Kyle went back up to finish unpacking his things.

Later that evening, Alex came back in from spending quality time with his wife and daughter, to talk over his plans with Marcose and Jarred, in the family room, including giving them each a full description of Philips and his car. "Pass this picture around, and tell the others when they get here, what's going on, so they can be on their guard if, God forbid, he were to ever come out here."

"Sure thing," Jarred agreed first, when his own wife walked in to join them, after seeing her cousin.

"Jessi filled me in," Jodi, Jessi's cousin, smiled. "And Alex, I see you're still up to your usual self," the brunette, who looked a lot like her cousin, teased.

"It's a hard habit to break," he laughed, when going up to give her a hug. "How is the antique business?"

"Slow, but once I hit a few estate sales we'll be picking up again."

"Will you and your girls be staying here with Jarred?"

"Yep!" she smiled over at her husband.

"Good. The more, the merrier," he established, when turning to see the young couple head out of the dining room, towards the front door, to go out around the side of the Inn, to go out back, where a large white gazebo awaited them. "Okay, for now, just keep your eyes and ears open, while we're gone," he told the others, before he and Ted headed out.

"This Philips guy," Jamie spoke up, from the family room doorway, when getting in on the last of their conversation, "won't come here, will he?"

"Not unless he hears that you're here! So whenever you or your daughter talks to Jason, don't, and I repeat, don't mention where you are. Don't even mention that it's an Inn that you're at. All he would have to do with that bit of information is start calling around, until he finds the right one. No matter how long it takes."

Shaking her head, she promised not to say a word.

"Does Lori know what's going on?" Jarred asked.

"No."

"Then one of us had better talk to her. We don't have to say too much, just enough to get her to understand the delicacy of this matter."

Alex looked out at the couple walking up onto the gazebo. "Not now, not while she looks so relaxed with her man at her side. Just take turns watching her. If nothing is said when I get back, I will then."

With that, everyone knew what was to be done, when saying their goodbyes, Ted and Alex were off to Camden, where Manning was just finishing his search of the house and ground.

Meanwhile, back at the Inn, Kyle and Lori were still sitting on a glider, in the gazebo, enjoying the brisk fall air.

"What are you thinking?" he asked, while holding her loosely in one arm.

"How peaceful it feels out here. And yet..." She stopped, and suddenly sat up.

"What?" he jolted, wondering what she had sensed.

Smiling, excitedly, "Horses...! I can smell horses! Does she have any here?"

"Well, yeah, there's a stable back off a ways, and to the right! Do you want to go down and see them?" *Damn...* he shook his head angrily. "Well, you know what I mean."

"Kyle," she smiled up at him. "It's okay! Mom and dad do the same thing!"

"Yes, well, do you?"

"Sure! I'd love to," she beamed, filled with excitement, as she got up to head off to the stables a little faster than she should have, when she inadvertently ran into one of the posts that led off the gazebo.

"Woe… there!" he teased, giving her a hand. "If you're not careful, someone may think you've been drinking."

"Yeah…!" she laughed sheepishly, while rubbing her forehead. "Did anyone see that?"

Looking around, he didn't see a soul, though Marcose and Jarred were watching from a safe distance. "No! No curtain calls for you this time."

"Kyle…!" she chived, smacking him, teasingly. "You're a brat!"

"Yeah, well you cut me to the quick, my lady!" he laughed, rubbing his arm, as the two made their way to the stables, where Hank was cleaning out a stall for Jessi's personal horse, Maggi.

Seeing them coming down the pathway, Hank stopped to greet them. "Hello!" he smiled warmly. "You must be Miss Roberts and young Kyle Moorsted. Ms. Jessi and Mr. Alex told me to be expecting you sometime this afternoon. Care to take a horse out for a ride?"

Looking to Lori, Kyle wasn't sure. "Well, Lori, what do you think? We could ride together if you'd like!"

"I…I…I don't know!" she exclaimed, looking slightly in Kyle's direction. "What if I… Well, what if I fell off?"

"Missy," Hank cut in, "you would simply brush yourself off and get right back on. In fact, I have just the horse for you. She's as gentle as a lamb and she knows the trails like the back of my hand. In fact, here comes the lady herself to tell you just that."

"What's that?" Jessi asked, while walking up with Craig, Jarred, Jodi and Jamie, while Marcose made himself invisible.

"What, no girls this time around?" Hank teased about Jessi and Jodi's two girls.

"No," Jodi announced, "they're all in watching a movie that was just released on DVD, including Kevin and Hannah, Lora's husband and their daughter."

"Lora?" Jamie asked puzzledly.

"My oldest," Jessi explained. "She's married and expecting her second in December."

"And she helps out here too?" she added. "How old is she?"

"Twenty. And too, my younger daughter, Cassi, eighteen, helps out, as well."

"Is Cassi married too?" Lori asked.

"No, yet there's one young man that's interested in her, but he's away at college right now."

"Andy?" Craig stated.

"Yes," Jessi laughed, remembering how broken-hearted he was to have to leave her behind.

"What?" Jamie asked, seeing her amused expression.

"Cassi doesn't want college right now, if ever, and I won't push her into going either. It has to be what she wants, so Andy has to go at it without her."

"Mom," Lora spoke up.

"Hey, there, I thought you would be watching the movie Cassi brought home to see!"

"I saw it already."

"Which one was it?" Kyle asked.

"The Day…"

"After?" Jamie smiled. "Of course…!"

"It sounded like a great movie!" Lori smiled.

"Would you like to listen to it when we get back?" Jessi asked, kindheartedly.

"When we get back…?" Lori asked, nervously.

"Well, we have plenty of horses, and you look light enough to share one with Kyle! How about it, Kyle? Care to share a ride with this pretty young lady?" Jessi asked.

"Mom…?" Lori cried more nervously now.

"Oh, but she is going too," Jodi returned, giving the girl's mother a look that could only mean to be supportive.

"You are?" Lori sounded surprised.

Having just come down and see them off, Jamie wasn't planning to do anything of the sort. But for her daughter sake, she agreed. "Well, sure, absolutely…! Kyle," she turned, "you will hold onto her, right?"

With a grin to beat all grins, he agreed.

"Well, shall we?" Craig laughed.

"You guys are crazy," Lori continued to groan.

Seeing this, taking a step toward her, Jodi placed a loving arm around her shoulder. "Lori, my name is Jodi. I'm Jessi's cousin, and married to her husbands' cousin, Jarred, who is standing right next to me," she explained, taking the girl's hand to touch Jarred's arm.

"Hi, Lori," his voice was gentle, while taking her hand to give it a squeeze. "You'll be fine. And sure, all this may seem overwhelming at first, but it's really okay!"

"Lori, it's me, Jessi."

"Yes, I know your voice now."

"What I'm going to do is have Hank, here, bring out my horse, Maggi. She is the most gentlest. Well, then again, they all are, actually. And when he does, I'm going to have you run your hand down her neck. If you get a feel for her, you may be able to relax some. And seeing you, she will know how kind of a person you are. Okay?"

"Yeah, okay!"

Looking to Hank, he nodded his sixty-year old, graying head.

It wasn't long then, while feeling a little nervous about the whole thing, Lori's mom stood back with bated breath, while her daughter was being introduced to Jessi's chestnut mare. Then they all saw the smile spread across her pretty face, and knew everything would be okay.

"I'm ready," Lori announced. "I want to do this. I've done it before."

"You have?" Jessi asked.

"Yes, lots of times."

"Then let me help you, by giving you a visual on what's to come, so it will help you to relax more. First, we'll start by closing your eyes and picture those times you've ridden before. Soon you will feel it all come back to you."

Doing so, she closed her eyes, and with the scent of the stable, she could see it all once again. "Mom...." she cried, anxiously, "it's so true...!"

"You're sure?" Jamie asked.

"Oh, yes, definitely. I'm ready to ride now."

"Okay then," Craig smiled, "let's get some horses saddled up."

Giving Hank a hand, the others soon had six horses saddled up.

Getting on first, Kyle reached down to take Lori's hand, when instructed to reach up to him. And with a little extra help from Craig, who was the closest, had lifted her left foot up into the stirrup with no trouble. Soon seated in front of Kyle, who had given her the saddle to sit on, he sat in just behind it, while the others went on to get up on their own horses.

Jamie, having chosen a pinto, named Sarge, Jessi took Lexis, a palomino, Craig hopped onto his black stallion, Joe, and the rest took the remaining appaloosas and quarter horses.

Feeling Kyle's arm holding her securely, the other one was manning the reigns. "You okay?" he asked softly in her ear.

"Surprisingly, yes," she giggled, until the horse took its first step. But then soon the jitters passed, when she leaned back against her man, while wrapping her arms around his.

Smelling the scent of fresh shampoo in her hair, he took in every moment they had together, while hoping she wouldn't push him away later, when they were alone again. *'Please, Lord,'* he prayed quietly to himself, while going on to enjoy their ride, *'I love her so much. Please help her to except what has happened so that we can move on with the plans we had, before all this had ever happened.'*

Pulling back on Lexis's reigns, while listening to them describe their surroundings, Craig too, reigned back.

"You felt it too, didn't you?" he asked his wife.

"He loves her. And well, what she is having to deal with..." Jessi stopped and shook her head sadly.

"Yes, it's getting in the way of their happiness."

"Uh huh."

He grinned his crooked grin. "Yeah, and you want to help them, don't you?"

"Craig..." she started.

"Jess, it okay. Just do what you can," he smiled, looking back at the lovebirds, as Kyle appeared to be telling Lori about Michigan's largest lake that ran along the backside of their property, Lake Michigan.

"What?" she asked, when he got quiet.

"The two of them," he smiled. "They really look good together."

With that said, the rest of the ride went pretty smooth. While back in Camden, all was quiet there, too, with Philips staying away.

"Manning," Alex spoke up, heading for the front door, "I want you and your k-9 on the back of the house, while Ted, you're inside."

"And you?" Ted asked, standing in the kitchen doorway with a cup of coffee in hand.

"Since it's been pretty quiet, I'll be parked across the street in the neighbor's driveway, where I can keep a better watch over things there."

"All right," he nodded, walking over to set his cup down on the coffee table, before checking his weapon.

"Oh, and Alex," Jason spoke up, laughing, just before Alex could open the door, "the Barrett's will keep you supplied with plenty of coffee, while you're there."

"Great, just as long as it's not too much," he laughed back. "Or they just might find me having to violate one of their bushes from time to time."

"Yes, I can see it now," Ted laughed. "Federal Marshal caught with his pants down, while on a stakeout. What do you think, Jason," he turned, grinning, "a misdemeanor or a felony?"

"Yeah, yeah, yeah, laugh it up now," Alex grinned. "Just remember, Ted, when it's your turn to go out, let's see how you would like it."

"Oh, but I thought you didn't think that was such a good idea!" Jason cut in, laughing.

"Yeah, well I changed my mind," Alex smiled, "seeing how the two of you are going to give me such a hard time, while I'm out there."

"Ah… do I here crying, coming from my buddy, here?" Ted ribbed.

"Uh huh, laugh all you want," he continued smiling, while switching over to his headset, before heading out.

Doing the same, Jason returned, "No, we'll leave you alone to entertain yourself. I've got to get ready for bed," he announced, tiredly.

"All right," Alex replied, closing the door behind him.

A short while later, and four cups of coffee to boot, Alex noticed the Barrett's lights go out just then. "Well, looks like the Barrett's are heading to bed now!" he exclaimed to his men over his headset. "Nope," he came back, seeing one of them come out to see if he needed anything more, before saying their goodnights. "No," he returned, saying his thanks, "I should be fine. If I do, my men are right across the street."

"All right," the man smiled, and went back inside.

Taking that time to look up some information on his laptop, Alex went searching for specialized cell phones, specifically ones that had a GPS built in. Finding what he was looking for, he wrote down the information and closed the lid. "Good," he noted to himself. "First thing tomorrow I'll go and purchase a half a dozen of them for Jason, his wife and daughter, and Ted and myself. Heck, while I'm at it, one for Jarred. I have a feeling he and Marcose will be needed here, when the Roberts get back."

As for the rest of the night, Alex and Manning took shifts so the other could sleep, while inside, Ted took light naps, keeping his headset on, in case something was to go down.

# Chapter Five

Back at the Inn, it was pretty much the same there, quiet, as Jessi and her people said their goodnights, after a busy afternoon of horseback riding, followed up with a great dinner, and a movie.

"Are you tired?" Kyle asked one very sleepy young lady.

"No. Well kinda. Why?" Lori softly smiled.

"Oh, I was just thinking, if it was okay with our watchdogs," he grinned, seeing Marcose and Jarred standing out on the back patio, off of the Inn's family room.

Hearing this, Jarred excused himself to come in and see what was going on.

"I was just about to come out and ask if I could take her out onto the patio to sit and enjoy the moonlight, before turning in. I kinda figured I would have to put it passed you guys first, though, with security being what it is and all."

"I see no reason why not. As for letting us know, we appreciate the thought. Make sure you never forget, as Alex and your parents," he looked to Lori, "would have our hides."

"Yes," she laughed, lightly, while Kyle took her by the arm to escort her out through the French doors.

As for their watchdogs, the two slipped off to go down and stand by the French doors of the two bedroom basement quarters, where Jessi and her girls once lived, years ago, when she first came into owning the Inn.

"Are you warm enough?" Kyle asked, looking down on her in the soft light streaming out from the family room doorway.

"Mmmm... yes," she sighed, taking in the soft breeze, as it blew a strand of her soft blonde hair across her face.

Moving it out of her way for her, they continued to stroll out a little further onto the patio. It was then the two heard a ruffling sound, off in the bushes, behind them.

"Kyle…" she cried, gripping tightly to his arm, "what was that?"

"I don't know!" he exclaimed, bringing her in close to him, while one of their guards went off to check it out, while leaving the other to come up and watch over them.

"Marcose…?" Jarred called out from the patio.

"It's nothing to be alarmed about. Just a possum looking for some food," he laughed, as it scurried away, when hearing him run up on him.

Looking back to the girl huddling close in Kyle's arms, Jarred motioned silently with his head to let Kyle know she was still frightened.

"Hey," he turned to glance down at her, "it's okay!"

"No, it's not!" she cringed. "Even when I could see, sitting outside my parents' house at night, and seeing those horrible things, they had always reminded me of oversized rats."

"Do you want to go back inside then?"

"Yes, but not just yet," she replied, while cuddling a little closer.

Loving the way she felt in his arms at that moment, he didn't argue, but looked to Jarred, and mouthed the words *thank you*.

"Sure," he smiled, leaving them once again, when Marcose returned to go back to their spot, until the two were ready to go back inside.

"Young love," Marcose smiled, quietly. "I recall a few other couples like that, but a bit older and not all that long ago," he laughed quietly.

"Alex and Beth?" he asked.

"And you and Jodi?" he went on laughing, while thinking about someone else, when Craig was but a troubled spirit. However, back then, in his state, no one would have thought it possible that he and Jessi could have fallen in love the way they did. Though, as the story went, not able to hold her in his past state, Craig's spirit, through the willingness of his uncle, stepped in to use Alex's body to be with the woman he loved, but only for short spells, as his strength would only deplete after awhile. For Alex though, unaware of what they would do with that time, he could only guess, for whenever he came to, he would sometimes find himself wet, as if from having just taken a shower, before being returned to his natural state. *'But then who was to argue,'* Marcose grinned respectively, *'she was, and still is a very beautiful woman. Those two indeed are very remarkable people.'*

"Hey, where were you just now?" Jarred interrupted, when seeing his smile turn into a grin.

"Huh? Oh, just thinking of the old days," he shook his head at another incident that took place out back of Craig's old farmhouse.

Jarred laughed quietly, knowing quite a few of those stories from the past. "Care to share some of them?"

He chuckled, shaking his head. "Yeah, well why not." Telling him about the time he heard a woman's scream, from a small lake, along the back portion of Craig's old property, Marcose laughed, and went on, "Coming up on the scene with guns drawn, Baker and I thought Belaro had gotten to her, during one of her visits to the farmhouse, without her girls. But then finding out later it was one of Craig's temporary possessions of his uncle's body, well that was some surprise. Heck, come to think of it, even Max wasn't bothered by what had taken place that night."

"No, he wouldn't have, since Alex had spent a great deal of time training her German Shepherd to sense out trouble. And that particular time, according to Alex, Alex, himself, wasn't even aware that Craig was going to do what he did, until afterward."

"Come to think of it, wasn't it while making one of his runs out at the house, when unaware that Jessi and Max was out back, where she was taking in a moonlit swim, while the dog lay nearby?"

"Yes, and from what Craig told me, Max didn't even make a sound when seeing what was thought to being Alex coming up on them quietly. As for Jessi, she was taken by surprise, thinking it *was* Alex at first, and not Craig."

"When did she figure it out?"

"When that unique smile of his came through. After that, well, you know what went on from there."

"Yes," he laughed quietly.

Meanwhile, thinking to himself, Jarred had his own memories of the past when it came to Jodi. Some sad, after years had gone by, since her grandmother told him he wasn't going to go out with her. Like Jessi, the two had both lost their true love in an automobile accident. And with his line of work, she didn't want her granddaughter going through it again.

But then, one stormy day, years later, having to find shelter for herself, and a load of antiques she was hauling, seeing her climbing through one of his windows, thinking his place was abandoned, somewhat like his cousin's, Jarred laughed, thinking how the habitant of his own place was very much alive, but in hiding until Alex could catch the man who tried doing to him what Belaro had done to Craig. Fortunate for Jarred, though, someone had seen the incident and called 911.

"Hey," Marcose nudged with an elbow, "we had better stay alert here. We can't keep thinking about what was, when we have to keep an eye on what is."

"Yes, you're right. But speaking of what was, after Alex's transfer from Detective to Federal Marshal, I am sure glad the Commander let us all team up again."

"Oh, but it wasn't all the Commander's doing," he grinned, knowing about the talk Alex and their old Commander had, before his leaving.

"What? Alex...?" Jarred asked with a humorous grin on his face.

"Yep!"

"Yeah, well, just wait until he finds out about our transfer to the higher power."

"Yes. After all, why should he be the only one to move on?"

"Yes, and I can't wait to join him."

"Then watch out bad guys, because the bad ass team is back to rock your world," Marcose grinned pridefully.

Shaking his head, Jarred turned back, sensing a storm was on its way, while seeing how the young couple was doing.

"Mmmm..." Lori was just saying, when hearing a soft rumble of thunder off in the distance. "Sounds like we're in for a storm? Oh... how I have..." She stopped, when recalling the storm that took her brother's life, that night, in the mountains of Tennessee. Feeling the pain of it all, she couldn't quite shake it, when all of a sudden she went into a panic attack. "Oh, God..." she cried out feeling her chest wrench in pain, as it put such a hold on her heart. Unable to catch her breath she tried getting Kyle's attention. But then, when all efforts were lost, she began to feel her body cave into an even deeper darkness.

"Lori...?" Kyle called out, when feeling her body go limp next to him. "Oh, God..., Lori...!" he called out again, while trying his hardest to get her to relax. "Lori...!"

Hearing the commotion, not only did Jarred and Marcose come running up the slight slope from the basement entrance below, but Jessi and Craig, as well, when hearing the cries from outside their main-floor quarters, just off the office side of the Inn, which Craig added along with the other things done to the Inn.

Reaching the two in no time, the four of them saw what was going on, as Jessi knelt down to check on her.

"Ms. Jessi," Kyle cried concernly, "we were just sitting here, enjoying the night air, when then we heard the thunder! Good, Lord, Ms. Jessi, Lori lost her brother in an accident that involved a storm."

"So I heard," she stated, "which may have thrown her into a panic attack, causing her to lose her breath. Lori…!" she called out, slapping her cheeks to get a response. "Lori!"

"Please…" he continued on, "tell me she's going to be all right…!"

"I sense she is breathing some, but I won't know until we get her to the hospital to get her seen. Craig…?" she turned.

"Right here," he announced, coming around to kneel by her side.

"Do you know if your father is on duty tonight?"

"Sure! He and mom both are," he replied, referring to his father, a semi-retired doctor, and his mother, a highly respected nurse at a nearby Memorial Hospital in Crawfordsfield.

"Jarred, go in and get her mother. Let her know what is going on, and then call Jodi and the others and tell them what's going on. Craig, we need to get her out to your truck, since it's the closest thing we have to get her there."

"Ok," he stated, just as he was about to pick her up.

"No, I'll get her," Kyle announced, while leaning down to sweep her up into his arms.

"All right. Jess," he reached out, taking her hand to lead the way in through the family room, passed the dining room, and on into the foyer, where they met up with her mother.

"Lori…?" she cried, looking her over, just as they hurried her out to Craig's truck.

"Jamie," Jessi offered on their way out, "Craig's mom and dad can take care of her at the hospital in Crawfordsfield, since he is a semi-retired doctor, and she is a register nurse at Memorial. They've seen things like this before. They will know what to do."

"Are we ready?" Jarred asked, while Jodi and the others gathered around, after his call.

"Yes," Craig announced, opening both passenger doors for his wife and Jamie.

"Jess, don't worry about a thing here. Just get her to the hospital," Hank stated, a few feet away, along with Annie and the others.

"Cass..."

"Mom, it's okay," she smiled.

"Annie..." Jessi then turned to the woman who had been like a mother to her.

"We'll be fine," she noted her concerns with the storm coming in.

"Jo," Jarred leaned down to give her a kiss, knowing she, like her cousin, wasn't a big fan of storms, "they're saying that it's not supposed to be too bad, and Marcose will be staying behind to keep an eye on things here, along with the others."

"Go," she smiled, kissing him sweetly on the lips. "We'll be waiting to hear from you guys."

"Jarred," Craig turned to his cousin once they were all in the truck, "you coming?"

"Yes." He studied his wife, before heading for his own truck. "Yes, let's get going."

Starting up their trucks, they were off.

While on their way, Kyle continued to hold Lori in his arms, while her mother sat next to them, praying. *'Blessed be the Father over His children. Be merciful unto us and protect my child from the nightmare of that horrible night. Please dear Lord, hear my cries for Your everlasting love and healing powers. In Jesus name, I pray unto You. A-men.'*

"Jessi...?" Craig looked quietly to his wife.

"I know," she returned, feeling the girls' pain, as he did.

"Yeah, sometimes I really hate these gifts of ours," he stated, while fighting to hold back the tears that threatened to fall on account of the girls' ordeal.

# Chapter Six

Reaching the hospital's Emergency entrance, being the closest to the door, Craig quickly went in to find his dad, a tall, older version of his son, though, in Bob's case, wearing wire rimmed glasses, and standing at the check-in desk, holding a patient's chart, as Craig called out, rushing up to take him by the arm, "Dad, we have a situation out in my truck that needs your immediate attention."

"Why, what's going on, son?" he asked, setting the chart aside to follow him out.

"A young female, from the Inn had a bad panic attack. She's currently unconscious and in the back seat with her mother and boyfriend."

Passing a male attendant, in blue scrubs, while on their way out, Bob told him to get a gurney and follow them out.

Once outside, where the rain was now coming down a bit harder over the canopy of the ER's driveway, reaching his truck, where Jessi was standing just outside the back passenger door, Bob went around to make a quick assessment of Lori's condition. "Son," he called out, "as soon as the gurney gets here, we need to get her inside, and have a cardiac cart waiting for us in exam Room Four."

"A cardiac cart…?" Jamie cried.

"It's only for precaution," Sue, Craig's mother, and nurse in her late fifties, explained, when joining them, to see what they had.

About that time, Lori began to come to. "Mmmm… Mom…?" she moaned softly, reaching out for her. "Mom…?"

"Right here, baby…" she called back, taking her hand. "You're going to be all right."

She didn't feel all right, when hearing other voices around her. Scared, she asked, when trying to set up, "W…where am I…?"

"At the hospital, dear," Bob explained, while attempting to listen to her heart through his stethoscope.

"Doc...," the orderly called out, when arriving with the gurney and one other assistant.

Giving them a hand, Craig reached in, as Bob moved aside to give him room. "Lori, it's me, Craig," he announced softly. "I'm just going to take you from Kyle's arms in order to place you on a gurney so that we can get you inside to be checked out."

"O...Okay...!" she uttered timidly, feeling the transaction out to the awaiting gurney.

Once there, they had her strapped her in, and about to roll her away, when fear took over once again. "Kyle..." she cried out, stopping them.

"It's all right," he called back, rushing to her side to take her hand. "I'm right here."

"Don't leave me...! Please... don't leave me...!"

"I'm not going anywhere. I'll be right here, by your side, for as long as they will let me," he assured her, while stroking her hair.

Seeing that he had her calmed down, Bob spoke up, ordering them to get moving, while Craig went around to park the truck in a nearby space. "Ok, people, let's get her into exam Room Four."

On their way in, taking that moment, Jessi quickly filled his mom and dad in on what had happened, including a brief story on how Lori lost her sight.

"Yes, we have seen something like this before," Bob explained, once they reached the exam room. "Sue," he turned, "once you have helped get her undressed, and into a gown, get her vitals and an EKG. I want to know all there is to know about our girl here."

"All right," she returned, heading for the curtains. "Ma'am," she asked, while holding off on closing them, "is this your daughter?"

"Yes. May I stay with her?"

"Yes. That would be wise in her situation. As for the rest of you, it'll be a little while before we know anything. You might want to wait out in the waiting room."

"Lori," Kyle leaned down to give her a kiss, "I won't be far, I promise."

"She'll be okay with her mother and I," Sue smiled, before turning to her son. "it won't be too awful long, sweetie. Get them all a cup of coffee or something, while you wait."

"Ok, Mom," he leaned in, giving her a kiss on the cheek. "I love you!"

She smiled up at him. "I love you, too. Now scoot." She patted him on the arm, and went back to her patient.

Back in the waiting room, time seemed to have drug by, while pacing the floor. "This is driving me crazy," Kyle groaned. "What if her attack could have caused her heart some damage on top of her blindness?"

"Then you will learn to deal with it," Jarred offered, flatly. "Because when you love someone, nothing gets in the way."

"You could say that again," Craig muttered under his breath, when going over to the coffee machine with Jessi to get them all some more coffee, and another cappuccino for his wife.

"You know, it isn't her heart we need to be concerned about."

"No...?" he asked, handing her, her cup.

"No. Her heart is just fine. It's the dreams she keeps having. It'll keep playing itself over and over in her head, until she can forgive herself for the argument she had gotten into with her parents, before they left on their trip."

"You're right. And heck, what had happened that night wasn't even in her control!"

"No, it wasn't," she agreed, with a heavy sigh, while the two shook their heads and carried the coffees back over to the group.

In a matter of minutes, Jamie and her daughter were brought back out to join the others.

Upon seeing them round the corner first, Kyle jumped up to go to her.

"How is she?" the others asked.

"She'll be fine. She just needs rest and a lot of support," Jamie told them, while taking out her phone to call her husband.

Taking Bob aside, Jarred reminded him who she and her mother were.

"Jason Roberts's girl..." he grinned. "Well I'll be. I haven't seen him, since he moved to Illinois all those years ago. In fact, that would have put her and her little brother just about..." he thought back a moment, "three and five?"

"Yes, well, her little brother is the one she keeps having the recurring dreams about. And I was told he was killed in an automobile accident, when going on a family vacation, two years ago, through the Smoky Mountains. During which time, a storm came up, blinding them. It was then that Jason had lost control of the car, when a by-stander saw what had happened and stopped to call it in. Afterwards, he got out to help get them to safely, all but Sam, that is. When going back to get him, the car exploded, and Sam was killed instantly."

"Good Lord, that had to have been horrible on them," he said, conveying his sympathy on the matter.

Meanwhile, back at the Roberts house, sound asleep on the couch, when hearing the phone ring, Ted jumped up like a shot and went right to Jason's room, wondering if it was Philips calling him. On the way, he called Alex over the headset.

"What's up?" his voice came back in a deep, grumbly state, having been jerked out of a restful slumber, while Manning kept watch for a few hours.

"We have a call, but I haven't confirmed who is on the other end yet."

"Find out. I'm on my way in." Putting the radio inside his vest pocket, Alex was out of his vehicle and on his way across the street by the time Ted had reached Jason's bedroom door.

Seeing the light on from beneath it, he tapped lightly, before going in. There, he saw the man lying in bed with one hand holding the phone, the other to his forehead. The expression on his face told Ted it wasn't Philips, but something yet closer to home.

"Is she there with you now?" he asked all choked up.

"Yes." Taking the phone to their daughter, Jamie told her it was her father on the line.

"Daddy…?" she cried. "Daddy, make it go away…!"

"The storm?" he asked knowingly.

"Yes…!" she continued, while thinking of her brother. "Oh, Daddy…!"

"I know, honey, we miss him too…! We… miss him… too…," he, too, cried, as he sat up in bed.

Just then, hearing Alex coming up behind him, after telling Manning to stand ready, Alex asked, "What's going on?"

"It's his daughter. From what I've been able to pick up so far, it's something about a storm and… well, I'm not sure without waiting until he gets off the phone to find out."

That didn't take long, when he told his daughter to put her mother back on the line. "Jamie, have you told me everything?"

"Yes. Bob's going to prescribe something for her to take, to help her get through the panic attacks."

"Bob?" he asked, looking to Alex.

"You know!" he laughed. "Doctor '*Gunshot*' Bob…! We would always call him that, because we were always going to him to have our gunshots fixed."

"Oh, Lord," he laughed, "I know who you're talking about…!"

"That's nice. Now how about sharing it with me," she laughed.

"The doctor, back home, who had always taken out the bullets whenever one of us had gotten shot!"

"Doctor Bob…?"

"Yes?" Bob turned, when hearing his name called out.

"Hey, honey, I'll talk to you later," she told him, when seeing the smile on Bob's face, as she was about to hang up.

"Okay. Tell my girl, I'll talk to her tomorrow."

Saying goodbye, they each hung up to talk to the ones they were with.

"That was Jamie," Jason explained. "It seems they are about to get a storm tonight, and Lori went into a severe panic attack, that took her breath away. When she passed out, they rushed her to the hospital in Crawfordsfield, where Bob was on duty."

"How is she?" Alex asked, concernedly.

"She's shaken pretty bad. That and they did an EKG for precautionary measures just to be certain her heart was affected by the attack."

"And…?" they both asked curiously.

"No damage, thank God. Now they want Jamie to take her home, have her relax, and try to get her mind of things."

"Home…? As in back here…?" Alex sounded alarmed, just then.

"No. Back to the Inn, where there is a lot around her to keep her mind occupied."

"And Jarred and Marcose, where are they now?"

"Jarred, along with Jessi, Craig and Kyle are with them at the hospital. As for Marcose, he's back at the Inn, keeping an eye on things there."

"Good. For now, what do you say we get some sleep? Tomorrow I have to run in and get some special cell phones we're going to start carrying."

"What's so special about them?" Jason asked, puzzledly.

"They're each built with a GPS, so if anyone gets into trouble, the others will know right where to find them."

"I guess it would be too much to ask, that there would be no trouble?"

"Sorry," Alex returned. "Not likely."

Meanwhile, back at the hospital, after their brief reunion, Jamie and the others headed back to the Inn, where Lori and her mother, went to their room to change for bed. While doing that, Jessi went to the kitchen to put on some hot chocolate for Lori, knowing that sleep was the last thing she would want, because of the dreams.

"Is that for Lori?" Craig asked, walking in.

"Yes. I'm hoping it would soothe her fears away and maybe help keep her awake a little while longer, so that when she does fall off to sleep, she would be too tired to dream."

"Are you going to stay up with them then?"

"For a short while, in case they need an extra person, if one of them gets too tired to stay up with her, she shouldn't be alone."

"Okay, I'll break out the cards then, since they helped us three years ago and again when Beth gave birth to Bethany."

"Bethany," Jessi laughed, at how he used to call Beth that, when Alex first introduced them. And when they were told she was going to have a girl that seemed to have been the fitting name to call her.

"Yes, thanks to me," he laughed, picking up on what she was thinking.

Once the chocolate was ready, Jessi took it into her, while Craig rounded up the cards and a few willing players, namely their cousins, and even Beth, when the storm woke her and Bethany, while staying in one of the cabins set up for them.

Coming in to see what was going on, Craig reached out to take his uncle's two year old. "Come here you little munchkin. I know right where you belong," he laughed.

Surprisingly, seeing Lori walk in just then, Bethany wanted to go right to her instead.

"What…?" Craig teased, seeing the girl looking a little lost at the moment. "Well, Miss Roberts, it looks as though Beth and Alex's little girl wants you to hold her."

"Me…?" she asked, just as surprised.

"Yep!" he smiled, while taking her over to a card table that was being set up.

Taking a seat, she was handed one loving little girl. "Oh, my," she smiled for the first time, since getting back.

"Lori?" her mother spoke up.

"It's her hair," she cooed, feeling it. "It's so soft!" Soon she had forgotten all about the storm that was nearly on top of them.

Walking back into the family room, Jessi asked, while she and her cousin brought in some drinks and something to snack on, "What are we going to play?"

"Well, that all depends on who's playing?" he asked. "Mrs. Roberts are you up for a friendly game of Five Hundred Rummy?"

"Kyle?" Jamie turned to ask.

"Count me in," he grinned.

"Uh, oh, you all had better watch out!" Lori laughed. "He is a pretty good card player, and gives no mercy."

"Well, let's see what you are made of," Jarred joked, while shuffling the deck.

With seven people playing now, they were going to need a second deck to make it more interesting.

It wasn't long after the game got started, little Bethany slipped off to sleep in Lori's arms. Holding her, she started thinking about the children they once talked about having, when once again her heart started aching at the memories.

With Kyle's help at the end of one hand, he took her over to the couch, where she could lie down with the little tike still in her arms, so not to wake her. "You okay?" he asked, seeing a tear make its way down her cheek.

"I was just thinking, is all."

"About our own kids if we had had any?"

"Uh huh!"

"They would be just as beautiful as their mother, and just as ornery, too."

"Look who's talking!" she teased, smiling.

"Okay, so she gets her beauty from you, and her meanness from me." Giving her a kiss on the cheek, he went back to playing, while from time to time, stealing a peek at the two of them cuddled up on the sofa together. *'Like a real mother and daughter would look,'* he grinned.

Meanwhile, as the game went on, so did the storm, though, not nearly as bad as they thought it would be. As for Lori, sleeping peacefully on the sofa, she did wind up dreaming, though this time it was about her and Kyle, holding their own baby. "Mmmm…" she cooed out openly in her sleep, when heard by just a few around the table.

"Was that her?" Jamie asked the others.

With a smile on his face, Kyle nodded, "It certainly was. And I would say she is having a dream about something nice this time."

Looking to her husband, Jessi smiled. "I would say it's about a baby, judging by the way she is holding Bethany."

"You're probably right," Craig smiled, knowingly, while looking on at the two.

Getting up from the table, both Craig and Kyle, Craig gently picked up Bethany, seeing how it would be hard for Beth to do, and Kyle carefully picked up Lori, so not to wake her.

"Momma Roberts," Kyle spoke softly, "if you will get the door to your room when I get her there, I will lay her on the bed for you."

Getting to her feet, Jamie hurried to their room and opened the door, then rushed over to pull back the blankets, while not once did Lori stir from her slumber.

"Thanks, Kyle, I'll take it from here," she smiled, while looking down on her peacefully sleeping daughter, with her own sweet smiling face, as she went on sleeping.

Taking their leave, the others turned in for what was left of the wee hours of the morning, before having to start another busy day at the Inn.

When morning came, finding herself in a strange bed, Lori called out for her mother.

"I'm right here, dear," she called back from the bathroom doorway with a washcloth in hand. "I was just getting ready for breakfast. Are you hungry?"

"Starving!" she replied, sitting up. "But where am I, and where is Kyle?"

"You're in my room, as it was pretty late when we all went to bed. As for Kyle, he's probably still asleep up in his room."

"Oh." She looked a little sad at first.

"Do you want to talk about last night?" she asked, going back in to finish up.

"Last night?" she asked puzzledly. "W…what do you mean?"

"The dream…! Most of us around the table heard you coo in your sleep. Were you having a nice dream?"

"W…wait! I was doing what?" she blushed.

"Cooing," she was saying, when coming back out to go over and sit on the bed beside her. "Now, tell me, what was this cooing about?" she asked, while placing a gentle hand on her daughter's.

"Mom… I don't know what you're talking about," she returned, while scooting passed her to get up.

Watching her closely, Lori felt her way around the room.

"Stop," she instructed. "The bathroom is six paces to your left, or as your father would put it, to your nine o'clock."

Finding it from that, Lori soon found the sink and washcloths.

Meanwhile, upstairs, Kyle was just about to get up, when his cell phone began to ring. "Hello?" he answered, while rubbing the sleep from his eyes.

"Kyle, it's Alex Storm."

"Yes, Mr. Storm. How can I help you? And is everything all right with Mr. Roberts? I mean, Jason?"

"Jason is fine, and you can call me Alex from now on, except for in public, in case we are being watched."

"Of course. Now, what can I do for you?"

"First, how is Lori?"

Smiling, "She's fine. The dreams of her brother didn't come back to haunt her last night, with the storm going on, and all, which has always been what had triggered them before. You did know about the dreams, didn't you?"

"Jason may have mentioned it last night. Now, for why I'm calling you at this time of the morning. I don't want you to be in a hurry to get back to the office."

"Oh?"

"No, as I'll be sitting in for you so that it will explain my continuous presence here," he returned, while already sitting at his desk, with brown hair and wire rimmed glasses. Though, keeping with his same icy blue eyes, not like when he used brown contacts, when he was in disguise before, while working on the Belaro case.

"Will you also be using an alias, like before, too?"

"Yes. Jordan Scott."

"I like that. So, what do you want me to do while you're there?"

"Help me, but from a safe place that Ted and I will have set up for us to work out of, in case Philips starts nosing around. He'll just think that Jason has sent you off somewhere to work a new case."

"And will I be expected to stay there too?"

"No. You'll be in an adjoining room, so not to be seen coming and going. And only when it's safe for you to come out, will you be allowed to."

"What? I won't be able to go anywhere?"

"Kyle, you are not even supposed to be back in town! Remember, you are supposed to be away on a new assignment."

"I'm sorry. Of course, you are right. Will I still be able to see or talk to Lori, any?"

"Yes, of course, but only when it can be made safe for the two of you."

Sitting there on the side of his bed, back at the Inn, his mind was going in all sorts of directions, while shaking his head glumly.

"Kyle, you still there?"

"Yes. Sure I am."

"Now, tell me, just where I can find O'Connely's file, and what all you have been able to find out on the case. Don't leave anything out."

Getting up to pace the room, Kyle told him everything he could remember. Clear up to finding the mystery envelope slid under his door.

"And that's everything now? You haven't left out a thing?"

"Yes, that's everything. Now, if it's okay with you, sir, I would really like to get ready for breakfast, as I don't want to miss a moment with Lori, if I'm going to have to stay away, even for a short time."

"It's for yours and her safety in mind, you understand? We are all just trying to make Philips think that Jason has backed off the case to a certain degree."

"I understand. And I sure hope it works for their sake."

"I hope so too," he offered, understandably, when Jason and Ted walked in to see him sitting behind the desk in his disguise, since he had gotten up and left, before they did. "Well, we'll be in touch if we have any more questions for you."

"All right," Kyle returned, saying his goodbyes, when returning the cell phone back into its carrier, while sitting there thinking sadly of his love downstairs.

Back at the office, Jason laughed, while closing the door behind him, "Jordan Scott, I presume?"

"At your service, sir!" he grinned, positively humorously, while getting up to go around the desk to shake his hand. "Kyle had just filled me in on what all he gathered, before getting off the phone to join the others for breakfast."

"Breakfast? I almost forgot," he grinned, favorably, while looking a bit hungry, himself.

"Is that a smile I see?" Alex grinned.

"Well, we should be getting something to eat, before digging into to all this work. Don't you think?"

"Do you have someplace in mind?" Ted asked.

"A diner we go to on the weekends. It's not far. What do you say?"

"Sounds good," the two agreed, while securing their service revolvers under their suit jackets, before heading out and locking up behind them.

"Mr. Roberts," Cindy announced, while walking up with a set of files in her arms to be put onto Kyle's desk.

"Cindy," Jason spoke up, "this is Jordan Scott. He'll be filling in for Kyle, while he is out. And to his left, is Mr. Green, his runner. Jordan, Mr. Green, this is Cindy, my secretary. If you ever need anything, she is the one to help you, if I am not in."

"Cindy," Alex and Ted both bowed their heads to the smiling secretary.

"Mr. Scott. Mr. Green."

Excusing herself, Jason saw the folders just as she was about to reach for the door, not knowing they had already locked up to leave.

"Cindy," he stopped her, "are those for Kyle?"

"Oh, yes, sir. I was just bringing them in to put on his desk."

"I'll take them from here. Thank you."

Handing them over, an envelope slipped out onto the floor, at his feet.

"What's this?" Alex asked, retrieving it for him.

Seeing the handwriting, Jason didn't have to guess, but recognized it almost immediately.

"Jason?" Alex spoke up, studying his expression, when turning to see that Cindy hadn't left yet.

"That will be all, Cindy," Jason said firmly. "Oh, and Cindy," he called out, as she turned to go back to her desk, "we're going out for an hour or so. Hold my calls, won't you, please?"

"Yes, sir. And Mr. O'Connelly, if he were to call?"

"Tell him to call my cell phone. But Cindy…!"

"Yes, sir?"

"Don't give it out to anyone else. And make sure there is no one around to over hear what you are giving him."

"Of course, sir." She turned then to head back to her desk, where there were calls coming in at that time. Luckily the calls were for his partner.

"Shall we?" he indicated toward the door, while pocketing the note.

Once at the diner, the three took a seat at a corner table, where they could talk privately. While there, Jason brought out the note and removed it from its envelope.

"Jason?" Alex leaned in to inquire quietly about its contents, as the man began to read it.

*Jason,*

*Well I see you have finally took my warnings seriously by getting your man off the case. Now be a good gent and leave the rest alone. Tell O'Connelly that there is just not enough evidence to pursue it further. If not, I'll be paying a visit to your lovely family.*

*P.*

At that moment, his expression paled.

"Ja..." Alex began again, when Jason handed the letter over to him.

Looking rather relieved that Philips had no idea they had gotten his family out of there, Alex turned to Ted. "Manning, is he still at the house?"

"Yes, we figured you wouldn't have minded if he were to get some rest, while having the K-9 keep watch."

"That's fine. Aramis is a great watchdog. He will get Manning up if anything were to go down. And then again, that's if he doesn't take care of the problem, himself," he laughed boldly.

# Chapter Seven

Back at the Inn, after breakfast, Jamie offered a hand at the front desk, when seeing Cassi, Jessi's younger daughter, become overwhelmed by incoming calls and guests wanting to checkout.

"That's fine," Jarred walked up, hearing her offer to help. "But let Cassi handle the phone, in case Philips was to call. We don't want him tipped off hearing your voice, in case he knows what you sound like."

"Okay!" she agreed, while being offered another chair to sit in next to Cassi.

Ready to take on the busy day, Jarred's cell phone rang, while the two took care of several guests, which in time filled the second floor and most of the cabins.

As for Lori, she offered to help Jessi's older daughter baby-sit Bethany over at Beth's cabin, while Beth worked in the Inns' kitchen with Annie, a short, average built woman in her mid fifties, who had been there since Jessi purchased the Inn, before Craig came along.

Seeing how she and Lora were doing, Kyle headed out to the stables to lend Hank, and Travis, an average height and wavy brown-haired man in his early thirties, a hand with the horses.

"Just hold him still, while I get these hooves cleaned," Hank yelled.

"I don't think he wants to have his hooves messed with," Travis yelled back, while trying hard to control Craig's black stallion.

"Here, let me help," Kyle offered, running up, having been brought up around horses since he was little.

"You know about these creatures, do you?" Hank asked, with sweat running down the sides of his face.

"Sure do. The greatest animals God graced the earth with. Does he have shoes on now?" he asked, sensing tenderness in his left hoof.

"Yes. They all do. Why?" Travis asked.

"It's just that he might have something lodged in that left one, is all."

Taking a look, the graying haired man, in his sixties, laughed, "Well I'll be. He does at that." Removing the object, Joe was set free to run the pasture, with only a slight tenderness to his hoof. "Son, I'm impressed. Been doing this most of my life, and I have to say, this is the first time I didn't think to check that out."

"Yes, well the smallest of things can sometimes cause the biggest of problems," he explained, while watching the magnificent stallion run with the rest of Jessi's horses. "Wow," he noted excitedly, "what a sight."

"They sure are," the two added from the open doorway, before getting back to work, with Hank issuing out orders on where the feed goes, before unloading a wagon of hay and straw.

Meanwhile, having gotten off the phone with Alex, Jarred turned to fill Marcose in on what took place back in Camden.

"That's good news!" Marcose stated. "Philips has no clue the man's wife and daughter are here, or even gone, as far as that goes."

"No, and to a certain degree Philips thinks because Jason had pulled Kyle off the case, he is pulling back, as well."

"Has he said what we are to do now?"

"Stay with them, I presume. Which reminds me, where are they now?"

"I've been watching Lori over at Beth and Alex's cabin. She's with Lora and her little girl, Hannah, babysitting Bethany. And Kyle, I figured, was all right going down to the stables alone to see if Hank could use some help, seeing how Lori was in good hands."

"Good. So I guess we decide who we want to keep an eye on, Lori, Kyle or Jamie! Which do you want?"

"I'll stay out here and watch over Lori. As for Kyle, Hank and Travis are good to keep an eye on him, since they know what's going on."

"That leaves Jamie, while I play the happy bellman," Jarred laughed, when turning to go back inside.

"Bellman? What happen to handyman?"

"Craig has me working on the cabin only when he's around."

"Where is he now?"

"Taking care of another job on the other side of town."

Shaking his head, Marcose laughed, while Jarred went running back into the Inn.

After hours of working out in the stables, on his way up to the Inn to get a shower, before joining the others for lunch, Kyle ran across Lori, coming back from Beth's cabin, with Lora, Hannah, Bethany, and Jessi's German Shepherd, Max. "Hey, there, beautiful…!" Kyle called out, attempting to get Lori's attention, when the others turned to see who was walking up.

"Well, thanks," Lora teased, knowing he was talking to his girl.

"Uh… sorry!" he laughed.

"Oh, you were talking to Max?" she teased, causing a giggle from Lori, just then.

"Well, he is all that and more from what I've been hearing," he smiled, while ruffling the black and tan Shepherd's coat. "Marcose says Alex has been working with him for years to sense if trouble were to come around."

"And to attach tracking devices onto someone's car, when we can't," Jarred added, when coming out to announce lunch was almost ready.

"Good, I'm starved," Kyle laughed, while leaning down to kiss his girl.

"Oh, Lord, Kyle…" Lori winced back, waving a hand across her face, "what have you been rolling in? You stink…!"

He and the others laughed, while he lifted the corner of his denim shirt to smell it. "Oh, that? That's mostly sweat from helping out with the feed, unloading a wagon of hay and straw, and a little bit of mucking out a stall or two. Travis and Hank elected to clean up out in the stable, where they keep a change of clothes, while I have to run up to my room where mine are, so I can shower and change there."

"You might want to do just that," Jarred continued to laugh. "I don't think they'll let you into the dining room smelling like that."

With that, even Max had to agree, when snorting at the smell that lingered in the air.

"Fine, Max," Kyle laughed some more. "Lori, I'll see you after I get cleaned up."

"Ok," she smiled, while petting the dog fondly.

"Well," Jarred spoke up, "Lora, are you guys on your way in, as well?"

"Yes, but I think we'll take another door in," she laughed, looking to the others, who agreed, joining her to go in through the family room doorway.

"Making fun of our guy?" Marcose asked, walking up.

"Yes, though for a Law Office Intern, he did work hard today," Jarred commented on his way in, while taking Max with him.

After getting his shower, Kyle came back down to find Cassi at the front desk, while seeing a guest off. "Cassi, is it?" he asked, seeming a little lost.

"Yes. And if it's your girlfriend you're looking for, she's out on the front porch with Jarred, Hank, and mom."

"Thanks," he nodded, heading out to see them.

"Well, don't you look good and cleaned up now," Hank smiled. "You certainly put in a good days work for a Law Office Intern. And it was greatly appreciated by both Travis and I."

"Thanks, but it's not anything I hadn't done before."

"Still though, from what Hank has told me," Jessi turned to face him, "I insist on paying you for your time, since you're a guest here."

"Well in that case how about putting it toward a stay in a cabin once things get back to normal?"

"All right, I can do that! Jarred, have you talked to Jodi lately? I really need her help."

"Yes, she and the girls will be here for lunch, just as soon as Karen gets to the shop to fill in."

"Good. I was hoping too that Craig would have gotten this job he had to do today done already, so he could give me a hand on the books and camp store tonight."

"Books…? Camp store…?" Jamie smiled. "Jessi, if you need some help, I can lend a hand! That's if you're talking about accounting. Something I majored in college, when the kids were little."

"Yes, but you and your people are guests here. I can't ask you to drop everything and do that!"

"Oh, yes you can," Lori smiled. "Mom loves to keep busy."

"Please…! Not to mention, it would sure keep my mind off of what's going on back home."

Sensing she was really bothered by this case, Jessi agreed. "All right, you got yourself a deal. How would you like to be paid?"

She laughed. "Just put it on our bill that which you hadn't been running, I'm guessing?"

"Yeah, well you got me there. The County, and now the Marshall's Office, has been covering a lot of it, whenever Alex has a case that needs the innocent ones hidden. That's how they wind up here."

They all laughed.

"Anyway, since it's been pretty busy around here with the remodeling and guests wanting to get their vacations out of the way before school starts, between Craig and his uncle, they have been great with figures. Lord, for what would take me all day to work some books, they could have them done in a third of the time. And then, like I said, there's the camp store, now, that needs restocking. And now, of all times, Sharon is out sick. So that puts me even further behind."

"Not anymore. We can do this, so the kids go out riding sometime."

"Good. Annie," she called out, seeing her just inside the doorway talking to Ashley.

"I was just about to come out and tell you that lunch is ready in the dining room," she announced, while smiling at Hank, before going back inside.

"Shall we?" Jessi suggested, while looking out over the driveway, hoping to see her husband and her cousin drive in.

"I'll call her again, while you call Craig in your unique sort of way," Jarred grinned on their way in.

"What makes you think we haven't already been talking our unique way?" she laughed.

"And…?"

"He's already on his way now. And Alex, how is he doing back in Camden?"

"It's been quiet, though he and Ted have been going through a lot of unexplained papers that aren't adding up."

"And Jason?"

"Stressing out! Which has Alex pretty worried. But the guy won't slow down."

"Something will give," she stated, going on inside.

"Yeah, well something though is about to change."

"What…?" she turned back to study his serious expression.

Pulling her aside, he filled her in about Kyle having to leave soon to help Alex and Ted without being seen.

"He's taking him back to Camden?"

"To be set up in adjoining rooms with Alex and Ted right there. He'll be safe. You know that."

"I may know that, but Lori, what is this going to do to her? And Kyle, does he already know this?"

"Yes, he's just trying to find the right time to tell her. That's why Alex is really counting on you and Craig's gifts to help her through it all."

"Sure, just like him to think we can pull rabbits out of our proverbial hats."

"Let's face it, since you and Craig had gotten together, the two of you have done some pretty amazing things," he smiled coyly.

"Yeah, and isn't it just a shame my cousin doesn't have our gifts too?" she laughed, and then headed into the dining room to get her a plate of food, before joining the others.

All that time, while on his way home, Craig laughed, loving his wife's temper.

*'Sweetie, I'm not alone here. You and I both have to help her get passed this, while he's away. Not to mention, how lonely she's going to feel, when he goes.'*

*'I'm with you on that. Anyway I should be there soon. So save me a plate!'*

*'All right. See you soon.'*

While getting their plates, Kyle carried Lori's back for her. "Lori," he started.

"You've heard from Alex, haven't you?" she asked sadly.

"Earlier. Yes."

"How long?" she asked, looking unhappy about it.

"I don't know. But he did say he would set aside some time for us to see each other. Although, it would have to be in secret, so that Philips wouldn't find out I'm back. Lord, that would be bad if he thought he was being double crossed."

"I don't even want to imagine what he would do to you or to dad if he were to know. In any case, can we please just change the subject? I don't want to think about it anymore."

"Yes, sure...!" he held her close, while they tried to eat.

"Kyle?" she sat her fork down, and fought not to cry.

"Yes?"

She turned to face him. "Can we go riding or something to keep my mind off of your leaving, please...? I mean once we are through with lunch?"

"Sure, but let me ask Craig first once he gets back."

Before she could say anything more, Craig walked in, still wearing his grubby work clothes. "Ask me what?" he grinned, while going over to give his wife a kiss, before getting himself a plate of food from the buffet.

"Horseback riding," she smiled up at him. "Would that be all right with you?"

"Yeah, well you're asking the wrong person that question. That's Jessi's area, since the Inn is hers to run."

"Oh, wow, I'm sorry, I should have known that," she cried, getting up to run out of the room, till Jessi came around to stop her.

"Lori, honey, no, that's fine," she smiled, looking to her husband. *'Craig..., a little help, here...!'*

*'Yeah,'* he turned, setting his plate down next to his wife's, while coming around to join her. "Lori, since being home now, I have the rest of the day to do whatever you two want."

"Riding horses?" she smiled through tear-filled eyes.

"Yeah, sure!" He looked up, grinning at his cousin. "Heck I would even think Jarred, here, and a few others could handle that too!" he teased, seeing Jarred's smile, while he and Jessi went back over to take a seat.

"Maybe you could stop off at our special picnic area, along the lake, too!" she suggested, while the two went on eating.

"Mmmm, and the fishing shack, as well, since we didn't get that far the first time out?" he smiled at her.

"Yes."

"Will you be going with us?" Lori asked, hopefully.

"I wish I could," Jessi replied regretfully, "but I still have so much yet to do. Though, now with your mother's help, I can get things done even sooner."

"Mom," Cassi spoke up from the end of the table, "Ashley can help Jamie with the books, and when Jodi and the girls get here, they can help me with the camp store. So go. You and Craig both! And don't forget to tell them about the ledger."

"The what?" Kyle asked, puzzledly.

"The ledger," Jessi explained, while getting up to clear away her dishes. "We had all gone out a few years back, while Alex and the others were here working another case."

"The Belaro and Delgado case?" Kyle asked.

"Well, by then it was just the Delgado case," Jarred explained, eating his food. "Belaro," he went on, "was a dead stick, you might say."

"Oh, yes, under a pile of rubble," Kyle offered, sensing quickly the delicacy of the subject, when it came primarily to Jessi and Craig. "I heard about it from Jason, back when he used to tell us stories about his infamous old partner," he explained quietly.

"Yeah, well, I wouldn't want to say the word '*old*' to Alex's face, if I were you," Jarred laughed. "He's a little sensitive about that."

"I'll keep that in mind," he laughed along with the others.

"Jess," Craig interrupted.

"Yes?"

"Why don't you give Jodi a call and see how soon she's going to be?"

"That won't be necessary," Marcose announced. "She and the others just pulled in."

"So you'll go now?" Lori asked again.

"Well, I don't see why not! But are you sure you and Kyle wouldn't prefer being alone?"

"With the exception of their bodyguards, they wouldn't be," Jarred reminded.

"Kyle?" Lori turned her head aimlessly, while waiting for his input.

Wanting to be alone with her, he reconsidered, knowing she could use the others company to help get her through it all. That, and he sensed a certain amount of compassion coming from Jessi and her husband. Though, he couldn't place a finger on it, they seemed to genuinely care, yet, not in the sense of pity. Still, he couldn't help but like them.

"Kyle?" Craig spoke up, cutting into his thoughts.

"Yeah, sure, that'll be fine!"

"Fine for us busting in on your time alone…? Or fine, like, sure, come along!" Craig teased.

With a blush traveling clear down beneath the top unfastened button of his blue flannel shirt, Kyle nodded his head, laughing. "The latter."

"All right then, what do you say, just after we finish here, we get started," Jarred suggested, while taking up the pitcher of iced tea to give himself a refill.

Going along with it, while they went on eating, Jessi filled Jamie and Ashley in on what needed to be done, while they were out.

"And Jodi and the girls?" Jamie asked, looking up, just as Jodi walked in with them.

"Did I just hear my name being mentioned?"

"Yes," Jessi looked up, smiling. "We were just talking about horseback riding."

"Yes, but will we have time to eat first? We are starving," she laughed.

"Sure. And did you tell the girls what they will be doing, while we're out? Oh, yes, and there's one small change. Kyleigh," she turned, "Lora and Hannah are over at Beth's babysitting. Could you take them over some food, and some for yourself, as well, when you go?"

"Sure," the brunette smiled, while going over to the buffet to get their food ready in some to-go containers.

"Hey, cuz," Jodi smiled at her knowingly, "are you bringing the ledger, too?"

"Of course, since most of us think it would make for good reading!"

The all went on laughing, while talking about other things, till they were ready to head out. At which time, Jarred got up to head for the door to go down and give Hank a hand with the horses.

"Oh, wait," Jessi called out, stopping him, "I don't know about Joe."

Concerned, Craig looked up. "What about him?"

"Hank mentioned to me earlier that he had picked up a small stone in his shoe. So he may be a little tender hoofed, yet."

"In that case, Jarred, I'll go down with you, just as soon as I change out of my work clothes, to check him out, if you don't mind waiting?" he asked, getting up.

"Sure, I can wait!"

"Good. Jess," he turned.

"Yes. Right behind you," she replied, looking back to her cousin.

"Go," Jodi laughed. "We'll be here, waiting, when you two get back."

"Thanks," she smiled, and hurried off, with him, to their quarters.

Once there, while Craig went on into the bathroom to get cleaned up, she went to their room to get the ledger out of her dresser drawer.

Looking it over, at how it all came about, she laughed, "Well now, let's just see how the others will feel reading through your pages."

"Jess..." Craig called out from the shower.

"Yes, be right in with your change of clothes...!" she called back, setting the book aside to go over to the closet to get something out for him.

Once done, she grabbed the ledger and headed back upstairs with him.

"Annie," she called out, going into the kitchen, while Craig went to see who all was waiting behind, "by any chance have you had time to put together some sandwiches for our ride, in case we're out longer than expected?"

"Got them right here, all but the refreshments. And that won't take me long," she smiled, just as Craig appeared in the kitchen doorway.

"Good," he spoke up, taking the bag, "we'll be heading out as soon as Jarred is through talking to Marcose out back."

"And the others?" Jessi asked.

"Out on the patio, waiting on us!"

"Annie..." Jessi turned.

"Go. I'll bring the tea out, just as soon as I get it made up."

"We'll be out on the patio, waiting, than," Craig announced, placing his free hand along the small of Jessi's back to head out of the kitchen.

Meanwhile, standing far enough out where the others couldn't hear, Marcose was saying with a grin, when it came to dealing with the bad guys, "Go, Jarred, if you're wanting to go. I can stay here in case we get any uninvited visitors!" he laughed. "Besides, I'll have the dogs to help change anyone's mind if they show up here without an invitation."

Jarred, too, laughed, "Okay, but don't allow yourself to get put out of commission like you did back at Craig's old place."

"Damn..., you just can't drop that, can you? How was I to know Frank was a dirty cop?"

"Yeah, well..." he laughed even more at the man's expense, over the Belaro case, "sorry, pal, old habits, you know. But still, we're all glad you and Baker made it out okay. And now for Mrs. Roberts," he turned, heading back up to the patio, when seeing Craig and Jessi walking out to wait with the others.

"Yes, I know, stay close by her," Marcose stated quietly, as they returned to the others. "Mrs. Roberts," he nodded, seeing her appear in the doorway.

"Marcose," she corrected, smiling, "please, call me Jamie."

"All right!" he grinned, while Jarred walked on up onto the platform.

"Jamie," Jarred intervened, "as I was just about to tell him, I want you to stay inside, while we're out, unless if you absolutely have to come out for some fresh air, do it back here, so to be out of sight of anyone driving by."

"All right," she agreed.

"Good. Now, then, shall we get the show on the road?" Jarred asked his cousin.

"Just as soon as Annie comes out with the tea," he teased, pointing out the bag of sandwiches and the ledger.

"Gotchya," he laughed, just as Annie showed up with the two containers.

"Thanks, Annie," Jessi smiled.

"Just have fun and watch the time. You don't want to run into any night fall, while on your way back," she replied in her usual motherly tone.

"If we see we're going to be late," Craig offered, easing her mind, "we'll give Hank a call to bring out the trailers."

With that, they were on their way to the stable to mount the horses Hank and Travis had saddled up for them.

"Hank," Craig called out, walking in, "how is Joe?"

"He's fine, now. But if he starts showing any signs of pain, just give me call and I'll have Travis ride Sarge out and bring Joe back."

"Good," Craig stated, looking his stallion over, before getting on.

"Are we ready?" Jarred asked, as the others mounted the horses they had ridden before.

"Craig?" Jessi turned, sensing his apprehension to ride Joe at that time.

"No," he returned. "Hank, let's go ahead and get Sarge saddled up. We can use Joe to carry our things, since they'll be lighter than carrying me on his back," he explained, running his hand lovingly over the horse's neck.

"Already done," Hank grinned, nodding his head toward his horse's stall.

With that, they were soon ready to head out, while telling Hank to be ready if it got late.

"Sure will," he called back, waving.

Along the way, with the sky looking somewhat peaceful, Kyle described more of the scenery to Lori as they rode along.

"Mmmm… it sounds so beautiful," she smiled up at her man.

Looking back on the two, while in the lead with her husband, Jessi smiled as well, when seeing the peaceful glow on Lori's face.

"Is she looking okay?" Craig asked, holding to Joe's reins, while on Sarge.

"She looks like an angel in love!" she smiled, looking on ahead.

Meanwhile, Jodi turned quietly to Jarred, while bringing up the rear, "Has there been any changes in the case?"

"Only that Philips thinks that Roberts has backed off it, since he thinks he had taken Kyle off the case."

"Then he has no idea otherwise?"

"No, nor does he know that Roberts has sent everyone out here."

"Good," she groaned, just as they arrived at their favorite picnic spot, along the lake.

# Chapter Eight

Spending an hour there, on blankets they had brought with them, they sat around talking about things that had gone on in their lives, while unaware of some dark clouds that had begun forming around them.

Then suddenly, without warning, a crack of thunder sounded off, nearly sending Lori over the edge with fright.

"Damn… where did that come from?" Jarred groaned, while getting to his feet with the others.

"I don't know," Craig returned. "I haven't heard a word on the weather channel about anything coming our way."

"Well, it looks like we got something coming now!" he exclaimed.

"Yes," Jessi added in, not liking what she saw of it. "And seeing how it's about here, we can't possibly get back to the Inn in time to beat it."

"No," Craig agreed, knowing she, and her cousin, both hated being out in bad storms. "That only means one thing." Taking her hand, he told the others, in good spirit, so as not to scare Lori anymore than she already was, to get to their horses.

"The shack?" Jodi laughed.

"Yes," Jessi called out, as the wind started to pick up.

Grabbing up their blankets, while hold to Lori's hand, Kyle asked, "How far is it from here?"

"Just up the line a little ways," Craig explained, while taking Joe's reins, before getting up on Sarge. When he did, Joe bulked in pain. "Damn, Joe, I'm sorry! Is it hurting you now?"

"Craig…?" Jarred called out from atop his horse.

"It's his hoof. We have to get him unloaded, and put everything onto Sarge."

"Yeah, but that wouldn't give you much room to ride," Jarred called back. "We'll split the load!"

"Then let's get it done. Jess..." Craig called out over another crack of thunder, "you and Jo know the way. Get them to the shack, before the rain hits."

"Okay!" she returned, reining her horse around. Taking that moment to explain what was going on, Jessi told Kyle to follow close behind. "They'll catch up soon," she smiled back at her husband.

After returning her smile, she and the others took off at a steady gallop to make the ride for Lori a softer one.

"Are you okay at this pace?" Kyle asked Lori.

"Uh huh!" she smiled, laughingly, while remembering the times she had gone riding on her grandfather's farm. *Remember, Lori, always remember to hang tight to the saddle horn,* he would say, smiling.

Soon Craig and Jarred had caught up to them, with Joe favoring his injured hoof.

Reaching the shack in plenty of time to beat the rain, everybody dismounted and hurried inside with their load, while the guys took care of the horses.

"Boy, just like the old days, huh?" Jodi asked, while going over to set the food and drinks on the table that occupied the one room shanty, along with a wood stove, a few chairs and a full sized brass bed.

"Old times...?" Lori asked. "This has happened before...?"

"Oh, yes," Jessi explained, lighting some lanterns, before going over to prepare the wood stove. Doing so, she went on to tell her what had happened, while describing her surroundings, so Lori wouldn't feel lost.

"Well," Craig and the others walked in, shaking off the rain, "it's here!" he laughed.

"The rain?" Lori asked.

"Yes," Kyle offered softly, while coming over to see how she was doing. "You okay?"

"Yeah, sure!" she smiled, nervously.

"Jess," Craig asked, "you still have the book with you?"

"Yes." She looked around briefly, while trying to recall where she had laid it. "Oh, here it is!" she announced, going over to take a seat at the table, while Craig and the others went to join her after getting something to drink.

Kyle, though, took Lori over to have a seat on the bed, where she could sit cross-legged, feeling even more herself.

Upon opening the book, Jessi remembered how it would start out sad. *'Oh, no, Craig, you remember how the story starts out...! What if this disturbs Lori somehow?'*

*'We'll know if it does, when picking up on her thoughts, if that's the case. And if it does, we'll call for a break, and the two of us will talk her through it,'* he smiled.

*'Ok. Oh, and did you call Hank to let him know what we're doing?'*

*'After getting the horses taken care of. He's going to let the others know. Marcose too, in case something springs up.'*

*'Let's hope not,'* she stated, while acting like they were getting more comfortable, before starting with the first page. Looking around the dingy room, she smiled. "Are we ready?" she asked, seeing how everyone was looking comfortable. "Ok...!"

> *August 27th, 1967:*
>
> *It was a rainy Saturday morning. Just a typical morning so I had thought, till my husband, after seven years, just told me he was dying of Leukemia. We had our whole lives ahead of us. A beautiful little girl name Katie Nicole, who is now five. How was I going to tell her that her daddy has only a few weeks to live?*

"Wow, what a beginning!" Kyle exclaimed, while Jessi went to turn the page.

"Go on," Jodi prompted, when her cousin went to clear her throat, before doing so.

"No, wait," Jarred suggested, while he and Jodi got up to take a seat on the floor nearby, with a blanket over them to keep warm.

Both Craig and Jessi laughed.

"Ok... are we ready now...?" she teased her cousin.

"Yeah, sorry..., just wanted to stretch out my legs and cover up."

"Well it is going to be a little bit of a read, in case anyone else wants to get a little more situated where they are," Craig suggested, grinning.

"Lori?" Kyle asked.

"No, I'm good!"

"Ok," Jessi continued, while Craig concentrated on Lori's thoughts from time to time, in case they ought to take a break.

*August 30th, 1967*: she continued,

*Sam was acting strange all day up in the attic, building something, but what? He wouldn't tell me. Just that it was for his little angel.*

*September 3rd, 1967:*

*When Sam came downstairs, we had a lobby full of guests for Labor Day weekend. His face was flushed and dripping with sweat. Wanting to know where his little angel was, I left the front desk to our helper and went to the kitchen, where Katie was last seen, helping the cook with her favorite cookies. Covered in flour, when we walked in, she had the cutest smile on her sweet little face, when she looked up to see her daddy standing there. Going over to pick her up, the three of us headed up to the attic to see what he had been working on for so long. And to my surprise, it was her very own special playroom that only she could play in. Later that night, Sam slipped out of the Inn. No one knew where he had gone off to, not even me.*

*September 4th, 1967:*

*Oh, my God, no! SAM..., he's gone...! He left me a note, Telling me he couldn't handle the pain anymore. We tried to find him, but he couldn't be found anywhere.*

Stopping all of a sudden, Jessi turned to Craig with tears welling up in her eyes. "I'm sorry, I can't. It's just as it was before, it's too sad...!"

"Here, I'll read it," Jodi offered, reaching for the book, before getting a little more comfortable in Jarred's arms.

Picking up where Jessi left off, while the storm continued outside, she went on.

*September 7th, 1967:*

*The local Sheriff, officer Samuel Mathis came to me with the worst news that I could have ever imagined. They found Sam down at the old shack, at the back of our property...*

"What...?" Kyle asked, quite suddenly.

"They found him here," Jarred explained.

"Yes, and according to this ledger, he died out here," Craig offered.

"If that's true, and I'm not disputing it," Kyle questioned, "but wouldn't you have been able to pick up on his spirit, like Jessi did with you?"

"What...?" Lori asked, sitting up more in his arms.

"You remember. Your dad was telling us all about it, after hearing from Alex!"

"Oh, my, I had almost forgotten about that. So, what Kyle is asking, wouldn't you have been able to do that too? Picked up on his spirit, I mean?"

"Not necessarily," Craig put in, while looking to his wife. "I called out to her. Sam, we assume, didn't!"

"It's so hard to believe that they are talking about this shack!" Lori went on, while Kyle got up to get them a refill.

"It sure is," he agreed, when coming back to hand her, her cup. "Here you go."

Reaching up, he put the cup in her hand. "So, does this mean the shack is haunted?" she asked.

"No," Jessi smiled, while looking to her husband. "We would've known it if it was, after all the time that we've spent out here."

"Hey," Jodi spoke up, while getting to her feet, "how about we have something to eat, while listening to the rest of the story?"

"Sure!" they agreed, while wanting another one of Annie's famous ham and cheese sandwiches.

"Wait a minute," Jodi spoke up, remembering something else she saw in with the things Annie had packed for them.

"What?" they stopped to ask.

"If I'm not mistaken, I think Annie put in some marshmallows, too," she laughed, seeing them.

"You mean these?" her cousin smiled, taking them out.

"Marshmallows...?" Lori smiled brightly. "Really...?"

"Do we have anything to cook them on?" Jarred asked, searching the cabinets for a meat fork, being the best suited, and safest to use at a time like this.

"Here we go," Craig returned, handing him one that was stored in the cabinet drawer, behind the stove, along with other essentials left behind for the shack.

With everyone getting comfortable again, Jarred stoked the wood stove to build up a proper fire for roasting marshmallows.

"Listen up," Craig announced, looking over the ledger. "This is where she had skipped a few months," he stated, while taking a seat to read on.

*7:15pm, April 3rd, 1968:*

*It's Thursday evening now, and it looks like it could rain at anytime. Katie is outside playing with her favorite doll that her father had given her, when she was a baby.*

*Oh, great!*

"What?" some of them asked, while taking a bite of their food.

"No. That's what she said in the ledger," he looked up and explained. "Anyway she says;

*Oh, great. The power had just gone out, and I can't see to write much in this light. I might as well go and check on my baby girl.*

*7:45pm April 3rd, 1968:*

*I brought Katie in, and went around handing out candles to the guests. Katie was crying, when I had gotten back to our living quarters. She had lost her doll, while outside, when it began to rain. I'll have to go out tomorrow and find it for her, or she will continue to be upset if I don't.*

*April 4th, 1968:*

*It's 2am. Katie has a high temperature now, because she had gotten herself wet, while playing out in the rain. I had to call the doctor, she was burning up, while all along, crying for her doll.*

*April 4th, 1968:*

*It's now 9am. I tried real hard to find it for her. It's as if it had vanished. God help me, she has never been separated from her doll before. What am I going to do?*

Craig had to take a moment to collect himself.

"Anyway; *April 7th, 1968:*

*My baby is fading away quickly now. The doctor said there was nothing left that he could do for her, she had picked up pneumonia and won't make it through the night.*

Stopping, he got up and put the book down. "I can't go on. It's just too sad for even me to read," he said, shaking his head, while walking over to the door with Jessi, when she too got up with him.

"Let me give it a try," Jarred offered, while reaching up to get it off the table. Picking up where Craig left off, he sat back, with Jodi taking the book to hold in front of her, for him to read on.

*Her last words that had been spoken were; 'Find my doll… I can't sleep without my doll…!'*

*I promised her, I would try. I had everyone looking.*

*April 8th, 1968:*

*Our little angel is now with her daddy in Heaven. However, at night I feel that I can still hear her little cries, asking for her doll.*

Looking up, Jarred commented, "She writes some other things in here about her husband's dreams of having cabins built."

"You mean the cabins out there, were her late husband's dream?" Kyle asked.

"Yes, and Jessi's too. But here's the paper to show what he had drawn up," Jodi offered, handing it to him, when he walked over to get it.

"Wow, just like the ones out there, now!" he noted.

"Yes, well it was just a coincidence that the both of their plans looked a lot alike," Craig told him. "We came across it, while we were reading the story for the first time, three years ago. Whereas, Jessi and Jodi worked on drawing up their own plans before that."

"Hey," Jodi went on. "It says here:

*April 7th, 1978:*

*It's been ten years now since our angel went to be with her father, and I can't take it anymore.*

"Take what?" Lori asked, while Kyle handed the paper back.

"You'll have to listen to understand," Craig explained, quietly, while Jodi went on.

*Hearing her cries at night from her playroom up in the attic.*

"Wait!" she cried, unable to believe what she had just heard.

"Yes, Lori," Craig laughed, "up in the far left corner of our attic, where I recall my wife telling me she felt a strange presence coming from that particular spot, just across from the attic's bathroom. In fact, you had even kept the attic locked up, because of it, didn't you, Jess?"

"Well, perhaps it was because of it. However, at the time I had decided to keep it locked up, I wasn't aware of these gifts I have."

"What sort of gifts?" both Kyle and Lori asked, with great interests.

"As you already know, she can pick up on the presence of troubled spirits," Jarred grinned. "And…" he hesitated, when looking to his cousin, "she can hear their thoughts, as well as they can hear hers."

"Like it was with you and Craig?" Kyle asked, seeing how they were always looking to each other a lot of the time.

"What do you mean, was…?" Craig laughed, wholeheartedly. "We still can! That had never stopped!"

"Though we thought it would have," Jessi smiled.

"So what you're saying is that the two of you still communicate telepathically?" Lori asked, amazed over it all.

"Yes, but there's more," Craig went on. "We can feel others emotions."

"Wow," the two concluded.

"Now, back to the attic," Kyle went on. "What happened?"

"Well, while up there," Jessi continued, "Alex had wondered why that particular spot was so different from the rest of the attic."

"Different? Different, how?" he asked.

"Maybe you should start from the beginning," Jodi suggested. "Or at least when Alex told you of the extra police officers he was bringing in to help with the case."

"The Belaro case?" Kyle asked.

"Yes, and mind you," Jessi explained, "he was unaware of the secret room when I had taken him up to show him the attic, before the extra officers, women, that is, had gotten here."

"Beth," Jarred spoke up, "having been one of them."

"And the other?" Lori asked.

Looking to Jessi knowingly, those who knew of the story shook their heads, while attempting to refrain from laughing.

"What?" Kyle asked, seeing their amused expressions.

"Terry," Jessi groaned, irritably. "She was all over Alex. Like flies on…"

"Jessi…!" Jodi broke in.

"Let's just say, she was trouble all the way around," Jarred explained. "And as for the attic," he laughed, "Alex was right, when having discovered the trick door, which kept the room a secret. Not to mention, the reaction they had gotten, when Jessi told him about the presence she picked up on at that particular spot they were standing near."

"What…?" the two cried.

"It," Jessi began hesitantly, while looking at Jodi. "Maybe I shouldn't say."

"Well," Jodi went on laughing, "let's just say, you couldn't tell by the way they took off out of there, that there was ever anything wrong."

"Oh…?" Lori laughed, while Jodi went on reading.

"Just to recap;

*April 7th, 1978:*

*I had to have the room closed off,* she began. *And as for the Inn, I can't go on anymore. I have to close it. People are beginning to go elsewhere. As for me, I haven't been doing so well, since the two most important people in my life have gone away. I just want to be with them!*

Turning the page, she continued.

# Chapter Nine

*September 14th, 1978:*

*Dear God, forgive me for what I'm about to do. I need my loved ones. I have no will to go on any l o n g e r_.*

"She must have written it out here, so she could feel close to him," Kyle thought.

"Then went and hid the ledger?" Lori commented questionably.

"Oh, sure!" he kidded. "And then, what, committed suicide?"

"No," Jessi spoke up. "She starved herself to death up in the attic, near the playroom, so the last thing she would hear would be the cries of her little girl, for her doll. At least that's what we found out soon after reading this," she explained, looking to Craig.

"You said you felt a woman's spirit, though not of this time!" he commented.

"Yes, hers."

"But then," Kyle spoke up, "how..."

"Did the book get out here?" Jarred asked. "We figured someone had to have brought it."

"But who?" he continued, when Jessi's cell phone went off.

"Wow, what a story!" Lori was saying, while Jessi went off to answer it.

"Sure was!" the rest agreed, while going around picking up after themselves.

Coming back after taking the call, she announced, "Hank is on his way."

"How are things up at the Inn?" Craig asked, while he and Jarred took care of putting out the wood stove.

"About like it was the first time we took refuge out here during that storm! It had pretty much blown over some of the tables and chairs out front, is all."

"So," Jarred laughed, "it looks like we have some work to do when we get back?"

"Not too much," she smiled back.

"Jessi," Kyle asked, changing the subject, "in all the time we've been here, I don't recall seeing an old well anywhere around the place."

"That's because it had been sealed up!" Craig explained, amusingly.

"Where was it?"

Unable to contain himself, Craig looked to his wife and laughed. "Once again, shall I?"

"Sure."

"Well, the two of you had been standing on it."

"What…?" Kyle looked to Lori.

"In fact, we all have," Jessi went on laughing.

Still looking dumbfounded, Kyle asked, "All right, where?"

"The gazebo!" the others laughed full heartedly.

"What…?"

Still laughing, Jessi laid a hand on his shoulder. "A contractor, by the name of Anderson, and his son, was called back by the previous owners, after learning they were the ones who closed off the attic room, wanted the well sealed off, as well. And in place of it, they built the gazebo."

"Cool…!" Lori chimed in. "All but it would have been nice had you restored the well, and put the gazebo in another spot that would be just as pretty."

"Well, actually," Jessi looked to Craig, "I have been giving it considerable thought, since it was a part of the property. Why not have the gazebo lifted and moved back and to the left a little so we can observe the stable and horses once in awhile?"

"I like that," he grinned, looking to Jarred once again.

"What…?" he laughed knowing that look all too well.

"Well Alex did say when I'm here you and Marcose could pose as two of my workers!"

"When do you want to get started on it?" he asked.

"Jess?"

"Right away! And if we're lucky, it'll be done, before Alex gets back!"

They laughed.

"Yes, this place really takes the cake," Kyle shook his head, amusingly. "Anything else?"

"No. Well at least not that we know of," they smiled, while hearing Hank pull up out front.

Walking in to see that everyone was okay, he shook his head with a hint of amusement. "The ledger, again, huh?"

"Yes," Craig laughed, "and a few changes are in the works, because of it."

"Namely…?" Hank asked.

"Well it's going to involve you, Travis, Jarred, here, and Marcose. Hank, my friend, we are going to raise the gazebo to move it back and to the left, so we can restore the old well, beneath it."

"Holy cattails," he laughed, running a hand over his graying head, "you're serious?"

"Yes," Jessi smiled, proudly. "And I'm thinking of using creek rock walls, a bucket on a rope, and a nice roof. But to make it proper, place a name plaque on it to commemorate the original owners."

"Well, I'll be. The next thing you'll be telling me is that you just might empty it to see what else you might find down in it."

"Sure. Jess…?" Craig looked serious.

"Go for it," she laughed, while he, Jarred and Kyle grabbed up a load to take out to the Hummer

Following them out, after seeing to it the lamps were safely out and the place looked okay, she closed the door and locked it.

"Wait," Kyle persisted, "what do you know about the ledger?"

"Quite a bit!" Hank laughed.

"Then you know what happened to Sam?"

"Yes."

"Well…?"

"Well, he died of Leukemia!"

"So he didn't take his life?"

"Goodness no…! And as for his wife, people have often wanted to know the truth of what had happen to the woman of the Inn. It's become a real live ghost story," he teased, while figuring they had already told them, but just wanted to stir things up a little.

"Great!" Lori laughed. "That's always nice to know."

Changing the subject, Jarred asked, "What about the horses? What are we going to do about them?"

"Well, what do you think?" Craig turned to the others, and smiled. "Do we ride them back, or load them up on the trailers?"

"Kyle?" Lori asked.

"Jarred?" Kyle turned.

"Well, once again it looks as though we'll be riding them back!"

"Well, all right then, I'll just take the trailers back," Hank laughed.

"Okay," Craig smiled, "we'll see you back at the Inn."

"Good enough! I'll let Annie know you'll be there soon. And once again she'll probably want to have something fixed for everyone," he announced, waving goodbye.

Meantime, having brought the horses around, everyone was on their way back, while laughing at what a day it had been.

"Yes, what a day," Kyle agreed, shaking his head.

Meanwhile, back in Camden, while going over reports his men had given him on Philips' whereabouts, Alex put in a call to Marcose. "How are things there?" he asked.

"Quiet, outside of the storm we had just gotten!"

"So I've heard. And our guests, how are they holding up?"

"They had all gone out horseback riding. But from what I've heard, they took shelter in the old fishing shack at the back of the property."

"Yes. I kinda figure so," he laughed, remembering where he asked Beth to marry him.

"Then you know, too, about some ledger?"

"Was it black?"

"Yes!"

With a roar, Alex shook his head amusingly.

"Oh, man, the famous ghost ledger?" he asked, laughing along with him.

"One in the same."

Laughing a little while longer, the two went on with why he was calling.

"So I assume Philips is under the assumption Roberts has backed off?"

"For now, but that isn't to say when he finds out that he will still have to go to court for his arraignment."

"Yes, and you'll probably want to beef up the security around that time, too."

"Damn straight."

"For now, what do you want us to do?"

"Stay with them until I let you know when to let them come back. I may even have you come back with them."

"Are you going to talk to the Commander about it first?"

"Yes, and now I've got to cut this short. Tell Jarred to call me later."

"Sure thing."

Ending the call, Alex turned to Ted, when he walked into Kyle's office.

"Jarred?" he asked, seeing his old partner putting his cell phone into his pocket.

"No. Marcose."

"Any news out that way?"

"They had a storm!" he laughed.

"A storm? What's so funny about that?"

With a raised eyebrow, he asked, "Don't you recall a ledger we found at the old shack?"

"Yes, what about it?"

Telling him what all had taken place, they both laughed wholeheartedly.

"I guess this means they have been well entertained, thus far?"

"Yes, sure, leave it to Jessi," he grinned, while looking back down at the reports in front of him.

"Well, seeing how things are quiet here, I'm going to head out front and keep an eye on things there."

Looking up from the papers, Alex nodded. "Sounds good. I'll let you know if we are going anywhere."

Taking his leave, Alex went back to what he was doing.

Meanwhile, back at the Inn, everyone was getting in from their ride, while Jamie was giving Annie a hand in the kitchen, since Beth wasn't feeling well. "Babies," she was saying, while opening a can of stew, "they are so beautiful holding after having given birth."

"But carrying them," Annie laughed, sympathetically.

"Yes. And this is her second one, how was the first?"

"It seemed somehow easier."

Shaking her head understandably, Jamie went on with what she was doing.

Meanwhile, back in Camden, heading for Jason's office, Alex ran into him out near the waiting room, where right away he noticed a man sitting there, appearing to be reading a magazine. He would have never noticed him, but something about the man didn't seem right. Then he saw it, the magazine was upside down. Taking that moment, Alex signaled Jason to be careful what he was about to say. "I think we have an eavesdropper," he indicated with a nod of his head.

"The man in the gray suit?" he whispered, lightly, while looking as though he were showing Alex a file he was to work on. "What do you want to do about him?"

"Follow my lead," he instructed. And with a silent nod of agreement, Alex cleared his throat, "I understand you want this done before Mr. Whiting gets here?"

"Yes. I would have Moorsted do it, but I have him working that new case in Atlanta."

"And not the Philips case?" Samuel Epstein asked, walking up to the two of them, just then. "What's going on with that case? I thought we had it in the bag!"

"Sorry, Sam," Jason had to think quick, not expecting to see his law partner at that moment, "I had to put that one on hold, since we didn't have all the information needed to convict him."

"Oh? And who is this?" he asked, looking squarely at Alex.

"This is…" He stopped, nearly telling him Alex's real name.

"Jordan Scott," Alex chimed in, seeing how his friend had nearly lost it. "I'm standing in for young Moorsted, while he is out on another case."

"Are you any good?"

"Frighteningly," he smiled brazenly.

"Hmmm, we'll just have to see about that," the man said cynically at how Alex had referred to himself. "Well, I'm on my way to court, now, and I'm running late as it is."

"Mr. Epstein," Cindy cut in. "This man is h…here," she turned to point him out, only to see an empty chair, and the magazine lying on the table haphazardly. "I'm sorry, but there was a man sitting right there, saying he needed to speak with you."

"Well, if he wanted to speak to me, he'll just have to call and make an appointment like everyone else," he said gruffly, while on his way out. Yet, stopping at the front door, he turned back, "Oh, and Mr. Scott, do a good job, and we just might have to add you on permanently."

"Somehow I don't think he would be interested," Jason laughed once the man left.

"No, I don't think so," Alex agreed, not liking the man's attitude.

"Yes, well I have some time on my hands, until my next appointment. What do you say we get out of here for awhile?" Jason suggested.

"Sounds good. Just let me grab some notes from my desk, and lock up."

While waiting on Alex, Jason went back to his own office to lock up as well.

"Ready?" Alex asked, when the two met up again, while walking into the waiting room.

"Yes. Cindy," Jason spoke up, heading toward the door with Alex, "we're going out for a bite to eat. Hold my calls for me, please!"

"Yes, sir," she smiled.

"Oh, and Cindy," Alex interjected a sense of caution, "don't tell anyone where we have gone. Do you understand?"

"Yes, sir," she returned, recognizing it being Alex in his disguise.

Reaching the sidewalk just outside the office, the two were temporarily blinded by the early afternoon sunlight.

"Well, we know this is going to be a nice day," Jason noted, while shielding his eyes for a moment, until they could get adjusted to the change.

"Yes," Alex agreed, looking for his men. Spotting Ted down the street a ways, he got on his cell phone to call him.

"Yes?" Ted came back.

"A short while ago. Not even fifteen minutes, did you see a man in a gray suit come out?"

"Yes. He got into a sliver pickup with another man, matching Philip's description, and drove off."

"By any chance, did you get a plate number off his vehicle?"

"Yes. It's registered to a C. C. Philips Corporation."

"That's one of Philips' other businesses," Jason stated.

"Did you hear that?" Alex asked his old partner.

"Sure did. Manning is on it now."

"How's that?"

"When I saw the man get out, leaving the other behind. I saw him carry in a white envelope, like the ones left under Kyle's door, and marked the same way. After running the plate, I radioed Manning to be ready to follow."

"Good work! Oh, and are you hungry? We were just about to go and get something. Do you want to join us?"

"Sure. Just let me call Manning and see how that's going."

"We'll see you at our usual spot, down the road from the motel, then."

Getting off the phone, the two headed for Alex's Blazer and were soon off.

Upon reaching the restaurant, Alex looked around to see if they could talk freely.

"What do you think?" Jason asked, taking a seat near the window.

Taking out his cell phone once again to make one more call, Alex nodded. "Yeah, looks pretty quiet! Just let me make this call, and I'll be ready to order."

"Who to?"

"A hotel not far from your office, but well within reach of your house. There, Ted and I will be staying, along with an adjoining room for Kyle and Marcose, when Marcose brings your family back."

"That can't be soon enough for me. But why Kyle, and in an adjoining room…?"

"To keep him out of sight, while helping me gather more information. Philips thinks he is still out of town, remember? And after our uninvited guest back at the office, by now he should have gotten the word out that young Moorsted is still out, working another case."

"Yes. Let's just hope he keeps thinking that."

"Well, that, and what you had told your partner! Which brings me to ask."

"What?"

"Your partner, just how well do you know him?"

"Sam? Well… shortly after moving here. Why?"

"It may be nothing, but something in the way he acted when he saw me. That, and he wasn't all that friendly about my taking over for Kyle, while he's out."

"Alex..."

"No, just hear me out. Ted said the man who went into the office had an envelope, just like the ones that had been left under Kyle's door. When he saw Sam walk up, I couldn't help but notice how he had gotten out of there rather quickly."

"You're right. He did. So does this mean you are going to have him checked out, too?"

"Would that upset you?"

Feeling dismayed at the thought of his own law partner conspiring with such a man bothered him. And now with all the threats against him! "No. Just do what you have to. I want this over with so we can get on with our lives."

"And if he *is* crooked?" Alex lowered his voice, when seeing a waitress heading their way with two glasses of water in hand and a few menus tucked up under her arm.

"Nail his hide to the nearest tree," Jason leaned in and thundered quietly.

"Give us a moment," Alex smiled at the waitress, in an attempt to throw her off of any part of their conversation she may have overheard, "we're waiting on one other person to join us."

"All right," the middle age brunet smiled back. "While we're waiting, would either of you want something to drink?"

"Coffee, black," Alex ordered, while pretending to look at the menu.

"Same for me," Jason added, doing the same.

"Okay. I'll get them right for you!" she continued to smile, and walked away.

# Chapter Ten

Their wait on Ted wasn't long. For when he arrived, he had some rather interesting news to share with them about Epstein. "Your partner," Ted began, when Alex handed him a menu, "met up with the man from your office, shortly after leaving there. And I must say," he lowered his voice, while looking around them, "Epstein was not one bit happy with him."

"Oh?" Alex grinned. "Was Manning able to pick up on any of the conversation?"

"Better than that, he taped it."

"What?" Jason asked, looking surprised to see the recorder Ted had taken out of his jacket pocket.

"Yes, Manning gave this to me, before leaving to come here. So the two of you just might want to listen carefully to what was said," he instructed, while placing it in the middle of the table, while the coast was clear. "Oh, and Alex, you might find it rather amusing, too. Not to mention, that there are some things on here that aren't so amusing."

"You've listened to it already, then?" Alex asked.

"Yes, in case there was something we needed to act on right away."

"And was there?"

"No."

"Good. But before we start listing, we best be flagging down our waitress, before she comes back in the middle of hearing it."

Shortly after giving their order, the three gathered close, once it was safe to hear what was taped, so not to miss a thing.

*'What the Sam hell were you doing there?'* Sam's voice came over the recorder clearly.

*'My job!'* the man said gruffly. *'So maybe I was a little early getting there. What of it?'*

*'You were told to wait until I left like all the other times I wasn't there, you idiot! Now we're just going to have to wait until another time to slip that note under Moorsted's door.'*

*'Yeah, but the guy isn't even there right now. Some other guy is taking his place, while he's out.'*

*'Yes, so I've noticed, and he doesn't look all that stupid either.'*

Stopping the recorder, Alex shook his head amusingly. "Was that what you wanted me to hear?" he laughed quietly.

"That, and this." Ted hit the play button again.

*'Yeah, well I wouldn't want to meet him in a dark alley, even if Philips were to order me to get rid of him, too. Hell no, he couldn't pay me enough.'*

*'You'll do it if you were told to!'*

*'Yeah, well what do we do now?'*

*'Wait. Soon Jason's family will be getting back from their trip. When they do, Philips will want to know in case this information on him was to become known. Therefore, if Jason was smart, and cares for his family, he had best bury whatever comes up, or else.'*

*'Yeah, well, what's in it for you?'*

*'Plenty. And for you too, if you do your job like you're supposed to. Now back to what you're supposed to be doing. Stay close to the courthouse in case there's anything to report back to Philips about.'*

*'Yeah, on his arraignment, I know. But I thought with the lack of information there wouldn't be an arraignment.'*

*'There isn't. Well, at least not now!'*

*'But he just wants to make sure the man doesn't change his mind, and dig up something on him later?'*

*'Exactly.'*

*'But wouldn't you, being there at the office, know if he did?'*

*'That wouldn't mean a hill of beans. If Roberts was to suspect me in any of this, he would simply clam up. Then how would I be able to find out anything? No, just do what you were told, and stick to the courthouse, in case the judge decides a ruling on just what he has.'*

"And that was all Manning was able to get," Ted explained, turning off the recorder. "After that, the man left and went home."

"Do we have an address on him?" Alex asked.

"Yes. And you were smart to change our location."

"The same motel we usually stay at, till now, that is?"

"No, but close. Just up the road from there."

"Great. Well in that case, we had better be getting our lunch ate, so we can get whatever things we still have there, out."

"Yes, but just to be on the safe side, let me handle it? With your disguise and all, the man had to have seen you at the office at one point or another."

"He's right," Jason put in. "Alex, he might see you and get suspicious."

"Yeah, you're right. In that case take our things here," he explained, writing their new location down on a napkin, so not to be overheard. "And I'll meet you there, later. I just have a few loose ends to take care of, and check with a man I have working at the courthouse, now."

"Why doesn't that surprise me?" Jason laughed. "Always thinking ahead."

"It has always paid off in the past!" he grinned. "But then you would have known that, if you hadn't gotten out of the law enforcement business. You are getting out of shape, old man," he laughed just as their order arrived.

Once the waitress left, Jason continued to laugh, "Yeah, well, I had decided that I wanted to keep my head a little while longer, too. Now, about my family, when will they be getting back? And what is your plan to keep them safe after hearing that Sam is a part of this?"

"Marcose will be escorting them back, and then Manning will be staying with them the whole time they are here."

"And Kyle," Jason asked. "I'm sure he won't be too happy, not being able to see Lori as much."

"I have that covered," Alex smiled.

"Oh?"

"With these new cell phones, he and Lori will be able to keep in touch regularly. Aside from that, when possible, one of us will get them together in some secret place that I'll have set aside for them."

"Uh, good," Jason answered, oddly. "Looks like you have it all taken care of."

Passing it off as having been a long week, they ate their lunch and talked about other things to get their minds off of what was going on.

Afterwards, Ted handled the bill, and went back to the motel to gather what things they had left, before checking out.

Back at the Inn, Marcose relayed Alex's message to Jarred. "He wants you to give him a call, when you got in."

"Thanks. I'll do that now, while they're putting their things away after the ride." Leaving the group, Jarred went into Jessi's office, and closed the door behind him, to make his call.

"Jarred?" Alex spoke candidly, while sitting in Kyle's office.

"Yeah," he laughed. "How are things there?"

"Somewhat quiet, you might say."

"Uh oh, what's going on?"

"We were able to pick up on a recording of one of Philips' men he has working for him. Are you ready for this?"

"Sure," he stated, taking a seat.

"Jason's own law partner is in on it."

"Epstein?"

"Yeah."

"That had to have hit him hard! How did you find out?"

"The recorder I was telling you about! He was on it. And to make it all more interesting, we met at the office. You could tell he wasn't all that happy to see a new face in the building. And from what I was able to pick up on," Alex laughed, "he doesn't find me to be all that stupid-looking either." Hearing Jarred cut loose, Alex went on, "So, I hear you all went out for a ride, and took the famous ledger with you."

"Yep!" he chuckled.

"So, now, they know about the attic?"

"Yes, and the well!"

"What...?"

"You heard me. Like you, they wanted to know where it was all this time."

"What did you tell them?"

"Same thing you were told. They have been standing on it."

At that they both laughed.

"Great," Alex commented.

"Yes, well you should have seen the look on their faces, when they heard how you and Jessi flew out of the attic that day she first took you up there."

"What...? You didn't tell them that too, did you?"

"No. My lovely wife did it for me."

"Remind me to ring her neck, when I get back," he laughed.

"Sure thing. Oh, and Jessi told me, when I hear from you, to let you know how Beth is feeling."

"Oh? Is she all right?"

"Yes, just feeling pretty achy throughout her back, is all. She's back at the cabin, lying down, right now."

"All right, I'll give her a call to see how she is doing."

"All right. And as for our visitors?"

"Marcose will be coming back with them in a few days. And when he does, he is to drop Kyle off at the Hilton Motor Lodge, where I'll have an adjoining room for him to stay in, so he won't be seen, until it's time."

"Okay. Oh, and Alex, I'll be coming with him. You will need my help, as well."

"No. I want you to stay there and keep an eye on Beth for me. I have everything here covered already."

"Sorry, uncle, but I'm already cleared by the Commander to go. Besides, Jessi and Jodi can keep an eye on her, just as well as I could," he informed him, without stating which Commander he was referring to, when it came to the team that Alex had put together years ago. That which included Ted, and Marcose, who was just as determined to keep the team together. Now Jarred wasn't about to let his uncle rain on his parade, as his mind was set to climb the rank of being a Federal Marshall, like his uncle. They were partners before hand, until Alex got his promotion, leaving Jarred and the others behind. And after a lengthy talk with Jodi, who had already lost her first love in a motorcycle accident, she came to the conclusion that Jarred was happiest at what he does, and would never take any unnecessary risks with his life.

"Jarred…" Alex growled.

"Enough said on the matter. Marcose and I have already discussed it. So we'll see you when we get there. Now, call your wife," he smiled, triumphantly, hanging up.

"Was that Alex?" Jessi asked, walking in.

"Yep!" he continued to smile, while getting to his feet.

"Uh huh, and I guess that smile means you had blatantly disobeyed an order he had given you?"

"He doesn't want me to come to Camden, when the Roberts' go back."

"Why?" she asked, as he was passing her by in the doorway.

Turning back, "He wants me to stay behind and keep an eye on Beth."

"But I can do that. Not to mention, everyone else who is here…!"

"Exactly! And now to go and talk to Marcose," he grinned, taking his leave.

Shaking her head, smiling at the thought of Alex not getting his way, Jessi went on over to her desk to get started on some paperwork, before it had gotten too late. *'Huh, poor Alex,'* she mused, *'you should know better than tell your own blood what to do, knowing that Jarred is just as stubborn as you are,'* she laughed lightly at the mere thought of his temper, when it came to someone other than herself defying to take orders from him.

Back in Camden, having left the office, once he was certain things were all right, arriving at the hotel to find Ted getting their things unpacked, just the look on Alex's face said it all. "You heard from Jarred, I take it?" Ted asked, knowing about the transfer Jarred and Marcose had been waiting on, after their talk earlier that day.

"Yes," he growled. "And he had just informed me that he was coming with Marcose."

"Did he say why?" he asked, hiding his amusement.

"He said I would need his help, as well. Damn him, Ted," he continued frustratedly, while going over to give his friend a hand with their things, "he informed me of his decision, not asked, but informed me."

"Alex," he stopped and put a caring hand on his shoulder, "you have to start trusting that he won't get hurt. After all," he grinned, "just look at who he has taken after."

Laughing, he had to agree. "Damn, you're right, we are a lot alike. So much so, it scares me."

"Scares you? What about those poor slobs out there, breaking the law? They would have to change their pants when the two of you start…"

Realizing what he was about to say, Alex nailed him right away. "Start…? Start what?"

"Nothing," he attempted to drop the subject, when his cell phone began to ring. *Thank God for cell phones,* he grinned, seeing Alex's expression only get hotter.

"We're not done with this," he growled, quietly. "Not by a long shot. You know something, and I'm going to find it out one way or another."

"Yeah, sure you are," he continued to grin, but soon that came to an end when Manning's voice came over the other end, sounding alarmed. "Alex, hold on, it's Manning!"

Seeing how serious he became, Alex leaned in to try and hear what the man had to say. Unfortunately for them, his voice was barely audible.

Taking the phone, Alex started in, "Manning, we can barely hear you. Where are you?"

"At Roberts' office, like you told me. He's on the phone now with Philips. That's why I'm not able to speak up!"

"Can you make out what is being said?"

"Pretty much the same thing. He's reminding him of his earlier warning."

"And Roberts, what is he telling him?"

"To back off, before he changes his mind. The case had been dropped, as asked."

"Damn, sounds like he has heard otherwise from his man at the courthouse."

"I don't know. What do you want me to do?"

"Stay there, but out of sight," he ordered, pulling his weapon from his shoulder holster to check. "Ted and I are on our way, now."

Getting off the phone, Alex filled Ted in on what was going on, while returning his weapon to its holster, before the two headed out, taking separate vehicles.

Stopping at the driver's side door of his, Alex looked over at his old partner. "Oh, and Ted," he growled, "as for this other matter concerning my nephew…"

"Alex," he interrupted, looking up over the top of his black truck, "Jarred had asked me not to say anything. You know he will tell you when he is ready."

"Tell me what, though? That's what has me bothered."

"You will know when the time is right."

With that, they got in and headed out, not wasting any time getting to Jason's office, short of running a few traffic lights along the way.

# Chapter Eleven

By the time they arrived, Alex walked in, trying to look composed so not to draw any attention to himself. As for Ted, he stayed outside to keep an eye on the place from where he was parked, down the street.

"Cindy, is Sam in?" Alex asked quietly.

"No, not since you two left!"

"Thanks," he returned, heading for Jason's office. "Oh, and Cindy," he stopped and turned back, "let us know when he gets back."

"Yes, sir."

Leaving her to her work, Alex hurried on down the hall to check on his friend. Reaching the door, he went on in. "Jason, what's the word?"

"It's the same old thing," he grumbled, tiredly.

"You're sure? Is it possible he may have heard from his man at the courthouse? And if so, it had to have been after I talked to my guy!"

"Yes, and no he didn't hear anything. I asked if he had, and he said no."

"Then what's his problem?"

With his face turning a shade of red that Alex hadn't seen before, the man grumbled even angrier, "He says he just wants to keep me on my toes! On my toes, Alex…!"

"Yes, but from what I heard," he watched him closely, "you told him to back off, or you *will* go right to pursuing the matter."

"Damn straight I will…!" he nearly yelled, pounding his fists on his desk. By then his face broke out into a sweat, when he began to shake.

"Jason…" he warned, seeing this, "take it easy, buddy, before this gives you a heart attack!"

"Damn it, Alex…" he thundered. Just as he did, his breathing became labored with nearly every other word spoken. "I a…am so t… tired of his threats a…and now to h…have to w…watch… what I am h…having to s…say… and d…do… in m…my own o…office…" He stopped suddenly, and clutched his chest.

"No…! Jason…!" Alex called out, rushing to the man's side. "Damn you, Jason…, don't you dare go and have a heart attack on my watch. You hear me…?"

"Alex…?" Manning rushed in, hearing the commotion from nearby.

"Manning…, give me a hand, getting him over to the couch," he yelled, taking one of Jason's arms to place over his shoulder.

Once the two had him on the couch, Alex began loosening his tie and belt.

"Come on, man, don't you do this to me!"

"A…Alex, m…m…my pills…!" he cried, digging into his pants pocket for them. "Th…they're here, i…i…in my po…pocket!"

Getting them, Alex quickly got one out and placed under his tongue, where it would have the quickest result, and then waited fearfully for what seemed like forever to take effect. "Come on, damn you, pill," he groaned.

"Alex, look…!" Manning called out, seeing the man begin to relax.

"Jason…? Jason, is the pain beginning to go away any?"

With a nod of his head, the color was starting to return to his face.

"Thank, God," both Alex and Manning sighed.

"Do you want me to call 911?" Manning asked, seeing how Alex had control of the situation.

"No," he replied, studying the man's composure. "Ted and I will get him to the hospital, but we will have to go by way of the back door, so no one sees what has happened here."

"What about Epstein?"

"No, I don't want him, or Philips getting wise of Jason's condition. Is that clear?" he turned, asking, angrily.

"Yes, sir. But…"

"What?"

"What if one of them shows up, while we're taking him out?"

"For Jason's sake," he looked back on his friend, "let's hope we won't have to cross that bridge if it comes to it."

"And if at some point Epstein were to start asking questions?"

"I'll inform him that Roberts has left me in charge of his cases, until he returns. All he has to know is that Jason had decided to join his family for a while."

"Yeah, that ought to set well with him!" he grinned.

"Yeah, well that's just the way things go," Alex grumbled at what all this case was doing to him, not knowing his friend had already had a heart condition to begin with.

Contacting Ted, Alex explained what had just happened.

"I take it I am to meet the three of you at the back door then?"

"Yes, and Manning is to stay and keep an eye on things here, until I get back. When I do, I'm going to put the word out that I'll be taking over his cases, while he is out with his family."

"And Kyle?"

"He will be helping me secretively with anything that may come up."

"That's all well and good, but what about any court dates that might come up?" he asked, bringing his truck around back.

"I'll call the chief and fill him in on what has happened. From there, he will call the judge to put off any cases that may arise."

"And when Jason gets out of the hospital?"

"I'll take him to Jessi's to recuperate."

"Will I be going with you?"

"Possibly. Although, I could really use you here if any of the others have anything to report."

"In that case, you're right about me staying."

"You really don't mind?"

"No. And after all the times we've worked together," Ted smiled, recalling them, "I would be the likely choice to stay behind."

"You're right about that! Now, where are you in adjacent to the back door?"

"Coming up on it now. And you?"

"Just about there," he fudged, getting Manning to help him get Roberts to the back of the building, quickly and quietly, before anyone saw what was going on.

Getting him out of there, and to the hospital, without being seen, was no problem. However, making sure the hospital kept his presence quiet took calling his boss, Chief, Tom Broadey, who in turn called the hospital.

Afterwards, Broadey called Alex back to be filled in on what went down.

"Listen, Tom," Alex returned, hurriedly, "I have to keep it short, the doctor has a few questions for me."

"Okay. But call me when you're ready to head out of state with him," he ordered, sternly.

"Yeah, sure thing."

"Oh, and Alex, just so you know, I plan to put a few extra men on this, while you're out, and a few others, when you get back, just to make sure nothing goes wrong."

"Yeah, let's just hope nothing does go wrong," he growled, getting off the phone.

After talking with the doctor and getting his friend settled in, Alex put in a call to Jamie, who was beside herself with grief when hearing the news.

"Oh, Alex, I want to be there for him."

"Jamie, you can't. But just as soon as he is strong enough, I'll be bringing him to you, so he can recuperate."

"And he *will* get stronger, won't he, Alex?"

"Yes, sure he will," he returned, not wanting to worry her.

After the phone call, he contacted Manning to come to the hospital, where he would leave Jason in his capable hands, while heading back to the office with Ted, to see if Epstein came back.

"How is he?" Ted asked, while walking back out to his truck.

"In bad shape, I'm afraid," Alex said, gritting his teeth. "And I'll be damned if those two mess with him or his family anymore."

On the way back, Alex filled him in on what he was going to be doing.

"Okay!" Ted returned, grinning, while waiting for Alex to give the all knowing word.

Alex just laughed.

"Well, I know you're going to say it."

"Yeah, you know me so well. Okay, fine. Taylor Green, it's time for you to get into character," he grinned.

"All right…! Now that wasn't so hard…!" he laughed, arriving back at the office.

"Yeah, well you do have what you need with you, right?"

"Right behind my seat!" he smiled, after coming to a stop, before reaching in behind him to pull it out.

Straightening back up, Alex was thrown by the transformation, when seeing a nicely trimmed goatee and wire-rimmed glasses. "Okay! Now let's get in there and show them who's boss."

Walking in together, Alex stopped at the front desk. "Cindy," he instructed, "take out your note pad and follow us."

"Sir?" she began, only to see the look of seriousness in his eyes. "Yes, sir." Doing what she was told, she got up, reaching for her pad and pen, and followed them to Jason's office. Though, surprised he would go there, and not Kyle's, she couldn't quite understand.

"Cindy?" Alex turned, seeing her puzzlement.

"Sir, I don't understand," she spoke up, once inside the room, "why are we in Mr. Roberts's office?"

"This is where I will be until he returns from his trip with his family."

"I…I don't understand! Why didn't he say something to me about leaving? I should have been told of this."

"Well consider yourself told, Miss Granger. And I'm sorry it has to be this way, but I can't go into why he had to leave so suddenly. And yes, I would appreciate it if you would not convey any of this to anyone, specifically Epstein, or anyone who was to call for him. As for now on, all calls will come straight to me. Do you understand?"

"Yes, sir."

"Oh, and Cindy, you have got to start calling me Mr. Scott if we are to get to the bottom of these threats to Jason, and now his family."

"Oh, my, of course, sir. I mean, Mr. Scott, sir."

"Thank you. And now, you do remember Mr. Green, don't you? He will be replacing me, while I'm in here," he explained, while going over to take a seat at the desk. "And now, if you'll please," he turned to the two of them, "have a seat so we can get started."

Doing so, she opened her pad and waited for further instructions.

"Are you ready?"

"Yes."

"To Mr. Epstein, until further notice, Mr. Jordan Scott will be sitting in for me, until I return from vacation with my family. All incoming calls and court cases involving me will be handled through him. Replacing him in young Moorsted's office will be Mr. Taylor Green, who has come highly recommended. As to reaching me, go through Mr. Scott, as well. Signed, Jason Roberts, Partner of Roberts & Epstein's Law Firm. Oh, and Cindy, date it as of this morning, too. And make sure you bring it by me first, before doing anything else with it."

"Yes, Mr. Scott, I'll get it typed up for you right away," she complied, before taking her leave.

After seeing her out, Ted turned back, closing the door behind him, and grinned, "Not bad!"

"Yes, well let's just hope Epstein doesn't start nosing around, while we are out."

"Yes, and speaking of Epstein, wouldn't Jason need to sign that memo, before sending it to him?"

"Yes, and just as soon as she is done typing it out, I'll run it over to him to do just that."

"Good. And now tell me just what I am supposed to do as your assistant."

"Dig a little deeper to see what else Philips has been doing. And check and see what properties he owns, especially warehouses. I don't want to take any chances that if anything was to happen to one of his family members, they may have them held up in one that we didn't know about."

"Okay."

"Oh, and Taylor," Alex called out, as Ted opened the door. "Take this key. It's for Kyle's office. And do try to be as discreet as possible, when gathering the information on our new case," he winked, before going on to speak more guardedly. "You know, so not to draw any unwanted attention to the firm, specifically to Roberts."

"Got it," he returned, quietly, while heading out of Alex's new office.

A short while later, Cindy returned with the memo for his approval.

"Yes, this looks good," he said, closing the door behind him, after she walked in. "Have you seen Mr. Epstein yet?"

"Briefly, just before coming here to show you that," she explained, while he walked back over to the desk with it.

"Oh, did he have anything to say?"

"Just that he doesn't want to be bothered. Oh, and he did asked if Mr. Roberts was in. I simply shook my head, and went back to what I was doing."

"Huh, so he didn't try to press you for more information?"

"No. He just looked preoccupied, and walked away, but not before looking down the hall toward Kyle's office."

"Wow, I wonder why?" he grinned, taking out his phone to call Ted. "Cindy, give me a moment to fill Ted in, and too, to see if he has anything new to tell me," he instructed, before putting in the call.

"Hello. Mr. Green speaking!"

"Hey, it's me."

"Yes?"

"Did you find any envelope, slipped under the door, when you got there?"

"No, everything looked pretty much normal, why?"

"Just that Epstein is back, and I was told that he looked down toward your office, before going to his own."

"What do you think, trouble?"

"No, I don't think so, but be on your toes, in case it was to come. Oh, and we have extra help on the way."

"Great, we may need it."

"I'll let you know when it comes. Hopefully soon, I need to slip out of here for an hour, at most."

"Go ahead! I'll be fine, until you get back."

"Yes, but I don't feel good about leaving you alone with Epstein here, just yet. So I'll just wait for the help to get here, if you don't mind."

"Okay."

Getting off the phone, Alex couldn't help but notice the amused look on Cindy's face. "What's so amusing?"

"All this!" She gestured with a wave of her hand, over the office. "It reminds me of my father, when he was a cop!"

"Your father, a cop? Where is he now?"

Looking away, sadly, he knew the answer.

"I'm sorry. Was it while he was on duty?"

"Yes, a bad drug deal that someone had ratted him out on. And because of it, they had him killed!"

"And that's why you have been so cooperative with all this?"

"Yes. You seem to be a really good person. Not to mention, Mr. Roberts had been raving about you, before you had even gotten here. And this, man, Mr. Green, he is your friend, too?"

"Ted Jones. Yes, from back home," he smiled. "Like Jason, we have been through a lot. And now, seeing how late it is getting, if you don't mind, I have a lot to do, before having you send this memo through to Epstein."

"All right!"

After Cindy went back to her desk, he groaned even more when seeing it was already after four. "Where is my backup?" he continued, impatiently.

Just then, Cindy called in to let him know there were two men to see him.

"Give me a moment, won't you, before sending them in?" he told her, while pulling out his phone to call Ted back.

"Yes, sir," she returned, just as Ted answered his phone.

"Ted," Alex returned, ending his connection with Cindy, "I think our help has arrived. So join me in talking to them."

"Sure. I'm on my way," he returned, getting to his feet to hurry out the door.

Once there, they greeted the two men together, as they were shown into Alex's office.

"You understand the situation at hand?" Alex asked the two.

"Yes, the chief filled us in," the taller of the two, yet muscle bound, answered.

"James, I take it?" Alex asked.

"Yes."

"And you are..." he turned, looking to the younger one.

"Roland, sir," he replied.

"Good. For now, go with Ted, but never, unless told otherwise, call him by his name. He's Taylor Green, and I'm Jordan Scott."

"Yes, sir," they nodded, waiting on Ted at the door.

"Alex," Ted spoke up just as he was about to head out of the room, "before I show these two around, are you going on over to see your pal?"

"Yes, and the sooner I get him to sign this memo, and get it to Epstein, the sooner I can set Epstein straight on what I'm going to be doing here in Jason's place. That's where these two come in. As for Marcose, and, God forbid, Jarred, that hard head."

"Yeah, yeah, yeah," Ted laughed, "a chip off the old block."

"Yeah, laugh it up," he growled, lightheartedly, while locking up on their way out to the waiting room.

Once there, Alex turned to Cindy. "Well, I'm on my way out to take care of some business. While I'm gone, forward all my calls to Mr. Green, here, please. Oh, and these two gentlemen are our new investigators, which Mr. Roberts had suggested to help on our newest case. They'll be here helping Green, while I'm out."

"Yes, Mr. Scott," she acknowledged, while smiling up at the youngest one.

# Chapter Twelve

Taking his leave, Alex hurried over to the hospital to find Jason sitting up in bed, talking sports with Manning and a nurse. "Well, I leave you in a broken state, and come back to find you talking about sports of all things," he laughed, walking in. "I guess this means you're ready to join up with your family."

"You've got that right. When can we go?"

"Just as soon as the doctor says you're strong enough for the trip," he laughed, with a great sigh of relief.

"Oh, but I am strong enough," Jason announced, turning to the nurse. "Tell the doc to have my paperwork signed and ready for me to get out of here. I have someplace to go, and I want to go now!"

"Yes, sir!" she smiled. "I'll see if he's still here."

Leaving them to go in search of the doctor, they went on talking.

"So, Jason," Alex growled, thoughtfully, "you really have to take it easy. I don't ever want to see you go through that again. Okay, buddy?"

Smiling, Jason nodded his head. "I just want to see my wife and daughter, is all."

"Yes. Well before I take you to see them, I need you to sign this memo first."

"Sure, what's it about?" he asked, reading it.

"It's just so I can monitor all your incoming calls, while you're away."

"And my cases, too…?" he asked, looking to his friend, puzzledly.

"Yeah, well the chief has already called the judge about that, asking that he doesn't breathe a word of your absence."

"In that case, fine. You just had me worried, is all."

"Well, to be frank, I was concerned that your partner may try and muscle in on your cases, to see if you had dropped Philips'."

"Then no doubt, stick to my office like glue."

"Plan to," he grinned. "Right along with Ted, Jarred, and Marcose, when you and your family come home."

"I will certainly be glad of that."

"Yeah, well, get yourself better, before thinking about coming back to work. And don't worry about Cindy handling all these new changes. She's a real trooper, just like her father."

"She told you about him, did she?"

"Yes, sadly."

"Yeah, well, he was a good man."

"You knew him, too?"

"Sure did! He did some work for me."

Suddenly a thought came to him.

Seeing that look, Jason asked, "What?"

"Were you working where you are now?"

"Yes, sure! Why?" He suddenly thought. "No…! Epstein again…? You think he had something to do with ratting on Franklin…?"

"Makes sense, don't you think? I mean who else would have known he was a cop, working undercover?"

"Okay, but let's cross that bridge later."

"Sure we will, but while I'm checking out Philips' background, I think I'll do a little more gardening in Epstein's backyard. Like right about the time Franklin was killed. Starting with when the bust went down."

Knowing his determination the way he did, Jason just shook his head, when the nurse came back with his doctor.

Soon his release papers were signed.

"Now remember," the doctor spoke firmly, "no stress for quite some time."

"Yes, sir," Jason returned, getting to his feet to change back into his own clothes.

Once done, Alex and Manning took him home to pack a few things.

On their way, Alex wanted to stop off at the office first. Calling Ted, he shot him a heads up that they would be there soon. "Take one of the men and meet me outside."

"Why, what's up?" he asked, making his rounds throughout the building with James.

"I have the memo to give you, before taking Jason to his place to get some things put together for our trip home!"

"Oh, all right!" he agreed, turning to James, once they got off the phone.

"Where to?" James asked, sensing a change in plans.

"Back to the Reception area, where we are to go out front to meet Alex. He'll be here soon, before heading out."

"Ok."

After that call, Jason asked Alex, "Calling Jarred?"

"Yes," he stated, keeping his eyes open for Philips, or any of his goons.

Soon Jarred was on the other end, while keeping an eye on Lori, who was talking to her mother.

"Jarred?" Alex spoke up

"Yeah."

"We're on our way with Jason, now, to get some of his things thrown together. Meet us at the state line."

"What about his family?" he asked, turning away to talk more privately.

"Marcose can watch them, while you're out. Besides, Kyle is there to give him a hand."

"All right. Oh, and Alex, how is he doing?"

Looking to Jason, he gave a slight smile. "He has a ways to go."

"All right. I'll just let the others know, and meet you, in what, a couple of hours?"

"Sounds good."

Seeing how everything was falling into place, Alex felt at ease about leaving, when recalling what Tom had told him. *'Good!'* he thought to himself, when getting back on the phone to call Broadey back.

"On your way so soon…?" Tom asked.

"Yes. I would feel a hell of a lot better having him out of town, and out of harms reach."

"Do you have enough coverage to get to where you're going?"

"Manning is with us now. And once we get to the state line, Jarred will be there to join us, as well."

"Yeah, well I'd feel a lot better if I'd send a couple more guys, just to make your trip that much safer. They're in the area now, waiting on word to follow along if I were to give it."

"No, that won't be necessary. I've been giving it some thought to take Ted along, too, while having James and Roland monitor things here."

"All right, but be quick about it, or there will surely be trouble on the way if Philips was to hear what's really going on."

Just the thought of Philips, concerned him, when picturing him, or one of his goons, following them to Indiana to see where he was taking him. But then, to think what danger it would put his own family in. Not to mention, all the others at the Inn. "Yes," he came back, clearing his throat, "consider it done."

Getting off the phone, just as they reached the office, Alex turned back to Manning, once he got parked. "Stay with Jason, while I go and talk to Ted," he ordered, shutting off the Blazer.

"Yes, sir," he replied from the back seat, as Alex hastened out of his vehicle to meet up with Ted and James outside the building.

"Alex?" Ted spoke quietly, seeing a hint of urgency on his face.

"Back inside. There's been a change of plans," he ordered quietly, while opening the glass door.

"Sure," Ted agreed, leading the way.

Stopping at the front desk, Alex turned to Cindy with the memo in hand. "Cindy, here's the memo with Roberts signature on it. But wait until tomorrow to give it to Epstein."

"Tomorrow?" she asked.

"Yes. I'm going to need time to get things squared away first."

"All right. Oh, but Mr. Epstein has already left for the day," she announced quickly.

"Oh? When?" he asked, looking alarmed.

"Shortly after you did," Ted grinned right away. "But not to worry, he didn't see which way you went. I saw to that."

"Oh…?"

"Yes," Cindy laughed for the first time, since meeting them. "He acted a little clumsy, when Mr. Epstein came out, as soon as you left."

"That had to have made him mad," Alex laughed, humorously.

"Oh, yeah, just a little," Ted smiled.

Shaking his head, Alex turned to James, "Okay then, this is what I want you to do. Keep an eye on things here, and report to me if there is any trouble."

"Wait!" Ted cut in. "I thought that was why I was staying behind."

"Yeah, well I'll tell you about that in a minute. Just let me finish."

Backing off, Ted waited.

"Anyway, as I was saying, Philips for one, I don't want him around here. If you see him, call for backup, as I may be too far away to do you any good." Going to the door, Alex looked around to see a few of Broadey's men nearby, in case there was trouble, before they could get Jason out of town. "Good, they're here."

"Who?" Ted asked, going over to the door to see what he was looking at.

"You'll soon find out," he announced, calling Tom. Soon they had their answer, when Tom called his men to nod their heads in confirmation of who they were. With that, Alex turned to Ted. "And now the change I was referring to," he grinned. "It's you."

"What?"

"Yes. I decided you were going with me, after all. Besides, it just wouldn't be the same if you didn't," he laughed.

"All right," he agreed, going back to lock up his office.

"Roland, Cindy, lock up, too," Alex ordered. But then stopped, when a thought crossed his mind. "Cindy," he smiled coyly, "are you involved with anyone?"

"Well, no! Why?"

"Well, it would explain having Roland around you a lot. As the two of you have all of a sudden become an item," he laughed, seeing her cheeks go red. "Do you have a problem with that?" he turned to ask the blond haired, brown-eyed officer.

"Huh, no…!" he shook his head, frowning. "Not a problem, at all!" Going up to put an arm around her shoulder, he teased, "Well, sweetie, shall we lock up and go get a bite to eat?"

Pulling away to walk up to Alex, she went up on tiptoes to give him a daughterly hug. "Thanks, Alex," she smiled, while hugging him a bit longer, before returning to stand by her bodyguard.

"Just stay close to him," he growled seriously. "And Roland, you and James, watch your selves out there."

"Yes, sir," they replied right away.

Heading out after making sure things were locked up tight, Alex kept watch on his surroundings, until making it back to his Blazer. "All right, Manning, go ahead and return to your car. When we pull out, stay in behind Ted, and keep your eyes open. Ted," Alex called out on his radio after getting into his vehicle, "you're behind me."

"Copy that," he returned from up the street.

Soon everyone had their orders, with Ted staying behind Alex, Manning and his K-9 behind Ted, as ordered. And though, Alex didn't feel he needed the extra men, Tom had sent, they stayed close anyway, by simply blending in with the traffic, until Alex and his people were safely on their way, after getting Jason's things.

Once that was done, when seeing they weren't being followed after getting out a ways from town, Tom's men faded out of sight, and returned to their assigned posts, until Alex and the others returned.

After an hour had gone by, the trip to the state line was a success. Getting a crossed it, however, Alex caught a glimpse, out his side mirror, of a man on a motorcycle, coming up on his left. Seeing it was Jarred, he laughed.

"What's so funny?" Jason asked.

"My nephew, Jarred. Yet it doesn't surprise me that he would show up on his bike. That, like my Blazer, is our babies."

Seeing what he was talking about, he, too, laughed, while Alex got on his radio to call back to Manning.

"Yes?" he replied.

"You do know to go back to Jason's place to make sure it hadn't been tampered with?"

"Yes. Do you want me to head back now?"

"No. Let's wait until after we take a break at the truck stop up ahead."

"Okay."

"Alex…?" Jarred called out over his headset.

"Yeah…?"

"Who's all with you?"

"Did you see Ted, when you rode up?"

Looking back at the black pickup, he grinned, as Ted flashed his lights to say hello.

"And behind him, who's that?"

"Manning, with his bomb sniffing K-9."

"Good! Is he staying with us?"

"No. He'll be heading back, once we're done at the truck stop, to keep an eye on Jason's place, while he's out."

"Did I hear you right, about the truck stop ahead?" Jarred asked.

"Yes, figured we would stop off there before Manning heads back."

With a nod of his head, Jarred road ahead to secure their tables.

Once everyone else got there, getting out they stretched their legs, before going in to take a seat at a large table Jarred had picked out.

"What do you have, boys?" a waitress asked, robustly, while coming up to take their orders.

"Coffee, and your daily special," Alex put in, first, while looking around to see the usual truck stop faces.

"And for you, boys?"

"The same," they each said, setting their menus down.

As soon as she left with their orders, Alex went in right away on what was to be done in his absence. "Any problem, your best bet is to call the Chief, since we'll be too far to do you any good. But nonetheless, call me too to let me know what is going on," he ordered firmly.

"Sure will," Manning returned, seeing their waitress bringing their food to the table.

With that they ate in silence with the exception of a few light conversations on what was going on back at the Inn.

Later that evening, pulling into the Inn's driveway, tiredly, Beth was right there with their daughter to greet her husband. And was Alex ever so glad to hold them in his arms.

"Hey there, Rookie," he pulled back, grinning. "How's my lady been feeling, since we last talked?"

"Better. I think I just missed your back rubs, is all," the strawberry blonde smiled up at him happily

"Mmmm… and I've sure missed my two girls," he smiled, while going to pick up his daughter.

"Daddy…!" she squealed.

"What…?" he laughed, while the rest came out to greet them.

"Just in time…!" Jessi smiled, while carrying a couple of pitchers of iced tea. "I thought we would have something to drink out here, if that's okay with you?" she asked, while going over to set them down on one of the Inns' white iron tables, set up for the guests and other inhabitants to use.

"Sure! Sounds good!" Alex agreed, setting his daughter down, when Jason's wife and daughter walked out to greet him.

"Hey," Jason hugged them warmly, "did you miss me?"

"What do you think?" Jamie returned, pulling back with considerable amount of worry on her face. "Are you all right? Alex called and…"

Cutting her off, Jason didn't want Lori to know about his heart attack. "She doesn't," he whispered, placing his hand to his heart.

Shaking her head, Jamie looked to Lori, who started wondering what was up with the coded message.

"All right you two," she frowned, "what's going on?"

"Jason, you should tell her," Jamie suggested.

"Yes, well…" Going up onto the porch to take a seat, the two followed close behind.

"Daddy…?" Lori cried out impatiently, once she was seated.

"Lori," Jason took her hand to comfort her, "everything is all right now. I wasn't feeling too good, and your Uncle Alex, here, took me to the hospital to be looked at."

"But you're okay now?"

"Yes," he looked glumly to Jamie.

Reading the expression in his eyes, she knew too well he wasn't. While trying to conceal her tears from the others, she asked quietly, so that only he could hear. "You're not, are you?"

Shaking his head, he tried to smile, until looking over at Kyle, who sat there, looking at him, knowing what had happened back at the office.

Getting up, Jason went over to take a seat next to him. "Why so quiet?" he asked.

"Alex told me what happened back at the office!"

"Everything…?"

"The…" He indicated in the same fashion. "And what he and Ted are doing, while you are here recuperating. Sir, we both know how

Epstein is about outsiders. Heck it took what seemed like forever to get him to except me being there. How is it going to look with those two running the show, when they haven't been there but just a short while?"

"Yes, I can only imagine. But I know Alex, and he won't put up with a man like Epstein. Not to mention, the team he and Ted are putting together."

"Team?" he wondered.

"Yes, aside from Ted, he has his nephew, Jarred, and Marcose from here, and Manning, over there, along with a few other good men his chief has put together for when they go back."

"Are you referring to my Camden team?" Alex looked up, smiling.

"Yes."

"Good," Jarred grinned, thinking Jason was referring to him and Marcose. "This man we are up against won't have a chance with us!"

"Yes, well Philips isn't the only one we have to deal with," Ted announced, grimly.

"Oh?" Marcose asked, having gotten himself a glass of iced tea, before going over to stand at one of the corner porch post, "Who else?"

"Epstein, himself," Alex announced.

Looking to Jason, both Jarred and Marcose were surprised to hear his own partner was behind any of it.

"I don't understand," Jamie returned, looking to Jason. "Your own partner...? How, and why...?"

"It's a long story," Alex offered, bitterly. "Jason can fill you in later. But I can tell you this," he turned to the others, "the man sure as hell crossed the line, when he had an undercover officer killed."

"Daddy...!" Bethany spoke up, shaking her little finger at him. "Bad word."

"Yes, sweetie, daddy should not have said that," he laughed, softly.

"Alex," Jason interrupted, with a groan.

"Sorry, buddy, but I can't let this one go."

"No," Jarred spoke up. "And being one of his old partners, you ought to know there is a certain code of honor we law enforcers have to live by."

"Yes, yes you're right. I'm sorry. Franklin, as I said, was a good man, and I think Cindy would be ecstatic to know her father's killer will finally be caught. So what can I do to help?"

"Just get better, and when the time is right, get yourself back to work," Alex stated.

"But you're going to be needing information on the case, and on Franklin's old case, if you are to catch his killer!"

"Kyle," Alex looked over to see the young man, now sitting with his lady, and grinned, "can help out with that."

"Well, for now," Jessi spoke up, "it is getting to be time for dinner, and after that, I can think of a few people who are going to want to head off to bed."

"Oh?" Alex asked.

"Me, for one," Craig announced. "I have a big construction job waiting for me, and the company I'm contracted with isn't going to want to see their contractor looking like he had been out all night."

"And our project…?" Jessi hinted too.

*'Got that covered. Besides, with Alex here, we can't do too much out in the open, until he goes back to Camden. As for tomorrow, I'm only going to be out long enough to get Jim and the others set up. After having told him what's going on here, he was thrilled and would like to lend a hand with it, as well.'*

"Craig, Jessi, what's this about a new project?" Alex asked, smiling at the look on their faces, when waiting for them to get through with their private conversation.

Craig laughed. "Oh, just something that's still in the works!" he grinned, knowing Jessi wanted it to be a surprise.

"Alex," Beth spoke up, tiredly, "when we're done with dinner, will you be coming home with us? Aside from me, our little one here can barely keep her eyes open."

"Yes, that goes for me too," he had to admit. "After all that had taken place today, I am beat."

"Well then, let's get inside and get something to eat," Jessi suggested, while she and Craig lead the way.

That evening, the dinner table was filled with light conversation, while keeping off the subject of what was going on back home, except when Alex gave out the new cell phones.

"We'll talk about them later," he announced, "after we've gotten some rest."

Later, after everyone went off in their own direction, Kyle and Lori went out to the gazebo, with their bodyguards, so he could remind her what he would be doing once he returned to Camden.

"But then that just means I won't see much of you!"

"Oh, but that's not true!" he smiled. "Like I said earlier, Alex is going to make sure we have time for each other. And these new phones he gave us will insure we can call each other without any trouble!"

"That's not all," came a man's voice from the shadows.

"Alex..." Kyle called out, trying to focus on the direction of his voice.

"Right here," he spoke up, once he arrived at the first few step of the gazebo.

"What else?"

"What I didn't mention earlier, is that they also have a built-in GPS, so we would know where everyone is that has one," he explained, pulling his out. "Here, let me show you."

Gathering around, he punched in the number for Ted's cell phone, who had taken the time to drive off into town, before Alex was to call him. Once he answered it, Alex was able to pick up the signal of his location.

"What do you have?" Ted asked, sitting on a picnic table at one of the town's parks.

"A clear fix on your location," he laughed. "Now move around and let them see what the monitor does when you do."

Getting back into his truck, he headed back to the Inn. However, he took a few different ways, before getting back onto the main highway, leading out of town.

"Looks good!" Alex announced, while Kyle watched over his shoulder. "You see what it does when he is moving?"

"Yes, and that's what ours will do too?" Kyle asked.

"Yes, and until we get back, I want you to help Lori with hers, so she will understand how to use it, and remember where the buttons are. Plus, I took the liberty, too, to put into memory her home number, her dad's office number, yours, and of course ours. And now, I hate to cut your time short out here, but we have some guys who need some rest after having watched the two of you all day."

"You're right," Lori smiled. "And, too, I am getting kinda tired."

Saying their goodnights, the two went back inside. And just when Alex was about to head over to his cabins, where Beth was waiting up for him, he ran into Jessi, just as she was coming out to do her nightly meditation.

"Hey, you, I thought you would have already turned in for the night," she smiled, while walking on up onto the platform.

"Just heading that way, but had a few last minute things to do, before calling it a night."

"And have you gotten them done?"

"Yep. And you? Coming out to meditate, as usual?"

"Wouldn't go to bed without it!"

Shaking his head, he laughed wholeheartedly, before saying his goodnights.

"Alex…!" she called out, stopping him. "Thanks."

"For what?" he asked, turning back to look upon her in the soft light that streamed out from her new quarters.

"For not turning my Inn into a war zone."

"Oh, but it's not over yet!" he teased.

"Alex," she closed her eyes, shaking her head, "that's not even funny."

"No, you're right. I'm sorry, but until we get them back to Camden, we have to be careful that our friends haven't gotten wise to our location."

"Well then, let's just hope they haven't!"

"That makes two of us," he agreed, giving her a hug, before leaving her to do her meditating. But then an idea hit him that only she and Craig could do to help this case along. "Jessi…?"

"Alex?" she turned back.

"This gift of yours and Craig's, I've seen you try to use it on David's parents. Can it be used on others?"

"You mean, can we pick up on Lori's situation?"

"Well, I kind of had something else in mind." Coming back up on the platform, he filled her in on Philips' threats to the family. "God forbid, he was to carry it out. But if for any chance he would, would these gifts be able to locate someone if they were to call out mentally for help?"

"Well, quite frankly, I had never thought of it like that."

"But could it be done?"

"Alex, do you know what you are asking?"

"Yes, and God, Jessi, I know it's a long shot, but Jason and his family…"

"I know how you feel, but I can't say one way or another, as it hasn't been done before."

"But what if you can? Think of how many lives you two could save with this gift."

"You make it sound like you want us to do this on more than just your friend and his family. Alex, Craig and I, we have our own family and work here to deal with. We can't just up and walk away from it quite so easily. Oh, but don't get me wrong, if it could work, and I'm not saying we wouldn't try and help, but not every waking moment of our lives, please!"

"Then, just maybe you'll think about it?"

"Think?" she asked, being the operative word. "I would have to discuss it with Craig first. And then try it out to see if we can pick up on one of their thoughts." Jessi already knew the answer to that. She and Craig had picked up on Lori's feelings, only because they were pretty strong. Yet there is a fine line between feelings and thoughts. *'Could we hear their actual thoughts, and at what distance?'*

With mounting excitement, he went up and gave her another hug, and went off to be with his family.

Watching him heading for his cabin, she shook her head. *'Oh, Alex, you have no idea what you are asking of me, or of Craig for that matter.'*

*'We can only try,'* Craig came back, while walking out to join her.

*'For Alex, yes.'*

"Will you be much longer?" he teased, walking up onto the platform to wrap his arm around her.

"Mmmm… not anymore… you sneak…!" she turned, smiling up at him, before claiming each other's lips.

# Chapter Thirteen

The next morning, waking to the sun shining in through their windows, Jamie and Lori were the first of the guests to arrive in the dining room for breakfast.

"Where is everyone?" Jamie asked Annie, while giving her daughter a hand at the steam table.

"Didn't you see Jessi on your way through the foyer? She's giving Lisa a hand taking in calls for yet another busy weekend. As for the others, they are probably still sleeping in!" she smiled kindly, while filling a tray with bacon.

"And Lora?" Lori asked, feeling her way to the table.

"She called to say she wouldn't be in today, on account of having a doctor's appointment to see how the baby is doing."

"How far along is she?" Jamie asked, having noticed she didn't look that far long.

"Four months."

"Wow, Jessi must be excited about having another grandchild," Jamie went on, while joining her daughter.

"She is!" Annie replied, giving the scrambled eggs a stir.

"And Cassi," Jamie went on, "any man in her life?"

Annie laughed, thinking how many that girl had lined up at the door.

"That many, huh?" she laughed as well.

"Yes, but one particular one stands out the most."

"Oh?" Jamie asked, but then stopped, when seeing the disappointed look on her own daughter's face. "What is it, honey?" she asked, placing an arm around her shoulder.

"Kyle, he hasn't been down yet."

"No, he hasn't," Annie returned, before leaving the room.

"Mom…"

"It's okay. He's probably up getting himself ready now!" she offered sympathetically. "So while we're waiting, what do you say we start in on this delicious food here?"

Taking a sudden disinterest in her food, Lori sat stirring blindly at the scrambled eggs on her plate, until they heard familiar voices streaming in from the foyer. "Kyle?" she perked up hopefully.

"Right here," he smiled, coming in to give her a light hug.

"I was disappointed to hear you hadn't come down yet."

"I would have," he explained, while going over to get his plate of food, "but I had a lot on my mind last night, and didn't fall asleep until sometime early this morning. Heck, if it hadn't been for my alarm clock going off, I probably would have still been sleeping."

"Well, you're here now!" Jamie smiled, while getting back up with her plate of food. "So why don't the two of you enjoy your meal together, while I get a plate to take back to our room, and see how your father is doing."

"Is he all right?" Kyle asked, concernly.

"Oh, yes," she smiled reassuringly. "He's just a little sluggish is all. But give him a few days, and he'll be ready to start barking out orders again, just like his old self."

With that, they laughed, as she finished getting her husband's plate ready, before making her way out of the dining room.

Shaking his head, "Man, I sure hope he bounces back," he stated without thinking first, when taking a bite of his food.

"What…?" Lori cried out fearfully. "And just why wouldn't he?"

"Oh, Lord," he came back, seeing the look of alarm on her face. "I…I didn't mean it like that, Lori…! I'm sorry…!" he offered, while quickly placing a reassuring arm around her shoulder. "It's just that, well, you know?"

"No, I don't…!" she flumed, pushing his arm away.

For the first time he was at a loss for words, when feeling her about to slip away, as the two sat quietly, till the others started pouring in.

Seeing the look of sadness on his face, being the first to walk in, Alex went over to take him aside. "What's wrong?" he asked quietly.

"Like a real dope, I said something to upset her," he groaned miserably, looking back on the woman, sitting silently at the table.

"Was it about her father?"

"Uh huh!"

"His heart?"

"No. Well… maybe, indirectly. But no, that would have sent her right over the edge."

"Then give her some time, she'll come around."

Shaking his head sadly, Kyle sighed, "I hope so."

Going back over to join her, she got up to excuse herself.

"Lori?" he called out after her.

"Go with her." Alex ordered. "Don't let whatever you said cause a rift between you."

"But what if…"

"What if, nothing. Go!" He nodded toward the woman, leaving the room. "Tell her you screwed up. Tell her anything. Just don't let her walk away without some sort of explanation."

Taking his advice, Kyle was out of the room, and in the foyer, taking her arm, before she could say anything.

Meanwhile, back in the dining room, Beth looked to her husband admiringly.

"What?"

"What you just said to him," she smiled.

"I just didn't want to see him make the same mistake I did all those years ago."

"By not telling me how you really felt?"

"By not keeping you in my life, regulations or no regulations."

"Honey, we were both cops, not allowed to fraternize with one another."

"I don't care, damn it. Beth, I had fallen in love with you back then. And for whatever reason, we were told that we had to end it."

"But now we are together. I am no longer an officer of the law, but working for Jessi. Whereas you, my darling husband, are out worrying me to death, working these other cases now that you have gone off to be a Federal Marshal."

"Yeah, well, if I had my way, this case would be over in no time."

"Don't we all wish that," Jarred agreed, looking to his own wife, who had just walked in behind him with her cousin and each of their two daughters.

With a knowing smile, she went up to give her man a loving kiss, before getting her own plate of food. "And yes, it's what you do," she offered, while picking up a plate. "Each and every time a case like this comes your way, we pray like crazy it will end soon, with all of you coming back home to us safe, and in one piece."

"And we do," he smiled, sensing her concerns, while they each got their food, before taking a seat.

Out on the front porch, with Marcose watching over the Roberts family, Annie brought out a plate for him to eat, not knowing Jamie had given him hers, when she and Jason went out to sit at a table.

"Thanks," he smiled, appreciatively, before taking a seat at one of the other tables, "but Jamie had already beat you to it."

"Your plate?" Annie asked her.

"Jason wasn't feeling up to eating all his food. So I gave my plate to Marcose, so Jason and I would share from his plate."

"Well then I'll just take this one back inside, unless someone else would want it?" Annie asked, smiling, when seeing Baker, a tall, light brown haired man in his forties, walk up, just then, for a visit.

"Did I hear you right?" he laughed. "Is that plate for me, then?"

"Yes, dear," she laughed, as well, knowing his appetite, while setting the plate down near a vacant chair, by Marcose, before going back inside.

"Lori…" Kyle went on, while following her out onto the porch, where she was met by her father, when he got up to help her to a chair, "I'm sorry I said what I did to upset you!"

"Then what did you mean by that?" she returned, sadly.

"I…" he looked to her father, knowing he had to lie to keep from telling her about his heart attack. "I just meant that I hope nothing else goes wrong, is all."

"That's all?"

"Yeah, sure! And I know, it was stupid of me not to think first what it would sound like when it came out, but it did, and I can't take it back. I can only tell you that I'm sorry."

Not sure what to think, or believe, she said nothing, and sat there in silence, pondering over what he could have really meant.

As for her parents, all they could do was look to one another and hope she would eventually let it go.

*'How can she?'* Jessi thought, looking to the three of them. *'They will have to tell her sometime!'*

After breakfast, Alex looked to Baker, "How are things with you?"

"Quiet, compared to what's going on here!"

"Yes, well things have a way of changing, just be ready if I have to call on you."

"All right. Until then, I'll head on out of here."

Watching him go, Alex wished he could have asked him to stick around, but there was already enough going on, when looking back to see the others waiting around.

"Alex…? Baker…?" Jarred spoke up, asking, while watching Baker drive off.

"Not just yet," he returned, sensing what his nephew was wondering. "We have enough going on now. Let's just get the others and go on out to the gazebo to go over the plans for when we get back to Camden, while Lori and Jamie stays pretty much in the Inn," he explained, leaving out the part of Jessi and Craig, until he knows how they would fit in, if at all.

"Sounds good," he agreed, looking to Marcose.

Once out back, Alex went into what was going to go on back in Camden.

"And the neighbor," Marcose inquired. "They're up for staying with other family members, until all this is over?"

"For as long as it takes, yes," Alex nodded, and grinned.

"Oh, oh," Marcose laughed, knowing that look. "You have a plan."

"Well, of course, and that is, how are we to explain the two of you being there?"

"Okay…" he continued sheepishly. "How are you planning to pull that off?"

"What else? The two of you have to make it look like you are doing some work on their place. Craig gave me the idea last night, when he said something about work. And with him being a contractor, why not?"

"Are you saying what I think you're saying?" Jarred asked, uncomfortably.

"It's possible!" Alex returned, while still thinking about the conversation from the other night with Jessi. But not having forgotten what he had to go through, when they had lost Craig once before. *Thank, God for second chances*, he smiled inwardly.

"Possible…?" Jarred nearly came off his seat, glaring at him. "I know you haven't forgotten what it was like a few years back, when you found him and all."

"I'm well aware of that," he returned the glare. "Just trust me on this. I have a plan. But until I hear back from Jessi…"

"Jessi…?" Marcose spoke up this time. "What does she have to do with this?"

Shaking his head, he wasn't quite ready to indulge them on this new piece of information just yet.

"Alex," Jason looked to his friend thoughtfully, "I have a feeling. And it's usually a good one, that you have a plan brewing up there somewhere. So you might as well bring it out into the open, and let us all in on it."

Placing his head down in his palms, he grumbled, until hearing Jessi in the background, talking to Travis. At that moment, he shot up, looking her way with a renewed smile on his face. "Hold the fort a moment guys, I'll be right back." With that, he took off like a shot across the yard to catch her, before she headed back inside.

"What was that about?" Kyle asked.

Jarred, knowing his uncle all too well, grinned, shaking his head. "I can't say for certain, but I have an idea that, whatever he is up to, it's sure to be a doozy."

Ted knew of course, having been told about it once he had gotten back from town the other night. "Oh… yeah, a real mind twister," he grinned, shaking his head.

Once their conversation ended, Alex came back, looking like he could bust.

"Good news?" Jason asked.

"She said they would do it. But just so we know, only for the sake of this case."

"You want to enlighten us?" Jarred laughed.

"Think about it. What is the one thing she can do for this case if, God forbid, Jamie or Lori," he stopped to look to Jason and Kyle, "if one of them were grabbed by Philips, or one of his men, to get you, Jason, to drop the whole thing. If of course it was to leak out that you are still working on it?" he asked, looking now to Jarred, with a knowing grin.

With a baffled squint of his eyes, he stared questioningly at his uncle. Then after thinking it through, it slowly came to him. "Her gift…?"

"Both, hers and Craig's. Just think about it. If something was to happen. And I'm not saying it will. But having them around, hoping that they will be able to pick up on their cries, silent or otherwise, it would sure help in finding them."

"Yes," Jason put in, "but isn't that what the GPS is for?"

"Nothing is fool proof, Jason. We learned that the hard way. I just want to be certain that I have all the bases covered, when it comes to family."

"And I appreciate that, Alex. Let's just hope we never have to put it to the test."

"That makes two of us," Kyle added.

"Question?" Jarred spoke up. "How and when are they going to be a part of this?"

"Craig has a good and strong right hand man to stand in for him on the job he is doing now. Jessi says the girls, along with her friends, and of course Jodi, can take care of things for her here. As to where they are going to stay, while there, we are still working on that. And for the story about working on the neighbor's house, by getting a couple of old pickup trucks, and put some made up signs on them to look as though the two, or I should say, three of you, Craig included, were actual contractors, working on the place. I have a feeling you could make it look quite real. You have the look to pull it off. Just don't shave for a couple of days."

"Great. Jodi will love that," he grinned.

"Marcose, what about you? I haven't heard you say anything for awhile?" Alex asked.

"Sure, that sounds good!" he agreed with a smirk. "But then no plan comes as a surprise when you're behind it!"

The two laughed boldly.

"And the office?" Jason asked, in an informal, but amused sort of way.

"A piece of cake," he went on wholeheartedly.

"Yeah, sure it is," Kyle laughed. "After all that I have seen you do so far, you can just about do anything you put your mind to do, if you want to."

At that moment, they all let out a humorous roar, before going on with their plans on how to deal with Epstein.

"Let's just hope he doesn't catch on to what we are doing," Ted commented, when they all had gotten quieter.

"First sign of trouble, we'll just have to tighten up on our men. Now," Alex went on, "Kyle, what, if anything, do you have to put in this?"

"Well," he though carefully, "I would rather be there at the office, myself, but..." Looking to the others, he knew that was out of the question. "Guess not, huh?"

"No," Alex stated, flatly. "Any other questions?" he asked, before getting up to head in to see his wife.

"Can Lori and I go for a walk along the trails?" he asked, getting up.

"Marcose? Jarred?" Alex turned.

"If you don't mind Ted taking this round, I would really like to stay behind," Marcose suggested.

"Sure. Ted?"

"Glad to do it."

"What about you, Jarred, are you going?"

"Sure. Just give me a couple of minutes to talk to Jodi first. Maybe we can make a picnic out of it."

"That sounds good, since it's such a nice day!" Jason put in. "And I know she would really love the time she has left with you to do just that," he smiled just when they heard the women walk up to join them.

"Love what?" Jamie asked, while Lori kept hold of her arm, until they reached the gazebo.

"Remember the walks we used to take back at your folks' place?" Jason asked, smiling. "The breeze in the air..."

"Let me guess," Kyle teased. "Would carry the scent of..."

"Kyle," Jamie cut in, seeing the look of mischief on his face. "It wasn't all that bad. It was more along the lines of honeydew."

"Sure it did," Jason laughed. "Because as it was, there was a lot of it along the roadside."

"Granny couldn't stand the smell of the pigs, and wanted to put her favorite scent out along the side of the house, but grandpa wouldn't have it. So he tossed the seedlings out along the side of the road."

"Where they grew each and every year. And from then on out they ate honeydew melons every summer," he teased.

"Wow," Jessi chimed in, "I can see why she would want to kill the scent of pigs. They're cute when they are small, but nasty when all grown up. So, what's this about a picnic?"

"They," Jarred began, while placing an arm around his wife, who, too, had walked up to join them, "were talking about turning their casual walk into a picnic along the way."

But then turning back to Kyle to see what he thought of the idea of making it a group effort, Jessi asked, "Unless the two of you want to be somewhat alone."

Looking to Lori, he wasn't sure how she would feel about the idea. And like before, maybe having the others around would soothe the moment for the two of them. "Lori?"

Looking away, she tried not to think about all that was going on back home, but the thoughts kept invading her mind. *Anything,* she thought quietly, *anything to stop these horrible thoughts, even if only for a while.* "Sure, let's all go," she agreed, turning back. "I really like having the others around to talk to. Really, I do."

Sensing something was troubling her, Jessi kept it to herself until she could get her alone.

"Great," Jarred commented.

"Okay," Jessi smiled, "I'll have Annie put something together for you guys. How many are going on this walk?"

Turning to Jarred, Kyle began, "Jarred…"

"It's not for me to say." Looking then to his wife. "Jo?"

"I don't have a problem with it. Karen's covering the shop, while I'm out. And the girls are out riding with their cousins. We were just coming out to see if they had gotten back yet."

"Jason?" Jarred turned.

"If it's okay with our two lovebirds, and my wife is up for it, sure, why not? The walk will do me good!"

"Are you sure?" Jamie asked quietly.

"Darn it, Mom," Lori spoke up, unable to take any more of their whispering, "I'm blind, not deaf."

"Honey," both her parents turned worriedly.

"Just stop, already. Ever since dad got here, you guys have been trying hard not to let me know what is really going on. Obviously something is wrong, and I want to know what it is. Daddy?"

"Right here, sweetie."

"Did something happen back home? Did that man go after you and try to hurt you somehow?"

There was silence. Everyone, but Lori was looking to each other for answers, when Alex stepped forward. "Lori."

"Uncle Alex?"

"Your dad is fine now. And no, the man didn't hurt him. It was just the stress of what all was going on. So Ted and I are going to step in to help out a little."

"I know that much. I just want to know that my dad will be all right. Daddy?"

Hugging her warmly, he smiled, "I'll be fine. Now what about this walk of yours?" he pulled back to ask, "How do you feel about having some company? Or would you two want to be, as Jarred had put it, somewhat alone for awhile?"

"Kyle, it's really okay with me," she turned softly.

"Okay then, that's settled. I think having the others come along would be nice!"

"Now that just leaves us with how many are going?" Jessi replied.

"Alex," Jason spoke up, "with Marcose staying behind, how about you and Beth joining us?"

Turning to Beth, Alex asked, "Would Annie let you off to go along?"

"Jessi?" she asked, hopefully.

"What about Bethany?" someone suggested.

"We can take her with us," Jodi offered. "Beth, you still have that child carrier, don't you? And if she gets to be too heavy to carry, one of the guys, apart from you, Mr. Roberts, can take over."

"What about you?" Alex looked to Jessi. "Aren't you going too?"

"No, Alex, some of us has an Inn to run," she smiled coyly.

"Okay, just thought I'd ask. You looked as though you could use a break."

"Thanks, but that comes later, when my husband comes home." With that, she counted heads to see how many were going, before going back in to fill Annie in on their plans.

# Chapter Fourteen

Meanwhile, the others headed back in to get what they would need. Still, Kyle didn't know what to say, or do, to make things any easier between him and Lori.

"It's going to all work out," Jamie offered, pulling him aside, just before reaching the stairs to go up to his room.

Watching Lori go off with her father, he looked back to Jamie, "It slipped out...!" he explained, regretfully.

Worried of what he had said to her daughter, she asked, "About his heart attack?"

"Yes. Well... not exactly."

"Which was it?"

"I didn't come right out and tell her about his attack. She just, well..."

"Assumed the worse?"

"I think so."

With a heavy sigh, she looked off toward the direction they had gone in.

"Mrs. Roberts..."

"No." She turned back. "It's okay. We'll just wait and see where this all goes. And if the subject comes up, we will deal with it then."

"And me? What about what I said? Will you and your husband forgive me for slipping up and saying what I did?"

Smiling at the poor lad, she patted him on the arm. "It's going to be all right. You were just acting out of concern for her father, it's understandable."

Taking their leave, each of them went off to get their things together. When they were finished, everyone got together in the dining room, where Annie had their picnic baskets waiting for them.

"Do we have enough blankets?" Jarred asked, having one folded over his arm.

"We're taking an extra one for Bethany," Alex offered, when seeing the smiles light up on his wife and daughter's faces.

"And we have ours," Jamie offered with a raised arm to indicate hers and Jason's blanket.

Standing all this time in the doorway of the dining room with Annie at her side, while watching the group in amazement, Jessi walked on in to offer a suggestion, "You know, before any of you get very far, your arms are going to be worn out from all that you have to carry. And then what's the use of trying to enjoy Annie's wonderful food if you are too tired to eat it? How about I get Hank to come up and gather all this stuff, and take it out to our favorite spot? That way you can enjoy the scenery around you. And Alex, you and your men can concentrate better on your surroundings, as well," she smiled, while conveniently leaving out if they had to act on any possible trouble that may come their way.

"Sounds good to me! Shall we?" he turned to the others.

"Absolutely," they all agreed.

Doing so, Jessi made her call, while Alex made one of his own to one of his men in Camden.

"It's been pretty quiet so far," Manning offered, while sitting across from the law office.

"Good, and Philips, has he been in lately?"

"Yes, from what I've just learned from one of the other guys you have on the back door, he was spotted going in just a few minutes ago."

"I wonder what's going on."

"Wish I could tell you, but…"

"I know." Thinking to himself, it was obvious in order to get in on any of their conversations, Epstein's office was going to have to be bugged. *That will just have to wait until we get back,* he thought, before ending his call. "Just keep an eye on what you can, but stay out of sight. You hear me?"

"Sure thing, sir," he returned, before hanging up, just as two men came walking out of the building. Looking both ways, the two split up, going off in different directions. "James!" Manning called out over his radio.

"Right here. What's up?"

"We have movement. Get up here right away. It looks like Philips is about to get into a dark green Suburban."

"Is he alone?"

"No, the other was Epstein, who is now getting into his own vehicle."

"You want me to take the Suburban?"

"Can you?"

"Sure. I'm rounding the corner now, and have him in sight."

"Hold up a minute."

"What's up?"

"Let's just make sure that it is Philips."

"You think it may have been someone else? Damn, if that's the case, then who did I see going in the back door?"

"Philips, himself, if not an impostor."

Just as their vehicle went by, Manning was able to see the man in it was a fake, made to look like Philips. "Damn…" he swore over his radio. "It's not him. James you have got to get back there and see if he had left yet."

"I'm already on it," he returned, when Manning saw James' black pickup do a U-turn in the middle of the busy street, before disappearing back into the alley.

It was moments before he heard anything from the other officer, while trying to keep an eye on Epstein's car. Then soon he had his answer.

"Manning?"

"Talk to me."

"I have him. He's heading up front now. Do you want me to stay on him?"

"No. Take Epstein. He's in a dark blue Chrysler Town car, about to pull out… now!"

"Got it."

And get it, he did. Without too much notice on his part, James was able to maneuver his truck around to take up the rear, while Manning made his move, though not as easy.

Within a matter of minutes both men were staying at a safe distance from their targeted vehicles. When then, without warning, Manning's man took a sudden change in lanes and soon lost his tail, making Manning fit to be tied.

"Damn him…" he cursed heatedly, when slamming his fist to the steering wheel. "James! Come back James. I lost him. He switched lanes and took off like a bat out of hell."

"Don't worry. Alex took care of that."

"What do you mean?"

"The day he went out to get those cell phones, he picked up a few tracking devices. He had me put one on both vehicles, in case we had trouble."

"Do you have the monitor with you?"

"Sure do."

"Great, what am I suppose to do in the meantime?"

"Give me a minute. Somehow I have Epstein now, pulling into his driveway, while still able to track Philips on the monitor."

Finding a place to pull off, while waiting on the other man to see where Philips was going, Manning put in a call to Alex.

Out on the trail, everyone was enjoying the heavenly breeze, when Alex's cell phone went off.

"Alex…?" Beth looked to him, worriedly.

"It won't take but a moment. Go on ahead without me. I'll catch up soon."

Doing so, Beth went on, though, not Ted or Jarred, who sensed something may be up, waited behind, while Alex caught the call on its third ring.

"What's up?" he asked, Manning.

"Philips. I was on his tail, but he gave me the slip."

"What…?"

"It's okay! James is just down the street from Epstein's place now, where the man had just pulled into his driveway."

"And Philips…?" Alex asked.

"James is working on that now, with the monitor, that is!"

Just then, James came back with the information.

"Hold on, Alex, James has something. Go ahead, James."

"He looks to be heading out of town, now!"

Hearing this for himself, Alex's expression changed, causing alarm for the others. "Which way is he heading?" he asked hurriedly.

"James, which way?" Manning asked.

"East. It looks as though… Oh, crap…! He is heading for the Interstate."

"No…! He couldn't have known of our location," Alex thundered concernly.

"Alex, I can't say. But if he had somehow, what do you want us to do here?" Manning asked.

"Get to Epstein's place right away, and have James follow the monitor to see if he can catch up to the SOB. And Manning…"

"Yeah?"

"Tell him, I want to know something as soon as he does."

"Where are you now?"

"At the Inn, but not inside."

"Oh…?"

"No," he looked to the others, worriedly. "We're…" he hesitated, "out on the trails, taking a walk!"

"Who's all with you?"

"The Roberts', Kyle, Ted, Jarred, Jodi, Beth, and…"

"And…?"

"My daughter…!" he groaned, raking a worried hand through his hair. "God, Manning, you have got to tell James to catch up to this guy. Don't lose him!"

"I'll tell him. And Alex…" He was quiet for a moment, feeling bad for what he had done. "I'm sorry, sir. I'm really sorry."

"It happens, Manning. Just keep your head and take over for James, so he can bust his rump finding Philips, before we have real trouble."

"Sure thing."

Filling James in, the two switched places, so that James could continue after Philips.

Back on the trail, Alex filled Ted and Jarred in, while keeping an eye on the others.

"What do you think happened?" Ted asked, while the three walked slowly behind so not to lose sight of them.

"Epstein must have gotten suspicious, when Jason had been out so long. Damn…, I was hoping that we would have had time to implement my plans…!"

"You still might!" Ted commented.

"You have an idea on just how we could do that? Because if you do, I sure would like to hear it!"

"If Philips was to know where the Roberts' were, we could get them out of here and to another location."

"Sure," Alex agreed. "Just long enough for him to finish recuperating, before going back to Camden, that is."

"And afterwards?" Jarred asked, curiously.

"Bring them back?" Ted indicated toward Lori, who at this time was leaning more on her father's arm than Kyle's.

"Lori…?" Alex asked.

"Yes. With her blindness, she is apt to feel more uneasy being in another strange place. So why not get her back to the Inn, as soon as it's safe for her?"

"Good point." With that said, Alex made one more call, before catching up to the others.

"Who now?" Jarred asked.

"James," he mouthed quietly.

Soon James was on the other end, while following the signaling device that had been placed just inside Philips' left turn signal lamp, where it would not be detected, even at night.

Not waiting, Alex asked, "What do you have for me?"

"It's weak, but I'm on the right track."

"And you're sure he is heading this way."

"No doubt about it."

"Damn, that's not good. Well stay on it, and call me once you have him in sight."

"You got it."

Ending the call, Alex punched in the number for the law office.

"Roberts and Epstein Law Office! How may I help you?" Cindy's voice came across clearly.

"Cindy, it Alex Storm. Did Epstein pressure you about Roberts where abouts?"

"Oh, Alex…" she cried, "he did, and oh how upset he was when I wouldn't tell him. He had even threatened to have me fired for insubordination if I didn't."

"Did you?"

"No, sir, I didn't. I told him I was given strict orders not to. And because of that, there was nothing he could possibly do to me to get me to disobey those orders."

"Did he ask who gave them to you?"

Hearing a little giggle, he knew she had to say something to aggravate the man.

"Oh, oh, what did you tell him?"

"I told him, Mr. Scott said so. And that he was in charge, until Mr. Roberts got back."

He laughed. "You did fine, Cindy. You stayed right with what was placed on the memo. Now, one more question. Who else was in to see him, besides Philips?"

"Mr. Philips? I'm sorry, sir, but I didn't see him in here today. However, there was another man here. Funny, now that you mentioned Philips' name, though!"

"How is that?"

"When Mr. Epstein left for the day, the man with him looked an awful lot like Philips."

"Yes, he was wearing a disguise."

"Yes, of course, that had to be it."

"Thanks, Cindy. Call me, or one of the other's watching the place, if anything else transpires."

"Yes, sir."

Once he was off his phone, Ted and Jarred were eager to hear what he had learned so far.

"I can't say just yet, but to be on the safe side, I think I'll give Craig a call and see if we can use his new place that he and Jessi use from time to time."

"The old farmhouse location, inwhich Tony's body was recovered from?" Ted laughed. "Aren't you afraid the man's spirit might be lurking about out there?" he teased.

Laughing back at his old friend, he shook his head. "If that were the case, don't you think Craig and Jessi would have noticed it?"

"Yeah, besides, after all the work you guys put into it, it would do for the Roberts to stay there for awhile. At least until we know the coast is clear."

"Then that's what we will do. And while I am on it, I'll call our old Commander and see if I can borrow Baker, since he knows the grounds so well."

"Good. Then we can try and enjoy what time we have left out here?" Jarred asked, when seeing Jodi's smiling back at him.

"Yes," he grinned, knowing how much he wanted to spend time with his family, before things got too intense around there.

# Chapter Fifteen

Arriving at their picnic spot, Hank was just about to leave, when Alex called out stopping him. "Can you hold up a minute?"

"Yeah, sure, what's up?" he asked, through the open window of his pickup.

Walking over to speak more privately, while Jarred went over to join the others, Alex filled him in on what was going on.

"Sounds oddly familiar, huh?"

"Yes. Let's just hope we can get them out of here, before he gets here."

"Just tell me what you want me to do?"

"Go back and fill Jessi in on what we just learned. See if she, with your help, can get all their things taken over to Craig's old place. Oh, and Hank..., make sure you're not followed."

"And if I am?"

"You got a cell phone?"

"Right here!" he patted the side of his belt. "And if necessary, I can take my rifle long with me."

"Good. Use it if you have too."

"What about Marcose? Do you want me to tell him anything?"

"Yes. Tell him to watch the road. If he sees anyone come up, act the part of the desk clerk." Turning to Ted, who had heard that last comment, when walking up, the two laughed, since that had always been his part during the last two cases.

"Better him than me," he grinned.

"Yes, well Philips may have already seen you back in Camden. If not, I don't want to risk it."

Agreeing to the plan, Hank was off to see Jessi as quickly as he could.

"Alex?" Jason walked up to see if something was wrong.

"Nah… everything's fine!" he tried sounding positive, but knew his friend wasn't buying it.

"Nice try. Now tell me something a little more believable."

Taking his arm. "Then let's go over here to talk, while the others are setting up. Ted…"

"Got it covered," he returned, while going off to lend the others a hand.

Once they were sure not to be overheard, Alex told him everything he knew so far. "My nephew, Craig has an old, well the house isn't anymore, but just the same, I want to get you guys over there, as soon as possible, to avoid detection. Marcose is going to stay behind to play desk clerk in case Philips was to stop in to see if you guys were here. He knows what to say, and he'll let us know when the coast is clear."

"How much time do we have?"

"Frankly…" He looked to the others, but when stopping at his wife, who happened to catch the look of concern on his face, he shook his head sadly.

"Alex…? Alex?" Jason was calling out his name.

"Y…yeah?"

"You didn't answer me, how much time?"

"Very little."

"What…?" he nearly cried.

"Jason, damn it, take it easy, and try recalling those days of being a cop. Think like that cop I once knew. Okay…?"

"Yes. Yes, okay. So what do we do now?"

"Wait on Baker. That's just as soon as I call to have him meet us out here."

"But isn't that a little risky? Wouldn't he have to come by way of the Inn?"

"No. On my last two cases, when I posed as a groundskeeper, I found an easement road at the backside of the property. He'll come in through there, and then go back out the same way."

"When can he get here?"

"Soon. For now just go back over and join the others. I'll be there soon."

Shaking his head, he turned about the same time Beth walked up, leaving their daughter with Jodi, who was already suspicious of what was going on. Though, because of the sensitivity of it, she didn't push for answers, knowing they would come soon enough, as they always had.

"Alex?" Beth spoke up quietly.

"Yes."

"Yes, as in what, or yes, as in, we have trouble coming our way?"

"Trouble."

"How soon?"

"Possibly two hours, give or take."

"You have a plan?"

"When do I not?" he smiled for the first time, since getting the news. Taking out his phone, he called Baker, while she stood by waiting.

Once he relayed the order, he hung up and took her arm. "Let's go eat, I'm starving."

"Alex," she pulled back to study him, "does this mean Bethany and I will have to go back to the Inn without you?"

"No, it means you, Bethany and Jodi will be going back to the Inn, as soon as I call Hank to come and get you."

Not liking what was about to take place, as soon as she was at a safe distance from her husband, she pulled out her old service revolver she had held onto, since her days of being a cop, before the two had gotten married.

Seeing this, Jarred walked up to see what she was doing. "Beth," he spoke softly, so not to draw attention to them, "please tell me that isn't what I think it is."

"Jarred, I'm not going to just stand around and watch you guys take this man on, when I still have what it takes to do my old job."

"Beth, I understand how you feel, but you're not a cop anymore. And in case you have forgotten, you are *very* pregnant, and have a child to protect."

"No, I haven't forgotten. And as for Bethany, Jodi can take her for a short while so I can be where I am best needed."

"You're not going to back down, are you?"

"No. And if you are any kind of a friend, you will back me up, when Alex reads me the riot act."

"The riot act about what?" Alex asked, walking up.

Looking to Jarred, she shook her head. "Fine. At lease go talk it over with Jodi, and I'll talk to Alex."

"I already have. It's already been taken care of."

"Excuse me!" Alex spoke up again. "What had been already taken care of? And what about a riot act? What the sam hell is going on here?"

"She's…" Jarred looked to Beth. "Sorry, Alex," he turned back, "she's going with us."

"What…?" he yelled heatedly.

"Alex, you need me," Beth stated stubbornly.

"Have you lost your mind…? I need you alive, along with our unborn baby here. No…!"

"Don't do this, Alex. Don't treat me like I can't cover my ass. You're going to need another woman out there to help watch over Lori."

"And that woman would have to be you? Why? Give me one good reason, and maybe, just maybe I'll let you go."

"Do you remember the first time you met Jodi? Remember when she didn't want to leave her home? What was it I told you then?"

Seeing the same look come over her, he felt the same pain in his own chest. "You knew how she felt about having to give up something that was hers." Turning to hide his emotions from the others, he quietly agreed to let her come along. "Just don't make me regret this."

"I won't." She turned him back to face her, before going up on tiptoes to kiss away his sadness. "I love you, Alex. Don't you ever forget that. You hear me?"

"I hear you. Now we had best be getting this show on the road, Baker will be here soon to collect everyone, and I still have to call Hank to see where he and Jessi are with getting their things out to Craig's place."

"So it's true?" Jamie asked, walking up with her husband and daughter.

"I'm afraid so," Alex explained, sadly. "But not for long. Just as soon as Philips is on his way back to Camden, we'll bring you back to the Inn, where the women can keep an eye on the three of you."

"On the three of us…?" Lori asked fearfully.

"Kyle will be coming back with us to lend a hand on what we don't know about this case," Ted offered, sympathetically.

"Remember what I told you out at the gazebo. You two will be able to talk on those cell phones I got you."

Smiling, she turned to feel for Kyle, who wasn't far from her side. Finding him, they held onto each other, until they heard the sound of an approaching vehicle, an SUV. One that Baker had borrowed from the Commander to get everyone over to their new location.

"Are we ready?" Baker asked, getting out to go over and shake Ted and Alex's hand. "Man, this is great working with you guys again," he grinned ominously at the two.

"Yes, well this time try not to get tied up again," Alex teased.

"Hey, that's not fair…!"

Laughing, everyone got their things loaded, before getting in.

"What about Hank?" Jarred asked.

"Give me a minute," he groaned, taking out his cell phone to call him.

"Yeah?" the man answered.

"Where are you in the moving of their things?"

"Just got everything loaded and ready to pull out."

"Make absolute sure there is no sign of their having been there."

"Jessi's doing that now by looking over the books to make sure they hadn't checked in."

Turning to the others, he asked, "Did you guys ever check in when you first got here?"

"No!" Jamie quickly replied. "I didn't think you wanted us to."

"I didn't." Turning back, he told Hank what he was told.

"Good. Hold on a minute, Jessi's coming out now."

"It's all clear," she announced. "As well as Kyle's room, too."

"Alex, did you hear that?"

"Sure did. Listen, Baker is here now. So we're about to head out the back way. Have Jessi go and grab my black duffle from our bedroom closet that has my equipment in it, and a change of clothes for us too."

"Do you want her to toss it all into the Blazer, to bring out to you, then?"

"Yes, while you follow behind, to meet us over there, as I'll have a few people needing a ride back when you get there."

"Oh, who would that be?"

"Jodi and Bethany. And Hank…?"

"Yeah?"

"Guard my daughter with your life."

"And Miss Jodi, too, I presume?"

Looking back to Jessi's cousin, he laughed, "Yeah, her too."

Sensing what was being said, Jodi smacked him on the arm, after having hung up, only to get another laugh out of him.

"Is daddy being silly?" Bethany asked, sweetly.

"Yes," the two returned, while giving her a huge hug, before getting in for the trip to Craig's old place.

"Oh, and before I forget," Alex added. "You'll love the neighbor, Allen and Rose McMasters. They have a pool and love to cookout a lot."

"Sounds wonderful!" Jamie responded, happily.

"Will you be coming out from time to time?" Lori asked Alex.

"We will all be out there, until we go back to Camden."

"Lori," Jodi spoke up attentively, "Beth will be out there too, if you'd like."

"Sure! And Jessi, too…?"

"When she can…!"

"Okay," Alex spoke up, "let's get going. We're burning precious time standing here."

Doing so, they pulled out.

The ride there took nearly an hour. Though, when arriving at their new location, pulling in around back, getting out, Alex went in first to check out the place. There, on the kitchen counter he found a note from Craig, letting them know that Allen and Rose would be by later with supper so no one would have to cook that night. "Huh," he noted, reading on, while the others slowly made their way in.

"From Craig?" Beth asked, from the back door.

"Yes," he smiled at the note. "He says; there is plenty of firewood out back if it gets cold at night. As for food, he stocked up the cabinets to help get us through for a while."

"Good," she smiled, as he shoved the note down into his pants pocket, before heading into the living room.

"Well, there's plenty of room here," he announced over his shoulder. "Three bedrooms up, and one down, as well as two full baths, one on each floor. Jason," he turned, "if you want, you, Jamie, and Lori can take the bedroom down to avoid the stairs. Beth…"

"The sleeper-sofa so that I can listen for any trouble?" she inquired.

"No," he laughed, recalling the time she took the sofa in the past. "I was about to suggest taking one of the rooms upstairs, and let Baker take the sofa this time."

"Wait!" Lori called out. "Can I share a room with Beth?"

"Are you sure, honey?" Jamie asked, sounding surprised.

"Yes! Besides, you and daddy need time together, and I like talking to Beth. Is that all right with you, Beth?" she asked, looking off in her direction.

"Sure!"

"What about the other two rooms?" Jarred asked.

Thinking about Craig's old room, though not so old, with the new farmhouse built over the old site, the place was identical to what was once there, all but the first floor bedroom. And because of certain memories that had once been shared there between Alex, Jessi, Craig, and Beth, Alex didn't want just any one taking that particular room.

"Alex," Jarred spoke up, seeing how he was in such deep thought.

"Yeah, sure, the rest of us can split into two groups and take the other two rooms. Yet, if Craig and Jessi were to come out, some of us would have to take the air mattresses that are stored in the hall closet, and put them here on the living room floor. Is that all right with everyone?"

"Sure!" they all agreed, just as Jessi and Hank showed up with their things.

Going out to help get it unloaded, Jessi asked if Jodi and Bethany were coming back with them.

Looking to her husband, Jodi knew the last place she would want to be is home without him. "No," she shook her head, "I can't. Beth," she turned back, "would you mind if Jessi and the girls watch Bethany, until the guys leave for Camden? That's if Lora is up for it," she asked, looking to Jessi.

"She probably won't be with Kevin working so much overtime, but Cassi might if I were to ask her," Jessi offered, understandably.

"Great. Alex," Jodi turned, looking to him.

"Fine," he laughed, "since I've learned my lesson, when it comes to my two nephews and their women."

"Oh, Alex, you have gotten softer in your old age," Jessi laughed, wholeheartedly, along with those who knew the story of how he couldn't keep either of his nephews, or their women apart from each other in the last two cases he worked.

"Jessi…!" he grumbled teasingly.

"Ok," she smiled, while going up to give him a hug. "I'll see you, before you guys head out."

"Yes, and call to let me know if Philips shows up after all."

"I will." Turning to Bethany, Jessi asked, "Are you ready to go and get spoiled by Cassi?"

"Mommy…? Daddy…?" She turned back to see the sad look on their faces, when it suddenly hit to be separated from their daughter.

"Oh, God, I can't do this," Beth cried, looking to Alex.

"Yeah, me neither," he painfully agreed, when going to their daughter, and dropping down on one bended knee.

"Wait," Jodi cried. "Why not let her stay with the two of you, since this guy doesn't know about this place?"

"No, he doesn't," Alex agreed. "And if he were to come out this way, James and I both have a monitor with his signaling device to show us where he is."

"That'll give us plenty of time then to get everyone to safety," Jarred acknowledged.

"Well, I guess that's decided. Bethany will stay here with us!" Alex grinned.

Unable to believe her own ears, Beth reached over to give her husband a huge hug, and then her daughter.

"I don't have to go back with Cousin Jessi?" Bethany squealed, happily.

"No." Alex continued, while looking to Beth. "Besides, I would rather she would be here, and not at the Inn, when and if Philips was to show up there."

"Speaking of Philips," Jarred asked, "where was his last location on your monitor.

"The Interstate. After that I hadn't checked it lately, since we left on the walk," Alex stated, getting the monitor back out to have a look.

"Yes, well let's just hope history doesn't repeat itself, where he might check-in at the Inn like our other not so friendly visitors," Ted announced, while waiting to see what Alex found out.

"He won't" Jessi announced, firmly. "I would simply tell him we are booked for the month."

"Well folks," Hank spoke up, "I hate to cut this short, but if we are expecting this man to show up, Ms. Jessi, you and I had better be getting back there."

"Give me a second," she returned, looking to Alex. "Anything?" she asked.

Looking up from the screen, he announced, "He's still a little ways out."

"Where?" Jarred asked, having a look for himself.

"Judging by the signal," he noted, "he must have made a stop along the way."

"Then we have time to get back to the Inn, to be better prepared, if he were to show up some time today?" Jessi asked

"Yes. And Baker, since we have enough guys here, go with them and hide amongst the trees to watch the road. If you see him, let them know. But then once we're certain he is gone, take an alternate route and get back out here."

"Ok," he returned, heading for the SUV.

Meanwhile, going around to get in on her side of Hank's truck, Jessi turned back, "Oh, and Beth, I put some clothes in the other duffle for you, once I heard you were going too. As for Bethany, when I get back, I'll get some things put together for her, depending on how long you guys will be out here. And Jodi, you and Jarred could use some of our things that's up in our old room, since you're both about the right size!"

"Oh, and Ted," Hank spoke up, "we brought your things out too, when some of the guys brought your truck out, and then rode back with Travis."

"Thanks," he laughed, as Hank was about to leave.

"Hey, wait," Alex called out, stopping them, when not seeing Ted's truck. "Where is his truck?"

"In the garage, where it won't be seen," Hank pointed out passed the house, to where the old block garage still stood, and smiled.

Shaking his head, Alex thought of their head groundskeeper, in his early thirties, who was known to be headstrong, and not afraid of anything.

After the two left, everyone went back in to get comfortable.

"Boy," Jamie spoke up, rubbing her arms, "I don't know about the rest of you, but it's getting a bit nippy in here."

"How about us guys go out back and bring in some firewood?" Jarred suggested.

"All but you, Jason," Alex teased. "While they are out doing that, the rest of us can check out the kitchen cabinets and see what all Craig stocked it with."

Taking the hint, Jason stayed in, while some of the guys went out back to get enough wood to do for the night.

"Jarred," Ted spoke up, once they reached the wood pile, "how about I hang out here and keep an eye on the road, while the rest of you are inside?"

"No, Alex has his monitor, and unless we hear something from James, Baker, or Marcose, we should be all right for a while. But then, if it's for the fresh air, you can!" he teased, while they went on to grab a load.

# Chapter Sixteen

Later that evening, the McMasters' came by with enough food to feed a small army, and to extend a warm invitation over to their place, while they were there, for a swim and a cookout. After they had left, Craig and Jessi came out to visit and play cards, while bringing the girls, Cassi, Madison and Kyleigh, with them.

"Any trouble?" Alex asked Craig, while setting up the table in the kitchen.

"No. But then you would have heard from your man if he was any closer."

"Yes, and no, he's not."

"Meaning?" Jason asked, joining them, when hearing their arrival.

"Only what I had suspected! Which is, Philips had decided to pull off at the same truck stop we did, along the way?" Alex explained, while getting out his deck of cards from his jacket pocket, on the coat hook, by the back door.

"Sure, but what's he doing now, though?" Jason went on.

"Still eating, from I've heard. Craig," Alex turned, "we're going to need a few more chairs."

"Got some in the hall closet," he returned, while going off to get them.

"Alex," Jarred commented, "it's still early yet."

"Yeah, well not that early. I would have thought by now he would have already gotten to the Inn, or at least darn close to it."

"Alex," Craig asked, returning with the chairs, "what exactly does this man want with you?"

"It's not me he wants, it's Jason. He wants to keep tabs on him, to make sure he doesn't go back on his word with this court date. As of now, the man thinks the whole thing had been thrown out of court due to lack of evidence."

"So what you're saying," Craig grinned, "he doesn't trust him?"

Alex laughed. "No, he just wants to be sure he doesn't double cross him, and find himself going to court after all."

"So for now...?" Craig asked.

"For now..." Alex sighed, looking concerned, "we just wait and see what his next move is."

"Sure, sounds good," Craig agreed, picking up on what was going through his uncle's mind.

"Hey, guys," Kyle walked into the kitchen, just then, "the others are starting get a little tired of hearing about Philips. Can we get this game going, since this whole subject is starting to wear on some of their nerves?"

"You're right," Jarred agreed, while the others came in to take their seats.

"Girls..." Jessi called out from the kitchen, "keep an eye on Bethany, while we're in here, okay?"

"Okay," they returned, putting in a movie they had brought with them, only for her to have fallen off to sleep half way through it.

After hours of playing cards, the men went out to get some fresh air, while the women cleaned up their mess.

"Still no word from the Inn?" Jodi quietly asked her cousin.

"No, but in a way, I'm glad."

"Why's that?"

"Just maybe this Philips guy doesn't really know where they are. Besides, I've been watching Alex checking his monitor most of the evening."

"Yes, me too," Jodi commented.

"Yes, well, think about it. It looks as though the man has decided to hold up elsewhere."

"Or..." Jodi looked off at Jamie and Lori.

"Don't say it," Jessi interrupted.

"Jessi, it's possible, and you know it."

"What's possible?" Jamie asked, walking back in after leaving Lori with Cassi and the others, once Beth had help taking Bethany up to their room to put her to bed for the night.

"It's possible," Jodi lied, "that we may get some rain tonight, and that always…"

"Cut the crap," Jamie scolded. "You are not talking to some green horn, here. Jason was a cop, before becoming a lawyer. So out with it."

"Sorry, Jamie," Jessi returned. "We didn't want to alarm you, or your daughter with any of our suspicions."

"Well then, how about you filling me in on some of them. As I have a few of my own."

"Well, from what I could tell," Jessi went on, "this man should have already been to the Inn, by now, to see if your family has been there."

"And since he hasn't?" she asked, inquisitively.

"Well, either he is holding up somewhere else…" Jodi was saying.

"Or he went and got himself a rental car, so he wouldn't be noticed, if he happened to have run across one of Alex's men," Jessi concluded.

"So… he could be out there, anywhere…?" Jamie cried quietly

"My guess," Beth spoke up, when coming back down to offer a hand, "he is parked down the road from the Inn, watching it."

"Good guess," Jarred grinned, while he and Craig walked back in.

"Where are the others?" Jamie asked, looking around his tall frame.

"They're out, sitting on the front porch, reminiscing," Craig announced, grinning, when going over to the counter to get some more of Rose's fried chicken.

Joining her husband, Jessi asked, while the others stayed behind to finish up, "Are you all right?"

"Yeah. Oh, you mean about what had happened all those years ago, when the old house was still standing?"

"Uh…you could say that."

Leaning back against the counter, heavily, he shook his head, "Jess, we have been out here how many times, since then? And… yes, that was the worst time of my…"

"Unlife," she corrected prematurely, while gazing up into his beautiful blue eyes. "And for me…"

"Yes…?" he grinned his crooked grin back down at her.

"Making love to you the way we did was so magical. In fact, one would never know just how magical a spirit like yours working through his uncle could be so great. As for what came the day you had to even the score..." She broke off, fighting back the tears that had threatened to come.

"I know." He, too, felt the pain of losing his best friend, when taking her into his arms. "God, I miss him too!"

Standing there in each other's arms, neither one of them heard Alex, nor the others, come hurrying in, until they heard the commotion coming from the living room.

"Jamie," Jason spoke up, hurriedly, "get Lori and the girls upstairs."

"Is something wrong?" she asked, going in to get their daughter.

"It's nothing to be too alarmed over," Ted offered, not wanting to frighten anyone. "We had just heard from Marcose, is all."

"Mom..." Lori cried, when getting to her feet with Cassi's help.

"It's okay, dear. I'm just taking you up to your room so you can get some sleep."

"We can take her," Cassi offered, looking to her mother.

"Yes," Madison agreed. "Beside, we're all kind of tired anyway, and need to get some sleep so we can be ready to go over to Rose's in the morning for that cookout."

"Thanks, girls," Jamie smiled, slightly, while watching them head on up the stairs. Once they were out of ear shout, turning back to the kitchen to join her husband, she opened up, "All right, boys, out with it. What's really going on now?"

"Alex, you want to tell them?" Jason asked.

"Marcose called just after Craig came back in," he announced, somewhat gravely.

"And...?" the women quickly asked.

"James was found just outside of Gary, Indiana, at the same truck stop we had stopped off at, when coming back home."

"Alex..." Craig asked right away, "is he all right?"

"Yes," Jarred cut in instead. "Just a nasty bump on the head."

"What could have happened that had gotten him hurt?" some of them asked worriedly.

"It seems Philips had made him, while James was sitting outside the diner. In doing so, Philips had somehow slipped out the back way, and came up on him, and knocked him out," Alex announced.

"Where is James now?" Jarred asked.

"Getting picked up by some of our people to go back and get checked out," Alex returned.

"And Philips…?" Jessi asked. "Where is he now?"

"We lost his signal after what looks like he may have gotten himself a…"

"Rental car…?" Jamie asked.

"Yes," Jason put in, studying her for a moment, when surprised of her knowing.

"The good news is the rental place gave us a make and model of the car he has," Alex grinned. "Now all we have to do is get everybody together, though, not the four of you, to come up with a new plan." Alex said, pointing to Kyle and the Roberts'. "I want you four to get some sleep, while we think up something."

"What about us?" Jessi asked.

"Well, knowing how you guys had probably planned to stay the night. It would be a lot safer if you do. So, as I was saying, the rest of us are going to have to come up with a new plan."

"Which probably doesn't include us women," Jessi teased. "So, while you guys do what you do to keep us safe, I think I'll go and check on the others, before turning in. Jamie, Jodi, did either of you want to go with me?"

"Sure. We'll," Jodi and Jamie declared, while Beth stayed behind to learn more.

After seeing them off, Ted spoke up, suggestively, "You know, while Craig and Jessi are here, the rest of us can take the floor in the living room, as if we weren't going to anyway," he laughed.

"Yeah, well, that brings us to Jodi and I," Jarred laughed, as well, looking to his cousin. "Now that the three of you *are* here, where do you want us to sleep?"

"You guys can have the back bedroom," he laughed.

"No," Alex disagreed, "that won't work. I'm going to need Jarred down here with the rest of us. Sorry, Jodi."

"That's okay! We're at least under the same roof!" she smiled up at her husband.

But then Beth spoke up, feeling hurt, "Then does this mean what I think it does, that you won't be joining me either, when you aren't keeping watch?"

He knew he couldn't say no to her, being in the condition she's in. But then seeing the look on Jodi's face, when she turned, hearing what she had. "Fine," he grumbled beneath his wife's slightly playful pout, and shook his head defeatedly, "you two win," he laughed. "We'll be up to join you later. But since we are doing that, we might as well take the back bedroom and let the girls stay where they are."

"What about Kyle?" Jason asked.

"He can stay down here with the others. Oh, and Jason, you and Jamie should be fine where you are. Just leave the curtains closed, while I keep a man out watching that side of the house."

Just then, coming back down to join them, Jessi spoke up, having just learned that the girls had been invited to stay over at the McMasters' the following day. "That should thin things out quite a bit around here. As for Craig and I, we will be going back to the Inn later tomorrow to keep an eye on things there."

"Craig?" Alex turned, worriedly.

"Yeah, well we can't keep bailing out on our responsibilities there, now, can we?" he laughed.

"No, but just the same, be careful. And Jessi," he turned back, "how long will the girls be over there?"

"A couple of days. Allen wants to try and win back some of the money he lost after the last card game Cassi played against him."

Laughing, he asked, "Is he ever going to give up? She is too good for him."

"Not a chance," Craig continued laughing.

"Well, in that case, with them staying over there for the next few days, leaving Lori alone in that room, Jodi, how would you and Jarred feel about sharing the room with her after the girls go, that is, while Beth and I stay in the back bedroom?"

"Sure!"

"Well I don't know about the rest of you," Ted spoke up, "but what do you say we get those mattresses out, and aired up, so some us can get some sleep around here?"

"Sure, but don't we still have the rest of that chicken to finish off?" Jason teased, when going over to see the large bowl still half full.

"Chicken…? That does sound good!" they agreed, joining him.

# Chapter Seventeen

Later that night, once everyone was asleep, the guys went out to walk the grounds.

"You know it's going to be a long night," Alex commented, while making their rounds.

"It could be worse!" Jarred returned, while looking over the area.

"Rain?" Alex grinned.

"Maybe!" Jarred turned, grinning at Ted.

"Not funny, Jarred. Not at all funny," Ted laughed, just as they walked back up onto the front porch.

"Yes, well, Jarred and I will be back out in about four hours to relieve you."

"All right," Ted nodded, as the two went on in to join their wives.

Meantime, back at the Inn, with the doors locked for the night, Marcose took Max with him to walk the grounds, while staying nearby.

"Well, Max, what do you think? Is it going to stay quiet tonight?"

Before long, he had his answer, when his cell phone started vibrating, due to being outside, so no one would hear it.

"Baker?" he asked quietly, when slowing to stop.

"We got company," he announced, catching the moonlight reflecting off a person's windshield, "and it's sure as heck, just down the road."

"To your left, or…"

"My right, and not far from the easement road that leads back to the fishing shack."

"Damn, just like Alex was saying earlier."

"That Jamie was thinking our guy just may show up, and park down the road from the Inn?"

"Yeah…" he growled, finding a cluster of trees to duck behind, while looking off in that direction. But when turning to look down at

Max, he asked, seeing the dog's head cocked, while looking up at him. "What is it boy?" he whispered, kneeling down to his level.

With a low bark, Max pawed the man's leg, as if to say, *growling is best left to dogs, because you suck at it.*

He laughed. "Oh, is that it? You don't like my growling, yet you don't seem to have a problem when Alex does it."

Again, Max pawed him.

"Oh, I see," he ruffled the dog's coat, "he's your pal. Okay, let's get serious here. We have a bad guy parked not more than seventy yards from here. So aside from calling Alex, what would you suggest?"

"Are you asking me, or Max?" Baker laughed on his end.

Forgetting he had him on the line, Marcose laughed, as well. "You caught all that, did you?"

"Yes. So what's the plan?"

"Are you still across from the Inn?"

"Yes."

"Stay there, and let me know if you see anyone outside the car."

"What are you going to do?"

"Head that way till I can see his car, then call Alex, once I'm certain it's him."

"Yeah, well be careful that he doesn't hear you coming, because so far I don't see anyone moving around just yet."

"All right, call me the moment you do," he ordered, hanging up. Soon he was on the move, but just as he got within twenty feet of the man's rental car, Max seemed to have picked up on the man's scent and took off running back to Alex's cabin. Having been trained by Alex to seek out what would be needed to do the job, Max retrieved one of the tracing devices Alex had left behind, in a pacific place that only he knew Max could get into.

"Great," Marcose grumbled, seeing the dog retreat, "so much for your dog training theory, Alex." Taking out his new phone, he put in the call to fill him in on what was going on.

"Where are you now?" Ted asked, taking the call for Alex.

"About twenty or so feet from his rental car, while tucked away amongst some trees, and well out of sight," he explained, quietly.

"And Baker?"

"A crossed the road from the Inn, hiding in the tree line."

"Ted?" Alex walked up, unable to sleep.

"It's Marcose. He has Philips in sight."

"And Baker?"

"Across the road from the Inn, hidden in the tree line."

"Ok. Give me the phone." Doing so, Alex perched himself on the porch step. "Marcose, it's me. Do you have Max or Maggie with you?"

Marcose laughed quietly.

"What?"

"Max," he returned, telling him what had happened.

Grinning broadly, he laughed, "That a boy… all right."

"Alex," Marcose came back, slightly miffed, "your boy, as you put it, just ran off!"

"Yes, and if I'm not mistaken, he'll be back soon with something in his mouth for you to attach to Philips rental car. And now for Philips, is he in the car?"

"Yes, drinking coffee, so it seems."

"Ok. And where are you in position to the car?"

"Twenty feet inland of the passenger side, and not far from the easement road to the fishing shack."

"Ok. Now, when Max gets back, can you get to the bumper without being detected?"

"I should!"

"Yeah, well we can't take any chances on getting Baker to do it. Philips will see him cross the road for sure. So I have to know, if he hears anything, even the slightest bit of noise, we'll lose him again. And we can't chance that, not when he is so close to our loved ones."

"No, we can't," he admitted, looking around his surroundings. "Damn…"

"What is it?"

"There are too many fallen twigs and dry leaves scattered about. Sorry, but it doesn't look like I can without hiking down the road a little ways further."

Growling to himself, Alex knew this meant only one thing, "Marcose, is Max back yet?"

Looking in the direction he ran off in, he heard the dog's breathing when getting closer. "Well I'll be, he's here now!" he whispered, while reaching out for the small black box he had in his mouth. "Give it here, boy!"

Doing so, Max dropped it into his hand, followed by lifting his paw in the air.

Looking amazed at what just happened, Marcose relayed the event to Alex.

"Is his paw up in the air?"

"Yes…!"

"Well…!"

"Well, what?"

"Shake it, and tell him good job!"

Shaking his own head, Marcose took the dog's paw, "Good, boy. Now what?" he turned back to Alex. "Unless I track down the road a ways, he may see me come up from behind."

"No." Alex had to think for a moment, and then told Marcose to put the phone up to Max's ear.

"What…?"

"Just do it. Put the phone up to Max's ear! Trust me. I trained him well to recognize my voice in any surroundings imaginable. So do it. We're losing precious time here. Oh, and Marcose, take the device out of its box for him."

"Ok…!" he laughed quietly. "Well, Max, the boss wants to talk to you." Doing what he was told, Marcose removed the device, while holding the phone to Max's ear.

"Max, do you know who this is? If so, give me a little woof, but soft enough that only Marcose and I can hear."

Bucking his head up, he gave out the softest sound of a bark as possible.

"Good boy. Now I need you to take the device as I had trained you, and go to the back of the bad man's car, and put it where I had showed you. Can you do that for me?"

"Rrrr…oof."

"Good boy. Do it now, but remember, not the slightest sound."

Taking the phone back, Marcose watch in amazement at what the dog did next.

Moving ever so slowly through the brush, not a single twig snapped, or leaf crackled. It was like watching a cat seeking out its prey.

Making it to the bumper of the car, Max crawled beneath it and attached the device without the slightest sound, and was back in hardly any time.

"Good boy, Max," Marcose hugged the dog, before getting back onto the phone with Alex. "It's done. What do you want us to do now?"

"Get out of there as quietly as possible. We'll monitor him from here. And Marcose, keep me on the line, until you have made it safely back to the Inn."

As he was about to leave, Marcose looked back to see Philips raise a pair of binoculars to look out. "Damn!"

"Marcose…?" Alex called out concernly.

"I'm here," he whispered, "but I'm going to have to be extra careful."

"What's up?"

"He has a pair of binoculars. So to keep out of his range, I'll have to track a little more inland, and sneak up to the back of the Inn to avoid detection."

"Then do it, and really watch yourself, the man is obviously smart."

Doing his best, he went inland to stay out of the man's range, and soon came upon the backside of the Inn. "All right, I'm at the back corner of the Inn now, and it looks like he may still be at his car."

"Don't trust that. Use the set of keys I had given you earlier, and go in through the family room's back door, and down to Jessi's old quarters to get Maggie," he ordered, referring to their Rottweiler. "She's the best sniffer, when it comes to intruders. She'll scare him off."

"Okay, I'm doing that now," he announced, taking out the keys.

"Good. Then call me back and let me know how it goes. And Marcose…"

"Yeah?"

"Call Baker and see if there had been any changes, as of yet. With Philips around, I don't want him doing anything that could put him or the others in danger."

"No, he won't. I told him to stay put, and let me know if there had been any movement thus far. Now, about Max, what do you want me to have him do?" he slightly chuckled, while locking up behind him, before making his way to the door that lead down to Jessi's old quarters.

"Keep him close, until it's safe to get Baker back over to give you a hand."

"Okay." Ending the call, Marcose headed for Jessi's old quarters, while getting Baker on the phone.

"Is that our guy for certain?" Baker asked, looking out his own binoculars.

"Yes, and I need you to keep an eye on him, while I go and get Maggie to search the grounds, in case he had gotten out, since we had recently tagged his rental," Marcose laughed.

"Who's we?" he asked, keeping his eyes on the car.

"Max and I. But listen, I need you to hang on a minute, while I get Maggie," he announced, reaching the door.

"Okay, but first I have to ask. Are we talking about Jessi's horse, Maggi, or their Rottweiler, Maggie, with an E?" he laughed quietly.

"Funny. Their Rot."

"I thought as much. But too, I often wondered, why would they have called both horse and dog by the same name?"

"Because Jessi had gotten the horse first, and when getting the dog for her older daughter, the previous owner had already given the dog the name, Maggi, without the E, and Jessi changed it to keep them straight," he explained, opening the door to go slowly down the stairs into the semi lit living room, where he found the dog lying near the small fireplace, at the foot of the stairs. Setting his phone aside, Marcose knelt down and called out to her. "Hey, girl, remember me?" he smiled, while holding out a hand for her to sniff.

"Rrrr…" she growled a moment, not sure who he was.

"Ok, well how about this, Alex has a job for you to do."

Hearing Alex's name, she shot up right away.

"Well, I see he has you trained, as well! So let's go, you have an intruder to run off."

Hearing this, she was up the stairs and waiting at the front door for him to let her out.

"Ok girl, take it easy. I have to make it look like I'm just letting you out to use the bathroom, in case Philips is standing anywhere nearby." Yet, with his service revolver where he could easily reach it, Marcose returned to his phone to see if Baker had any news.

"Yeah, the front is all clear, let her out."

"All right. I'm letting her out now," he announced, opening the door. "Okay, girl, go to the bathroom!" Just as the words were out of his mouth, she ran out into the semi darkened yard, heading right for Philips' rental car, when catching his scent in the breeze.

"Wow that was certainly fast!" Baker grinned, watching from his perch.

As for Marcose, reaching in to get his, now, cold cup of coffee off the desk to give off the appearance of being a desk clerk, he called out to Maggie, pretending he was concerned of how far she was getting. "Maggie, my girl, don't you be runnin off to far, now! I got to be stayin' close by the phone in case we get a call…!"

Just then, he heard the sound of a car starting up, along with the continued sound of her barking, when soon the car and its occupant drove by, not looking all that happy, either.

Once he was far enough away, Marcose and Baker met out near the road to watch his taillights disappear in the distance.

"Awww…, did we disturb your peace and quiet?" they grinned ominously, before hearing Maggie return, panting.

"Good girl…!" Marcose reached down to pet her, but then felt something damp along her right shoulder and front leg. "Oh, God, no…" he groaned, kneeling down immediately to get a closer look. "What's happened to you, girl…?" he asked, fearing the worst.

"Marcose, can't you smell it?"

"Coffee?" he asked, recognizing scent. "Thank God. I nearly lost it there, thinking the man had used a silencer on her. But then, without a doubt, it was the coffee I'd seen him drinking earlier. So what do you say, girl, we get you inside and cleaned up, while I put a call into Alex?"

"No, I'll get her cleaned up, while you call Alex, so he's not having to wait on what's happened out here," Baker offered, taking her inside.

"Ok," he commented, bringing up the rear, after having one last look down the road for any signs of Philips or his rental car. Seeing nothing to be concerned about, he walked on inside, closing the door behind him. "Alex," he called, once dialing his number.

Filling him in, Alex laughed. "Good. I'm relieved that everything turned out okay. As for the tracking device, it's fully operational, which makes our job a little easier. So get some rest and I'll call you in the morning to let you know what's going on so far. Oh, and to let you two know, Craig and Jessi will be back tomorrow evening without Cassi."

"And Beth and Bethany?" Marcose asked, locking up.

"They'll be staying here with us, until I feel it's safe for them to come back, as well."

"Okay."

Getting off the phone, Alex turned to the others and filled them in. "Max was a great success in getting the device planted on Philips' rental car. And Maggie…"

"She did well, as usual?" Ted grinned, having done the same with her, when Tony was alive, while sneaking around outside the Inn. "Yes, she sure is a great guard dog."

"Just like Max!" he grinned. "And now, about tomorrow. I want Jarred to stay here with you."

"What about me?" Jarred asked, when it was time for him to take watch with his uncle.

"You'll be staying here tomorrow with Ted."

"What will you be doing?"

"Playing Mr. Scott, who will be coming to look for his boss! It seems we have a new case that only he can take care of. So if Philips is around, let's just hope he overhears that the Roberts canceled their reservation to go fishing up north, somewhere, where the fishing is plentiful."

"And will Marcose be the one to act as desk clerk, telling you that they had changed their mind about staying there?" he asked.

"Marcose, or Jessi, if she were to get back, when, and if, Philips were to actually come to the Inn to see for himself. Either way, we'll have his location on the monitor. And when it shows that he is close by, I'll make my appearance."

"I wish I were there to see it," Ted commented, sheepishly. "It'll most likely be your best performance."

"You just might. But for now, why don't you get inside and get some sleep."

Taking his leave, Alex and Jarred walked around, looking up and down the road, while listening for anything out of the ordinary.

# Chapter Eighteen

By the next day, everyone was getting up and ready for breakfast, while Alex was monitoring the tracker.

"Any news?" Ted asked, walking in from having taken a shower out in the man-made shower Craig had built long ago.

"He's held up at a motel just outside of town."

"How can you be certain of that? He may have left the car there and went out to the Inn on foot!"

"Because Marcose is across the street with his binoculars, while Baker gets some sleep. That, and the Chief put a man on the back side of his room."

"Good," Jamie said from the kitchen door, while Jessi was in scrambling eggs. "Now maybe we can relax a little."

"Alex," Jessi called out, "why don't you guys show them the small lake out back? Craig had stocked it with some fish, last time we were here."

"Fish…?" Jason looked hopeful.

Telling Jason of his plan to go back to the Inn, acting as Mr. Scott, looking for Jason and his family, the man laughed so loud, it could be heard outside. "Gone Fishing up north, huh? That is a great cover up, since it is so well known around the office just how much I love the sport."

"And don't I know it," Alex laughed.

"Let's do it then. Craig," Jason turned, "do you have any good poles and leers here?"

"Plenty!" he grinned.

"Wait just a gosh darn minute," Jamie, Jessi, and now Jodi, complained.

"After breakfast, boys. You got that?" Jamie scolded.

"You heard her? She's not one to be messed with if she has something cooking in the kitchen," Jason laughed.

Seeing that look, Craig grinned, as well. "No, I wouldn't think of it."

After breakfast, not only did the men take their dishes in to get washed, but did them their selves, before heading out to do some fishing. While back at the motel, Philips was on the phone with Epstein, fuming.

"So they have a guard dog," Epstein growled. "Surely it's not out during the daytime. So go back and act like you are a friend, looking for them."

"And if they're not there?"

"Ask. Just ask."

Hanging up, he got up to go to the window. Seeing the slightest movement in the curtains, Baker, having gotten his sleep out, backed the binoculars away, remembering what Alex had said about the light reflecting off the glass. So from on top the roof, where he perched, across the street, he just watched.

Meanwhile, staying in cell phone contact with the man in the back, in case Philips had a radio that would pick up their signal, Baker filled him in on what was going on up front.

"We should let Storm know," the middle aged man suggested.

"Yeah, but let's wait and see what the man is going to do next."

During which, the two sat by quietly, while out at the farmhouse, Jessi was getting ready to head over to the McMasters to check on the others.

"Can I go with you?" Lori asked from across the room.

"Sure! Jamie? Beth?"

"I'll come with you, too," Jodi added, when walking back in from the bathroom.

"Thanks," Jamie returned, while working on some cross-stitching she had brought with her, "but I'll stay here and wait on the men to get back."

"Beth?" Jessi asked, seeing how she looked so comfortable in Craig's favorite recliner. "Are you staying behind?"

"Yes, I think so. But why not take Bethany with you? Grandma Rose and Grandpa Allen would just love having her around."

"Okay!" she smiled, while gathering up a few things for the walk over, since it wasn't too far away.

"I'll carry her, while you hold to Lori," Jodi politely offered.

"Are we ready then?" Jessi asked, while heading for the front door.

Once outside, she spotted Ted off to one side of the porch, while talking on his cell phone to Alex.

"Hold on a second, Alex. It looks like Jessi, Lori and Jodi are heading out somewhere. Let me see what's going on."

"Is that Alex on the phone?" Jessi asked.

"Yes."

"Let him know the four of us are going over to Rose's to check on the girls, while Beth and Jamie stay here."

"I heard that," Alex came back. "I assume the fourth is my little girl?"

Smiling, "She sure is," he returned.

"Are they walking?"

"Yes."

"Okay, but tell them not to be gone too long."

"No," Jarred spoke up. "Tell them we'll come and get them, when we're through here."

Relaying the message, Jessi nodded her reply and started out across the front yard to the road. Just then, Lori pulled back sharply with the look of pain etched around her eyes.

"Lori, what is it?" she asked right away.

"Mmmm… it's nothing now, just a slight headache, is all."

"Do you want to go back inside?"

"Oh, no, let's keep walking. It was probably the light."

"You can see lights?" Jodi asked thoughtfully.

"Lights and some shapes once in a while."

"That has to be nice, in place of total darkness!" the two agreed, while getting closer to the McMasters place.

Seeing that Craig's parents were there, too, Jessi thought, while watching her closely. *Just maybe I'll have Bob take a look at her, while we're there.* Getting there, she didn't waste any time seeking him out, when finding him and Allen sitting at a chess board that was set up on the kitchen table. "Bob," she called out, while walking over to tell him of Lori's headache. "It happened, when reacting to the sunlight, while on the way over here."

"Sounds like her eyesight may be taking a change! She was telling me about the surgeries she had undergone right after the accident. I'll have a look right after we get done here."

"Who's winning?" she asked.

"Allen, but I have yet to make my famous Matthew's move," he laughed, when all of a sudden he called, "Check Mate."

"That is the fifth time you have done that this week," Allen jived.

"Are you ready to concede to my winning?"

"Might as well," he grinned, looking across to the young lady, who looked a bit in pain, "since it looks as though your services are going to be needed soon. She doesn't look like she is feeling too good."

Rubbing her temples, Lori sat hunched over, while the others were talking to Rose, who now had Bethany bouncing on her lap.

Slowly, Bob eased himself down on the couch next to Lori, so not to startle her. "Hey there, young lady, Jessi tells me you have a headache. Can I have a look at those pretty blue eyes of yours?" he asked, taking out his pin light.

"Who are you?" she asked, pulling back.

"I'm sorry! I'm the one who saw you at the hospital the other night when you had your anxiety attack, and I'm the one who had always fixed up your dad and Uncle Alex, when they were partners awhile back."

"Yes, I remember you! Dr. Bob…! Do you think you can tell me what's going on with my eyes?" she asked, looking in his direction.

"I'm certainly going to try," he offered, while getting a fairly good look at them. Unfortunately, it wasn't as good as he had hoped, when shaking his head. "How about we go over to the table, where I can see a little better? The angle here is just terrible."

She smiled at the way he worded it, and got up with his help.

"Sue, could you give me a hand here? You remember Sue, don't you?"

"Your wife, and the nurse from the hospital?"

"Very good! Well she is going to hold the light for me, while I get a closer look. And Rose, if you don't mind getting the blinds, I'm going to need a little more darkness to do what I need to in order to see into these lovely eyes of hers. Now, don't be nerves, it won't hurt me a bit," he teased.

She laughed, while getting herself comfortable.

Once the lighting was dimmed, Bob went to work, looking deep into her eyes. "Uh huh," he muttered with each change of position. "Uh… huh." Then pulled back to study the pigment of her irises.

"Bob?" Jessi asked, softly.

"Where are your folks right now, young lady?" he asked with a hint of bafflement.

"Why?" Jodi asked this time. "Is something wrong?"

"Jessi…?" Lori cried, reaching out for her hand.

"I'm right here. It's okay," she assured, when looking to Bob. "Her dad is out back, fishing with the guys. Should I call her mother? She's at the house with Beth."

"I think perhaps you should."

"Should I get the curtains?" Rose asked, reaching up to open them.

"No. Let's wait on that. Oh, and Jessi, if her fella is around, have him come too. I think he may want to get in on this."

Calling Craig through the use of their telepathy, instead of calling Jamie, she told him what was going on.

*"We're on our way,"* he explained, looking to Jason, while getting to his feet.

Seeing the look on his face, while knowing about their gifts, Jason was up, pumping him for information. "What was that about? That look on your face, just then? Is something wrong back at the house?"

"Jason," Alex interrupted, "slow down and take it easy. Craig, looks like you just got a message from Jessi. What's going on?"

"Yes, but there's no danger, we just need to get the others, and get over to the McMasters place. You too, Kyle! It seems that Lori has come down with a headache, and any bright lights seem to be affecting her blindness. Bob and Sue are with her now."

Not wasting anytime, getting back to the house, Jason called out to his wife, while walking in through the back door.

"What's going on?" she asked, when Alex walked in to get his own wife.

"Alex?" Beth spoke up, looking worried.

"Just come with us. It's Lori."

"Has something happened to her…?" Jamie cried out, on their way out the door, while Craig and Jarred locked up.

"All I know is that Jessi got in touch with Craig, and said we need to get over there right away. Something about a headache and blinding lights."

Not wasting any more time, the ride over was short, when reaching the front porch, Rose was right there to open the door.

"My baby…!" Jamie cried out, going inside. "Where is she…?"

"Right here," Jessi spoke up, when stepping aside to let them be with their daughter.

"Honey," Jason was right at her side, "what's wrong?"

"Kyle…?" she called out, reaching for him.

"Behind you."

Seeing how crowded this was going to be, Bob suggested moving back into the living room. And in the living room they all went, with some having building excitement, while hoping it was good news.

Once she was made comfortable, the others stood back, giving Bob room, Jamie on her right, Jason, her left, and Kyle standing in behind Jamie.

"Okay, and now why I asked you all to be here," he smiled hopefully. "Jessi informed me that this young lady was affected somehow when stepping out into the bright sunlight. This in turn, brought on a slight, but painful headache. Now I went ahead and gave her something for the pain, strictly safe of course, Tylenol for headaches. But what caught my attention was what I had seen in her eyes."

"Doc, please!" Jason insisted, anxiously.

"The irises have changed in color."

"What…?" her family and boyfriend cried.

"Is this bad?" Jessi asked.

"No, not at all. In fact this may be the best thing to have ever happened to her. Lori, I'm going to have Rose slowly open the blinds. Now, what I want from you is to close your eyes, and wait for me to tell you to open them. When you do, do not strain to see around you. Can you do that for me?"

"Uh huh!"

"Okay."

Looking to Rose, she slowly twisted the rod, which opened the blinds. As she did, little by little the room began to light up.

"Stop right there," he motioned. "Lori, open your eyes slowly." As she did, he moved around to take a look at them. "Now, look at me."

She slowly lifted her head.

"What do you see?"

"I…I see a blur."

"That's enough," Jason groaned. "She had already been through enough, with one doctor, then another."

"No, wait…!" she cried, looking to her father, and then her mother. It wasn't until she came to the one standing in behind her, that things began to get clearer.

"Rose, the blinds. Open them all the way," Bob smiled.

Doing so, something lit up in Lori's eyes, when right away her mother saw the blue returning to them, as she cried, covering her mouth.

"Kyle…?" Lori cried, reaching out to him.

"You can see me…?" he too cried, while the others shed a few tears of their own.

"It's like looking through a glass, but yes, I can see you!"

Wanting to get right in there to hold her, Bob held them off for a moment. "Folks I know how exciting this must be, but until she has fully regained her sight, I must caution you, she must wear good, strong sun glasses for a while to avoid any possible damage to her retinas."

"Of course," Jamie cried right away. "She'll have the best there is."

"Count on it, Doc.," Jason added, while feeling he was about to burst.

"Yes, well just remember not to strain your eyes," Bob reminded, smiling.

"All right," Lori nodded.

"Doctor Bob, can I…" Kyle asked, eager to hold his lady.

"Go ahead," Bob continued to smile, while stepping aside.

Turning to give one another comfort and joy, Jamie held tight to her man, as well, while looking up to Jessi with appreciation, and then to Bob, just for being there.

"Thank you so much," she and her husband said, getting to their feet to shake his hand.

"Lori?" Kyle cried tearfully, while holding her.

"Yes?"

"I…I love you!"

"Ditto," she smiled through tear-streamed eyes.

"You know," Bob went on to saying, "I may have just the glasses she needs out in my car. I was thinking about getting a hold of Alex to see if you could use them." Going out to get them, it wasn't long before Lori had them on and anxious to go out and try them out.

"Mom? Dad?" she asked excitedly.

"But just out back," Alex told her, cautiously.

Being lead out through the patio doors, the sun, at that time, was tucked in behind some clouds, making it easier for her to see without any pain.

"Lori?" her mother asked, softly, from behind.

Not answering, with Bob standing off to one side, watching her closely, he could tell she was seeing something, and yet, she was squinting a little.

"Does it hurt any?" he asked.

"No. It just feels… kinda… different."

"Like what, sweetie?" her mother asked.

"Like I've been in a cave most of my life, with very little to see by. And now it's so beautiful. Oh, my…!"

"What?" Kyle asked.

"The pool! Is that how big it is?"

"Can you see it clearly?" Bob asked.

"Not real clear, but I can see that there are chairs around it!"

"Okay, that's enough for now," Bob suggested. "It's time to get you back inside to give your eyes a rest."

"Now…?" she cried, wanting to see more.

"Afraid so. You don't really want to push it too fast the first day. Besides, inside you can relax the optic nerve, and still see some things around you."

"Like the people that have been good enough to take us in," Jason mentioned, graciously.

"There is one I've been dying to see ever since he came back into our lives."

# Chapter Nineteen

Once inside, taking off her glasses, she looked around the family room for that one familiar face in the crowd. Seeing it, she went to him with tears of joy in her eyes. "Uncle Alex."

Trying to wipe away his own tears, he took her into his arms and held her for what seemed like a lifetime. "Lori, i…it's so good to see you smiling again," he cried, holding her, like a father holding his own.

"Yeah, well, it's been awhile," she pulled back, rubbing her eyes.

"Rose," Jessi quickly gestured for a cool washcloth.

"Sure thing." She hurried off to the bathroom to get one, while Lori was ushered over to a recliner to lay her head back.

Once the cool cloth was put into place, the feel of it worked its magic right away.

"Jason," Bob spoke up with a hint of concern, "as soon as you can, you need to get her in to see her doctor. Until then, don't let her strain her eyes anymore than necessary, or she could lose her sight again."

"Yes. Yes of course," Jason agreed, looking back on his daughter from the kitchen doorway.

"Well, people," Alex spoke up, "some of us need to be getting back to the Inn. Jessi? Craig?" he turned his attention to them. "We have a certain gentleman to convince that the Roberts' are somewhere up north, fishing."

"Well, I guess we should be going then," Craig grinned. "Mom, Dad, see you two later?" he waved, heading for the door. "And you too, Mama Rose and Papa Allen," he laughed.

"Cassi," Jessi turned to hug her daughter, "see you in a few days. And if you decide to go over to the farmhouse, let Jarred know that you're coming."

"Okay!"

"Beth," Jessi then turned, "I'll let Annie know you'll be out for a while."

"Thanks, and little David, here, thanks you too," she smiled, rubbing her belly.

"Well, you just tell him to behave. See ya later. Jodi?" she turned to her cousin.

"I'll call you," she smiled.

"I guess this means that you are staying out here, too?" Alex asked at the doorway.

"Yep! At least until the girls are ready to go home," Jodi announced.

"Fine. Shall we?" he said, turning to the others. "Jarred," he called out, looking back to his nephew, while still standing by his wife, "you and Ted are in charge, while I'm gone. Call me if you have any trouble."

"We will."

"Hey, Alex," Ted called out, stopping him, while on his way out, as well.

"Yeah?"

"Watch your back?"

With a sheepish nod, the three left for the Inn after Alex turned back to give his wife and daughter a hug goodbye. Though on their way, with Jessi and Craig bringing up the rear, pulling out his phone, he called Craig to fill them in on his plan.

"She can do that!" he replied, looking to his wife.

"Good, but before I get there I'll need to pick up a car the chief has for me to use so that my Blazer isn't recognized."

"Is the plate going to be registered in your alias name?"

"Yes."

"Good, and do you know where Philips is now?"

Looking at the tracker, on the seat next to him, the signal hadn't moved. "No change."

"Meaning what?"

"He's still at the motel. But just to be on the safe side, I'll give Baker a call to be sure."

"All right, call us back."

Putting in the call, Baker confirmed his whereabouts. "He left once, but only to go to the store and back. And too, he's been on his phone with Epstein, but no doubt, mad."

"About?"

"The guard dog, maybe?" he laughed, watching the front door and window through his binoculars, while the sun was still behind some clouds.

"Oh, well, listen, I'm on my way back, but first I have to pick up a loaner car. It's time for Jordan Scott to pay the Inn a visit."

"Why?"

"To send out a bogus message that Scott is looking for the Roberts, due to a new case that the client only wants Jason to handle."

"Good thinking. And us?"

"Stay put until I call you," he ordered, getting off the phone to call Craig back.

Once that was done, he arrived at the pick up point to get his car, while the others went on ahead without him.

"What do you have for me?" he asked the garage man, wearing coveralls, smudged in oil.

"The chief said to give you the top of the line. You know how he is? Nothing is too good for the best detective around!"

"Federal Marshal, George," he corrected with his broad grin.

"Oh, yeah. Moved right on up to the big time, did you?" Pointing to a shinny, black number, he nodded his head. "A real beauty, that one is."

"The Pontiac GP?"

"Yep!" he nodded, tossing him the keys. "Already filled up and ready to go."

"Thanks. Oh, and hide my baby for me. I'll have one of my guys come by and get it later."

"Sure thing."

Pulling out onto the highway, he wanted to open it up and see what she had. And why not take it by the motel, where Philips was staying.

Getting there, Alex saw the man standing outside his room, on his phone, shaking his fist in the air and pacing between two of the posts closest to his door.

"I don't care how long it takes, find the man, Scott, or ring it out of that secretary of his. I don't care. Just find him," he growled, getting off the phone.

"Wow," Baker whispered, reaching for his phone. "I've got to call Alex and warn him. He is going to want to call his man in Camden about this!"

The wait wasn't long, and he didn't have to say much, as Alex was already within ear shout of the man.

"Thanks, Baker, but I already heard it all first hand," he nodded his position up to the man on the roof. "And now I have to call Roland and have him get Cindy out of there."

"Sure, but how are you going to explain why no one is at the front desk?"

"I won't have to. Roland will watch the front desk for her," With that said, he cut the call short, to do just that.

"Yes, I'm here with her now," he said, smiling down at her.

"Good. I don't have much time to fill you in, but you have to get her out of there, now. And if she refuses to go…" he growled. "Knock her out if you have to. Just get her out of there."

"And do what?"

"Take her place, and if anyone asks, tell them she left, because of how she was being treated after our leaving, and that she won't be back until one of us returns."

Laughing, he agreed, and took care of the matter right away.

"But why…?" she cried stubbornly.

"Because your life is in danger if I don't get you out of here, and now."

"Okay, you have convinced me." Grabbing her things, they headed for the door, when then seeing Epstein pull up out front.

"Damn," he swore, running his hand over his head.

"The back door…!" she cried.

"Good. Let's go."

Making their way through the office building, they got out just in time to clear the alley, while he made a quick call to one of the men Alex had sent to get them.

"Where are you now?" he asked, looking up and down the main thoroughfare.

"At the alley and 3rd!"

"Hang tight. Be right there."

"What are you driving?"

"A white Dodge pickup."

"Yes, I see you now."

Getting her to safety meant going to Roland's house on the north side of town. "It's not much, but it's home," he explained on their way.

"Nice! How long will I have to stay there?"

"Until this is over, I suppose!"

"But I'll be needing some things from my place!"

"I'll get them. Just tell me what all you'll be needing."

"Uh huh!" She looked at him questioningly.

Making a face, he blushed. "Oh, those."

"And some other clothes and pictures. Like that of my father."

"Sure."

Telling him where everything was, after dropping her off, he went right over, using his old beat up Plymouth to get her things, and was back in no time.

Meanwhile, back at the Inn, watching closely to the monitor, Philips was on the move, and looked to be coming their way.

"Ted, Marcose, it's show time! Jessi…"

"I know. He's on his way," she acknowledged, while looking around her surroundings to see who all was there.

Looking to her concernedly, Alex asked, "Are you sure you want to do this?"

Before she could reply, Craig walked in. "She won't be alone," he announced.

"No, sir," Hank added in, upon his arrival, too, "I'll be here, as well."

"Me too," Travis spoke up, coming up onto the front porch.

"And Marcose," Alex turned, seeing Maggi at his side, "just what do you think you're doing with her?"

"Well, he already knows she's here! And Travis, here, said something about running her."

"That'll explain his presence!" Alex agreed. "Hank, what's your excuse?"

He looked to Craig for help, having been told on the fly of their impending situation.

"He's here to lend me a hand with…" He looked around quickly for an answer. "Landscaping…!"

"Fine. Let's get into our roles then. Marcose, give Travis the dog. Maggie," he knelt down to ruffle her coat, "if the bad man gets angry, show him whose boss."

"Rrrr...uff," she responded.

With very little time to spare, they went over their plan one last time, when just then a car pulled in the drive with a middle age couple in it.

"Is that him?" Craig asked, seeing how Alex ducked inside the doorway to watch the oncoming car.

"No."

"Jess..." Craig started to ask, when realizing Hank needed to get his garden tools to make their part look real.

"Hank, aren't you missing something?" he gestured to his empty hands.

"Yeah, you're right!" he chuckled, hastening off to the garage, where his truck was parked, to pull out his tools.

"Hold up there," Craig called out, following after him, "I'll give you a hand!"

Soon the two were back and had things laid out, looking like they were busy, having to dig up some of the plants so as to get them replanted. As for the couple who had just arrived, they were people from Ohio, and had been there once before.

"Mr. and Mrs. Shelling...!" Jessi greeted warmly. "How wonderful it is to see you again. Your room is all ready for you, and if you'd like..." she had to think quick of a made up name for Marcose, "Franklin, here, can carry your things up for you."

"That'll be nice," the two smiled, and handed their luggage over to Marcose.

"Room 2, Franklin!"

"Ma'am!" he nodded. Though, on his way up the stairs, he gave Alex a frowned expression.

Laughing quietly, Alex checked his disguise in the hall mirror, when, then, Philips pulled in. "Great," he grumbled, seeing the man. "Heads up," he signaled Jessi, who in turn signaled Craig, who passed the word quietly to the others. "Marcose... Franklin...!" he corrected, seeing how he was still with the new guests, at their door.

"Is he here?" he asked, setting their things down inside it, to check his service revolver.

Seeing it, the couple gasped, while Alex relayed the message.

"Sorry folks, I'm a Detective, moonlighting as a Bellhop," he frowned once again, though, sheepishly that time as he headed down to ask where he was to go.

Looking into the boutique, Alex quickly called Renee over. "I don't have time to fill the two of you in, but you both need to pose as guests, looking at the merchandise. Can you do that for me?"

Seeing the urgency on his face, and knowing Alex for who he really was under his disguise, Renee was quick to agree. "Yes, sure, but I should warn you, I'm a flirt," she smiled playfully to ease the moment.

"Fine. Let's do this then," he agreed, and just in time, when Philips was just about to get out of his car.

Nodding his head at Jessi, she readied herself to act as though she were about to help her so-called guest, just as Philips was about to walk up onto the porch.

"Sir," she said politely.

"It's Mr. Scott. Jordan Scott," he corrected in his roll, while placing his hands on the desk to make it look as though he were upset.

"Yes, Mr. Scott. However, as I was saying, I'm sorry that you had to waste a trip over here, but the Roberts family had a change of heart, and canceled their reservation at the last possible, inopportune time…!"

"Did they say why?" he asked heatedly.

"Yes, something to do with a cabin, and fishing. To be more précised, I believe the words he used were; the best catch of the season."

"Where would that be?"

Hank couldn't resist chiming in at that moment. "Sir…! Why that would be up in the northern point of Michigan. Right along Canada some would say. Yep, if n' you want to get in on the best there is, Michigan and the Canadian border that'd be the place, all right."

"Is that it? Is that where he said they would be going?"

"Sorry…" she shrugged, pretending to act helpless, "that's all I know, is somewhere up north. Oh and that they had only a certain amount of time if they were to get in any kind of fishing, before he had to get back to the office, that is."

"Damn it, Jason," he growled, pounding the desk, before shoving passed the so called guests to leave, as they came out of the Boutique, carrying their packages.

"Hey... what's your problem...?" Renee shouted at him, while acting as if his actions hurt her shoulder.

"Sorry," he grumbled, when stopping at the door to look back at her, but only to see where Philips was standing in adjacent to his path out of there.

"Yeah, well just watch it next time, will you? You could really hurt someone with those shoulders of yours," she commented, while running her hand over one. "Yes indeed. Mmmm... you sure could."

"Ma'am, if you are done, here, I really must be going."

"Oh, but of course!"

Grinning quietly, Alex turned to see Philips standing close enough to the door for him to purposely run into, and so he did, while on his way out to his car, grumbling the whole way. Getting in, he slammed the door and got on his phone to make-like he was calling someone, while all along Philips watched. "Jeffery," Alex nearly shouted into the receiver, "it's Jordan Scott," he announce, while waiting for the right amount of time to lapse to go on. "Yes, I know they want Roberts, but he is out of town. No... I wasn't able to catch him. Yes, it seems like he has already gone up north and probably won't get back in time to help them out. So if they call again, just tell them that he handed their case over to me to take care of. Yes, I'm well aware of that, damn it! Just do it!" he yelled, hanging up, before starting up the car, to spin out of the driveway, still acting mad as all get out.

"Some temper that one has," Marcose commented to his supposed boss, while watching the man peel out of the driveway.

At that moment, Craig walked in. "What was that was about?"

"He said something about a new case and that the CEO wanted this Jason Roberts to handle it personally. What was I to do? The man called a few days ago and canceled his reservation. Lord, I took the call myself!"

"Yeah, well from the looks of it, he won't be coming back here at any time," he muttered.

"No, I seriously doubt it," she agreed, turning to the others. "Okay now, whose next?"

"They are," Philips offered, while standing back in the doorway, thinking what his next move would be, when then looking across the way at the Rottweiler.

Seeing his expression turn grim, the others pushed on talking and laughing as nothing was wrong.

# Chapter Twenty

"Sir," Jessi turned to Philips, while Ashley and Renee went upstairs, but only to sit and wait on the attic steps, until word was given to return, "can I help you, now?"

"Rooms?" he asked sternly. "Are you all out of them now?"

"Just rented the last one to those two women," she pointed. "And the cabins, I'm afraid, are booked up until September. However, I have been telling people that if they want to get in on one, they need to call three months in advance."

"And this family who canceled?"

"They called just the other day. Though, had of you been here then you could have gotten one of their rooms, which as of just a short while ago had all been rented out to a family here for a large reunion. Couldn't say for sure how long they will be here. Did you want to be put on a call list if I were to get an opening?" she asked, pulling out a book that was nearly full of names, making it look like he would have quite a long wait ahead of him.

Looking at the number of people in it, he shook his head, "Thanks, but I'll be heading back to Illinois this evening." He turned then, and walked back out to his car, but not without Maggie bearing her teeth at him.

"Maggie, heel girl," Travis commanded. "Sorry, Mister," he fought back a grin, "I don't know what's gotten into her."

"Yeah, well just keep her on the leash, until I get out of here," he growled, while steering clear of her.

Watching the man leave, Travis turned back to the others and smiled.

"Glad that's over," Jessi commented, while she and the others walked out onto the front porch to join the rest of them.

"Yes, but which way did he go? Did any of you see?" Marcose asked, being the last one to join them, after having told the others to come back down.

"Same way Alex did," Hank indicated with a nod of his head.

"Hello! Did I just hear someone mention my name?" Alex asked, with a grin, from the doorway, having started them with his unexpected appearance.

"Where did you come from?" Travis asked, looking up at him puzzledly.

"The back easement road. Oh, and by the way, that car does great across the pasture!" he laughed.

"Oh…?" Jessi asked. "And just where is it now?"

"Back behind the stable, covered with a tarp," he went on laughing, just when Annie walked up to announce dinner was ready.

Just before going in, Craig turned back to Hank. "Have Travis give you a hand with getting those flowers replanted, and then come on in to eat, the both of you," he ordered.

"Hank," Alex turned back to offer his thanks in a job well done. "You too, Travis. And that goes for the rest of you. Thanks for jumping in when you did."

"You're welcome!" they all put in proudly.

Excusing himself, Alex went in, using Jessi's office, to check on Philips' where abouts, and to call Jarred.

"Has he left the area?" Jarred asked, while still out at Craig's old place.

"Yes, but he hasn't gone all that far yet. And from the looks of it, he is still heading west, toward the state line."

"Where is Baker?"

"Seeing if he had checked out of his room yet."

"Good. Will you have someone on him once he gets back to Illinois?"

"Damn straight! For now, we can rest up a little, but keep our friends out there for now. And speaking of our friends, how is Lori doing?"

"She and Kyle are out at the lake, taking in the scenery."

"Is she wearing her glasses?"

"Oh, yes. She doesn't want anything going wrong with her eyes now."

"Are you with the two now?"

"Jodi and I both are, but at a safe distance, and still able to see them."

"Good. I'll be out later to see Beth and my girl, and to fill the Roberts in on what all transpired here."

"Okay. See ya when you get here."

Finishing up with his business, he joined the others at the dinner table for some good ribbing, when it came to his acting temperamental. As to the rest of the evening, Philips went back to Camden with a new tail on him, and arrangements were made to pick up the Blazer and tracking device from the rental car. As for Cindy, she was quite happy where she was.

Later that evening, as planned, Alex went out to see the others, with Jessi and Craig tagging along. "Once we get there," Alex was saying over his phone with the two on speaker, "I'm going to take Jason out back for a walk and talk to him about what I have planned for the office. While I'm doing that, Craig, I want the two of you to talk with Lori and Jamie about this gift of yours, and the idea we have to utilize it if, God forbid, either of them were to get grabbed."

"Sure, but Alex, they already know about our gifts," Jessi announced.

"What?"

"Yes, she had already told them about it, when we went out riding the other day," Craig explained.

"Then test it out on them. Damn it, we have to have a backup plan if those cell phones don't work!"

"Alex," Craig cut in to assure him, "it's all right...! We can try it out, out here, and see what happens...!"

"Sorry, but I can't help but have a sinking feeling that something is going to go wrong, when we get back. I can feel it."

"Well if this will help any," Jessi smiled. "They don't know that she is getting her sight back."

"That's true, and when we get there, I'll have to tell Jason to keep that bit of news under wraps. And, too, she has to take it easy on how long she exercises the use of them for long periods of time."

"All right," they agreed, when arriving at the house.

Going in first, Craig and Jessi greeted Jamie by asking how Lori was doing.

"She's doing pretty good! She and Kyle are out back talking. Why?"

*'Hummm, they must be further out than the backyard!'* he thought out to Jessi.

*'The path back to the lake, maybe?'*

*'Still…?'*

*'Well, it is still a nice evening, and they do still have their bodyguards with them!'*

"Craig…? Jessi…?" Jamie asked, seeing how they were looking to each other.

"Yes, well," Jessi spoke up first, "Alex has an idea that might come in handy if, God forbid, something were to go wrong with the new cell phones."

"Oh, but I thought those were a sure thing!"

"Yes, well nothing is 100 percent," Craig offered. "So he came to us a short time back to see if there was something we could do to help. That's if any possible wrinkles were to come up in this case, we would be like a plan in reserve."

"What sort of wrinkles?" she asked worriedly.

"If, for instance, and that's a big *if*," Jessi assured her, "that something were to go wrong with those new phones, there would be a backup plan."

"What sort of backup plan?"

"Us," Craig indicated to him and his wife.

"If you're talking about going in undercover, well let me stop you there. First, neither of you could pass yourself off as Lori or Kyle. And secondly, it's just too dangerous."

"No, that's not what we would be doing," Jessi explained.

"What then?"

"Do you remember the day we went out for our first ride? The subject about our gifts?" she asked, smiling.

"Yes."

"That's what Alex has in mind," Craig grinned. "To see if we can tap into either of your thoughts, in case either of you got into trouble."

"So, while they're out there, we're just going to see if we can or not, while…"

"Alex keeps them occupied?" Jamie smiled.

"Yes, but understand," Craig explained, "it's just an experiment to see if it will even work, since it hasn't been done before."

"Telepathy, wow," she laughed. "Well, it certainly sounds like it would be fun!"

"We're glad you think so," Jessi smiled. "But when it comes to your husband, we're afraid he may think otherwise."

"And he would," she agreed.

"So does this mean we have your cooperation on the matter?" Craig asked.

"Yes. Just let me go and get my daughter."

While she was off doing that, the two looked to one another. "It could go either way," Craig said unsuridly.

"We have to try though, for their sake."

"Yes. And with Alex taking Jason out back to talk, it'll give us the whole house to practice in."

"And Beth…?" Jessi wondered.

"She'll be fine."

"What about Kyle?" Jessi looked worried. "What if he insists on coming back with Jamie and Lori?"

With a heavy sigh, Craig shook his head. "Send him back to join Alex and Jason."

"Telling him what, that Alex wants to go over the plans more in detail?"

"Just not around the women," he cleverly suggested.

At that, they both laughed.

"Listen," Craig changed the subject, seeing they had time to go over other things, before Jamie got back with her daughter, "while we're waiting on them, there's the matter of this project we're wanting to do out back of the Inn."

"The restoration of the old well, yes," she said glumly.

"Well, I've had time to talk it over more with Jim, and with this case taking us to Camden to help Alex, Jim has offered to step in and take care of things, while we are out."

She smiled hesitantly, before turning away to look elsewhere.

"What?" he asked, sensing remorse.

"The gazebo," she sighed, turning back to look at him. "Oh, Craig… after thinking it through, I…"

"Can't bear the thought of moving it now, after all the times you've gone out to meditate on it?"

"That, and all the other times we have all spent on it. It's just not practical to move it further out, as I had thought it would be."

He smiled.

"What's that about?"

"I mentioned that very thing to him too, and we came up with a plan that would work all the way around."

"Well…?" she asked anxiously.

"Relocate the old well with all its rocks and water source back to where you wanted to put the gazebo, along with a few bench seats for anyone wanting to sit out near it and the lilac bush."

"You two thought all this up without me knowing it? How were you able to keep me from picking up on it?" she laughed.

"Oh, believe me, it wasn't easy," he laughed, hugging her.

"Is this a bad time?" Jamie teased, walking back in along with Lori.

"Kyle?" the two asked, not seeing him.

"Oh, I told him to join the others," Jamie laughed.

"Did you tell Lori what was going on?" Jessi asked, smiling.

"Mom said the two of you had a game you wanted to try out," she replied, while going over to take a seat on the sofa.

"Yes," Craig explained, "but first, where is Beth and Bethany? It's been too quiet around here, since we had gotten back."

"They're up, napping," Jamie replied, while going over to join her daughter.

"Well, shall we then?" Jessi asked, apprehensively.

"Lori," he began, "I want you to clear all thoughts from your mind. Then I want you to think of only one thing."

Looking to her mother, puzzledly, she took off her sunglasses.

"It's okay," she smiled. "You'll love it!"

With a nod, she closed her eyes, and cleared all thoughts, but one that remained strong, as a smile creased her lips.

"That's okay," Jessi smiled, too. "I can't stop thinking about my man, here, either. And oh yes, he is so hot."

At that, Lori's eyes shot open. "But how…"

"You were thinking about your guy, right?" Craig grinned.

"Yes!"

"Of all the thoughts you were clearing from your mind, Kyle's was the one that refused to go," Jessi explained. "And now for you, Jamie."

"Sure, okay, but I have to ask, do you really think Philips would go after me?"

"Anything is possible," Craig stated.

"Yes, but how, when Alex has so many men out there, watching us, already?"

"That's just it," Craig stated, "Philips isn't stupid. He obviously knows that something is up with all the new faces, but doesn't know what? So we have to go that extra mile."

"By using telepathy," Lori understood.

"Yes," Jessi returned. "That, and the fact that no one knows yet that you are getting your sight back."

"So then exactly, what's the plan?" Jamie asked.

"Just in case one of you were to get taken by Philips, or one of his goons, be ready for anything," Craig announced.

"Even chloroform," Jessi added cautiously.

"Chloroform?" Jamie cried. "But that knocks a person out!"

"Yes, if they aren't ready for it," she explained. "Ok, picture this. Someone comes up from behind. They grab you…"

Seeing their confusion, Jessi turned to Craig. "Let's show them," she suggested, by going in to get a folded washcloth from the bathroom. "Okay," she continued, when coming back, to give it to her husband, "now here's what you'll do."

Putting herself in front of him, he put his arm around her waist, as if being her attacker. Then with the hand holding the washcloth, he started to put it to her mouth, until she stopped him.

"This is where you grab his arm and push it away as hard as you can. Then take a deep breath and hold it. Because when he succeeds in covering your mouth, and he will, if no one comes to your rescue, by doing this, you will be ready. Now watch, by holding your breath, act as if the chloroform did its thing and drop, acting as if you had passed out. Once he thinks you have, he will remove the cloth to carry you away. Remember though, keep your eyes closed and act as if you are unconscious and breathe normal, but quietly. This way you will know more of your surroundings, and when it's safe, start calling out mentally for help. We will do the rest, as we will also be there in Camden, and more than likely in a hotel that Alex will have set up for us."

"What? But that's crazy. You can stay at our place," Jamie protested.

"No. That wouldn't be a good idea," Craig informed her. "Your place may be watched, and a hotel would be less conspicuous. But then, there is that supposed project, with the neighbor's house, my uncle was telling me about."

"Sure!" Lori cried. "Then that way we can continue to practice, so when we do have to act on it, we'll be ready!"

"Craig, she has a point," Jessi agreed, while turning in his arms.

"Well, for now let's try having the two of you go to separate rooms, and try thinking about crying out for help, but not verbally. When we can detect it, we'll tap on that particular door to let you know we found you. Kind like hide and seek."

"Sure! Mom, are you ready?"

"As ready as I'll ever be!"

"Let's do it, then!" Jessi laughed. "You two go on up, but remember, separate rooms, and then start thinking. Jamie, you first."

While the two went up, Jessi and Craig stood back, waiting.

"You know, it was easy hearing their thoughts from the same room," she commented, concernedly. "I just hope this will work, when there's some distance between us."

"You and me both. Yet you and I were miles apart, and look how that went."

"Yes, it did," she smiled, but then her expression changed.

"You have something?" He detected from the look on her face.

"Not fear, but I hear her."

"Well, then, Mrs. Mathews-McMasters, shall we go hunting?"

Getting to the top of the stairs, Jessi took the lead, while Craig just smiled. "Go for it, sweetheart," he teased, having a fix on both women already.

Passing his room slowly, as Jessi went on listening, the thoughts came more strongly, as she turned and walked over to tap on the bathroom door.

Opening it, Lori smiled.

"Okay, honey, it's your turn!" Jessi beamed, sweetly, at her husband.

Turning back, he didn't take as long, when going up to tap on his bedroom door.

"Wow…" Lori laughed, when her mother walked out. "Let's try it again!"

"This time we're going to put even more distance between us," Craig suggested.

"Outside...?" Jessi laughed.

"Yes, but first I need to call Ted to get it cleared."

While he was doing that, Beth walked out of her room with Bethany. "What's going on?"

"We're playing hide and telepathy," Jessi teased.

"Hide and what...?"

"Telepathy," Lori returned.

"In case Alex needed a backup plan, if someone loses their phone," Jessi explained.

"So far it has worked. Jessi and Craig have both been able to find us, when we hide and think out the word *help*!" Lori smiled.

"And now we are going to take it outside to see how far we can go!" Jessi added.

"Well, that's done," Craig was saying, when turning back to see Beth standing there. "Oh, hi, Beth!" he grinned mischievously.

"Craig," she laughed, shaking her head, "you all look like you're having too much fun with this."

"At first I wasn't all that sure about it, since we haven't used it that much. But as long as it's being used for a good reason, we just want to see if we can pick up on their thoughts if either of them has to call out for help! Anyway, Ted said the coast is clear. He'll come and get Jamie, and Baker, who is back, now with Max, will get Lori."

"Max, as in my dog, Max...?" Jessi asked.

"Yes. Ted said Alex wants him to be a part of this team, in case our telepathy falters somehow. Besides, Ted knows the story of our gift, but Baker, Ted felt, should be left in the dark, in case it was to get out."

Soon the two were walking in through the back door with Max.

"Craig," Ted spoke up, asking, "Alex said I am to ask you if you have a set limit on how far you want us to go?"

"Stay within the property line for now. Then stretch it out a ways each time we succeed."

"All right, are we ready?" he looked to Jamie.

"Let's go hide!" she laughed, taking their victims, while Jessi and Craig stayed behind with Max, Beth and Bethany.

"How much time are you going to give them?" Beth asked, while going into the kitchen to get something to eat.

"Ted will call on his old phone, so we won't pick up on his GPS," Craig returned, while going in behind her.

"And Alex and Jason?" she added.

"They'll be watching," he explained.

"Jason knows now?" Jessi asked.

"About our game…? Yes, when he started to get suspicious."

"How did he take it?" the two inquired.

"Well…" Craig returned, shaking his head, "he wasn't too thrilled."

"Craig," Jessi spoke up, sounding concerned, "his thoughts, they could interrupt this whole thing…!"

"Alex thought about that, and explained it to him."

"And now…?"

"Well against his better judgment, he has finally come to grips with it. So he won't interfere. He wants whatever it takes for all this to be over."

"We certainly know how *he* feels, don't we?" Beth grinned.

# Chapter Twenty-One

Soon the call came, but before they headed out, Jessi pulled back.

"What is it?" Craig asked, masking their thoughts.

"I know that may sound a little premature, but I want to say a prayer that this will work so they will be safe."

Bowing their heads, Beth included, they joined hands and silently prayed.

"A-men," Jessi whispered heartfeltly.

"Well, good luck you two," Beth offered, before the two walked out, taking Max with them.

"Thanks," they turned back, smiling, as she closed the door

"Well, do you feel them?" Craig asked, looking to his wife.

"Yes, over there," she pointed, and then ordered her dog to go and find Lori.

"That's cheating!" Craig laughed, as the two ran after her dog.

"No it isn't..." she laughed back, cutting through the woods to the far, back corner of the property.

Soon she had her mark, as Max barked triumphantly.

"No way...!" Baker was astounded at how fast they showed up.

"Yes, well someone, here, cheated a bit," Craig laughed at his wife.

"Well, we did sense things, when coming out! Now for Jamie."

Listening to their surroundings, Craig picked up on her whereabouts right away. '*Why you, Alex,*' he thought telepathically.

"Rose's...?" she smiled.

"Oh, yeah."

"Now who's cheating?" she laughed, shaking her head. "Let's go!"

Choosing to walk, they all crossed the woods together, but when coming up on the McMasters property they decided to be sneaky about the whole thing, and hide behind some trees to scope-out the area.

"Anything…?" Baker asked.

"No, no sign at the pool," Jessi commented.

"The house," Craig laughed, seeing Allen peering out the back door window.

"What's the plan?" Lori smiled eagerly.

Looking around, Craig pointed back in behind them. "We go back that way to avoid being seen, and then up front." Just as he said that, he picked up on Ted's thoughts. "Well, well, well," he grinned, spotting Ted up by the front corner of the garage.

"What?" Jessi asked, looking around.

"There, on his phone," he pointed Ted out.

Jessi shook her head. *'Why that dirty little sneak, he's on the phone with Alex.'*

*'Yes, but he hasn't seen us yet.'* Turning back to Baker, he asked, "I need to know, did you know anything about this?"

"About them taking Jamie across the line?"

"That, and Ted keeping Alex informed of our whereabouts?"

"I didn't know that part of it, but yes, I knew Alex had something up his sleeve. When doesn't he?"

"Then the next question is, whose side are you on, ours or theirs?"

"And Baker," Jessi warned amusingly, "remember whose Inn you're staying at. I can make your stay really uncomfortable for you just by cutting off Annie's good cooking, and making you sleep out in a stall from now on."

"Wow, you would do that, too, wouldn't you?" he grinned.

"You really don't want to try her, do you?" Craig laughed quietly.

"No, and hell yeah, I'm on your side. What do you take me for, an idiot? The stall I could get use to eventually, but going without Annie's cooking…?"

They all laughed, and headed back inland, taking Lori's hand to help guide her.

"Where to?" Jessi asked.

"The woods, behind their house," Craig stated, but then abruptly stopped.

"What?" Baker asked, taking out his service revolver, thinking Craig had seen something out of the ordinary.

"No, put that away," he stated, seeing Lori's frightened expression. "It's our new cell phones."

"What about them?" Baker asked, not thinking how Alex could monitor them by their GPS signals. Then it hit.

"Yes. So if he can change the rules, so can we by shutting them off long enough to get a jump on them, and then turn them back on again once we're inside, and within their reach."

"Sweet," he agreed, "but we'll have to move fast, this will no doubt piss him off a little," he laughed.

Doing so, they all hurried around to the other side of the house, where Craig knew a way in.

Once there, though, Craig turned back to Baker, and whispered, "Wait here, till we get inside, before turning our phones back on. Afterwards, casually go up to Ted and say, 'what's up?"

He laughed, "Sure!"

Turning to the other two, he smiled, "Let's go in quietly. Once there, Jessi and I will listen in on their thoughts, before turning our phones back on so we can get a jump on them."

They agreed, smiling.

Once inside, Craig and Jessi did just that, while hiding in behind David's old bedroom door to stay out of sight.

Meanwhile, sitting in the kitchen, eating a piece of cake, was their mark.

"The kitchen…?" Jessi smiled.

"Yeah. Let's go," Craig returned, heading out of the room, and into the hallway.

Seeing them out of the corner of her eye, Rose smiled quietly at the three coming up the hall. "What could be taking them so long?" she asked from the doorway.

"I don't know," Alex grumbled. "I lost their signal four minutes ago. Ted, do you see them? Ted…"

Having picked up on something Baker was thinking, Craig and Jessi laughed, coming around the doorway with Lori in tow. "I'm sorry, but Ted's a little tied up right now!" the two continued to laugh.

"What…?" The others turned to see the three of them standing next to Rose.

"Baker..." Craig called out, as they turned their phones back on, "bring him in now!"

Opening the front door, the two walked in, Ted first, with a huge grin on his face, while shaking his head embarrassingly.

"Ted..." Alex laughed loudly, "no... not you too...?"

"Shut it," he laughed along with them.

"Well it just came to me," Baker continued to laugh, while pretending to have Ted in an arm hold.

"Yes, well I would say we have a plan," Alex grinned.

"And if I hadn't seen it for myself," Jason shook his head, disbelievingly.

"I don't understand," Kyle asked. "How did you find them so quickly?"

"Never mind that," Alex interrupted. "We need to test it a little further away. Like, say, the Inn?"

"When?" Craig asked.

"Tomorrow, before Ted, Kyle and I head back to the office."

"What about me?" Jason asked.

"One more week," Alex grinned. "For now, get in that fishing you've wanted to do. As for you ladies, practice, but not without your bodyguards."

"Yes, sir," Lori smiled.

The following morning, the guys were up getting ready to head over to the Inn, having decided to take the Roberts' with them, after finding out the coast was clear.

"What, no breakfast this morning...?" Jamie asked, walking out of the kitchen.

"Annie has it on back at the Inn for us," Alex returned, while strapping on his shoulder holster. "We'll all need to be getting ready to head out, as soon as everyone is ready."

"Okay. I'll just go and get the others up," she offered.

"Jamie," He stopped her short of the living room, "were you already getting something started in the kitchen?"

"No!" she said, sounding a little miffed. "Okay, I was thinking about it."

"I'm sorry, but I had already called the Inn to check on things there, and my man said Annie had things started already."

"Yes, well I was just thinking how nice it would be to do something special for you and the others, for all that you have done for us, and all."

Smiling his handsome smile, Alex thanked her just for the thought alone. "Perhaps once we get back to the Inn, and Annie knows what it means to you, she will relinquish the kitchen for a time to let you do just that."

"Sure, and I know just why you are doing that. You miss my homemade beef stew."

Going over to give her a big hug, he grinned, "Darn straight, woman. No one can make it like you do. It ought to be canned and sold for a high price!"

"Go on with you now," she blushed. "I have some sleepyheads to be getting up."

"Sure, thing. I'll be out getting the vehicles ready," he laughed, turning to Max. "Ready, boy…?"

Together, the two headed out, taking their things with him, when Craig walked up with some more of their things to put into his truck.

Seeing Alex on his cell phone with what might be Annie, he smiled to his uncle, when hearing part of what he was having to sweet talk the cook into doing, while they were on their way in. Once he was done, Craig asked, "What time are you guys heading back to Camden?"

"Noon, or soon thereafter. I've had Roland sitting in for Cindy all this time."

"Yes, and I just bet Epstein was thrilled, seeing, yet, another new face," Jarred put in, joining them.

"Yes," laughing, Alex returned, "he sure was. Roland called last night to let me know how livid he was, when he demanded that Roland removed himself from the building."

"That had to have gone well!" Craig grinned.

"It certainly did! When Roland stood up, quite literally, he towered over the man, and told him he was there under orders by his current boss."

"And that of course would be you?" Craig laughed.

"Yep!"

"And Epstein's reaction to that?" Jarred asked, taking a seat on the back step, with the morning sunshine, shining brightly overhead.

"He backed off," Alex laughed, "as if he had been hit by an unexpected wave of energy."

"Yeah, but who would have thought that a man like Roland would have it in him? Tall, but quiet," Ted grinned from behind, when joining in.

"Yes," Alex laughed, shaking his head," tall and really quiet."

"Yeah, sure, till Epstein sees you return to the office," Jarred went on laughing at his uncle.

"Yes, well, speaking of Camden, we might have a little problem," Alex uttered.

"What? What would that be," Jarred asked.

"Philips has seen Craig, Jessi, and Marcose, now."

"That's easily remedied!" Craig offered, smiling.

"Yes, we can always get the two of you into a disguise!" Jarred laughed, looking to Alex, with his still in place

"Or keep them out of sight," Ted suggested.

"No, we can't do that," Alex stated.

"Which?" Craig and Jarred both asked.

"Keep them out of sight. We need to put them in disguises so they can be accessible at all times," Alex grinned, and turned to go back in and tell the others they were about ready to go.

"What about the girls?" Jodi asked, coming down the stairs with a few things in her arms.

"Call and tell them to be ready. We're close to being on our way over now," he returned, while taking his daughter from Beth's arm, before offering her a hand.

After making the call, Jodi laughed, walking out the back door, as Craig went around locking up the rest of the house.

"What's up?" Jarred asked, seeing her amused expression, when it came time for the girls to have to get up so early.

"They were just now starting to get up, and told me they hadn't eaten yet."

"They can eat back at the Inn," Alex grinned, remembering how late they liked to sleep in.

"I told Rose the same thing, and thanked her," she smiled, while getting into their own truck, followed by the others, getting into theirs.

"Ted…!" Alex called back, waving him up to the Blazer, where Kyle and the Roberts' were seated.

"What's up?"

"I'm going to take Jason and his family on ahead of the rest of them. Stay with us," he ordered, while calling Jarred up to fill him in.

"Yeah, what's up?"

"Ted and I are going on ahead so we can put some distance between us and Craig and Jess. With that, I want to see if they can still pick up on their thoughts. Let them know."

"Are you going to call them when you're ready to test them?"

"Yes, but wait for the call, before leaving the McMasters," he grinned. "That way, too, it will give the girls more time to wake up."

"All right, I'll pass the word," he acknowledged, in the same manor, while turning to walk back to his truck. "See you when we get there!"

"Be ready, though. I plan to hide them, well," he went on mischievously.

"That's just great. What about their new cell phones? They're not going to want you to pick up on their GPS!"

"Fine. Once they get there, they can turn them off again."

Jarred laughed, looking to his cousin.

*'Uh, oh, dear,'* Craig laughed, *'I have a feeling my uncle is up to something again…!'*

*'Yes, testing our gift some more, so that we have to go looking even harder for them?'* she smiled coyly.

*'Well, we do have to see if we can still hear them with more distance between us!'*

Walking back to pass the word, Jarred saw the look on their faces. "Oh, great, you both know, don't you?" he asked, walking up to Craig's side of the truck.

"Yep, sure do!" he laughed.

"In that case, it's safe to say that nothing gets passed either of you, huh?"

"It's not as if we're trying to pick up on you guy's conversation. But let's face it, when he has that look on his face, we all know he has something brewing in that head of his."

"That's for sure," Jarred shook his head, grinning, while heading on back to his own truck.

At that time, everyone headed out, with Max riding with Craig and Jessi, they and their cousins headed south to get the others from the neighbors, while Alex and his people went north, back to the Inn.

Thinking to himself along the way, Alex wondered where to hide the Roberts', when a thought came to him.

"Alex," Jason spoke up, see how his friend was so deep in thought, "what's going on in that head of yours?"

"The final step, before we, hopefully will not have to put it to a real test."

"To see just how strong their gifts are?" he asked.

"Yes," he responded uneasily, while the rest of the trip went on in silence.

Once back at the Inn, Alex went straight to the kitchen to talk to Annie, and put a call out to Hank, while Beth got Bethany settled in with Ashley, who offered to sit for her, until the others got back. As for the Roberts', they quickly brought their things in and dropped them off, before Alex returned to get them.

"I wonder what he has planned on where to hide us," Lori pondered, while standing out in the foyer, waiting on her parents.

"Don't know," Kyle returned, while admiring her zeal over what the last few days had brought them. "Lori?"

She turned, looking up into his smiling face, as the blue in her eyes grew more and more brilliant with every passing moment. But before either of them could say anything, Alex walked up, and then her parents.

"Jamie," Alex spoke up, "everything is set up with Annie. Just let her know what you will need, she will get it for you, if she doesn't already have it here."

"Great."

"And now, are we ready? Keep in mind, they are an hour away. So concentrate hard, like they have told you. Clear your thoughts and concentrate solely on crying out for help. And while you're at it, give a little description of where you are, but leave some mystery to it solely for the practice, but not the real thing if it were to happen. And too, so that you know, we have a list of all of Philips and Epstein's properties.

Including any warehouses they might own. So when Craig and Jessi get there, they will be shown each of them when it's safe to show them."

"Sounds like you have thought of everything," Jason spoke proudly of his friend.

"Can't afford not to," he looked to Jason, and then his family, caringly. "Wait."

"What is it?" Jason asked, concernly.

"Lori's walk. Now that she can see, she has altered the way she's been walking now. We need to keep it looking as though she is still needing help getting around, in case she's being watched."

"You're right," Jamie stated, taking her arm, as Ted walked in.

"Alex," Ted spoke up, "Jessi's on the phone, wanting to know if we are ready yet."

"Give us fifteen more minutes, and then have them start out." Turning to the others, "We have to get moving."

Once Ted was off the phone, Alex suggested a few places on where to take Lori and Kyle. "But explain to him what to do and what not to do. I'll take Jason and Jamie with me."

"Where are you going?" Ted asked, so not to take them to the same spot.

"Just the other side of the shack."

"Good. One of the unoccupied cabins seems like the likely place to go," Ted returned.

"Okay, shall we? Annie should have something for us to take along to eat. And Hank will have some horses saddled up for the three of us to take, as it's a little far to go on foot. As for comfort, we'll stop off at the shack to get some blankets that had been left out there, for when we go to take a break."

"Sounds good. Let's get going, then," Jason suggested, just as Annie walked up with the containers of food.

Leaving, Ted, Kyle and Lori headed over on foot to cabin 4, where they got comfortable on an old sofa and an overstuffed chair. As for Alex, Jason and Jamie, they headed down to the stable to mount up a few horses Hank had ready, and soon were on their way.

Meanwhile, back at the McMasters, they were all saying their goodbyes, and taking some sweet rolls with them to eat on the way.

"Are you sure this is going to work?" Rose asked, having been the first to know about Jessi's gifts.

"We hope so," she returned, looking to Craig, who was already picking up on some of the Roberts' thoughts, even then.

"You have something, don't you?" Jarred grinned, seeing that all knowing look.

Smiling broadly, he turned, taking his wife's hand. "Let's go!" he called out, on their way through the living room.

"Craig..." Jessi called out, not hearing them yet.

"You don't hear that?"

Standing just outside their house, she concentrated quietly for a moment, while crunching up her brow. "No," she shook her head, while only able to hear faint thoughts. "It's just bits and pieces. Like static on an old phonograph, being played."

"That's okay. It'll get clearer as we get closer."

"Hey," Allen hollered out the front door, after them, "how is it that you hear it, and not her? And too, how is it that you don't hear other people's thoughts?"

"Who's to say we don't?" he returned. "Neither one of us, in that regards, will do that, unless the thoughts are so strong that they can't be ignored. As for me, having a few more years of experience helps!" he explained, grinning, when saying goodbye once again, while heading for their trucks.

At the Inn, everyone was at their hiding places, waiting patiently for their supposed rescuers.

"This can be a lot of fun, but at the same time, mentally stressful," Jamie was saying, while lying back on her blanket to rest her mind.

"Then go ahead and give yourself a break!" Alex suggested, while calling Ted.

"Yeah?" he came back on his end, while looking out a window.

"It seems that it may take them a while to get here. Tell Lori to give herself a break."

"For how long?" he asked, looking back at her.

"Five to ten minutes, but no longer. And to think, if she were actually held captive, it could be hours before finding her. So with that in mind, she'll have to give herself a couple of minute intervals, between thought patterns, so not to burn herself out too soon. The same goes for any of you. And at the same time, let the other person know when you're not practicing. We don't want to overdo it."

"Ok," Ted returned, hanging up.

Meanwhile, looking up at the sunlight, streaming through the branches, Jamie wasn't aware she was sending out thoughts of how beautiful the view was, when halfway home, Jessi picked them up pretty clearly. Smiling, she looked out her window, as Craig did the same.

"It is beautiful, isn't it?" he asked.

"What?" Cassi asked, puzzledly. "Are you talking in general, or are you repeating their thoughts?"

Both looked back, into the extend cab portion of the truck, at Cassi, and lightly laughed.

"Oh, honey," Jessi smiled, "I think Jamie was just thinking that, while looking up at the sky!"

"Does that mean you have an idea where she is?" she wondered.

"Out along the trail, I would guess. Right," Jessi asked, looking to Craig.

"Yes, but where exactly, I couldn't say."

"What about Lori?" Cassi went on asking.

Craig smiled, knowing where she was, but wanted Jessi to figure it out on her own.

"Thanks," she laughed.

"Well…!"

She thought for a moment. "It's kind of dark. Perhaps inside," she thought some more. "Not the Inn, maybe a cabin."

"Or the shack," Craig asked, knowing she wasn't.

"No," she smiled knowing he knew better. "It doesn't look that rough. The attic…? No, one of the cabins. It has to be."

"What else can you see?" he asked, getting closer to the Inn.

"Wood walls. Rooms." Realizing what it was, she laughed. "Oh, yes, one of the cabins for sure!" she turned, smiling even more. Seeing his, she knew she was right.

"Now all you have to do is figure out which one!" Cassi laughed.

*'Come on Lori, tell me the number,'* Jessi called back, knowing what she was asking was futile.

*'Honey, she can't read your thoughts! And if their heads were covered, they wouldn't know anyway.'*

*'I could hope!'* she laughed.

Craig laughed, as well, as the Inn came into view.

Pulling out her cell phone, she called Hank to saddle up some horses. "Cassi, would you like to go riding?"

"Sure, but does this mean I'm going out to help you find them?"

Before she could answer, Craig told Cassi, no. "We have to do it ourselves, but you can go along for the ride!"

"Okay, but what about Lori, aren't you going to find her first?" she asked, when coming to a stop near the front door.

Getting out, they looked to each other.

"That's true, she is closer," he agreed, shutting his doors quietly. "But let's not forget to shut off our new phones, too, just in case they up and move them."

"And if any of them need to get a hold of us?" Jessi asked softly.

"They can call our old ones."

After turning them off, Jessi stood still, and listened for a moment, before looking over at the cabins, one by one, till coming to number 4. "There," she pointed excitedly, and headed over to knock at the door, but then stopped to look at Craig.

"What?" he asked.

"I have an idea," she carefully explained, taking his arm. "Let's go around to the bathroom window, where we can slip in as quietly as possible."

"Are you sure you want to do that? What about Ted, after what we did to him at Rose and Allen's? Wouldn't he be a bit agitated at us for doing that to him again?"

"We're not going to tie him up, just sneak up on him," she grinned. But then another thought came to her, when pulling out her old phone to call Jodi with a brilliant plan.

"I love it," Jodi returned, looking to Jarred, sweetly.

"Good. Oh, and Jo, did you two remember to shut off your new phones?" she asked, as they went on to get closer to their targeted cabin.

"Oh, no, you're right, our new phones," she turned to Jarred. "We need to shut them off."

Doing so, the two laughed quietly about her cousin's idea.

"Jo, will he go along with it, though?" Jessi asked, quietly, when stopping a few doors down from their targeted cabin.

"Oh, he'll go for it, or I'll make life unbearable for him," she smiled.

Figuring by the way she said that, Jarred knew he would live to regret refusing her, if he had.

"What, sweetheart...?" she asked, hanging up her old phone.

"You and your cousin," he laughed. "Why am I going to hate this?"

"Because it entails you to call Ted, to get him to meet you at the garage, as soon as possible. Tell him anything, but get him out of the cabin. Heck, tell him that Jessi and Craig went out to find Jamie first."

"And if I don't?" he laughed.

Whispering something in his ear, he grinned, and groaned painfully, "You wouldn't?"

She raised an eyebrow and smiled.

"Oh, Lord, you are bad..., bad, bad, bad," he continued to laugh, while taking out his cell phone to put in the call. Doing so, he went on looking at his lovely wife, grinning.

Soon Ted was on the line, seeing it was Jarred. "What's up?" he asked, from the window.

Hearing him, the three quickly ducked out of sight.

"We just heard from Jessi. They're heading out in search of Jamie first. So how about meeting me up by the garage? I've got to discuss something with you, while we have the time."

Looking to the others, he shook his head, thinking, *'Go or not go?'* "Oh... okay, but we have to make it fast."

"Sure," he continued to grin, shaking his head. "I'll see you there."

"So...?" Jodi asked, while he hung up.

"What do you think?" he laughed.

# Chapter Twenty-Two

At the cabin, the others hid around back, waiting for Ted to leave, while inside he was letting the others know what was going on. "Listen," he said, heading for the door, "that was Jarred, letting me know that Craig and Jessi went out to look for the others first. But for some reason he wants to see me, while they're out. So stay put, I shouldn't be long," he announced, closing the door behind him.

Seeing him leave, Jessi pointed to the bedroom window. "Let's go in through there instead, and take them out to hide in another cabin. Though, we ought to attempt to do the chloroform to see if she would remember what to do."

"But won't that terrify her?" Cassi asked, worriedly.

"Sure, at first, until she sees it's us! Oh," Jessi stopped outside the bedroom window to hand Cassi the master keys, "go and unlock cabin 6. We'll be there, soon."

With a nod of her head, she slipped off quietly, while Jessi and Craig made their move.

Soon they were inside, listening to the two talk in the other room.

*'Are you sure you want to do this?'* he asked telepathically.

She nodded, making sure the two weren't looking their way, when pointing off toward the bathroom, where there was a folded washcloth on the counter.

Seeing it, Craig slipped off to get it and was back without making a sound.

After handing it to her, she nodded toward them. *'You get Kyle, while I get Lori.'*

*'In case he tries to struggle?'*

*'Yes,'* she nodded.

Soon the two made their move, with Craig coming up behind Kyle, just as she took Lori. Once nabbing the unsuspecting victims, covering each of their mouths to keep them from screaming, the two fought like wild animals, until hearing Jessi's voice.

"Kyle, Lori, it's us," she announced, quietly.

"What…?" Lori screeched, once Jessi removed her hand. "Why did you do that? You scared the h…e…l…l… out of me."

"That's just it. I had to see if you would remember to push your attacker's arm away, and you did. Did you happen to remember to take in a breath and hold it, too?"

"Well, no…! But I will if we practice that again!"

"Lori," Craig shook his head, "had this been for real, you may not have had a second try."

"Ok, I'm sorry. I understand what you two are trying to get across to me," she returned, shaking her head.

"Lori," Jessi placed an arm around her shoulder, "we're not trying to be hard on you. We just don't want to see anything happen to you, is all."

"I know. I've heard it from dad many of times, when he was a cop. I'm okay."

"Good."

"Kyle…?" Craig turned, grinning at how excited he was.

"Man," he laughed, "what a rush that was, though!"

"Yes," he too laughed, "so why don't we just rush this little group right out of here."

"Yes," Jessi suggested, looking out the front window, "Jarred isn't going to be able to keep Ted entertained for long."

"You're right," Craig agreed. "Let's go."

"Where to?" Kyle asked, on their way out, using the back window to avoid detection.

"Cabin 6," he pointed, while closing the window behind them.

Taking their people to the new hideout, Jessi put a call into Annie to have her call Jodi.

Filling her in on what she was to say, Annie laughed lightly, "Okay, I'll do it. And Ms. Jessi, you guys have fun, now."

"We will."

Soon after hanging up with her cook, they were on their way, and safely inside, when Jarred got the call from his wife.

"Okay, let him go!" she laughed.

"Okay!" Hanging up, he turned to Ted, "Sorry, Jodi, she's waiting on me."

"Yeah, well I had better be getting back to what I was doing. Anything else?"

"No," he fought hard to keep from grinning, while still having a hold of his phone. "See ya later."

"Yeah, later," he said, sounding a little puzzled at Jarred's strange behavior.

Watching him head back to the cabin, Jarred turned quickly and ducked in behind the garage, where Jodi had quietly snuck up to. "Boy that was intense," he sighed heavily, while stealing a peak around the corner, along with his wife.

"Oh…, but you're not done yet," she laughed, quietly.

"What…?" he laughed, turning back to look at her. "But I did as you asked…!"

"Yes, well, you had best be calling Alex, before Ted does, or something is going to be hitting the fan."

"Damn, you're right, and tell him what?"

"What Jessi and Craig have done…, silly…!"

Doing so, Alex roared out laughing.

"What?" Jarred asked, laughing in return.

"Craig has already called to let me know that they had just paid me back. Damn, Ted is going to be really pissed, when he gets back there, only to see that he is the hunter now."

"You know he'll be calling you soon."

"Not if he doesn't come looking for you first!" he announced, while letting out another roar, before filling the others in on the joke.

Meanwhile, Jodi's girls snuck up to see what was going on, when Jarred turned, getting off his phone. "Sorry girls," he grinned, grabbing their hands, "I don't have time to explain, but we have to get out of here, and now…!"

"What? Why…?" Jodi asked, while holding up the line.

"Jo…, we don't have time for this," he laughed, "Ted is going to be coming after me, once he finds out that he has been duped!"

"Well, yes…, I kinda thought he might…! But what better place to hide, than the cabin Jessi and the others are hiding in?" she laughed, while turning back to spot a good way of getting there, without being seen.

Agreeing, once she pointed out a way, the four slipped off to the backside of the cabins, until reaching the back window of cabin 6, where Jodi tapped on the glass to get Jessi's attention.

"What are you guys doing here?" she asked, puzzledly, while letting them in. "You know you could have used the back door, right?"

"Yes, but what's the fun in that?" she laughed quietly, getting their help.

"So, are you going to tell us?" Jessi laughed at how they looked, doing so.

"Well, you might say we're hiding from Ted, too!" Jarred laughed even more, while straightening himself up. "Alex says, he is going to be after my hide, once he discovers that he has been double crossed."

Just then, they heard Jarred's new phone go off.

"Are you going to get that?" Craig grinned handsomely, while the others laughed quietly so not to be heard outside.

"Are you mad…?" he laughed, looking sheepishly at the name printed across the caller ID, and shook his head.

"Well?" they asked again.

"Fine," he said, taking the call, when having to hold the phone out away from his ear.

"You lousy SOB…!"

They all heard, when suddenly, remembering the phones Alex had given out, Craig snatched it out of his hand and hung it up.

"What the hell?" Jarred asked, puzzledly.

"The GPS…!" Craig reminded him. "Did you forget to turn your new phone off, when Jessi reminded you guys?"

"Oh, God," he groaned, "I turned Jo's off and forgot to do my own…!"

"Oh, no…" Jessi cried, "Ted will know now that we're close by…!"

"Not if we get out of here, before he gets here," Cassi suggested, hurriedly.

"Let's go then," Craig laughed, while heading the group out the back door, and just in time, as Ted was coming across the courtyard.

"Where to...?" Jodi asked.

Looking to the next cabin, Jessi saw one of their guests standing out back, smoking a cigarette. "There," she pointed.

With that, they made their way quietly, while leaving the window to cabin 6 open.

"Mr. Cavanal," she called out, quietly, "can we borrow your cabin real quick?"

"W...what?" he asked, confusedly.

Taking him by the arm to shove him inside, she explained quickly what was going on, while the others rushed in, closing the door behind them. "Do you understand now?"

"A game...? All of you...?" he laughed, quietly, when his wife walked in just then to see them all standing there. Quickly he put out his cigarette, and told her what was going on.

"Well that would explain the man outside, fuming over something!" she laughed.

"We're not out of the woods yet folks!" Craig interrupted, while going over to the side window to watch Ted go around back to check out the cabin they were just in. "Come on," he waved toward the front door, "I have an idea."

Not asking any questions, they all, but the couple staying there, followed him out quietly to run back over to the cabin Lori and Kyle started out in. Going around back, Craig told Jessi to get them inside and have a seat. "Jarred, you, Jodi and the girls sneak back over to the Inn. Better yet, get to the stable and take the horses that Hank has saddled up for us, and get out to the old shack. Just the other side of it, about twenty feet or so you will find Alex. Tell him we will be out soon. And tell Hank to saddle up the rest of the horses, we'll be needing them too!"

"You got it," he grinned, hurrying off with his family.

Getting inside and closing the window, Jessi followed Craig to the front room to check on Ted. By then he was walking out the front door of 6.

"I can't keep doing this to him," he laughed, going to the door.

"Wait. What about Jarred and the others?" Kyle asked.

"They'll have time to get away," he smiled, while opening the door.

With a deep, friendly scowl, Ted walked over, shaking his head. "Where is he?" he asked, hinting payback.

"Uh, who?" Jessi asked, innocently.

"Funny," he laughed, short of the door, when pushing his way passed the two to have a look inside.

"Hey… it's just the five of us, here," Craig grinned, and went on to fill him in on what all took place.

"Not a bad idea," he agreed to the attack strategy.

"Well, what do you say we go find the others?" Jessi suggest, when sensing Jamie's thoughts again.

"Are you picking up on something?" Craig asked, seeing her expression change.

"Yes, Jamie is getting tired."

"Let's go, then," Ted suggested, heading out first, while Jessi closed and locked the door behind her.

"What about cabin 6?" she asked, holding the key. "Did you lock it up, before coming over here?"

"Yes."

"Okay."

Arriving to the other's hideout, everyone got their laugh out at what all happened. Soon after, they rode back to the stable to turn in their horses, and then headed up to the Inn, where Jamie rested up a bit, before starting on lunch.

After lunch, sitting back to loosen his belt, Alex spoke openly of his love for her beef stew. "Well, Jamie, as usual, that was the best beef stew around."

"Thank you, and when we get back, I'll have to cook up some extra, while you guys are at the hotel."

"That would be nice," he was saying, when he caught a glance in Kyle's direction. The look wasn't a happy one, knowing he wouldn't be able to see Lori as much. Since the return of her eyesight, the two had been inseparable. "Kyle," Alex spoke, sympathetically, "I know what you're feeling. I don't want to be away from those I love either, but we have to think about what is going on at the present. Sure we could always stay together in one place. That would probably make things a little less complicated, but…"

"Why can't we, then? I mean if it's okay with Lori's parents, why couldn't we stay there? You could watch over them better if we were all in the same place! And if anyone asked, the pipes in your place busted and they are going to need you out of there for awhile to clean up the mess!"

"Alex, I think the lad just might have something," Jason grinned. "Sure, stay with us! We had just finished out the basement, and it looks great down there."

"We even put in a bathroom and an extra bedroom," Jamie added.

"Uncle Alex," Lori put in hopefully, "now that I'm getting my sight back, it sure would be nice to quite literally see you. Please, not only to have Kyle close by, but you too. And you as well, Ted!"

"Thanks," Ted declined the offer, "but if Craig, Jessi and Jarred are going to be across the street, using the neighbor's house, I should stay with them. Although, I could occasionally stay with you folks from time to time, when I am needed there."

"Then it's decided," Jason declared. "No hotels for any of you."

With that said, before leaving, they went over the final touches of their plans, after the girls had excused themselves from the table.

After nearly an hour had passed, looking at his watch, Alex saw how it was time for some of them to get going. "Did we cover it all?" he asked, getting up from the table.

"What about disguises for the two of them?" Ted asked.

"Craig? Jessi?" he asked grinningly.

Looking to one another, Jessi thought of the disguise Craig's friend, David McMasters, used in Alex's first case. *'Dusty,'* she smiled, proudly.

*'Yes, Dusty.'*

"Craig?" his uncle sensed something in the way the two were looking to each other.

"Dusty," he turned, smiling.

"David's…" Alex couldn't go on, as the tears came on suddenly. Getting to his feet, he walked out of the dining room, through the family room, and out onto the patio to clear his head.

"Alex," both Jessi and Craig joined him, followed by the others, with Beth carrying their daughter, who seemed to have brought a sad smile to Alex's face.

"Alex, are you all right?" Jason, who soon joined them, asked, knowing about David's unique death, which gave Craig a second chance.

"It's just the memory of losing him, is all," he chuckled. "He had once used a disguise of an older man, while calling himself, Dusty."

"Why Dusty?" Jamie asked.

"When we all used to play ball together," Craig went on, smiling, "he would always slide into home, getting himself all dusty."

"From that, I presume you were thinking of using that same disguise?" Jason gathered, sensitively.

"Yes," he smiled, turning to Jessi. "As for my wife, here, she can be Mrs. Miller, Dusty's wife."

"Yes, but with a little extra padding, temporary hair color, and contacts," Alex suggested.

"Let me guess," she laughed. "Grey hair?"

"Well… graying," they laughed.

"Yes, sounds good…!" Craig laughed, teasingly.

"Keep it up, old man," she laughed with the rest of them.

"Okay now," Alex cut in, "we need to be heading out. And Jason, we'll be coming back to get you soon. So get yourself fit and ready to take over your cases."

"Sure will," he chuckled a bit, with a slight twinkle in his eye.

"Kyle," Ted spoke up, "sorry, bud, but…"

"I know," he turned to Lori. "See ya soon?"

"Alex," Craig took him aside, "Jessi and I can bring the Roberts' with us, when we come, if that's all right with you."

"Yes, but use my Blazer, it'll be safer with the tinted windows, and all. And to make sure your trip stays that way, I'll send Baker over to assist," he explained, while pulling out his phone to call Hank, to have him bring his loaner car up.

Once he had gotten off the phone, Craig asked, not having seen Alex's other man around, "What about Marcose?"

"He's already there, giving Baker a hand in getting the neighbor's house ready for everyone."

"And I assume in disguise, as well?"

"Yep, and you will see that when you get there," he laughed, while turning to go back inside to get ready to head out.

It wasn't long before he returned, when seeing some sad faces, that of his wife and daughter for one.

"Alex," Beth spoke up first, while coming up to give him an endearing hug, "watch yourself out there, okay?"

And then Bethany, who had really broken his heart, when giving him his little-girl hug, "I…I love you Daddy…! You come back now, o…okay…?" she stammered sadly.

"I will, baby," he returned, hating himself for having to leave so soon. "Jason," he turned back, once handing her back over to her mother, "see you soon. Jamie! Lori!" Turning then, one last time, he reached over and gave his wife and daughter another kiss goodbye. "Damn it all…, I love you both," he groaned, just when Hank got there with his car. Taking his leave, he took Kyle with him so they could go over their itinerary, while Ted took up the rear.

"Are we going straight over to the Roberts' when we get back?" Ted asked over the phone, on their way.

"Yes, and I'll have Baker come over and stay with you, while I go over to check things out at the office."

"All right."

Before reaching the Roberts' place, Alex checked the monitor to see where Philips was. Shaking his head angrily, he saw that he was parked down the street from his friends' house. "Damn him!" he growled, calling Marcose to see what was going on.

"Yes, Alex we know. It seems he has been waiting on the man to come home for awhile, now. However, there is an upside to this."

"I sure as hell hope so."

"Well," he laughed, "he won't be much longer."

"How's that?"

"Anytime now, he will be asked to move on."

"Local police?"

"Yep! And to top it off, they agreed to stay in the area, because of some senior officer who had been killed awhile back, name, Franklin something or other."

"Cindy's father," he spoke regretfully.

"Jason's, Cindy?"

"Yes. So, getting back to Philips, what's the word on him?"

"Well…" he eased up to the road to get a better look, "uh… yep, he's rolling out of here now."

"Good. I'm right down the street from there, and I was going to have Baker stay with Kyle, but if you can."

"Say no more. See you real soon."

Arriving within moments of their conversation, Alex hit the house with a listening device, detector to see if there were any planted. Once done, he left to go to the office, where Roland was on the phone, making an appointment for Jason.

"Roland?" Alex greeted, when walking in, in his disguise, while carrying a briefcase that had his equipment in it.

"Mr. Scott!" Roland stood to hand him all of Jason's messages, and a few for him, as well.

"What's this?" he asked, flipping through his own.

Looking around to be certain the coast was clear. "Some were from the man," he hinted quietly of what he said. "The other, well, I guess I don't have to tell you!"

"Philips?" he mouthed.

He nodded, and then carried on like the secretary he was portraying, "Mr. Scott, will Mr. Green be in today?" he asked, while Alex read the note.

"Possibly," he read on, shaking his head.

"What?" he asked, quietly.

"He has invited me to represent his new company. Thinking, since I'm not a partner here I would want to start my own firm, with him as my biggest client. He also says I can bring my secretary, meaning you, of course, because he has never known anyone with such strong devotion. Well, just wait until he meets Taylor Green," he laughed quietly. "Is Epstein in?"

"No. He had a late court appearance that's sure to take him until 4:30 or 5:00."

"Okay," he replied, being careful what he said, when taking out the same device used at the Roberts' house, while going over the office complex to see if Philips or Epstein had put any listening devices out.

Checking Jason's office, after going over the waiting room, he found two, and then two more in Kyle's office, as well as the break room. Not to mention, phone taps on all the phones.

"Great," he growled, taking each one out of their hiding places.

Writing a note, Roland asked what he was going to do with them.

Alex pointed to Epstein's office, where he headed off to right away. Getting there, he used a credit card to let himself in to go over to the man's phone and attach one of the taps there, and then placed the listening devices around the room, in places that were never thought to have hidden one. With ample satisfaction, he turned to his man and walked back out, while locking the door behind them.

"What about the house?" Roland asked.

"Did it," he announced, going back into Jason's office to call Ted.

"I'm on my way," he said, checking his weapon, before heading for the door.

"Ted, don't forget your disguise."

"Got it," he laughed.

Getting to the office, Roland told him that Alex was in Jason's office. "I believe Mr. Scott is expecting you, sir," he smiled.

"Thanks," he nodded, and headed off in that direction. Once there, he saw that Alex was on the phone with someone. And by the look on his face, it was Philips.

"Thanks for the offer, but Corporate Law isn't my favorite forte. I'm doing this for Mr. Roberts, because of his tight schedule, and too, because of the horrible accident two years ago that took his son's life, which if you can only imagine, had really knocked the wind out of him."

"His daughter too, I hear had lost something in it, as well. I had offered my condolences by offering him the same position as I have offered you, but he had declined it."

"Think about it, he was representing your former partner. That would have been a conflict of interest, wouldn't you say?"

"Yes, but that case was thrown out, due to lack of sufficient evidence."

"Yes, sad to say, and a great loss of time and money for this company, too! And now, Mr. Philips, it's been a pleasure talking with you. Oh, however, there is just one last request."

"Name it."

"Your listening devices. Keep them out of our office, or you will wish you hadn't met me."

"So, you found them, did you?" he sneered.

"Mr. Philips, bugging devices are illegal. So unless you want to find yourself with a new address, I strongly suggest you lose them, along with any wiretaps I have found here and at his home."

"Just exactly who are you, Mr. Scott?" he asked, angrily.

"One very ugly attorney who hates having their privacy invaded. So stay the hell out of this office and the Roberts' home, or plan to meet your worst nightmare. Do I have your attention, Mr. Philips?" he growled venomously.

"Fully."

"Good. Now have a good day," he said coldly, while hanging up.

"Philips, huh?"

"Yes," he reported, while switching off a recording device he had hooked up to the phone.

"Smart!" Ted grinned.

"But of course! And now, seeing how late it's getting to be, let's go see how everything else is going."

"With Cindy?"

"That's one, and to let you know, our boss has seen to it to put the local police department on this case, now that they know who may have had her father killed."

"Yes. Though, that ought to be interesting."

"Why, because cops hate cop killers?" he growled hatefully.

"Yes, and now that we have that out of the way, what are we going to do when we leave here?"

"Go shopping," he announced, "since we both could use some more suits. That and I want to be sure both places have enough food and other supplies. Oh, but before we go," He stopped short of rounding the deck, "I'm having a man come in to put an added alarm system on both offices, since Epstein already knows the one they have now."

"Yes, well that should get his attention," Ted laughed, when there came a knock at the door.

Answering it, Alex recognized the man of being one of their own. "Come in. You know what you are to do."

"Yes, sir," he replied, while getting started on the door first.

While doing that, Alex went back over to the desk to look over one of Jason's files, concerning the case they were working on. "Ted?"

"Yes?"

"Stick around, I might have something for you."

"Sure thing," he returned, while watching the man do his work.

"William O'Connelly," Alex muttered to himself, getting Ted's attention.

"What?" he asked, coming over to the desk.

Not answering, he shook his head and read on, while Ted peered over the top of the desk to see what it was that had him so miffed.

In the file, it read;

> *...With the man hidden away in a safe house, ever since it all began, due to seeing how valuable evidence was overlooked.*

Just then, it hit him, as Alex read it again, only so that the two of them could hear. "When seeing how valuable evidence had been overlooked'. Damn...!" he growled, taking out his phone to call Kyle.

"Alex," Ted tried getting his attention to ask what it was about.

"Hold that thought. I have to ask Kyle what all this means." Soon Kyle was on the other end. "Kyle, what the hell is all this stuff in the footnotes?" he pointed out to Ted, in case he had missed something, "And why isn't there any paperwork on it?"

"I wasn't sure how important they were, when Jason started to get those threatening phone calls and notes!"

"Then we need to get on it right away. With this, we can put a rush on Philips' trial. In fact with all these threats and listening devices he has been leaving behind, I think we can file for him to be restricted to the city limits, until we can put him behind bars, even. As for Epstein, he's going away sooner for the murder of Officer Franklin Mosley"

"Yes, but isn't that going to make him even more mad?"

"Not if we get all the evidence together in one fell swoop! And I can take care of that with one phone call."

"Then if I were Jason," Kyle laughed, "I would say: What are we waiting for? Let's nail the bastard."

"Consider it nailed." With that said Alex was off the phone with him and calling his boss to fill him in on what he found.

"I'll have that done for you right away, and then personally deliver it to you as soon as I have all the information together."

"Thanks, Tom," Alex returned, hanging up, to recap everything with Ted.

"Looks as though we can have this wrapped up by the end of the week!"

"We can with Epstein's case. However, I'm not so sure about Philips. He isn't going to want to go to prison any time soon."

"Then without a doubt, he's still going to go after his family?"

"Count on it."

"Sir," the alarms specialist spoke up, putting his things away, "I'm all done here. And as you requested, here are keys for you, Ted and Mr. Roberts."

"Good. Now for the other office, down the hall," he ordered, while he and Ted showed him the way.

"Yes, sir," he returned, following them out.

It wasn't much longer, when he got through and left, that the other two left, too, using their new keys to lock up.

# Chapter Twenty-Three

That night, Alex called Jason, Craig and Jessi, to fill them in, including what was found in the foot notes of one of Jason's files that Kyle had kept to himself, until Alex came on board, fearing Philips or Epstein would find and destroy it. "Craig, how soon can you guys get over here?" he asked, sitting on Jason's couch, with a cup of coffee to help keep him awake for the first watch.

"Just give Jessi and I time to get into disguise, and we'll gather up the others, and be on our way."

"Good. I'll have Baker switch with Marcose, and send Marcose out to meet you at the truck stop, along the way. Oh, and Craig, I've had a change of heart about the neighbor's place."

"We're not staying there?"

"No, that hasn't changed, you're all still staying there. I just want Jarred on the ground, and ready to spring into action if we need him too. So with that in mind, I concluded that you guys could be landscapers, since you did such a bang-up job out in front of the Inn the other day," he teased.

"Thanks!" Craig laughed, knowing where that came from.

"Sure. And I'll have a few old trucks lined up for you with made up signs put on the sides, too."

"Ok, then. See you in a little while." Hanging up, Craig turned to Jessi, "Well, Mrs. Miller, it's time to get ourselves ready," he laughed.

"Good, I already sent Annie to the store to get most of what we will need. Alex, I presume will have the rest?"

"Yes."

"Craig," Jason spoke up from the family room doorway, "I heard what was just said, and we'll be ready soon."

"Just remember, we will be going in the Blazer. And as for the neighbor's place, there has been one slight change."

"What's that?"

"We're landscaping it now, instead of reroofing it."

"Oh?"

"Yes, Alex wants Jarred on the ground, in case of any excitement."

"Sounds good," he agreed readily, when Annie returned with their things.

While getting ready, Jessi filled Beth and Jodi in on what to do around the Inn.

"Sorry, cuz, we're going too."

"What?" Craig turned, hearing what was just said. "No…, Alex sure isn't going to like that. And to boot, not again…!" he laughed.

"Beth," Jessi even had to speak up in Craig's defense, "the farmhouse was one thing, but this is taking it so far off the reservation. We're talking ground zero, here, where not only you would be putting yourself into danger, but Bethany's, and the life of your unborn baby. And Alex, have you thought about how distracted this would make him…? I know you want to be there for him, as the officer you once were, and can be again someday."

"Beth, we all love you so… much, but this isn't the day," Craig stated concernedly.

"I know, and don't worry about me or our kids. I wouldn't dare put them in harm's way. You've got to trust me on this. I know what I'm doing, and I will deal with Alex in my own way," she announced confidently, just as Jarred came in to join them.

Though, not looking one bit surprised to hear her declaration, he grinned.

"You know about this…?" Craig turned, seeing the look on his cousin's face.

"Sort of! And after the other day, out at the picnic site, when she was so bound and determined to go to the farmhouse, I knew not to get in her way. Besides, she and Bethany's being there will be good for Lori. It'll take the edge off of what's going on around her."

"Yes, but that was when she was blind," Craig argued.

"Sure, but you know how Beth is when she makes up her mind about something," Jarred came back.

"Craig," Jessi spoke up, "I have to agree."

"What…? But you were just saying…"

"Yes, I know, but a lot of this makes sense," she replied, so compassionately. "Honey, if that were you, miles away, I would want to be with you too…!"

"But you will be."

"Yes, sure," she laughed, "so blow my defense out of the water, why don't you? A woman can change her mind, and see the other side of the coin when she wants too!"

At that, they all laughed.

"Fine," Craig turned back to Beth, sternly, "but no police work. You hear me?" Then looking to his cousin, "I mean it, Jarred, or Alex will have us both for lunch," he stated, getting up to go and get ready.

"Jess," Jarred turned, smiling, as she got up to follow Craig out.

Smiling back, she left the others to talk, while joining her man in their quarters. "Hey there," she was still smiling, when walking in on him, "are you going to call Jim to tell him that we're going to be leaving earlier?"

"Yes," he answered quietly, with his back to her, while getting some clothes out of the closet.

"And Max," she asked, going over to their dresser to get a few things put together, "are we taking him?"

He nodded his head, while they went on getting ready.

After a few more lingering minutes of silence, Jessi turned to her husband. "Craig, are you mad at me?" she asked, sensing his silence.

"No," he said, slumping down onto the bed. "When Beth wasn't pregnant, Alex wouldn't have worried about her as much."

"But now…?"

"But now he has two… No, make that three that he has to be concerned about."

"It's not just them you're thinking about, is it? You're thinking about me. Worse yet, the day he found you back at the farmhouse?"

"God, Jessi…" he turned back, looking to her, as he nearly cried, "that day nearly killed him. How is he going to survive if something happened to his family now…?"

"With all of us being so close in one area, he won't have as much to worry about. Craig, honey," she came to join him on their bed, "it's like what Kyle was saying, Alex's men wouldn't be so spread out, watching us, if we were all together in one area."

He thought for a moment, knowing she was right. 'Alex would worry, wondering if Philips had suspected who he really was, and sent a few of his goons to deal with his family, here.'

Sensing his concern, she placed an arm around his shoulder, and hugged him dearly. "So, what do you say, let's finish getting ready so we can get on the road? And we will just have to deal with Alex's fury when it happens."

"Sure. Just one more question. What about Cassi?" he asked, looking to her.

"She'll be staying behind to help out here," she announced quietly, while glad that she wasn't going.

Back in Camden, after sending Marcose out to get them, Alex and Ted went out to walk the ground, while setting up their own alarm system, in case Philips or one of his men were to show up.

"He's going to be one unhappy fellow if he were to trip one of these lines," Ted laughed, quietly, while setting the tension on the fishing line.

"Yep, sure is...!" Alex agreed, though his mind seemed to have been on other things, while wrapping up there.

"Hey, I've been meaning to ask, the Roberts', I thought you weren't going to have them come back for awhile longer. You know, to give the man some time to get stronger!"

"Yeah, well, I got to thinking how I was when I had been laid up for awhile. It about drove me nuts."

"Yeah, well, he isn't as young as you were back then. Good, Lord, we are talking about a heart attack, here."

"Yes, but the stress of not knowing what is going on can be just as deadly, and when it comes to a man who is used to being in the driver's seat, Jason hates being left in the dark for long. So, yes, I am bringing him back. But I am not putting him back to work. He can recuperate here at home, just as well as back at the Inn. And too, this way I can keep a better eye on him and his family, while I'm doing what I need to be doing."

"Yes, not to mention, Kyle's thrill of having his lady here with him."

With that, they both went on working on the traps, until they were finished.

After an hour and a half had gone by, their work was done.

"Well I'm going in to get cleaned up. What about you?" Ted asked, watching Alex walk up onto the patio to sit at the table.

"Monitor the tracking device for awhile, while Baker keeps watch up front."

"Okay." Going on inside, it wasn't long, when Ted was back, with more coffee, to join him.

"That didn't take you long!" Alex stated, looking up, just as Ted was handing him a fresh cup.

"No. And the neighbor's have just left the nest, too."

"Oh…? Good, it shouldn't be much longer, when Jarred and the others get here."

"Any news on Philips?" he asked, taking a seat to see where the man was on the monitor.

"Yes. He's been over at Epstein's, since shortly after our conversation."

"What do you think they're talking about?"

"Definitely not the weather!" he groaned, rubbing the back of his neck, tiredly.

Alex was definitely right, back at Epstein's house, they were certainly not talking about the weather. In fact, the only storm brewing up over there was in the ongoing heated conversation.

"So, you thought you would threaten to turn me in when you were about to be arrested for the connection to the cop's murder, huh?"

"We both were connected to that, and you damn well know it," Samuel growled, turning his back on him. "So why should I be the only one taking the wrap for it?"

"Because after all we have done, why should we both go to prison, while leaving all that money tied up in some offshore account, not getting used?"

"Well you should have thought about that before sending your goon out to kill Franklin," he snarled back, while pouring himself a brandy.

"Speaking of cops," Philips laughed sarcastically.

"What?" Samuel turned, looking back at him, red-faced.

"Your new faces back at the office."

"They're not my new faces!"

"Fine. Jason's then."

"What about them?" he asked, taking a sip.

"Don't you think it odd to take off, leaving two new, so-called, attorneys we know nothing about, to go on vacation?"

"Jason wouldn't have, had he not had them thoroughly checked out."

"Checked out…?" Philips nearly yelled, while pulling out a concealed folder from his suit coat, tossing it onto the end table nearest Epstein. "This Jordan Scott, AKA Alex Storm, is a Federal Marshall, and Roberts' partner, back in Langley, IN, Crawfordsfield County to be precise, when they were fresh out of the police academy. You fool…! He went and called his old friend to investigate our dirty deeds. And this Taylor Green is Alex's other partner, Ted Jones, after Roberts left the force."

Epstein's face went white, while sitting his glass down on the table, after hearing the name Storm, knowing about his infamous record to get to the truth of whatever case he was working on.

Seizing the opportunity as Epstein turned away, feeling his world about to crumble around him, Philips quietly went over to the fireplace, and grabbed the iron poker from its stand. Turning around quickly, he came back, taking that moment to forcefully bludgeon it over the back of Epstein's head again and again, until he dropped to the floor, dead in his own blood.

Wiping the tool clean of his prints, Philips placed it back into its carrier, and came back to get the folder on Alex, when then hearing a car pull up out front.

Going over to the window to see who it was, he saw two uniformed officers get out. "What…?" he growled, looking back at his accomplices' dead body, lying in a pool of blood, on his living room floor. "Oh, no you don't," he growled, darting from the living room to exit out the back door. As he had, he was oblivious to the fact that one very important piece of the file had slipped out of its folder, lodging itself beneath the table Epstein had set his glass on. Yet, that wasn't the only thing going against the man. Philips' fresh set of prints left on the back door knob, as well as the tracking device still planted in the left turn signal of his own car that continued to give away his position.

Meanwhile, across town, while drinking their coffee, Alex and Ted were keeping their eyes on the monitor. When suddenly they shot up in their chairs, seeing the beacon start to move.

"Damn... he's on the move," Alex announced, setting his cup down to study the monitor.

"Yeah, I see that, but where to, and why so fast?" Ted asked, while fixed on the screen.

"It's too soon to tell. But damn, look at how fast he *is* moving. As if something spooked him, or had certainly pissed him off."

"Yes, it sure looks like he's running away from something. But what?

"Or... who...?" Alex questioned, looking to Ted, when then hearing a vehicle pull in up front.

"Jarred?" Ted asked, getting up to head for the door.

"No," Alex grinned, setting his cup down, to take the monitor with him, "if that would have been Jarred, that would have been my Blazer pulling in. That would have to be Marcose."

"Okay! But what about Philips?" he asked, walking into the kitchen

"He's far enough away to give us time to get everyone settled in. But we have to move quickly, I don't want to be off the monitor any longer than necessary."

"Sure."

Reaching the front door, Baker walked in first to announce their arrival, followed by the others.

Upon seeing Craig and Jessi, Alex laughed wholeheartedly. "Nice...! Now I don't feel so old anymore."

"Yeah, well this isn't all," Craig stepped aside to let Beth and Bethany in, followed by Jodi.

Silence quickly filled the room, so much so one could cut it with a knife.

"What the..." Alex stopped, when Bethany, while in her mother's arms, reached out for his hand. "Ted," he groaned, reaching over to give his daughter a quick kiss on the head, "get the door closed. No, wait, we have to hide the Blazer first," he ordered somewhat heatedly. "So, take Baker, and get their things unloaded, before hiding it, then get back in here."

"Let's go!" he nodded toward the door, sensing that his old partner was about to explode at any moment.

Once they were gone, Alex turned back to Jarred and motioned him into the kitchen, where the rest eventually followed. "Damn it, Jarred, I don't have time to go into this right now!"

"Trouble?" he asked

"Possibly," he explained, taking a seat at the table, to open the laptop, and view the monitor.

"Is that…" Jarred started to ask.

"Philips? Yes."

Watching it quietly, everyone gathered around the table, holding their breath, while anxiously waiting on Alex to say something.

With a heavy sigh of relief, he shook his head, and sat back in his chair, while the others took a seat.

"Alex, don't keep us in suspense," Jason queried.

"Philips just left Epstein's' place in a rather big hurry," Alex explained. "But at this point we don't know why."

"Do we at least know where he is now?" Jamie asked, taking Lori's hand, when Ted returned with most of their things.

"Back at his place, for now, so it seems!"

"What do you mean, 'so it seems'?" Jodi asked.

This time it was Ted who offered an explanation, "The way he was driving, just as you guys pulled in, looked as though he was running away from something."

"Or…" Alex started.

"Someone…?" Kyle finished.

"What do you think, Alex?" Jason asked, turning to his friend. "Do you think he caught onto who you really are?"

"My guess…! I can't be all that sure. But I can be certain about one thing, tonight Epstein was going to finally pay for what he did to Cindy's father, when having him killed."

"But I thought that was Philips' goons doing," Jason questioned.

"It was, but evidence pointed to Epstein, as well. As for Philips, I think being there, talking to Epstein, followed by seeing the officer pull up, scared him. Thus, he probably slipped out the back way, got into his car, and started out slow at first, and then took off like a…" He stopped, when noticing his daughter resting her head, tiredly, against Beth's shoulder.

"What do we do now?" Jarred asked, noticing how tired they all were getting.

"Baker…?" Alex called out.

"He's outside, keeping watch," Ted informed him from the kitchen doorway.

"All right, but still, I want you and Baker to go and keep an eye on our friend. If he so much as much as runs, I want to know where. And call me every hour, on the hour. You got that? I don't care what time it is, just do it. And you two." He turned his attention heatedly onto his nephews, when Jason intercepted.

"If this is about the others being here, blame me for that."

"No," Beth spoke up, only to be cut off by Jason's daughter.

"Uncle Alex, it was my doing. With all that's going on, I asked her to come. To help keep my mind off of being so scared. As for Jodi, well..."

"That would be my doing," Jodi confessed, looking to her husband.

"On the way here," Jarred went on, "we were tossing around a few ideas."

"Good ones, I hope," Alex grumbled, "because if this goes sideways, I want everyone that is not a Fed or a Detective out of here, and back to the Inn, where Hank and the others can keep an eye on you."

"Yes," Jamie smiled, "I would absolutely say they're pretty good."

"Well, let's hear it then."

"We thought to include Jodi as a part of our landscaping team," Craig grinned. "As for Beth's appearance, well that would make her Aunt Beth, coming to see her beloved niece, not knowing the neighbor's had left for awhile. So she and Bethany will be staying there for a time, while in disguise, and staying out of sight, in case Epstein and Philips were to have learned your true identity."

"God forbid, if that's the case," Alex groaned miserably, "I can't send them back to the Inn, where either one of those men could just as easily send their goons to harm them, or the others."

"No, but while they are here, Craig and I could stay on as the Millers," Jessi smiled pompously, just to goad him.

Looking at her warningly, through icy blue eyes, Alex broke suddenly into a grin, realizing she had him from when he first arrived at her Inn, years ago. "Okay, now can we please try and stick to our plans? No more surprises?"

"Yes," Beth smiled. "And just so you know, Craig drilled me good about my not being a cop anymore, and how dangerous this case has gotten. So you have my word, I will stay in the shadows, along with Bethany, to keep us safe and out of harm's way."

"That couldn't make me any happier," Alex smiled, while reaching over to kiss his wife. "But don't think for one minute that gets you off hook so easily, Rookie. I am beyond mad right now that you would just show up like this, without so much as a phone call to talk about this first. So, we *will* be discussing this later, just not right now, seeing how tired and hungry everyone is."

With that said, Jamie got up to warm up the pot roast Annie had sent with them.

"Alex," Jason spoke up, while Jamie was doing that.

"Yeah?" he responded, while keeping an eye on the monitor.

"Sleeping arrangements?"

"W...What? Oh, yeah."

"Hey, pal," he laughed lightly, while handing the monitor off to one of the other guys, "why don't you let someone else watch the monitor for a while, while you and your family gets something to eat, before getting settled in? In fact, why don't you, Beth and Bethany take the spare bedroom that once belonged to our son? And Kyle," he turned, "how about you and Ted take the family room, downstairs? If that's okay with you, Alex," he turned back to ask, only to see how tired he was really getting. "Alex?"

"Yeah, downstairs with Ted. That's when he is here," he stated, getting to his feet to help himself to some iced tea Jamie had just made. "Thanks, lady," he grinned tiredly. "As for the rest of you," he announced, looking back at the table, "across the street, once we get done here. That's provided our buddy isn't in the area, when you're ready to turn in. Oh, and Ted, when you're finished eating, if you don't mind, how about watching the monitor for a spell, so Marcose can catch a few winks, before relieving you?"

"Sure."

After their late dinner, everyone, but those going across the street, got ready to turn in, all but Alex, Jarred and Ted.

"Alex..." Beth turned back, after Jamie offered to take Bethany off her hands to get her ready for bed.

"I'll be in soon, once we check the monitor one last time."

"Oh, okay!" she replied, sensing he was still bothered by her not discussing with him her decision to just show up."

After she had left the room, Alex turned to the others. "Though, none of us has heard anything from our guys watching each end of the street for potential trouble, why don't you guys go on into the living room and wait, while we check to make sure the coast is clear."

"Okay," they agreed, tiredly, and left them to do just that.

Turning to Ted, who by then had the monitor in hand, and was about to go into the living room to get comfortable on the sofa, Alex and Jarred smiled.

"Okay, and then off to bed for the two of you," Ted hounded lightly, while setting the monitor back down on the table for the three of them to have a quick look.

Once they saw that Philips was back at his place, Alex turned to Jarred, "Looks safe enough for the rest of you to head on across the street, where Manning has been keeping watch on things there for you."

"Yes, and none too soon," he stated, looking into the other room to see Jodi leaning her head on Jessi's shoulder, while the three were seated on the sofa, waiting on word.

"In that case, I'll say my goodnights, now, and turn in, as well," Alex grinned at the others, while heading on down the hallway, while they got ready to grab their things.

"Jo," Jarred grinned, while going in to give her a hand up, "shall we head on over, now?"

"What, we're not there yet…?" she yawned, welcoming his arm, as he held onto her, for support.

Once in the privacy of their room, seeing how Beth was still awake, Alex removed his weapon to set aside on the nightstand, before removing his vest and shoulder holster.

"Alex," Beth spoke up softly from her side of the bed, "I can see you're still unhappy with me."

"You would think by now I would be used to you guys' stubbornness, but this case is not just some walk in the park kind of case, it's…"

"I know, dangerous. And I know I should have called and discussed it with you. But would you have said yes? No, you wouldn't have. And yes, bringing Bethany along was crazy to say the lease. It's just that I was thinking like a…a…"

"Cop…?" he stated sharply. Yet felt bad for having gotten so tough with her. "Beth, honey, I know you must be missing the action, but with us about to have another baby on the way, it's not safe for either of you to be here."

"You're right. And yes, I do miss the action, but I missed having you home, safe, like it was before you became a Federal Marshal. Alex," she reached out to him, as he sat heavily on his side of the bed, "I meant what I said, when I got here. I will stay inside and do everything you say to do. I promise. Just don't be upset with me."

"I'm not upset. Well, I am that you didn't call and tell me you were coming so I could have altered my plans. But then when it comes to you, Jessi and Jodi," he laughed, "any plans I make, I usually have a spare just waiting to put to use in case any of you would happen to show up like this."

"Oh, you are such a smart ass," she laughed, smacking his arm.

"Yeah, well just so happen a little birdie called and told me to expect some extra company, but not to be too hard on you when you got here. So I had a little more time to prepare for your arrival. Now, before I change out of my clothes, is there anything you need from the kitchen?"

"A glass of Jamie's iced tea would be nice."

"Okay. I'll get us both a glass," he smiled, getting up to go and get them.

Getting back, he found her asleep, looking so peaceful. Smiling, he set their glasses down and went on to get ready for bed.

Sometime during the night, after seeing Philips was on the move again, Ted called Marcose to let him know that he and James was heading out to check on his whereabouts. "Keep an eye on things here, while we're out, won't you?"

"Okay. Just call if you need more backup, though."

"We will," he said, as he and James followed each other out in their own vehicles.

An hour or so later, Ted called Marcose, who patched the call into Alex, to let him know that Philips had packed up some of his things and went to one of his warehouses on the eastside of town. "From the looks of it," Ted went on, while watching from his perch, near a dumpster, "I don't think he planned on being there alone."

"Why's that?" Alex asked, quietly, while getting up to take the call into the living room, so not to wake Beth or their daughter.

"I'm looking in one of the windows, now, at the far end of the building, from on top of one of their dumpsters. I see a room, fixed up all in pink, quite possibly for a young lady."

"Someone like Lori…?" Alex asked quietly.

"Yeah, I would presume so."

"Ted," Marcose asked, "is he there, now, and if so, what is he doing?"

"Hold on and I'll patch you both in with James, too! He'll be able to tell you what's going on at that end."

Soon the three way connection turned into a four way.

"James, it's Ted. Alex and Marcose are on the line, too. Tell them what you can from your end."

"He's here, in his room, now, at the opposite end of the building from where Ted is."

"What is he doing?" Alex asked hastily.

"Pacing the floor, while clinching angrily to a folder. He looks really pissed."

"Any idea why?" Alex asked.

"Something about a missing page, from what little I could hear."

"Hear…?" both Alex and Marcose asked, puzzledly.

"Yes. He was yelling. But from my location, all I could pick up on was something about a missing page from the folder he has clinched in his hand."

"Great. Well that takes care of where he is, if he were to nab Lori in hopes to keep Jason from going through with this case," Alex pondered, wondering what was so important about the missing page.

"Sure, but you do have the chief working on the rest of the evidence, right?" Ted asked, moving quietly down from his perch to join up with James.

"Yes, hoping to get his butt locked up, before he goes after her. And Ted…?"

"Yeah?" he asked, sensing remorse.

"What if this missing page, he is so bent on, has anything to do with our being here? God forbid, he has irrefutable proof who I really am, and about my own family being here, now."

"Alex, he won't go anywhere near them. I promise you that," Ted assured him in a hushed-like voice, when nearing the other end of the building.

"You can't promise me that, Ted."

"No, but if I have to personally watch over them, they will be safe," he swore, heatedly.

"We all will," Marcose swore, as well.

"Yeah, well you both might be doing just that," he growled, slamming the phone back into his pocket, before rejoining his wife, while Marcose kept watch over the Roberts', that night. "You both just might be," he repeated, quietly, once he reached their room, to see his wife and daughter both still sleeping peacefully.

# Chapter Twenty-Four

The next day, when Alex and Jason got to the office, Roland greeted them both, as they walked in, with three cups of coffee and an assortment of fresh pastries from the coffee shop next door.

"Roland, careful there," Alex teased, while getting out his new key to open Jason's door for him, "you will have people thinking you really are a secretary."

"You think?" he laughed, following them in, while they went over to set their briefcases next to the desk. "Oh and here are your morning papers, sirs. I took the liberty to stop on my way in to get you both a copy, which you will certainly want to see what's on the front page," he pointed out.

Taking his, Alex read the caption, first, to himself. Shocked at what he read, he called out in astonishment, "Well, I'll be…! 'Prominent Attorney slain in his home' it says."

"Samuel Epstein," Jason read on, "prominent attorney found dead in his upper Camden home late last night. Cause of death, the man was apparently bludgeoned by a fireplace tool. At this point an ongoing investigation is underway to find the person or persons responsible for it. As of now, burglary has been ruled out."

By then, both Alex and Jason were shocked at the news, when Alex took out his phone to call his chief.

"I know all about it," Broadey came back. "Epstein was brought in for questioning earlier the other day, when we found sufficient evidence to hang him on Franklin's murder. But then he told us about some evidence he had on Philips' case, and how the two were connected in some corporate embezzlements, which he would give up if given a lesser sentence."

"Did he say where he kept this evidence?"

"Somewhere in his office. Oh, and Alex," he had sounded pretty grave about it, "you guys have got to find it, before Philips does."

"And we will, but there is something else you should know."

"What is it?"

"Philips was at Epstein's house last night, sometime before nine, until just before midnight."

"How do you know that?"

"I started monitoring him shortly after finding out he was involved. When he left, it looked as if he were in an awful big hurry."

"Just before midnight, you say?"

"Yes, why?"

"One of the officers on the scene reported the incident at eleven forty-eight. That would mean…"

"We have him…" Alex growled, looking to the others in the room. "And we know where he can be found."

"Where?"

"A warehouse, he owns, on the eastside of town. And Broadey, you will want to be there for this."

"Why's that?"

"It looks as though he was planning to kidnap Lori Roberts," he stated, before thinking of what his comment would do to Jason.

"He, what…?" Jason cried, sitting himself down hard in his chair.

"Roland," Alex pointed to Jason, "watch him closely, while I finish filling Broadey in."

"No," Jason waved him off, "I'm fine. I want to know more, and I want to know why I wasn't told this at breakfast, this morning?" he demanded.

"I didn't say anything, because I didn't want Lori or Jamie getting upset over it, till we had more information on it," Alex explained, while Broadey remained on the phone with him. "As we can tell so far, he has a room all set for her on the opposite end of the building from where he planned to stay."

"That doesn't sound good," Broadey stated.

"No, and damn, we have to get him! And we have to get him now…!" Alex groaned, turning back to see the pale expression on his friends' face at what he had just heard.

"And we will, Alex," Broadey assured him. "We will. But, as for investigating Epstein's murder, I know you want front row seats, but don't. I have a strong feeling Philips has his goons watching the place to see if you show up."

"Broadey…!" Alex protested heatedly.

"No, Alex. You, nor any of your people, are not to go near the place. I already have a man on it, and he is good."

"What are you saying? That he's better than me?"

"Never, my friend," he laughed. "No one can beat the record of the infamous Alex Storm! Nor do I know of anyone else who has had his vehicle windows bullet-proofed, because of your impeccable record. Just that word has it, you and Roberts were partners many years ago, when you two first got out of the academy. So just let me handle things on this end. You have enough on your plate with Jason and his family back in town."

"That's not all," he grumbled.

"What?"

He laughed, "I have Craig and Jessi here too, doing what they are gifted at. And…"

"Let me guess," he laughed, knowing the story of Jessi and her cousin's temperament. "With Jarred there to help out, Jodi refused to stay back in Indiana?"

"Beth, too. But we have everything covered to protect them."

"Good. Last thing we need is for something to go wrong with her and the baby."

"Yeah, well, now I have to ask, you *are* wanting to be in on this take down, right?"

"I wouldn't miss it for the world," he grinned.

"Good. Hey, Tom, give me a minute to fill Jason and the others in on what's going on, then I'll get my team together and meet you at the warehouse."

"Okay."

Getting off the phone, Alex did just that.

"But you just said Philips had a room set up for Lori!" Jason cried.

"It looks like it from what Ted was able to see the other night. But there is one other piece of information you need to know. Somewhere in Epstein's office is the evidence to nail Philips. Can you and Roland find it, while I get the others ready to storm Philips' warehouse?"

"Yes, sure!"

"Hey, you are going to be okay, right?" Alex asked, concernedly. "No heart attack, right?"

"No. Just get that son of a…"

"We will." Looking to Roland, Alex reminded him, "Stay with him. And in case Philips was to slip away, I'll have a few extra men on each door, watching this place, like Fort Knox."

"Yes, sir."

"Good." Alex then turned and called Ted.

"Yeah, he's still here," Ted returned, quietly into his headset, while on the roof of another local coffee shop, dressed like an AC repairman.

"Good. The chief is on his way, and the rest of us will be there soon, in full gear."

"Good. I'm in mine, underneath my repairman's gear! Oh and what about the Roberts place? Are you going to leave someone there, in case he slips away?"

"Yes, and the office, too. So let Baker know to get back to the house."

"Sure will. Oh, and I read about Epstein. Are we going to investigate that, as well, since we know Philips was there?"

"No. Broadey ordered us to stay away from there. He has a man covering it now, and knows what he's doing."

"What…? Someone out there is better than the infamous Alex Storm?" he laughed quietly.

"No. Just that he's concerned that Philips may have some of his goons watching the place, in case I, or any of my people, were to show up on the case. As it turns out," he groaned, "we were right, thinking he may be suspicious of all the new faces at the office. Word has got out that Roberts and I were partners, many years ago, when the two of us got out of the academy. So, Broadey wants to handle things on his end, since we have enough on our own plates with Jason and his family back in town."

"Yeah, and that's not all," he laughed. "Did you tell him who all came along?"

"Yes, and he laughed."

"So he knows you have Craig and Jessi here to do what they are gifted at. And..."

"The others, too," he laughed.

"Then he knows about Beth?"

"Yes. But I assured him that we have everything covered to protect them. Anyway, we had better be getting off here to get everyone ready, and put into place."

"Okay, see you soon."

Getting off the phone, Alex didn't waste any time calling the others to get suited up and ready. "We'll meet at Jason's place. Oh, and Jarred."

"Yeah?"

"Philips killed Epstein last night."

"Is that why we are moving in on him now?"

"Yes. So get everyone across the street to the neighbor's house, in case one of Philips' men was ordered to nab Jamie or Lori, while we are out busting his hide."

"All right." Just as soon as he got off his phone, Jarred rounded everyone up.

"What's going on?" Beth asked, feeding her daughter.

"Alex wants everyone across the street, and now. They are going over to bust Philips today."

"Today...?" Jamie cried. "Why so soon...?"

"He..." he hesitated. "He killed a man last night."

"One of Alex's...?" they cried.

"No. Epstein," he returned, gravely. "Now, come on, I have to get you all out of here, in case Philips has a man watching the place, while we are out to bust him."

Doing so, some of them took a few of their things with them. One of which, was Jason's medicine.

Once across the street, Marcose was just getting off his phone with Alex.

"Craig," Jarred called out, waving him and Jodi over, when Jessi happened to walk out of the house to see what was going on. "We have a crisis going on." Filling them in, Jarred turned to Marcose. "Are you ready?"

"Yes, but whose going to stay with them?"

Soon he had his answer, as Baker and Manning pulled up.

"Baker," Marcose called out, "why aren't you at the warehouse?"

"Alex says the chief will have plenty of men on hand. As for Manning and I, we are to stay here, while Roland is at the office with extra men there."

"All right then. Well I guess we ought to be getting ready," Marcose turned back to Jarred. "Wow, our first bust as Federal Marshals."

"Yes! Just let me change into my uniform," Jarred grinned, pulling out his gold shield.

"Yeah," Marcose did the same.

Soon Alex was there with a few other men following behind. "Craig..." he called out from across the street, while getting out of the loaner car to go up and open the garage door, "the local police have been notified of our operation, and they are going to be sending cruisers over to help keep an eye on things here. Don't let anyone outside, until you have heard from me. And make sure it is *me* that you hear it from, no one else."

"Gotcha," he grinned.

"Daddy...!" Bethany cried out, wanting to toddle out to him, but was stopped, until he had crossed the street, while the others were getting into their bulletproof vests, after he had already put his on.

"Hey there, pumpkin, you're going to have to stay here with mommy, while daddy goes after a bad man with Uncle Jarred."

"Then you be back?" she asked, sweetly.

"Count on it, sweetie," he smiled assuredly, not only to her, but Beth, as well, who hated to see him go. "Beth," he reached over to his wife, and kissed her passionately. "I will be back. I promise."

"You had better be," she choked back on her tears, while hating to let go.

"Same here," Jodi stated, kissing her man, as well.

"Oh, yeah, count on it," Jarred grinned down at her.

"Okay, let's get this show on the road...!" Alex hollered on his way over to get into his own vehicle.

Pulling out of the garage in his shinny black Blazer, Jarred, having taken his uncle's advice, drove his burgundy, Chevy pickup, extend cab, with Marcose in his shinny Black Dodge Ram. Soon they were blazing a trail to Philips' warehouse, where Chief Broadey, a tall athletically built, forty-eight year old, with dark hair and eyes, was joined up by Ted, while having had the place surrounded.

Upon getting there with the rest of his team, they stormed the building, catching Philips' men, but losing Philips in the commotion, when he slipped through a hidden doorway, just behind the dumpsters that Ted had been on the night before.

Mad as hell, the chief started barking out all kinds of orders, while Alex pulled his men off to the side. "Ted," he asked, while checking his monitor, "did you get the tracking devices placed on all the vehicles that were here last night?"

"Yes, and I don't know how I could have missed that hidden door, when I was on that particular dumpster the other night, too!"

"Don't let it get to you," he explained, looking over the area carefully, when then spotting a busted street light. "There's you answer, right there," he pointed it out. "So, seeing how his car is still here, I'd say he is in another one. Did you by any chance make a list of what was all here last night and today?"

"Did that, and…" looking around them, while standing near the dumpster, Ted checked his list, and knew just which one was missing. "He's in a grungy brown Impala, 1976 to be exact."

Passing the word to the chief, Alex called Baker to let him know what to watch for, and then called Roland. "Bring the men in and lock the place down, but keep them at their appointed doors, and out of sight."

"All right. But do you have any idea which way he could be heading?"

"North. But why? I don't have a clue."

Getting off the phone, while Roland was getting the men inside and locking the place down, Alex was splitting up his team. Feeling Ted and Marcose were the best of his men, not saying Jarred wasn't, Alex just wanted to keep his nephew close by. "Ted, take Marcose and a few other guys and go after Philips. Use the monitor you have, while I go by the office and see if Jason has found the evidence needed to hang him. Jarred, I want you to get back to the others, and stay with them. I'll call you when we are on our way back. And Jarred," he stopped him, while looking concerned for his feelings, "I'm sending you to be with the others, because I know you would want to be there for Jo and them, not for any lesser reason. That, and you know what vehicle to watch for. So call me the moment you see it."

"Okay," he returned, smiling, while getting into his truck to rush off.

Just as Alex was about to get into his Blazer, Broadey stopped him. "What's up?" Alex asked hurriedly.

"It's from my man I had investigating Epstein's murder," he announced, looking gravely, when handing Alex a slip of paper.

"What's this?" he asked, taking it.

"A piece of paper, missing from Philips' folder, apparently on you and all who are connected to you. My man just gave it to me moments ago, telling me it was found lodged under an end table near Epstein's' body. And Alex, there's no longer any doubt, Philips knows you are on this case. So watch yourself, and tell the others right away. Don't wait on this."

Looking it over, his expression grew dark and stormy, before shoving it into his pocket. "I'll tell them right away," he growled, getting into his Blazer. Taking his leave, Alex made his calls, while on his way to the office.

Upon getting there, he spotted James, just inside, knelt down beside the filing cabinet, while holding his service revolver at the ready.

Seeing Alex at the door, James stood, letting him in. "Agent Storm, Roland filled us in. Any word on Philips yet?"

"No. But I want these doors, as well as the back ones to remain locked. And when we leave here, I want you and your other partner to stay and keep watch. Oh, and James…?"

"Yes, sir."

"Stay inside, and out of sight, just as you were. If Philips shows up, wait until he's inside, before apprehending him. I'll have a few men outside, watching the front and alley, just in case he was to bring company."

"Yes, sir."

Leaving James to guard the front door, Alex made his way to the rear of the office complex to check one of Broadey's men. "Baxter," he called out, before getting there, to let the average height, light brown haired man in his late twenties, know he was coming up behind him.

"Agent Storm…?" he asked from behind a tall artificial plant.

"Here. How are things back here?"

"Quiet, sir."

After telling him the same thing, Alex went to check on Jason and Roland. Walking in, he saw a planter overturned in a corner, and papers, now, sitting outside a small green trash bag on the desk, covered with that day's newspaper. "Well, did we find what we were looking for?"

"Sure did," Jason smiled, tiredly, with cold sweat running down his face.

"Good," Alex returned, seeing how he looked. "In that case what do you say we head home, and look it over there? Besides you look as though you could use a break."

"I'll get that break, but first I want to see what all this commotion was about that had our lives in such a tether."

"Jason, we can do that at home," Alex insisted, while picking up the bag.

"Yes, but look at this," he groaned, waving a few pages at him. "There are things here I have never seen before, dating clear back to when you and I were partners."

"That far back…?" Alex looked surprised, when taking them.

"Yes."

Giving them a quick once over, he shook his head, "Fine, let's go," he ordered, putting everything back into the bag, before ushering the two out into the hall, so he could lock up behind him.

"Wait! What about the mess?" Jason asked, pointing back at his office.

"It'll still be there tomorrow. For now, let's just get you out of here, while we can. You're starting to worry me."

"Okay. You're right, I am feeling kind of poorly."

Not wasting any time, with Roland's help, they ushered Jason out to Alex's Blazer, and got him in without incident.

Meantime, back at the neighbor's house, Jarred noticed the loaner car Alex had been using, still sitting out at the curb.

"What is it?" Manning asked, picking up on his concern.

"Alex's loaner car. We need to put it in the garage to get it out of sight. Would you take care of it?"

"Sure," he offered, taking the keys from Jarred. "Zeus, come boy," he ordered his K9.

"Manning, when you get done with that, check out the grounds there at the Roberts place, and here. But watch for the traps Alex and Ted had set the other night."

With a nod of his head, he put his K9 into the back seat, before getting in behind the wheel.

Back inside the neighbor's house, Jarred found the men in the living room, and the women in the kitchen, all but Lori, who had excused herself to take a nap.

In the privacy of one of the bedrooms, having slipped off to sleep, she began to dream. One that started out to be a good one, where she was alone, thinking over the past few glorious weeks. But then suddenly she was caught off guard, when a pair of hands came up around her. In one hand there was a rag coated with chloroform, which Jessi had warned her about, while the other was holding her around the waist. Recalling what she was told, she tried pushing the hand away to take in a deep breath and hold it. At that point the hand came back to cover her mouth, while the other tightened around her waist to drag her into a nearby alley. "Mmmm…" she moaned out in her sleep, feeling her lungs about to burst. But then, remembering to act as if she had passed out, she went limp, allowing her attacker to continue.

At that moment, thinking the chloroform did its job, the attacker shoved her into the backseat of an awaiting car. That was when she had heard his voice, *"Where to?"* he asked the man next to him, when getting in behind the wheel.

*"My warehouse, where I have a private nurse waiting to care for her,"* he growled, as they pulled out of the alley to look at her father's office, while driving passed it. *"You have been warned, Roberts. Now maybe you'll do what you were told, if you know what's good for you."*

*"Sir,"* the attacker interrupted the man's train of thought, while unaware of her blindness, *"Why the nurse?"*

*"I may be a ruthless man at times, but I was told that she had been blinded in an accident a few years ago. So I don't want to totally scare her, when she wakes to find herself in a strange place!"*

Meanwhile, with her father having worked later than planned, looked down at his watch and groaned seeing what time it had gotten. *"Darn…, I told Lori I'd meet her at the coffee shop at 5:10. It's 6 pm now...!"* he groaned, getting to his feet to shove his papers into his briefcase, before rushing out door, while closing off the light on his way.

Getting to the coffee shop, just as it was closing, Jason knocked on the glass door to get the owners' attention.

*"Jason. What is it?"* the owner asked cordially.

*"I was to meet Lori here. Is she still here?"*

*"No, she left half an hour ago. I thought to meet with you?"* he asked puzzledly.

Looking around, Jason didn't see any sign of her, or her bodyguard.

Seeing his concern, Ted came running up from his truck, while parked across the street. *"Jason, what is it?"*

*"Lori..."* he cried in her dream, *"she's not here, where we were to meet at 5:10. I was running late, and Frank said she had left a half an hour ago, having thought to be going over to the office, to meet with me...!"*

*"Damn,"* Ted too, groaned, taking out his radio to call Alex.

"Mmmm.... Alex...!" she called out in her sleep. Meanwhile, when he got on the other end, Ted told him what had happened.

*"Where's Manning?"*

*"I just left him back at the house, before coming back to join you!"*

*"What the hell happened?"* Alex growled.

*"I was across the street in my truck, while she was inside talking to the owner's wife. Next thing I knew, a van pulled up in front. After that..."*

*"Wait. A van...?"*

*"Yes, a delivery van. I assumed to drop off something."*

*"How long was it there?"*

*"Minutes. Not even long enough to go in and abduct her."*

*"My next question is, was the van a part of the abduction to block your view, or just bad timing for us?"*

*"I can't say."*

Taking the radio, Jason's voice came over the air, *"Alex, where is she, damn it...? Where is my daughter...?"*

"Oh, Daddy..." she cried in her sleep again, while the dream went on.

"Craig..." Jessi called out, coming to the kitchen doorway, just then.

"Lori. Yes, I hear her," he returned, getting to his feet, but not going to look in on her.

"Dreaming of her abduction?" she asked, picking up on the same thing he was.

"Yes."

"What...?" Jamie cried from the kitchen, when getting to her feet, as well. "Shouldn't we go in and wake her?" she asked, wanting to go and check on her.

"No," Craig explained, stopping her. "Most times, when a person has dreams like this, it's a way of telling them what's about to take place."

"Like a premonition or déjà vu," Jessi offered, getting some of the others attention around the room.

Meanwhile, as Lori's dream went on, Alex was trying to console her father. *"Take it easy, Jason. We'll find her. For now, call home in case she may have gotten a ride from somebody."*

*"She wouldn't have done that. She would have called, or come by the office to tell me. I had even asked Frank, but he knows nothing!"*

Hearing this only made Alex that much angrier. So much so, he threw his radio at the dashboard of his Blazer, when it shattered into pieces. *"Damn him..."* he growled, feeling the pressure of his blood rising to his brain. *"Wait!"* he groaned, reaching for his phone to call Ted, while recalling the new cell phones he had gotten for Jason, Jamie and Lori, in the likelihood something like this were to happen. Not to mention, Jessi and Craig's assistance. *"Ted?"*

*"Alex, what happened? One minute we were talking, the next you were gone!"*

*"Remember the coffee mug back, at Jessi's, awhile back?"* he laughed.

*"Gotcha. So what's up?"*

*"The cell phones! Ask Jason if he still has the new cell phone on him that I gave him?"*

*"Damn! You're right!"* Turning to Jason, he asked, *"Your cell phone?"*

*"What about it?"*

*"Not the old one. The one Alex gave you, your wife and Lori, while they were back in Indiana. Do you have it on you?"*

Pulling it out about the same time Alex pulled up, he grinned, *"I sure do."*

*"Good. Alex,"* Ted turned, *"he has it."*

Pulling out a matching one, Alex dialed her number, hoping she would have it on vibrate so that no one else would hear it. With it on, he would be able to tell where she was. *"Here,"* he called out. *"But she's moving."*

*"Where?"* they asked, gathering around to have a look.

*"I can't tell yet. Let's get back to my Blazer, where I can hook it into my laptop. That'll have a better point of reference, and a map to follow it with."*

Doing so, Ted and Jason left their vehicles behind to go with Alex and follow the signal.

Back at the storage building, while the two men reached into the back seat to get her, just before clearing her from the car, her phone slipped out onto the floorboard, landing just beneath the front passenger seat, where it couldn't be seen.

"No…! No…!" she cried out suddenly, bring everyone else out of their seats, as Craig, being the nearest to the hallway, took off first, followed by Jessi, to the room Lori was in.

# Chapter Twenty-Five

Hurrying in, Jessi went to Lori first, calling out to her. "Lori…! Lori…" she called, shaking her. "Lori, wake up, sweetie. You're having a bad dream! Come on, wake up, now."

"Mom…?" she cried out.

"No, Lori, it's Jessi. Can you hear me…?"

Opening her eyes, she looked to Jessi, horrified at first. But then remembering what she and Craig had taught her, sitting up, she hugged her. "I did it…! I remembered what you told me, and I did it…!"

"Honey," her mother spoke up, coming around to join Jessi on the other side of the bed, "what are you talking about?"

"In my dream," she turned to her mother, while taking Kyle's hand, as he offered it to her in all the commotion, "I dreamt I was attacked outside Frank's Coffee Shop, while waiting on dad to join me, but he was running late. So I had gone outside to watch for him. While there…" she looked up at Kyle, and smiled.

"What?" he asked, as Jessi joined Craig at the end of the bed to give Kyle room to sit with his girl.

"Well," she laughed slightly, "I had been so preoccupied, thinking about all the glorious days, since getting my sight back. But then it happened…!" She turned, looking back on at Jessi and Craig, "I was grabbed from behind…!"

"What…?" came a man's voice from the doorway.

Looking over at the open door, Lori smiled even more, when seeing her father, who hadn't been aware of the bad dream she had just awoken from. "Oh, Dad…!" she cried, happily, getting up to go to him. "It was so wonderful…!"

"Wonderful…? I'm sorry, sweetie, you've lost me," he stated, pulling back to look down at her.

"Folks," Craig suggested, from the end of the bed, "why don't we take this back into the other room, where we have more space to hear about this."

"Yes, and then maybe someone can explain what she is talking about," Alex growled, having heard what Jason had.

Once back in the living room, Lori, with Craig and Jessi's help, explained the dream, and the meaning of what she had learned from the attack.

"But I don't understand…!" Jason wailed. "How is this, a good thing?"

"Because, Daddy, I had maintained control! Like Craig and Jessi told me I could," she smiled triumphantly. "And now I know where, if he was to grab me, and too, when I would be grabbed. Therefore, I would be able to tell Craig and Jessi, so they can pass the word to Alex and his team."

"That isn't all, Lori," Jessi explained. "By having this dream, you now know what you must do to avoid any of it from happening."

"You mean like not going outside the coffee shop to watch for dad?"

"That's one thing!" Craig exclaimed. "Go on…!"

"My phone…?" Pulling it from her pocket, she looked down at it.

"Yes…!" Craig nodded.

"I should put it where it wouldn't fall out."

"And Alex," Jessi turned, "knowing now that Ted can never lose sight of her. Not even for a second. So you must put someone on that alley, and make sure her bodyguard doesn't leave her side either."

Feeling the weight lift from this new bit of information, everyone in the room was affected by it, all but Kyle, who continued to worry about her, but didn't want to spoil the moment, seeing how much joy it had brought her.

"Alex," Jason looked to his friend.

"I'll work on it. You have my word," he returned, sensing after all those years what he was thinking. Turning to Jessi and Craig, he grinned. "Thanks, you two, for your keen input."

"Yes. Yes, of course," Jason put in, looking even more poorly.

"Okay, you," Jamie ordered, recognizing what all this was doing to his heart, "it's time for you to get some rest. Alex and the others will take care of things from here. So let's go mister, it's to bed for you, after I give you your medicine."

Not arguing with her, he gave his daughter a hug, then turned back to Kyle. "That bag there that Alex is holding," he pointed out. "Go through it. There is some crucial information that he and his chief needs on Philips, right away."

"Okay," he returned, as Alex handed him the bag, and pointed to the study where he could work on it.

"And Kyle, I want to know right away if you find anything in that mess that will hang Philips out to dry."

"Yes, sir," he replied, turning back to Lori with a soft smile, before leaving the room.

"Jessi," Alex turned, "I have a question for you."

"Go on!"

"The car in her dream, what color was it?"

"Lori?" she turned.

"I'm not sure!"

"Lori, think back," she urged. "You fought the chloroform, while he was dragging you to the alley. At any given time did you peek to see anything around you? Even the doorframe, or the interior of the car?"

Playing back that part of the dream, she vaguely remembered seeing the door, as he put her into the back seat. "Dark. Yes, it was dark."

"As in brown…?" Alex asked, thinking of the loaner car he had recently driven.

"Mmmm, no, more like dark blue or black."

Shaking his head. "Are you sure, Lori? Are you sure it wasn't brown?"

"Alex, what is it?" Craig asked.

"He's in a brown car now," he explained, looking frustratedly to Craig.

"Who is to say that he doesn't change cars again?" Beth asked, when Alex's phone started to ring.

Taking it into the kitchen, he answered it.

"Alex we have him cornered again," Ted announced, watching through his binoculars.

"Let me guess, in his north side warehouse?"

"In the vicinity, why?"

"Checkout all the cars around there. Do you see a dark blue one, or a black one?"

Looking, just as he was about to say no, he spotted one tucked away with a man waiting in it. "I see it, and there is a man waiting in it. What do you want me to do?"

"See if you can get close enough to tag it, and then run the plates. Let's see who he is."

"I'm on it," he returned, putting the phone back into his pocket. "Marcose, watch my back."

"What's up?"

Pointing out the car, he filled him in on Alex's plan.

"Let's do it then."

Taking that moment, the two hurried over quietly, while watching all around them to make sure Philips wasn't watching. Not to mention, the man sitting inside the running car.

Once there, Ted pointed out the plates and the make of the car. Then using hand signals, told Marcose to write it down, while he pulled out a tracking device.

"Be careful," Marcose mouthed, as he was about to get the last number and its two letters.

Ted smiled, and proceeded, slipping through any obstacles in his way, until reaching the occupied car.

"Come on, Ted…" Marcose whispered, anxiously, once he was finished writing down the information on the car, to go back to watching the area for signs of Philips. "Oh, crap," he muttered, when spotting the man ducking in and out from behind some crates, heading for the same car. "Damn…!" Looking from the man in question to Ted, who was now sliding out from beneath the car, he waved quietly, "Come on…! Come on…!"

Getting back just in time to duck in behind another car, Philips ran up to the sedan and got in.

Calling it in, the chief radioed his men to follow, just as the car sped off.

"Now to get back to Alex," Ted returned, while moving off toward their trucks. Once there, he pulled out his cell phone.

"What's the word?" Alex asked, while watching the monitor, as the signal moved quickly through the city streets.

"Success," he announced, watching his own monitor. "Are you seeing what I am seeing?"

"Yeah, looks like he's in a hurry," he laughed.

"Yes. Have you heard from the chief, yet?"

"Just got off the phone with him."

"And…?"

"Just as planned. He is going to pull his men off soon, allowing Philips to think he has gotten away. Afterwards, we're going to put some men on that part of the alley, near the coffee shop, and an undercover, female, officer to pose as Lori. When he attempts to nab her, we will grab him and his goon."

Just then, overhearing Alex's plan, from the living room, a thought came to Jessi, when looking to Lori.

*'Jess, what are you thinking? We don't want to put her in the middle of it!'* Craig stated, concernedly.

*'No, but that has to be her choice. After all it was her dream. And with Alex and the others there to watch over her, she will be more than safe.'*

*'Are you going to be the one to ask her? And if so,'* he laughed, not intending it to have been quite so audible to the others, *'are you going to be the one to tell…'*

*'Alex…?'* she smiled, seeing some faces looking back on them.

"What?" Lori asked.

"Alex was just telling his man what the plans were going to be. Lori," Jessi, along with Craig, got up to join her on the sofa, before her mother returned, "this dream you had was telling you what's about to happen. Alex is considering bringing in an undercover, female, officer to pose as you. You could stop that if you think you could do it yourself, with the amount of men Alex and his chief will have to cover things."

"That," Craig spoke up, sensing a serious problem with Alex's plan, "would be better, since Philips has been studying your habits so well."

"What…?" Alex and Jamie chimed in at the same time, when walking into the room.

"Are you out of your mind…?" Jamie wailed. "You're not putting my daughter into the middle of this…! Alex," she turned, glaring at him, "I won't have it."

"Alex…" Craig spoke up in their defense.

"No…!" he thundered. "She's right. We're not putting her in the middle of this. Not when I can get a look-a-like to pose as her."

"Can she walk and talk like her in the short amount of time we have?" Jessi asked, glaring at him. "No doubt Philips has been studying her every move. And answer me this. Will the look-a-like be using a cane or walking without one?"

Alex looked to Lori, and for the first time, didn't recall seeing her with one. Shaking his head, he knew, once again, they had something there. "Lori," he turned, looking to her softly, "in all the time you were blind, I never saw you with one."

"I never really had to use it. Yet, right after the accident I did, but that was for such a short time. Only because of all the time I've gone to the Coffee Shop to see my brother, while he worked there, and to meet up with dad. And sometimes I used to make a game of it, when going over to the office, to count the steps! At first with my eyes open, and then closed! So when I had lost my sight, after getting passed the initial shock of not seeing, I delved back into my memories 'of the game of counting."

"Did you wear dark glasses, too, after losing your sight?" Craig asked.

"Yes, but only on sunny days."

"Alex," Craig turned, "no one could imitate her as well as she can, herself. And if this undercover officer was to falter in any way, it could put the woman's life in jeopardy."

"Lori," Alex came up to kneel before her, with tears in his eyes, "you have been like a real niece to me since the day you were born. If something were to go wrong…" he fought back more tears, and simply dropped his head, shaking it.

"Uncle Alex," she placed both hands to his cheeks, and raised his head to look at her, "I trust you more than life. You won't mess this up. You don't have it in your vocabulary to mess up," she smiled brilliantly.

"Okay," Alex conceded.

"What…?" Jamie cried.

"Mom, I'll be fine!" Lori assured her.

Seeing the confidence in her eyes, Jamie smiled back, just as there came a knock on the door.

"That'll be Tom Broadey," Alex announced, going to the door.

"Alex," Tom smiled, causing his blue eyes to sparkle in the afternoon light, "didn't know if you would be still here at the neighbor's house, or Jason's."

"Here for a bit till it's safe to go back across the street. Come on in. Ted and Marcose should be here soon with the others, and once they get here, we'll have an idea to put passed you, but not until then. This way everyone will hear it at one time."

"Okay," he agreed, walking in, nodding his greeting to those who were there, all but Kyle, who had been in the study, going over the papers that Alex and Jason had brought back with them.

Their wait wasn't long, when the rest of Alex's team showed up, before he could make his introduction of Tom to Jamie and Lori. As for Beth and the others, they knew him through Alex being a Fed.

Telling them what had transpired in their absence, there were a lot of disputes over the decision.

"No undercover officer?" Marcose groaned concernedly.

"No," Alex stated firmly. "Craig and Jessi made a crystal clear argument. So listen to what they have to say, before we go on. Craig, Jessi, the floor is all yours," he turned, smiling.

"Had of we gotten a look-a-like," Craig began, "you would have to ask yourself, knowing what kind of man Philips is, can she walk and talk like Lori in the short amount of time we have? No doubt Philips has been studying her every move."

"That, and answer me this," Jessi added. "Will the look-a-like be using a cane, or walking without one?"

They each looked to Lori, and for the first time didn't recall seeing her with one. Shaking their heads, they knew the two had something there.

"Lori," Tom sat in a nearby chair, while looking to her compassionately, "in all the time you were blind, had you ever used a cane?"

"I never really had to! Yet, right after the accident I did, but that was for such a short time. Only because of all the times I've gone to the Coffee Shop to see my brother, while he worked there, and to meet with dad. I used to make a game of it."

"What sort of game?" he asked, puzzledly.

"Counting steps!" she explained, but still saw a lot of confused faces, aside from his. "You see, when going over to the office, I would count the steps. At first with my eyes open, and then closed! So when I had lost my sight, after getting passed the initial shock of not seeing, I delved back into my memories of the game of counting."

"When you lost your sight, did you ever wear dark glasses?" Ted asked, standing next to Alex.

"Yes, but only on sunny days."

"Alex," Tom turned, "no one could imitate her as well as she can, herself."

"Yes, and if this undercover officer was to falter in any way, it could put the woman's life in jeopardy, as Craig had so put it."

"When Alex came up and knelt before me," Lori went on lovingly, while looking to her long adopted uncle, "with tears in his eyes, he told me how I have been like a real niece to him ever since the day I was born. And that if something were to go wrong. At that point, I stopped and told him, 'Uncle Alex, I trust you more than life. You won't mess this up. And..."

"'You don't have it in your vocabulary to mess it up'," Alex finished for her, smiling, with tears still in his eyes.

"Okay," Tom agreed. "This could work. But only with plenty of agents around in disguises to cover her," he ordered. "Mrs. Roberts..." he looked to Lori's mom.

"Jamie," she corrected.

"Sorry. Since we hadn't been formally introduced," he looked to Alex and frowned, while extending out a hand, "I'm Tom Broadey, Chief Federal Marshal over Illinois and Indiana."

"Jason's wife and Lori's mom," she smiled, shaking it.

"Well you certainly have yourself a fine family. And Jason...?" he looked around the room.

"He's in resting," she explained. "This whole thing has taken a huge toll on his heart."

"Sorry to hear that. I was hoping that the trip to the Inn would have helped out!" he offered.

"It had, till we came back to this!" she muttered. "Mr. Broadey..."

"Tom," he corrected.

"Would you and the others like some iced tea?"

"Sound good. Thank you."

"Jamie," Jessi and Jodi offered to help, while taking Beth, Bethany, and Lori into the kitchen, while the men went on talking.

"What…?" Lori asked, getting there.

"It's their time to go over plans," Jessi explained, looking back on Craig, who smiled, knowing the two were going to be listening in on their thoughts throughout the meeting.

"So what's the plan?" Tom asked, pulling out a notebook and pen to keep his own notes.

"We hide men in the alley, both side and back, and a few in Frank's Coffee Shop, as well as on top of a few selected buildings, and on the street," Alex explained, looking over his notes.

"All concealed of course," Jarred added.

"Concealed? In what fashion," Tom asked.

"Storefronts and three sided advertisement signs, like the one sitting outside of Frank's Coffee Shop. We have a man that would fit inside it perfectly!" Jarred laughed, thinking about one of Tom's smaller guys.

"Adam?" Marcose asked, laughing about the same guy.

"Yes. He's perfect for it. And he is the smallest Tom has."

"Okay, now that we have that part covered," Tom commented, writing it down, "what about the ones out in the open? And too, what about the shop owners and their customers? No telling what this man would do if aggravated, since he had already killed one that we know of."

"But from Lori's dream," Craig was quick to add, when picking up on a few red flags of concerns in the crowd, as well as, Jamie's, from the kitchen, "he's not wanting to hurt her."

"Dream…?" Tom asked Alex.

"That's how we knew what car he was going to be in, and where it all was going to take place. Craig," he turned, "would you care to elaborate?"

"Sure. Some dreams has ways of letting people know that something is about to happen. In Lori's case, the car and its color, and the place in her dream, telling her it was going to be the coffee shop."

"Yes, but there is other coffee shops in town," Tom stated. "Why Frank's?"

"Because…" Craig started.

"Philips knows she spends a lot of time there," Alex stated, "and at her dad's office. So it's apparent that he will try to grab her there."

"After all," Craig spoke back up, sounding a little agitated, "that is why the need for all this heavy security in the area, right?"

Tom looked to Craig a little puzzled, not knowing what all had taken place years ago at the farmhouse with David, Craig's best friend. To Tom, that was David he was looking at, at that very moment. *Yet it's David's body, but they call him Craig. Alex's nephew, Craig…?* he thought to himself.

"Tom…?" Alex spoke up, suspecting something was up, in the way he was looking at Craig. "Tom?"

"Yeah? Yeah, right," Tom agreed, looking back at Alex, questioningly.

Alex laughed, "I'll explain, what you're probably wondering, later."

"Then, it's true…?" he whispered, pointing back at Craig.

"Yes, but later, my friend," he hinted a need for privacy. "Later."

"Yeah, right," he agreed quietly. "Now, back to my question, disguises?" he looked back at Craig, shaking his head, uneasily.

"Casual clothing for those out in the open, along with their bullet proof vests under them," Alex ordered. "As for added effects, have a few of them carry shopping bags, from various shops, so not to draw any undue attention."

"What about the actual shop owners, and their customers?" Roland asked.

"Have them move to the rear of their store, when the signal is given," Alex stated.

"Yes," Jarred grinned, "and then the bastard is ours."

"Okay," Alex laughed, "I think we can end the meeting on that note! Ted, I'm going to need you to come up with another disguise, and then check the monitor to see where our guy is, before taking some of Tom's men to check on things in town."

"Okay," he returned, sensing Alex was about to fill Tom in on a little history lesson about Craig and the farmhouse.

As the meeting was about to break up though, Marcose spoke up, getting Alex's attention, "You know, Alex, speaking of disguises, now that the cat is out of the bag about you and Ted being in Camden, Jordan Scott and Taylor Green's disguises will have to be put into cold storage," he laughed, looking back at Ted, who was getting ready to go through his bag of disguises to find the right one, before getting changed.

"Yes…" Alex laughed. "So what's your point?"

"Well…" Marcose went on, while walking up a little closer to stand in amongst their immediate team, Baker, Jarred, and now Ted, who came back to join in the ribbing, while Craig stood back grinning his crooked grin.

"Come on, spit it out, Marcose," Alex continued to laugh.

"Well, as most of us, here know, you are well known for your various disguises. So, what's it going to be this time, huh?"

He looked around at the usual faces, and thought for a moment. But then looking back at Craig, and now Jessi, who couldn't stay away for that, came to stand in the kitchen doorway. "Well," he smiled at the two, knowing they could pick up on his thoughts. Turning back, he said, squarely, without so much as a smile, "you'll just have to be surprised, for when the curtain goes up on this show." Closing his notebook, he went on into the kitchen to get himself a glass of iced tea.

"Good one," Tom smiled, joining him.

"Yeah, well the thought did cross my mind to have a facial mask of myself made so I can peel it off in front of Philips to reveal Epstein's face. But then who would want to clean up the mess, when he shits his drawers?"

He shook his head, laughing. "Yeah, well I can only imagine those few who knew about the farmhouse incident, years ago, and how they took the news. Heck, when I caught wind of it, I blew it off as just being an office joke, a sick one at that, but still a joke at best."

Alex grunted, nonchalantly, while gesturing to Ted to get the newer guys out of there, so they wouldn't hear any of the conversation.

Nodding his head, Ted hurried into his new disguise, and checked the monitor for Philips' whereabouts, before getting them out of there.

Seeing this, Tom waited to say anything more.

But then, after the others had left, those who knew the story walked into the kitchen, smiling.

"Okay," Alex laughed at Tom's baffled expression, "I guess this is as good as time as any to let you in on a specific secret."

"Concerning what I had just felt out in the living room, standing next to a man I had assumed was David McMasters, since you became a Fed?" Tom wailed uneasily.

"Yeah, well it's something we don't go around and publicize," Alex smiled.

"Then it is true. Tony Belaro came back two years after having killed the wrong guy, when he had shot Craig, instead of David. And then for whatever reason David goes into the farmhouse, while the two of you," he points to Jessi and Alex, "were there. But then soon after, Tony shows up with his sidekick, Harry, and the house comes crashing down a short while later, as everyone comes running out, but Tony? Who, by the way, I read in the file, had gotten buried under the rubble."

"Yes. What else do you know?" Alex asked.

"Just that everyone has been calling this guy, Craig," he repeated, "your nephew, Craig."

"Yes, my nephew," Alex smiled at Craig.

"Not David McMasters," Tom stated, astoundedly.

"In body, yes," Craig explained, "but me in spirit. I had fallen in love with Jessi during that odd time, and married her later as David," he smiled lovingly at his wife.

"Yes," Jessi concluded, while smiling up at him.

"Wow, you two were really there, helping him to free his spirit, after wrongly being killed? And falling in love, to boot," Tom smiled, fascinated.

"Wrongly killed was the key word," Alex went on. "While we were up in Craig's old room, he was downstairs dealing with Tony, when Tony had tried to make a run for it out the back door."

"He had to be stopped," Craig explained, "so that my spirit could rest. In order to do that, I had to bring down that section of the house, thinking it wouldn't affect the part the others were in."

"But it did, when a beam from the ceiling came crashing down at me," Jessi added. "David saw what was going on and rushed over from the window to knock me out of its path. Doing so, he took the blow to the back of the head and shoulders himself, while Alex and Harry were both injured, when Tony had shot the two. Soon after, I called out to Craig, because of David's injuries. When he showed up, so did two angels, who had stopped the house, momentarily, of its shaking."

"Gideon, who had been the one that was there for me all along," Craig related, "and another angel to tell us how God had answered our prayers."

"Which were?" Tom asked solemnly.

"As it turned out, we each had been asking to be given second chances. All but David," Jessi looked sadly to her husband.

"What had he prayed for?" Tom asked puzzledly.

"Because he had been eaten up with so much guilt of my death," Craig explained, "what we didn't know was that he had been praying that God would take him, and give me back my life, as it wasn't my time to go. Thus, the angel told me that this was my chance to come back."

"As David," Tom affirmed in awe, when thinking how it was in the Biblical days, when Jesus brought Lazarus back the dead.

"Yes, but who are we to question God? He put us here for a purpose. Alex and his men to deal with the criminals, and Jessi and I to help the troubled spirits, and some of the living, as well," Craig smiled, picking up on his thoughts. "Yet, I have to admit, switching places with my best friend…!"

"But you did, and you and Jessi are together, because of him. What better gift could he have given you?"

"Yes, and I'll never be able to forget it either," he looked sad, losing his friend over it.

"Yes, but wait, what of David and Craig's parents," he asked, "How did they take it?"

"Knowing they would each have a part of their son, they accepted it," Alex explained. "Yet, all of this could have been avoided, had it not been for a crooked cop that took David's call to warn me of what was about to take place with Craig," Alex growled.

Shaking his head, Tom turned to Marcose and Baker, "And you guys? Were you there too at some point?"

"We were all there, at one time or another," Baker laughed.

"Yeah, well that's another part of the story the two of us would rather not talk about," Marcose growled.

"Ahhh, yes," Tom laughed, "something about that same crooked cop."

"Alex…" Marcose swore, acting like he wanted to change the subject.

"Go. See how Ted is doing, but try not to…"

"Shut up…!" he laughed, heading for the door, while leaving Baker behind.

"Wow, I guess that is a sore subject," Tom laughed.

"Wouldn't you think so had you gotten tied up by someone you thought was an honest cop?" Baker grinned.

"Yeah, well, you're right. And now about this gift the two of you have," Tom turned to Craig and Jessi.

"You mean, gifts," Alex corrected. "As in, sensing troubled spirits, and telepathy!"

"Along with hearing people's thoughts, too," Craig added. "That's why we're here, to help Lori if she were to get into trouble."

"And how long have you two been able to do this?" Tom asked.

"Me, a few years longer than Jessi," Craig laughed, looking down at her.

"Yes, well, as for me," Jessi laughed up at him, "I didn't even know I had the gifts, until I met him! And that was due to a storm he had created to get my two daughters and I off the road, and into his farmhouse, for shelter, until the storm was over. Oh… and what a time that was."

"Why?" he asked, getting himself a glass of iced tea poured.

"Because he was playing tricks on me at the beginning."

"Yes, well, until she had threatened to take the girls and leave!" he groaned. "I couldn't take that chance, so I made it so she could see me. From there I told her what had happened, and she offered to help."

"Yes, but getting your uncle to believe wasn't easy."

"Even though I've been there plenty of times after…" Alex turned away, not wanting to go down that road again.

"You found him. Yes, I know," Tom explained. "I read it in an old report, before taking you on as a Fed. It's all in the past now, and your secret is safe with me. So," he turned to Craig, "I suppose I'm to call you Craig, too?"

"Yes," he smiled.

# Chapter Twenty-Six

Later that day, while watching the man's whereabouts on the monitor, Ted commented to Alex about Lori's dream, "Kinda makes you wonder if she, too, is gifted."

"No. Jessi thinks it's because of all that she had heard us talking about, before going to sleep. As for the different car, and most of the other things said, I'm not taking any chances that they could have been warnings for us to watch for. Face it, she was right about the car, and she could be right about you're surveillance being cut short by a van pulling up in front of the coffee shop."

"You know, Alex, when it comes to Craig and Jessi's gift, you won't get an argument out of me."

"Ted, I know what you're going to say, but humor me. Let's make these changes. From here on out, I want you in the coffee shop, with her, whenever she is there. As for the van, I want it checked out if one were to pull up in the next day or so."

"All right, we'll do that," he agreed.

Taking one last look at the monitor, hours after Broadey was to have pulled his men off of Philips, the Chief had changed his mind, telling Alex about it, when he called.

"Fine, but you should know that I'm having second thoughts about letting Lori use herself as bate."

Telling him all about it, the man agreed to send out a couple of female officers for Alex to choose from, in case he did have a change of heart.

Getting off the phone, Alex was finding himself bothered more and more by her dream, and why neither Craig nor Jessi went to her, while it was going on.

"Alex," Craig spoke up, seeing something was bothering him.

"Yeah…?"

"Is something wrong? You looked troubled."

"Just a bit. Where's Jessi? I need to talk to the two of you in private."

"In with the others. I'll get her."

Not using telepathy like he sometimes did, the two were back in minutes, when Alex turned away from his monitor to study them for a moment.

"Have a seat," he suggested, while looking for the right words to say what was on his mind.

Doing so, they waited, knowing what he was already thinking.

"Craig, Jessi, when Lori was having her dream, did either one of you pick up on it? If so, why after all the practice at the farmhouse and the Inn, did you not go to her?"

"Alex," Craig explained, "we were aware of her dream, and had we gone to her, during which time, it may have cut it short. Thus, she would have not come up with the information she had."

"Alex," Jessi offered, "most dreams are a form of premonitions. Without them, we would not know what's about to happen."

"And had it gotten ugly," Craig added, thoughtfully, "we would have interceded right away."

"I'm sorry. You think after all I have learned from the two of you, in the past, I would know these things."

Smiling, Jessi patted his hand. "It's a learning process. We're still finding out new things about our gifts all the time!"

She and her husband laughed.

"Great," Alex laughed, as well, "does this mean there's more to come of your gifts?"

"Who knows?" Craig teased.

Running his hand over his graying hair, Alex continued to laugh, shaking his head, before getting up.

Later that day, after meeting at the neighbor's house with the female agents that Broadey had sent over, they found the right one to do the job if an officer was needed in place of Lori putting herself into too much danger.

"Agent Storm," Lori's look-a-like spoke up, "I'll do my best."

"I'm sure you will, but Officer Todds, the main thing here is to allow them to get you into the car. We'll do the rest from there. Just make sure your service revolver is in a place where it won't get dislodged, and fall out onto the floor."

"Will a leg holster do, then?" she smiled, raising her loose fitting skirt to reveal one just above her knee.

"That's perfect," he agreed, seeing the other unattached officers smile at her long shapely leg. "Okay, guys, roll your tongs back into your mouths, and remember what we are doing here."

"One more thing," Craig spoke up, while standing next to his wife.

"Craig?" Alex turned.

"When getting chloroformed, remember to push his hand out away from your mouth to take in a breath, and hold it."

"Pardon me!" she looked to Craig, not knowing who he was. "And why should I be listening to you?"

"Because, Todds," Ted spoke up sharply, "if you don't, you are useless to the rest of us."

"Todds," Alex spoke up, "meet my nephew, Craig, and his wife Jessi. They have been working with Lori in knowing what to do if she were to be chloroformed. So I strongly recommend that you listen to him, and listen well, so that if you want to remain conscious throughout this whole experience, you will."

"Yes, sir, I'm sorry. You were saying, sir."

"If you don't wish to get knocked out, because, trust me, when you do wake up, you will have wished you hadn't ignored my warning, as when his hand does come back to cover your mouth, and it will, because he is ultimately stronger than you, the chloroform will leave you with one hell of a headache, when you do wake up," he returned, angrily.

With that said, he looked to his uncle, before taking his wife to go into their room.

That night, while going over the revised plan, Alex took Ted, Jarred and some of his other men over to the coffee shop to scope out the area. While there, they checked out the back alley, looking for anyone who looked to be working for Philips, when they were met up by another one of his own men, who stayed hidden away in a darkened doorway.

"Morris!" Alex nodded.

The man nodded back, while they continued on to the adjacent alley that had the back entrance to the coffee shop.

Checking out all the doors and old fire escapes, Jarred commented, "Looks pretty quiet."

"Let's keep it that way," Alex demanded, when they appeared at the front entrance of the alley, once sure the area was clear.

Signaling his other men, they all came out, even the ones inside the office, while locking the front door behind them.

"Adam," Alex began, "I want you here when the time is right," he pointed out a six foot, three-cornered sign, for him to hide in. "Ted, you'll be inside the coffee shop, as you already know. James, once Philips thinks he has Lori in the car and set to go, when I call you, bring your vehicle up the alley from behind. Jarred, using one of the landscaping trucks, I want you blocking off the entrance to the alley. At that time, James, I want you to get out of your truck and come around to join Ted and Jarred. I'll be coming out, as well. As for Jason, Jamie, and our Lori, I will have Roland and a few other men keeping them under lock and key the moment we learn that Philips is in the area. The same for everyone back at the house, which will include Manning and Baker, along with the local police."

"They'll be here too, when it all goes down, right?" James asked.

"Sure will."

"What about our family?" Jarred asked.

"I've given a lot of thought about them."

"And…?" he looked concerned.

"With Jason and the others, while Craig and Jessi do their thing in a nearby shop, in case our monitors fail us."

"But then what's the use of Manning and Baker staying behind at the house if we're all in town?"

"To let us know if Philips was to show up there first. And Todds," Alex turned, "you will know to immediately pull your weapon, when you hear the commotion. So please *do* as Craig suggested, so that you are alert, when the time comes."

"Yes, sir. And again, I'm sorry for my behavior back there."

"Apology accepted. Now does everyone know their part?" he asked, looking to everyone standing there. "People, there can be no room for mistakes, and absolutely no casualties amongst us. Do I make myself clear?"

"Crystal," most of them returned in unison.

Ending their meeting, James and his man went back to the office with Ted, who made his rounds, while Alex and Jarred continued to discuss the layout.

"Do you have anyone watching this part of the alley at night?" Jarred asked.

"Me," Marcose spoke up. "And when I'm not on it, my replacement will be."

Wrapping things up, while leaving Marcose behind to watch over things there, Alex, Ted and Jarred headed back to the house to get some rest, while some of the others did the same.

"You know, Craig was a bit peeved, when that officer talked to him the way she did," Jarred commented.

"Yes, kinda reminded me of a certain blonde cop we sent away," Ted commented, when looking to Alex.

Glaring back at his friend, he grunted, "Yes, no doubt, she was out of line."

"Yep," Ted returned, getting into the Blazer with the others, "and had of we not nailed her on it, she would have been as useful to this mission as a wet noodle."

"Yeah, a wet, blonde…"

"Noodle," they busted out laughing, while heading on down the road.

The next few days went by quietly, while Philips had decided to keep low, until the heat was off. As for Jason, he went back to work with Alex, as himself, staying right with him.

"What a nice couple of days without any trouble," Jamie commented, while she, Jodi, Beth, and Bethany, along with their bodyguards, went shopping for much needed groceries and other supplies.

"You can say that again," Beth sighed heavily. "Alex, Jason and Kyle have been able to go through all those papers that were in Epstein's office, and gave them to Tom, once they were through with them."

"Yes, and once Philips surfaces, they will finally nab him after this so-called attempted kidnapping," Jodi added quietly.

Back at the coffee shop, Lori, Jessi, Craig, and Ted were enjoying a frappuccino together, along with Todds, so Lori could tell her about the counting game she played, while waiting for her dad.

"That would explain your not having to use a cane during your blindness," Todds replied.

"Yes."

"And the glasses I brought with me, in case I may have to slip them on," she patted them on her head. "One question, though, are you really okay with the change Agent Storm made at the last minute?"

"Yes. Kyle was really starting to worry that things may go wrong, and didn't want to lose me. So when Uncle Alex asked if I would consider being on lockdown with mom and dad, I gladly said yes, because Kyle would be there too."

Just then, Ted got a call from Jarred, who had been sitting in his assigned truck, drinking some coffee, while acting like he was reading a newspaper. "What's up?" he asked, looking out the window to see where his attention had gone.

"It looks like our van is coming up the street now! Get Lori out of sight, and tell Todds to put on her shades."

"Sure, but what happened to wanting her and the others on lockdown with Jason?"

"I don't know, nor do I see away to get her over there without being seen! Hold on a moment," Jarred called out, seeing the van wasn't stopping.

"It's not going to," Craig spoke up sensing the driver was looking for a specific address. "This wasn't their stop!"

"Their…?" Ted asked, as he and Jarred watched it drive on by.

"Ted," Jarred spoke up, "false alarm. Even the monitor shows Philips still on the north end."

"All right, let's get Alex on the phone. This was too close."

"Yes. So while you're doing that, I'm going to call Jo, and see what's going on there," he announced, concerned for his wife and the others.

"Alright."

Putting the call into Alex, he wasn't thrilled. "Get Lori over here, while I call the house and get them brought in. Jason has a small suite upstairs they can be put in till this is over. And Ted?"

"Yeah?"

"I can feel it in my bones, it's going to go down soon."

"Yeah. me, too." Getting off the phone, Ted turned to Frank, "Can you put together a few things to take back over to the office for an extended stay until this is all over?"

"Sure, I'll have it for you in a jiffy," he said, bustling around to get what they would need.

"Craig…" he turned, looking worried.

"I know. It's coming, and he just has enough time to get everyone here and locked down. Jessi, we need to get into place," he stated, getting to his feet, and taking her hand."

"Where to?" Ted asked, as the two headed to the door.

"Melody's Secondhand Shop, directly across from the alley, so we can pick up on Philips, as well as anyone else."

"So you're staying together," he looked on them hopefully.

"Yes," he looked to his wife, grinning, "I'm not letting her out of my sight. Are you crazy?"

"Jessi, take good care of him," Ted smiled, just as Frank showed up with their things.

"Oh, and I have a few things for the two of you, too," he smiled, handing to them, before they left.

"Lori," Roland spoke up, walking in with James, "Alex sent us to get you."

"And mom…?" she asked, worriedly.

"She and the others were out shopping for food and supplies with their bodyguards," Jarred announced, walking in. "They're getting some things put together right now, for the stay in the office suite."

"I'll call Marcose," Ted announced, "to see how the alley looks."

Getting the all clear, Jarred turned to Lori, "On the way out, I want you to stay tucked in amongst us, so not to be seen."

"Okay."

"Shall we?" he suggested, while looking in all directions, as he and the others got her concealed before heading over to the office, along with the things Frank put together for them.

After they left, Ted checked the monitor again, and called Marcose back to fill him in on the van encounter.

"Yes, I saw it, and how Adam looked pretty unsure of himself when it went by. Maybe we ought to get him out and brought into the coffee shop."

"You're right, and since things look all right on the monitor, how about you call Alex on it, while I get him out?"

"Alright."

Turning to Todds, Ted instructed her to act like Lori, even around Adam. "And that includes the shades. And Frank," he called out.

"Yes?" he hustled right out to their table.

"Do not let on that this is not Lori. In fact, from this moment on, start treating her as you had always treated Lori."

"Of course," he smiled, as Ted headed out to get Adam.

"What?" Adam asked, seeing Ted approaching him.

"You're coming inside to help watch over Lori."

"Oh, okay!" he returned, not wasting a moment to get free of his cramped hiding place.

As the time passed, everyone was safe and secure, and where they ought to be. Jason had is family and his medicine. Alex, though, standing watch at the front door, was elated to have his family near, while staying connected by headphones with everyone, as the clock on the waiting room wall clicked by second by second.

Standing at the window, near the entrance of the coffee shop, Ted looked down at his watch. "It's nearing closing time for Frank. Alex what do you want us to do?"

"Tell Frank to lock up like his usually does. As for you and your Lori, walk her over here like nothing is wrong."

"And Adam?"

"Tell him to sit tight and stay out of sight. If he sees anything suspicious, have him call you."

"Okay."

Before they could do anything, with Jarred back in his work truck, and Craig near the window of the secondhand shop, Craig called out over his headset, seeing another van. "It's here," he warned, "Get all the shop owners and their people back in their offices.

"Oh, crap," Jarred growled, seeing the look Craig's face, when nodding toward the dark grey box van, as it headed for Frank's Coffee Shop.

"Showtime…!" Ted told the others. "Frank," he called out, "get your people into the office and stay out of sight. Lady," Ted referred to Todds, "remember what Craig told you."

"Yes, push his hand away if he has the chloroformed rag in it, and take a quick breath and hold it."

"Yes, but don't forget to act like you have passed out from it."

She smiled her thanks, and hurried to the front door with one last glance over at Adam, and then Ted, who was on his headset, alerting Alex.

"Gotta go, Alex, she's ready."

"I'm on my way," he returned, calling Roland and James to stand guard over Jason and the others. "Stay here until you have heard from me. Roland," he turned back, before heading out to take his position, while alerting the police to be ready. "Roland, lock the doors behind me, after I go," he ordered.

"Got it, sir."

Peering out the front door of the building, he saw his chance to move, which was two car lengths in front of where the van was preparing to pull in. Seeing this, he concealed his weapon and acted as though he was going to ask the driver for help. In the meantime, Ted, Todds, Jarred, and Craig were watching him closely, while Marcose kept an eye on the alleyway, after relieving his man.

"Alex," Ted grumbled to himself, "what are you doing? That wasn't part of the plan!"

"Sir," Alex spoke up, reaching the driver side of the van, "can I get your help on something?"

"Wh…What…?" the man grumbled nervously, while keeping an eye periodically on the alley for his boss. "No…" he shouted, "I can't. So go away."

"Don't do it," Craig came over Alex's headset. "That's our van, all right."

Hearing this, Alex grinned to himself, while drawing out his weapon. "Oh, but I can't!"

"What?" the man growled, doing the same.

Grinning even more, Alex shook his head, "I wouldn't if I were you."

"And just why not?"

"Because," he nodded his head toward Ted, who was now standing at the coffee shop door with Todds and Adam, "my friends wouldn't like it."

Looking their way, the man saw all three weapons trained on him. Turning back with a whole new look on his face, he asked, "What do you want with me?"

"Your boss," Alex ordered.

"I…"

"Don't waste my time telling me you don't know what I'm talking about. Is it a signal he is waiting on to nab Miss Roberts? Answer me."

"Yes."

"What is it?"

Showing him the radio, the man was began to sweat. "I'm supposed to let him know when she comes out."

"Ted," he called out over his headset. "Send our lady out."

Telling her, she put her weapon back in its holster and somberly walked out, remembering to act blind.

"Now, call him. But one word of warning, and we won't be easy on you, when you are sentenced."

As the man did so, the others hid. Soon, their man in the back alley gave the word of his coming to Marcose, and from his vantage point he passed the word to James, who aside from Jarred, saw Philips just as the driver stopped, and jumped out, to come up and chloroform the look-a-like.

Doing what she was told, she took in a deep breath and held it, before her mouth was covered.

Once the driver had her in the back seat, he got back in behind the wheel, just as everyone moved in, shouting for him to put his hands in the air. As for the van driver, who was apprehended by Jarred, was passed over to a few local officers, before going after the driver of the car along with Ted.

At that time, Alex and Marcose made their grand appearance, at Philips door, while Todds came up out of the backseat with her weapon trained on the man's head.

"What the hell…?" Philips swore, seeing her gun, and then Alex and Marcose's, followed by Jarred's, all trained on him.

"Well, well, well, Mr. Philips. I would never have taken you for an alley man. And now, what was it I was saying about a new address?" Alex grinned, taking him out of the car, placing him up against the side to pat him down. "Oh, yes, the State Pen for you, he grinned, while reading him his rights. "Oh, and the part about finding you an attorney. Good luck on that, once the word gets out about what you did to Epstein, no one will want to even consider taking you. And to top it off, all your assets are in the process of being frozen, courtesy of the IRS, while you are under investigation for embezzlement."

"Storm, you think you are so funny," Philips growled.

"No. I'm a riot. Oh, and did I forget? Let's add to the list, attempted kidnapping of an officer," he laughed, while slapping on the cuffs.

"Detective, Detective, Detective…" Philips laughed, not seeming to sound all that worried, until hearing another man's voice correcting him, as he walked up from behind.

"That's Federal Marshall, Alex Storm, to you," Tom smiled.

"Yes, and your worst enemy," Alex and the others put in, laughing, as Todds got out of the back seat with Ted's help.

"What…!" he cried, when Marcose handed him off to Broadey, who hauled him away with a few other locals.

That night, they all celebrated the end of Philips' reign of threats. Even Cindy was brought back out of hiding to enjoy knowing her father's murderer had paid, though, not in the way anyone would have wanted, but still she could go on with her life more happily now, knowing he could rest in peace. Not to mention, a check she would receive each month from the Policeman's Pension Fund for fallen officers.

"I guess this means goodbye again?" Jamie looked to Alex sadly.

"Well, it's not like you guys can't come to Indiana to see us!"

"Mom," Lori spoke up. "You and dad have always talked about how much you've wanted to take that vacation. Well, now we can, and with my sight back, I could really have some fun. Besides, Rose and Allen wanted us to come back for a swim and a BBQ."

"That's right!" Jessi put in excitedly. "Now she and Kyle can really enjoy going out horseback riding, and take in walks along the lake, without a chaperon."

"Consider it our gift to you and your family," Craig offered, warmly.

"Oh, I don't know," Jamie replied, uneasily. "That is so nice of you both, but we have already taken up so much of your time, and all."

"No, really," Jessi insisted. "We would love to have you."

"Jason?" Jamie turned.

"Why not? And only if this means that Alex and I can get in some real fishing!"

"Count on it," Alex laughed.

"That reminds me," Craig turned to his wife, "Jim called. He and the whole crew pulled together and got the old well relocated without any problems."

"What, no buried treasure?" she asked, grinning.

"Nope, just a few trinkets that the little girl may have dropped down into it, and some change the previous guests had thrown in, when having used it as a wishing well."

"What...?" Alex chimed in. "Are you talking about the well back home?" he asked, looking surprised. "And just when were you going to tell us about the move?"

"It was something Lori had suggested, when we were out at the shack, reading the ledger," Jessi smiled.

"Yet it was meant to be a surprise to everyone, but Jessi, and those remaining behind. I had planned to do it with Jim's help, while you were out," Craig explained. "However, this case took me away from it. So Jim and our crew went on to do it for me, by raising the gazebo and moving it over to clear the old well. Once that was done, he had it drained into a large tub so to get a glimpse at what was at the bottom of it. That's when they found all the old change, along with a few trinkets the little girl must have dropped in. Afterwards, they trenched the wells water source over to its new location, so it would still be that of the old well with its original wall that held the water in, just extended out to where it is now. As for the old wall, once the rocks had time to set up, new rocks were used to build the above ground wall, so when we get back, what you will see is an old fashion well, with its rope drawn bucket, like it had been years ago."

"What about all the dirt?" Jessi asked.

"It was used to fill in the old location, before setting the gazebo back into place."

"And the new location for the well…?" Alex asked.

"Back near the stable and lilac bushes," Craig announced, "where I told Jim to add some benches. This way anyone sitting out there can still see the horses out in the pasture."

"And enjoy the scent of lilacs when in bloom!" Jessi smiled up at her husband. "You really did it."

"Yes. And as for the trenching through the backyard, Jim was able to save the grass, when peeling it back to do the piping, before laying it back down."

"Just one other question," Alex spoke up, grinning. "I assume no old skeletons were found that I would have had to have identified, when getting back?"

They laughed.

"No," Craig chuckled, "just a bunch of old change and a few trinkets that once belonged to the little girl. Unless you could count having found a very old Domino piece, which back then when they first came out were made of bone…!" he laughed. "Does that count?"

"No," Alex grinned, shaking his head.

Meantime, throughout their whole conversation, Kyle never said a word.

"Kyle, why so quiet?" Jason asked.

"Tired, I guess," he replied, looking quietly in Lori's direction, with only one thing on his mind, asking her to finally be his wife. And when they returned back at the Inn, he knew then just where he would ask her.

"Well I guess if we're all going back to Indiana," Jamie laughed, "we had better be getting some rest."

"Wait. What about the office?" Kyle snapped his attention back to Jason, and asked "Our things, when we thought we would have to be staying there till this was over?"

"We'll get your things brought back tonight," Ted offered.

"As for the office, itself," Jason replied, "I can get Bernstein to fill in for me while we're out," he announced, turning to Cindy, who had hardly taken her eyes off Roland. "And Cindy," he smiled, "it would be really nice if you and your friend here would join us in Indiana. That's if Alex says it's okay."

"I'm not the one to be asking that," Alex returned, grinning.

"Sure," Roland agreed, smiling. "I have some time coming to me. We would both like that."

It was settled, the next morning, after giving the neighbor's house a good cleaning, having done the landscaping, before hand, everyone was packed and on the road, with Roland and Cindy in the loaner car, while all the others in their own vehicles.

Along the way, all Lori could think about was how she would finally be able to see all she had been missing, having been to a few Bed & Breakfasts in the past. But then there was something even more special about this one, she was going with the man she loved.

# Epilogue

The trip back, while unaware what was to come of it, Lori had a feeling something wonderful was going to happen. What the others didn't know was that during the wedding ceremony, which was to take place one month from then, while out along the lakeside, Little David Storm, was going to make his grand entrance, at the exact moment the couple said "I do."

"Beth…?" Jessi called out, seeing her grabbing her stomach.

"Oh… Lord…! I think it's time…!" Beth cried out, as her contractions began.

"Are you sure?" Alex asked, taking her free hand.

"Uh, huh…! Oh, yeah, it's… time all right…!" she groaned.

With every step she took, the pain increased even more. Because of it, their baby didn't want to wait to get to the hospital, which meant only one thing.

"Looks like we're going to have to make a special delivery here," Bob announced.

"Right here…?" most of them, close to Beth asked.

"No, in the shack we had fixed up for the newlyweds!" Craig announced, while helping to make her more comfortable. "Hank…"

"Yeah. I'll get the Hummer," he called, rushing off to get it.

"No, I'll get it," Cassi called out. "I can get there and back faster."

"Then you'll need these," Hank smiled, tossing her the keys.

Before they knew it, she was off, and back undoubtedly quicker than Hank would have been. Soon Beth, Alex, Bob and Sue were loaded up, and headed for the shack, while the others took their chairs with them to sit outside, waiting for the blessed event to happen.

Meanwhile, inside, Jessi stayed at Beth's side, while Craig got the water going for his dad.

"We're going to need plenty of towels and sheets, when the time is right," Bob called out, while seeing how the baby was coming.

"Bob…?" Alex asked, coming back with the towels.

"Anytime now. Beth," Bob asked, "how are you holding up?"

"I want to push," she panted with each hard contraction.

"Soon. Just keep doing what you're doing. Alex do you want the honor of being on the receiving end, or help her push?"

He grinned hugely. "You mean…"

"Be the first to hold your son? Yes."

"Annie…? Hank…?" Beth called out, wondering where they were. "Where are they…?" she asked, looking tearfully to Jessi.

"Craig…?" Jessi looked to her husband.

"I'll get them."

Hurrying to the door, he went out and spotted them right away, talking to the Roberts', when Hank turned back to see the look on Craig's face.

"Craig… is everything all right…?" he asked, worriedly.

"Craig…" Jamie and some of the others, too, came up looking concerned.

"She's fine so far. Annie, Hank, she's wanting the two of you in there, too. Though, I can only imagine why. The two of you have been like parents to her, since you each met. So go, get in there, your daughter needs you."

Taking Annie's hand, the two hurried inside to stand at the head of the bed.

Moving around to give them room, Jessi joined Craig at the stove, where he held her close.

"Okay, young lady, are we ready now?" Bob grinned, while he, Sue and Alex stood ready to receive his son. "You can start pushing at anytime."

And with Annie and Hank's help, they began the process of pushing, until hearing the sweetest sound ever.

"Well, Alex," Bob smiled, while wrapping a soft towel around their precious baby boy, "say hello to your new son, David McMasters Storm."

"Correction, Bob," Alex grinned tearfully, while holding him close to his heart, "its David *'Dusty'* McMasters Storm," he announced proudly to everyone there, before looking to his wife, and then Craig and Jessi.

As he did, there came a soft, yet, magical breeze in through one of the side windows, as if to say their David in Heaven agreed, while those who knew him looked heavenward, and smiled, as laughter filled the room.

"Until our next case!" they all went on laughing, while opening the door to the others, after getting Beth cleaned up.

Printed in the United States
By Bookmasters